PHOENIX RISING

PHOENIX #1

ELISE FABER

Elise Faber
SNARKY BOOKS FOR SNARKY MINDS

PHOENIX RISING
BY ELISE FABER
Newsletter sign-up
This is a work of fiction. Names, places, characters, and events are fictitious in
every regard. Any similarities to actual events and persons, living or dead, are
purely coincidental. Any trademarks, service marks, product names, or named
features are assumed to be the property of their respective owners, and are used
only for reference. There is no implied endorsement if any of these terms are
used. Except for review purposes, the reproduction of this book in whole or part,
electronically or mechanically, constitutes a copyright violation.

PHOENIX SERIES

Phoenix Rising

Dark Phoenix

Phoenix Freed

ONE

"SORRY, LADY!"

The bump from the little girl could barely be considered contact—they'd merely brushed arms as they'd passed each other in the crosswalk—but Daughtry barely heard the apology because images were tearing through her mind, threatening to take her to her knees.

Fuck.

She'd broken her first rule of survival.

Never. Touch. *Anyone.*

The little girl and her mother walked on, the brief brush meaning nothing to them and *everything* to her.

Purple sparks that only she could see burst from her palms, clouding her vision. Nausea burned the back of her throat, and her legs went rubbery.

She tried desperately to throw up some mental barriers around the vision flooding her mind, but she'd never had any control over them. And her efforts were too late anyway. The scene was already playing through her head—

The mother bent to retrieve a bright yellow bracelet that had fallen to the road. But while she was distracted, her little girl tugged her hand free and lurched forward, a beautiful smile splitting her young face as she splashed up and down in a huge puddle.

That joy only lasted a moment—

The vision speeding through Daughtry's brain screeched to a halt, playing every detail of what happened next in excruciatingly slow motion—

The girl's jeans were soaked all the way up to her knees. One pigtail hung crooked and the other was glued to her head with dirty water.

Her mother rushed after her, but it was clear that she would be too late.

A tractor-trailer barreled down the road—

Daughtry's mental horror flick sped up, suddenly playing in fast forward—

The deafening wail of the truck's horn, an ear-piercing shriek of tires against asphalt as the driver attempted to stop the heavy vehicle.

He didn't.

Afterward, the little girl lay prone in the street, her body mangled and unrecognizable aside from one pink shoe dangling from the toes of her tiny foot—

As quickly as the vision came on, it vanished. Daughtry found herself on her knees in the middle of the intersection, the rough asphalt biting into her skin.

The irony stung. No big rigs were barreling toward her. She was a sitting duck, a bigger target, and yet no truck threatened to run her down.

What she wouldn't give to trade places with that little girl. She didn't have a death wish, but she wasn't so callous as to want to live in place of such jubilant innocence.

Unfortunately, her desire to help was restrained by her own abilities and, worse, by her own fear, because every time she altered a vision—every *single* time she attempted to make a person's death more peaceful—their end got worse.

Car accidents became terminal cancer.

Falling down the stairs turned into suicide.

Quick and painless became horrible and drawn out.

"You okay, miss?" Out of the corner of her eye she saw a hand reach for her.

"Don't touch me!" It was a shriek, which probably made her sound insane, but she was too raw to risk another vision.

"Okay. Fine. Jesus, lady."

She didn't even see the man's face, just his palms rising in a symbol of surrender. Still, that was enough to have relief coursing through her, the tension that had locked her spine fading away. *It's not you*, she wanted to say. It was *her* fault. After all, it was *her* vision, *her* curse that had ruined so many people's lives.

Daughtry staggered to her feet, doing a really great imper-sonation of a drunkard. That's when she saw the yellow bracelet. The same one from the vision. It was bright as sunshine against the pitch-black pavement.

That little slice of luminescence made her do something she'd been resisting for months.

Biting her lip, she scooped up the bracelet and followed the pair.

Perhaps seeing the piece of jewelry was a sign that *this* time she had a shot at helping someone.

Daughtry caught up with them, returning the bracelet and reminding the little girl lightly to hold tight to her mother's hand. It was hardly anything, only the smallest bit of interference, but relief coursed through her when the little girl smiled and tightened her grip on her mother's hand.

There shouldn't be any ill effects.

She walked back to her car, hope bubbling up within her, and she thought that maybe she could do it—actually be out and interact with the rest of society. Find a way to use her visions to help people. Talk with someone other than the voices in her head.

It would be so much better than staying in her apartment all the time and—

"No," she cried, pressing her hands to her temples, staggering and landing hard against a building as another vision raced through her, stealing her breath and making her eyes fill with tears.

She should have known!

She hadn't made things better for that little girl. She'd made them worse—*so much worse*.

At least the tractor-trailer would have been instant and painless. It couldn't dish out rape or torture.

Dammit, *why?*

Why hadn't she just left it alone?

Why had she risked that little girl just to assuage her own . . . conscience or mental well-being or—

It was selfish. It hurt people and made her . . . *fuck*. None of it meant anything, anyway.

It didn't matter.

Except it *did*.

And it was the reason why Daughtry kept trying. She *had*

made a difference. One time, a year before. One touch. One vision. One hastily spoken warning and she'd managed to change a woman's death for the better.

Somehow, she'd changed the future.

If only she could understand how she'd done it.

TWO

DAUGHTRY WALKED DOWN THE STREET, her head pounding, her tongue swollen and dry.

It hadn't been a good night. But then again, spending rent money on cheap vodka was never a smart idea.

Stupid. As in it was totally irresponsible and stupid but also . . .

It was the only thing that made the memories go away.

Sidestepping an elderly man teetering down the sidewalk, Daughtry sucked in a breath, jumping to the right as he lurched toward her, his worn leather house shoes coming within millimeters of her Nikes. That slight bit of contact would have been enough for another vision.

That had been way too close.

In fact, just walking down the street had become her personal version of Russian roulette.

After the visions from the day before, she already felt fragile, as if one more good push would shatter her forever. Especially with the vision replaying itself in her mind over and over again.

She was witness to horrific events that hadn't happened

yet, events she couldn't hope to stop. Daughtry saw the murderer every time she closed her eyes—a tall, pasty white, rail-thin male with irises that would have been the color of hot chocolate on anyone else, but on him instead they gleamed coldly.

She'd hardly slept the night before, even after attempting to drown out the vision with a series of over-priced drinks at her neighborhood bar.

Then there was the eviction notice that had been posted on her door that morning. A bright red paper with large black letters.

Nothing screamed failure quite like bold, block letters.

Sigh. She had nowhere to go, parents who wanted nothing to do with her, friends who'd long since forgotten about her— well, suffice to say she was beyond rock bottom.

Bedrock bottom? Crust bottom? Mantle bottom?

It had been too long since her geology class.

Too long since she'd felt like a normal member of society.

Because while Daughtry might not be a murderer, she'd caused more deaths than the average serial killer.

Which made her a hundred times worse.

Her eyes filled with tears, but she blinked them back. The drops of salt water were more of an annoyance than something she would give into—because emotions never solved anything, only served to expose her weaknesses to the world.

And also . . . there was no one in her life who cared if she cried.

That thought was enough to pause her feet on the sidewalk, to pull a sigh from her lungs. She'd go back to the apartment and pack her stuff. Pick somewhere new to start over.

Except, as she turned to go back, her eyes caught the sign on the building above her. The bar she frequented. The one place she'd allowed herself to hold on to. It made sense to go inside—if only to say goodbye. And maybe to gather some liquid courage for what needed to be done.

Inside, the space was a cliché through and through.

Neon beer signs adorned the windows, and the bar was sleek black granite. Modern metal stools stood rigid like soldiers in front of the polished counter. She perched herself on one and winced. They were as uncomfortable to sit on as they looked.

She missed the bar's old days. Back then it had been solid oak and sticky from years of beer spills and the grime of blue-collar men. The new owners had spent a boatload of money remodeling the place, but only succeeded in forcing it to lose its character. Now many of the patrons were middle-aged businessmen who, despite the wedding rings most wore on their fingers, hit on everything in a skirt. They stuck around for happy hour, pretended they were single for an hour or two, then presumably returned home to their waiting families.

The only good news was that what had once been a regular hangout for her friends had now become a laughing stock. No one was around to bear witness to her fall from grace.

The bartender plunked a vodka tonic with two limes in front of her and gave a wink. "On the house. Didn't expect you back so soon, Dee. How's it going?"

Daughtry smiled at the other woman. Darcy was as close to a friend as she came by these days. "I'm moving," she said, bypassing the loaded question completely.

"What?" Darcy asked, brows dragging together. "Why?"

A man approached the counter before Daughtry could answer. Not that she could give a real explanation.

Darcy gave the man his drink, tolerating a lingering caress on her cheek that made Daughtry shudder even though she was at a safe distance.

When he was gone, Darcy opened her mouth then closed it. After a moment she murmured, "You're not okay."

"Nope." *Okay* wasn't an adjective that described her life as of late.

"Want to talk about it?"

"No."

Darcy served a few drinks before she paused again in front of Daughtry. "If you need a place to stay . . ."

Daughtry's eyes shot up. Had she been that obvious?

". . . you can stay with me."

Her heart squeezed as she held back a grimace. The risk of a vision—and her temptation to change its outcome—was just too great. It was better if she were by herself. At least in the bar people mostly left her alone.

Of course, that was because she normally dressed in baggy T-shirts and jeans. Her red dress—the only piece of clean laundry she'd had—was garnering an entirely different type of attention.

And *that* was her cue to leave. It was time to kiss her apartment, her current life goodbye, to start over and hope that things might be different somewhere else.

She tossed back the rest of her drink and stood. "Thanks but—"

A hand on her arm prevented her escape. "Can I get you another, angel?" came his weaselly voice. The squeaky pitch was almost as bad as the preemptive nausea from his vision. She not so originally dubbed him Weasel Face as his death flashed behind her open eyes.

An audible sigh of relief slipped through her lips.

Not violent. In his sleep as an old man.

"You okay, angel?" Clammy fingers trailed down her arm. She swallowed hard. Puking in public wasn't exactly her idea of a good time.

Daughtry stepped back, pulling out of the man's grip, opening her mouth to tell him to back off. That she wasn't for sale, despite the way his gaze roamed her body, despite his grabby hands that were drifting toward her butt.

But something stopped her. An unhealthy darkness in her soul, a cruel piece of her mind had her hesitating. It all came down to money, and this would be an easy way to get some.

The businessman's eyes lit up as he helped her back onto the stool, his eyes glued to the skin so blatantly displayed by her dress.

Then she was trapped. Like the rollercoaster had taken off without her strapped in, and she was hanging on by her fingernails.

Daughtry ignored her conscience, which was screaming at her to run.

She didn't have to like this.

She just had to get through it. And then never, *ever*, do it again.

Darcy brought her another drink, which Daughtry pretended to enjoy, while the man prattled on about a merger.

She wasn't listening. Not really. Her brain buzzed frantically. The longer she sat, the louder her conscience got. On second thought, she couldn't do this, couldn't be this person. She had leave. Right *now*—

"How much?"

Oh fuck.

Daughtry shrugged, pretended not to know what the man was talking about, even as she searched for someone to intervene. But Weasel Face was obviously experienced in this kind of transaction.

"How about a thousand and a night at the Ritz?"

She tried to get Darcy's attention. It didn't work. Her friend couldn't see her past the crowd at the other end of the bar.

A protest was on her lips as Weasel Face gathered his coat and stood, taking her silence as acquiescence. Not surprising, considering how witless she had been up to that point. He tugged her to toward the exit while she tried to formulate some semblance of a response.

How about no? Or stop!

With that, the implication of what she was playing at finally hit her. She dug in her heels, passive participant no longer.

Ripping her arm away, she stumbled. A hand on her shoulder steadied her. She cringed at first, then relaxed when she felt . . . nothing.

She was too shocked by the lack of vision to even notice who had stopped her.

It wasn't until she had heard, "What the hell do you think you're doing, Daughtry?" that she realized it was John.

THREE

JOHN GRABBED DAUGHTRY'S ARM.

"Hey!" Weasel Face protested. "I—"

"Fuck off," John growled, shooting Weasel Face a glare that had him paling and clamping his mouth shut.

"Come on," John muttered, tugging her toward a quiet corner. His palm was hot against her bare skin and she found herself wanting to lean into the contact—it had been *so* long since someone had touched her without spurring a vision.

That frightened her more than anything.

It also pissed her off. Because John was interfering again.

"What are you doing here?" she said, trying to yank out of his grip. "Oh, wait. Maybe you've come to give me some more good news? Too bad I don't have another fiancé who needs you to do his dirty work. All my boyfriends break up with me on their own now."

John's head snapped back, a seemingly physical reaction to the venom in her words, and he rubbed his free hand across his face. "Shit, Dee. I deserved that. I should have made Jimmy tell you himself."

Yeah, like that would have happened.

She could still recall the stiffness of the paper, the roughness of the grains of sand that had stuck to the tape sealing Jimmy's breakup note.

It's over, Daughtry.

Yup. Had to give the boy points for creativity. Or maybe props for the bare minimum of words used.

Jimmy was also too cowardly—or perhaps that wasn't exactly fair, since he *was* serving in the Middle East, risking his life to protect the country. So maybe the truth was that he just hadn't cared enough about their relationship to give her the courtesy of a brush-off in person.

The worst part was that John had played errand boy for Jimmy, bringing the news with him when Jimmy couldn't be bothered to do it himself.

And so John had seen her at her worst—consoled her while she cried, wiped her tears as she'd sobbed, stopped her from setting Jimmy's shit on fire. The memory of him wrestling the lighter from her hands made her lips twitch, but then the fact of what happened next made that smile fade away like so much smoke.

Because he'd held her until she finally felt as though she wouldn't shatter, that all the hopes and dreams she'd been holding on to so tightly could be rebuilt. He'd brought her wine and ice cream, had checked in on her every day for weeks.

John had made her care.

He'd made her hope that they might have something between them—

Then he'd disappeared from her life.

And the visions had gotten so much worse.

From happening once in a while to monthly to weekly . . . until *every single* touch had caused one.

But never with John, now that she thought about it.

She'd had brief respites in the past few months, breaks from the images that sometimes lasted a few hours, sometimes several days, but eventually the recess would end and any hope she'd garnered that she could interact with others like a normal human was wiped away under an onslaught of blood and gore.

Still, for whatever reason, John had always been safe. For her visions, that was. Her heart, on the other hand? *That* hadn't been so safe.

Daughtry sighed.

John had fractured that last unbroken, untarnished piece inside of her.

"Let go of me," she said, her voice quiet and deadly serious.

He released her, but when she went to move away, he stepped closer. "You do realize that guy is an absolute fucking twatwaffle." He leaned down, met her eyes. "What about the ring? You only date married men now?"

The insult should have hurt, but if John knew the truth, he'd be even more disgusted. She cringed inwardly as she thought about what she had almost done. She'd stood there like a fucking mannequin and almost let herself be led out of the bar. To have sex. *For money.* She might have been pretending that wasn't what she was doing, but that didn't change the truth.

The absolutely disgusting truth.

She had just spent the last hour considering crossing a line that she'd *never* anticipated even coming close to.

Swallowing, she clenched her stomach muscles hard, trying to keep those drinks on the inside.

"Hey." John's fingers brushed her arm. "Talk to me."

Daughtry jerked away from his touch and turned for the exit, but before she could get there, he snagged her arm again and herded her into a booth. Damn, impractical heels. She should have screwed any inclination of fashion sense that morning and just rocked her sneakers.

The booth was lit with soft, romantic light, karma's version of a joke, considering that she had once thought the two of them could be—

Stupid.

That's what she'd been.

Holding out hope that John might be different.

Ugh.

She pressed her hands to the table and started to stand but he slid in next to her, preventing her escape.

Sigh.

But not just one borne of irritation, because despite her lingering resentment, she *had* missed John, missed his dark blue eyes that were always filled with compassion, with unconditional kindness. He'd been strong when she'd needed a friendly shoulder to cry on—and his were certainly broad enough for that monumental task.

He set his hand on her nape, pressed her more deeply into the leather seat. "Sit," he gritted out, glaring at her. "Stay."

Though this ordering her around, the anger turning his eyes a shade darker was different.

Before he'd seemed almost boyish, easy to smile, quick to laugh, a small swathe of freckles across his nose adding to the sentiment. Of course, the tight muscles she could see underneath his plain white T-shirt tended less toward adorable and more toward sexy—

"What the *hell* were you doing?"

A smile had been tugging up the edges of her lips when he spoke. His sharp question flattened the curve out.

As if anyone actually gave a damn about what she did with her life.

A narrowed glare in his direction. "You have no right to tell me what to do."

He'd left. He'd gone when she'd needed him the most.

But . . .

He'd also come when he didn't have to, told her the hard truth when Jimmy wasn't capable or willing. Which meant she should probably be the bigger person, express some gratitude for that.

Except . . . she was tired of talking, of fighting.

She just wanted to leave.

"Move," she said. "I'm going home."

For however long she had it.

John didn't reply, simply crossed his arms and stared.

All that quickly, Daughtry flashed back into anger. Her hands clenched as she rapped them on her thighs. "What? You think because you knew my a-hole ex-fiancé, you're obligated to watch out for me? Don't be ridiculous! I'm not some pity case or a damsel you need to rescue!"

Weasel Face chose that exact moment to reappear. "Look, we doing this or what? My money won't be good all night."

John burst out of the booth. "What did you say?" His hand went to Weasel Face's neck, his expression ferocious, the growl that escaped his mouth frightening.

"I–I don't want any trouble," Weasel Face said, hands up, face pale, and about ready to pee his pants. "She said she was available the whole night, but if you want her, I'll go." He pawed pathetically at John's hand. "Seriously, she's all yours."

Unthinking, Daughtry slid out of the booth and placed her hand on John's shoulder. She held her breath, waiting, but nothing happened. No nausea, no purple sparks, no images flashing through her mind. It was the first time that she'd initiated contact in nearly a year. Not since her visions had started, not since she'd realized it was touch that made them happen and not some mental breakdown as she took her bag from the guy in the drive-through window.

Was it possible that John was safe?

She was probably stupid to not quash the hope bubbling in her veins, but optimism had always been one of her better qualities. Maybe he—

Or maybe she *was* in the midst of a mental breakdown after all, because who had visions of other people dying?

"*Ergh.*"

Daughtry blinked, pulling her mind back into the present.

Weasel Face's hands were scrabbling at his throat, his skin turning a startling shade of blue.

"John," she said, and his head swiveled in her direction. The intensity in his gaze raised the hairs on her arms. "Please." She inclined her head to the man now hanging limp in John's hold.

There was a beat of silence before his fingers unlocked. Weasel Face's feet hit the floor with a *thud*. He gasped a single, long breath before throwing himself into the throng of people on the dance floor. Daughtry didn't blame the guy because, *fuck,* did John look scary. The aggression pouring off him was palpable.

A shudder seemed to flow through his body as he turned to fully face her, and then his features were carefully calm, and he resembled the kind Army Ranger who'd helped—albeit gently— break her heart.

Fortunately for her, before the past could ensnare her into another cycle of self-loathing, John's expression became judging and that was more than enough to get her hackles up.

His voice went soft, full of concern. "What are you doing, Dee? You don't need the money. I know Jimmy's parents set you up fine."

He looked closer, his blue eyes slightly unfocused.

A shiver skated down her spine.

"Do you have a drug problem?" he pressed. "Do you need help?"

She lifted her chin. "Why do you even care?"

His expression darkened, some unknown emotion playing across his face, but when all he did was stare unblinking at her, she decided that enough was enough.

"Just leave me alone," she snapped and pushed past him.

FOUR

DAUGHTRY STORMED OFF, weaving through the crowded bar, trying to avoid the gyrating bodies. John trailed her, and she sped up, almost running.

The foot came out of nowhere.

It knocked her off balance, propelled her headfirst into a dancing couple.

She barely heard their shouts of anger as a vision shot through her. Overcorrecting, she slipped on already wobbling legs.

Her shoulder glanced off someone else.

Car accident. No seatbelt. Ejected through windshield.

She straightened, was bumped from behind and, off balance, crashed into another person. Then another.

House fire. Two dead. Husband and wife.

Gunshot wound to the abdomen. Killed in Afghanistan.

Murder suicide. Wife, husband, three kids dead.

By the time Daughtry reached the exit she was sweaty, nauseous, her legs like rubber.

Outside, the late afternoon sun was blinding as she stumbled down the block and around the corner to her building. Leaning back against the brick wall that made up the first floor of her complex, she took a couple of deep breaths. The pain in her head faded to near manageable levels.

"Better," she muttered to herself, pushing off the bricks. "Bett —*oof.*" Her head snapped back, cracked against the wall. A teenager playing on his cell phone had knocked into her, hadn't bothered to stop or apologize.

She was too shocked, too hurt to yell at him for not looking. Then the vision had her and she was aware of nothing else except the horrible events leading up to his death.

Sociopath. Killed seven people before being gunned down by the police. Electrocution. Decapitation. Acid—

The keys fell from her numb fingers, landing in a dirty puddle near her feet. They were joined by the vodka tonics she'd drunk earlier.

As Dee straightened, her skin felt too sensitive, like every nerve ending was on high alert. With a sigh she rubbed away the goose bumps and sat heavily on the step. Her life was a mess. Every effort she'd made in the last months to avoid the visions had gone to hell in the span of five minutes.

There was also something she was neglecting, something she'd tried—failed—to forget. Because if it hadn't happened, then she wasn't obligated to keep trying to make a difference.

Except it *had* happened. She'd helped someone once. If she could call accidentally knocking a drink out of a drunk girl's hand helping. But that single, unintentional action had been enough. Daughtry remembered watching as the fibers of the girl's gruesome death had pulled apart like a tapestry being unwoven. They'd rearranged themselves, wrapped back together into a vision that had showed such a peaceful ending it had been almost laughable. It had seemed easy after that. Daughtry had just needed to set it up so that her interference had been accidental. Or arranged for someone else to do the intervening.

Neither had worked.

And she'd been forced to witness her interference making everything so much worse. So she'd retreated into herself, tried to avoid any visions so she wouldn't be tempted to intervene. *That*, at least, had been successful. Until yesterday, until today at the bar. Now she had death after death pinging around in her head.

Sighing, she slouched against the railing. There had to be a way to make sense of this. Someone she could talk to. Someone better than the section of occult books from the library or the crazy palm reader around the corner. Someone—

"Enough," she said.

Smothering the hope that made her vulnerable, she closed her eyes.

Daughtry wanted to help people, had to have been given this ability for a reason. But she needed to accept that her fantasy to be everyone's savior wasn't in the cards. It was time to stop screwing around with visions and the future.

It was all . . . just enough. She needed to leave and not look back.

The concrete step was hard and her back ached from resting against the iron rungs. She knew she should summon the energy to let herself into her apartment, but exhaustion had soaked into her limbs, rendering them heavy, almost useless.

She was so tired, in fact, that she barely registered the footsteps, the hand darting into the water to pick up the keys, being swept up into someone's arms . . .

It wasn't until she was halfway up the flight of stairs that she finally recognized what was happening. Thinking the teenage sociopath had come back and decided to make her his first victim, she freaked, kicking and scratching, but the grip on her only tightened.

"*Oof*." John grunted as a foot made contact. "Quit squirming or I'll drop you."

Panic faded at the sound of his voice, quickly transmuting into outrage.

"Put me down right now!" He ignored her as he continued to climb the stairs. Irritated, she grabbed at his arms, trying to pull them off her legs and shoulders. They didn't budge an inch. She might as well have been trying to bend a steel rod.

John made the ascent without tiring, without so much as a puff of air or another grunt. Of course he did—his biceps were huge, his thighs muscled. Paired with his square jaw, straight nose, and close-cropped blond hair, he was a jarhead through and through. A military man who wouldn't let a measly two flights of stairs fell him.

When they finally reached her apartment, John managed to let them in without fumbling the keys or putting Daughtry down. He strode over to the couch, knocked some of the old take-out containers and vodka bottles onto the floor, and lowered her none too gently.

"Jesus. You're a slob," he said, looking around the garbage-strewn apartment.

"Yeah, well, this may not be one of my better moments." She unstrapped her heels and let them fall to the carpet. Then flexed and curled her toes a few times to get the feeling back. Whoever invented stilettos should die.

John strode over to the fridge. The contents were meager, but she did have a bottle of water, which he grabbed, opened, and plunked into her hand before sinking into the worn arm chair opposite her.

Then he stared at her, blue eyes bright with kindness. So much so that it made her want to tell him about the visions.

She almost sighed.

Why would he believe her? She could already see how it would go. She'd tell him she could predict deaths. He'd bolt. There wouldn't be any hanging around to help the crazy chick after that. No matter how guilty he felt about his part in the breakup with Jimmy.

She shifted her eyes away to stare at the ceiling, concentrating on the almost artistic pattern of brown water stains as she forced down the tears that had filled her eyes.

By the time she got herself back under control, John's face was a blank mask.

He stood. "Pack a bag."

"Wh-what?" Her fingers went numb and she fumbled to hold onto the water bottle.

"We're leaving."

"I can't just *leave*." Sure she'd been planning to but—

John snorted, morphing some of her confusion into irritation. "You're getting evicted. You're broke and almost whoring yourself out—" He pressed his lips together then sighed. "Dee, there's no life for you here."

Her stomach churned at his words. "I'm fine," she said. Her throat was tight, but thankfully her voice almost sounded normal. "I can run my own life, John."

He pulled out his phone. "We'll argue about this later. For now, I just want you to pack a bag."

"But—"

He started dialing and turned his back on her.

FIVE

"STUPID," Daughtry muttered as she followed John's order by stuffing clothes into a backpack, still not entirely sure why she was doing as he'd asked.

Regardless, the red dress had been dropped to the floor, swapped for worn jeans and a tank top. On second thought, she reached way back into her closet to extract a hoodie. Even though it was warm this time of year in Northern California, she felt chilled.

The stress was taking its toll. *That* was why she was following a barked-out order without an explanation, not because she was weak or pathetic.

Ah, the lies she told herself.

With a sigh, she exited the bedroom.

John was on his phone. ". . . not yet. But I need to get her back. It's bad here—" He broke off as he saw her. "Yes. Tonight." Hanging up, he stared at her. "We need to talk."

"I'm fine."

He gestured to the disaster zone around him. "*This* is fine? This mess is fine? Selling yourself for a few hundred bucks is fine?" His voice rose with each question, until he practically shouted the final one. "What about *this* do you think is okay?"

"Nothing!" she yelled back, before forcing herself to lower her voice. "*Nothing*. I am so screwed up it is not even funny. Some days it would be better if I threw myself off the bridge, but I'm still here. I'm hanging on."

"Let me help you." John's voice was calm again, but there was an undercurrent of desperation that she thought was odd, given how little they knew each other.

"Why would you want to do that?" she responded warily. John had to have an ulterior motive. People always did.

His blue eyes were steady on hers. "Please, Daughtry."

It was the *please* that did it. It was so unusual for someone to ask her nicely that she agreed without really thinking.

Plus, she had nowhere left to go. At least with John—

"Fine," she said and waited for him to say something, to lay out a list of expectations and orders. That's what usually happened when she gave in to requests. When he didn't, she couldn't help asking, "Now what?"

"Snacks then gtfo." He pulled out a chocolate bar and handed it to her. Her heart melted a bit. Somehow, he'd remembered her addiction.

Don't get your hopes up, honey, the darkness in her taunted. *It not hard for a man to guess a woman likes chocolate.*

Daughtry shoved the thoughts away, but the damage had been done. Her eyes stung. Her chest felt too tight. The little bit of happiness in her soul had deflated.

In the midst of her swirling emotions, John plunked a can of diet soda into her hand—the right brand, no less—and, chest relaxing, she told her inner mean girl to stuff it. For whatever reason, John *saw* her. He didn't look past her like her parents had, but *at* her. As if she meant something to him. As if she were worth any trouble she might bring his way.

For a while the only sounds were the *pop* of her soda can opening, the rustling of wrappers. She leaned back against the couch. It was lumpy, uncomfortable, and yet, sitting there with John, having an approximation of a normal meal was nice.

"Why are you here?" she blurted, the words sounding harsh even to her own ears. Guilt flooded her as she opened her mouth to take it back. *Way to go. Alienate the one person who's been kind to you.*

John's shoulders tensed, but he turned to face her, lips tilted up slightly at the edges. "It's a fair question. I'm on leave."

Vague much?

"Any family in the area?"

"No."

Her teeth clacked together. "Sightseeing?" she ground out.

"Of a sort."

Frustration at the twinkle in his eyes made her snap. "How long until you leave?"

"Not too long."

That was it. She'd had enough. She pushed up from the couch and yanked open the door. "Out." This wasn't the time for games. He either needed to own up to why he was there being so nice to her or he needed to leave. "Unless you talk."

John straightened and stalked over to her, not stopping until his muscled body was close enough that she sucked in a breath.

"I'll tell you what you want to know," he murmured. "But you need to come sit down."

"Why?" Fear prickled down her spine, raised gooseflesh on her arms. Suddenly, she wasn't so sure that she wanted him to talk. What if John was there to tell her something bad again? What if—?

Gentle hands nudged her to the side, pushed the door closed, and flicked the lock. He tugged her to the couch and plunked himself down into the armchair.

She hesitated, emotions vacillating wildly—wanting to sit, wanting to stand, thoroughly confused and yet feeling like the next thing John told her would change everything. Her heart pounded, and her anxiety was sky-high.

John spoke softly. "It'll be okay. I promise."

Fear clawed at her insides. Somehow, she knew that it wasn't going to be okay. That everything was going to be jumbled and altered and—

He just sat there and waited, as if he understood the inner war going on within her mind. Finally, she forced her knees to bend and perched stiffly on the edge of the sofa.

Daughtry tried to force herself to relax. She knew John. Sort of. He was safe. *Maybe.*

But it wasn't John that had her worried. It was what he was going to tell her. She'd been hiding her visions for the better part of a year, knew that things weren't always like they seemed. What appeared good up front could end up being very, *very* bad.

"Dee." She forced herself to look up, meet his eyes. "There's something I need to talk to you about, and all I ask is that you give me a chance to explain everything before you throw me out."

"O-okay."

John cleared his throat, the noise loud in her quiet apartment. "It's about your parents." He paused and met her eyes. "Your *real* parents."

"What do you mean my *real* parents?" She stood. Her skin felt too small for her body as irrational panic flooded her senses. A distant part of her knew that her reaction wasn't logical, that John hadn't said anything outrageous.

He was probably just mistaken.

But a primal part of her was convinced that John knowing

the information was akin to the end of the world. Her palms went damp, her gut twisted.

"You were kidnapped—"

No one could know. It would mean her life.

The thought came from somewhere deep in her mind, a place she hadn't even known existed. John's words propelled her into motion, urged her to find a safe distance from the information. She wasn't supposed to know this.

Her lungs were tight as she reached the door, her palm making contact with the metal of the knob.

An odd prickling feeling trailed down her spine.

She glanced over her shoulder. "I'm sorry. I can't—"

"Get down!" John launched himself at her, slamming them both to the ground.

"What—?"

The front of her apartment exploded, and a volley of razor-sharp debris rushed toward them.

SIX

"STAY DOWN," John ordered, as wood and plaster rained down fast and furious. He pressed her face farther into the dingy carpet as his body covered hers from head to toe.

Eventually, everything went quiet. Daughtry opened her eyes, the mere prickling feeling she'd felt a few moments before almost unbearable now.

Standing just outside her apartment were two of the scariest things she'd ever seen.

Human, but wrong.

"Dalshie?" John murmured. "How can they be here?"

Pale, pale skin and red eyes were their most obvious attributes from the distance, but their palms, stained an inky black, were the worst. The marks seemed to undulate and move, almost lurching off their hands.

They made Daughtry's skin crawl.

The two men started forward, but their movements were abruptly halted when a wall of blue sprang up.

It was as smooth as the chunks of broken glass bottles that wash up on a beach. Rubbed almost velvety soft by the pounding waves and not quite clear, those pieces were still translucent enough to see through. But the wall of blue was also a visual contradiction because though the barrier was solid like sea glass, it was also fluid enough to curve itself around the hole in the front of her apartment.

The men pushed at the wall. Every hair on her body rose to attention.

Not right, her instincts screamed as she scrabbled backward.

John picked her up, shoved her bodily toward the opposite side of the room. The action cleared her head enough for her to focus.

"What are they?" she gasped.

"No time," John said, grabbing her arm, leading her to the window. There was a fire escape on the exterior wall. "We have to get the fuck out of here."

She nodded, knowing she'd gladly brave the rickety ladder over joining the two men trapped on the other side of that blue wall. So far, the barrier was keeping them out, but they were running their black palms over it, as though searching for any chink or weakness. She didn't want to be around if they found a way through.

"Open it," John grunted, nodding at the window. Sweat was pouring down his brow, darkening the hair at his temples.

Her hand stopped mid-motion as her eyes finally took in what was happening in front of her. *John* was making the barrier, strands of blue running from his body to the shield.

That wasn't possible. She blinked, trying to clear her vision. Maybe she'd finally snapped. Except—

She was seeing it with her own eyes.

Her mouth went dry as she saw barbed strands of black slither out of the palms of those scary-ass men. The oily threads crawled across the shield, searching for something.

She had the disconcerting feeling that it was her.

One of the attackers looked directly at her, pursing his lips in a frightening approximation of a kiss. She bit her lip to swallow a scream, not wanting to risk distracting John into dissolving the shield.

Screech!

Metal screeching on glass behind her shoulder shattered that intent. She let out a shriek that hurt even her own ears.

Another one of those *men*—

Monsters? Her mind struggled to classify them because up close they looked even less human. He stared at her through the window, an inky stain trailing up this creature's arms, emerging from beneath the collar of his shirt, encircling his neck like a malevolent necklace. All the while, the stain on his skin seemed to writhe in excitement, like it was trying to extricate itself to get closer to her.

Perhaps more frightening was the part of her mind that encouraged it. Something inside of her wanted to get closer to the darkness.

The man stroked the point of his knife along the glass again, the second screech of the blade loud enough to make her jump again. There was distinctly predatory gleam in his red eyes that had her shaking off any urge to get closer.

John cursed and yanked her behind him again, shuffling them sideways until she was pressed into the corner furthest away from the window and the giant hole in her apartment.

"Down." He shoved her to her knees when she didn't move fast enough, and a sharp piece of wood sliced her palm. Her fingers closed instinctively around it. She clutched it to her chest, thankful for any weapon. "Stay behind me," John said, shielding her with his body.

Daughtry crouched down and peered between John's legs. His knees were slightly bent, but his muscles were tensed, waiting. Before she could ask what was happening, the black strands of magic began battering themselves against the barrier.

She gasped, shoving herself further into the corner. *Oh God. Oh God—*

"Daughtry."

Her pulse skyrocketed, and spots clouded her vision.

This couldn't be happening.

"Daughtry." A hand gripped her chin. She looked into bright blue eyes, the color an exact match of the shield John had created.

"There you are," he said, breaking away and standing up. "Stay down. Ready?" he asked when she crouched farther into the shelter of the corner.

Not trusting her voice, she nodded.

"On three. One," A bolt of blue magic shot from John's palms, shattering the window as it knocked the creature there out of sight.

"Two." The wall disappeared. The black strands lurched in the sudden absence of the barrier.

"Three." The ebony fibers launched themselves at John.

For a moment, Daughtry thought he might be overwhelmed. But in an almost casual movement, he thrust his hands out, an equal number of indigo strands emerging to battle with black.

Near blinding light flashed as the magic connected. When her eyes adjusted, the colored strands were gone. In their place stood three red-eyed creatures, their rancid scent burning her nostrils even from her position behind John.

The scrape of metal against leather drew her attention, and Daughtry watched in a mix of fear and amazement as John extracted two swords from holsters hidden along his sides. They were short, frighteningly sharp, clearly meant for close combat.

"Leave the girl and we'll let you live," one of the trio said, his fetid lips curling up at the edges. He was presumably the leader by the deferential way the other two regarded him. "For the moment."

John didn't reply with words. Instead, he simply lifted his swords and waited.

He didn't have to wait long.

All three men charged at once, not giving John a chance to take them on one by one. Their weapons, knives with sick-looking black blades, clashed loudly in the otherwise quiet room.

She craned her neck to watch, then almost wished she hadn't. John's swords glinted, moving faster than her eyes could process. Unfortunately, she didn't miss the blood dripping down his arm, or the way he stumbled as he took a hit to his thigh.

Three against one was too much.

The leader backhanded John across the face, and he flew through the air. Daughtry's feet were moving before she even heard the sickening *thunk* of John's body against the wall. *Dear God, don't let him be—*

It wasn't until she pressed her fingers to his neck and found a pulse that she was able to breathe again.

"Aw, so sweet." A voice had her spinning around, clutching up one of John's swords. It was heavier than she'd imagined. She dropped her makeshift wooden dagger to grasp it with both hands.

The monster was only a foot away, his eyes twinkling in excitement as he raised his hand.

Daughtry barely resisted the urge to run.

Ebony sparks emerged from that inhuman palm. They burned like acid as they fluttered across the space between them, extinguishing themselves on her exposed skin.

"St-stay away from me." She brought the sword up, pointing it at the monster's stomach.

A sickening laugh emerged from rotten-looking lips. "Oh, no." He took another step forward. "I don't think I will." He pressed closer still and impaled himself on her sword. Then laughed as he pulled away.

"Stick me again," he said, a trickle of too-red blood dripping out of the wound before the skin began to knit itself closed. After a few moments, only the stained clothing and rancid smell remained. "I love foreplay."

"Hurry up. Let's get this done," one of the other men said.

Daughtry's stomach clenched. She didn't like the sound of that at all.

Keeping the blade close to her body, she took a subtle step sideways. Maybe she could make it out the door and draw them off long enough to get someone to help. Except— She held back a hysterical laugh. Who would believe her? And besides, who would be strong enough to take down the monsters who'd hurt John? He could do magic and had still ended up unconscious on the floor.

With a frightening smirk, her attacker cut her off. "Tsk. Tsk. I have plans for you." He took another step toward her. His hand moved to the button of his pants.

A frigid sort of calm had Daughtry antagonizing him back. Better that than being a quivering pile of fear. "No thanks. I don't do corpses."

"Bitch." Red eyes narrowed. "I'll show you how alive I am." He unbuttoned his pants. Inky fingers fumbled at his zipper.

"How about you brush your teeth first?" she shot back, flexing her hands on the heavy sword's hilt. They were cramping from gripping it so tightly. "Gum? Mouthwash? Heard of those?"

He growled and shot a kick at her coffee table. It crumbled, literally disintegrated into pieces and she took an involuntary step backward.

It was when she found herself pressed up against cheap, stained wallpaper that an idea finally pierced the fog of fear clouding her mind. Daughtry would run, draw the monsters away from John.

She'd head for the bar, the middle of the street, anywhere with a lot of people, and hope to hell that they wouldn't pursue her into a crowd. Pray that their pursuit of her would give John long enough to regain consciousness.

Decision made, she retreated toward the gaping hole that had once been her front door.

The monster smiled. "Lovely," he said, trailing after her. He spoke with the faintest hint of a British accent. "I do enjoy the smell of fear in the morning."

Daughtry ran for it.

In a flash, his hand latched onto her arm, the icy cold of his palm painful against her bare skin. Stinking breath puffed into her ear. "I'm going to—"

She wheeled around and plunged the sword straight into his heart.

It was a lucky shot.

The air stretched taut, the blade almost sucking itself into the monster's chest with a sick, popping sound that made her stomach clench.

He exploded into a thousand flecks of ash.

They coated her skin, choking her. She coughed, still clutching the weapon, and squinted through the suddenly dusty air.

"Thank God, you can die." She rubbed a hand roughly across her eyes, trying to clear her vision. Where were the other two?

"So can you." They charged her.

Sidestepping the lunge, she bolted for the window. A twenty-foot fall was nothing if it meant she lived.

They were faster.

Arctic fingers gripped her ankle. She fell hard and her head clanged against the hardwood floor, the sword clattering loudly as it fell from her grasp.

"My turn," one of the monsters said, shoving his companion away. His eyes flashed between red and murky brown, like he was struggling to hold on to some semblance of humanity.

Daughtry didn't have time to see more because his stained palms suddenly reached for her throat.

Flailing, she managed to land a blow to his nose. He cursed as blood splattered, cold on her face. She scrabbled backward, the sharp bite of the sword's metal blade a comfort.

Her fingers clamped around the hilt and she stood, her eyes locked on the monster in front of her.

He stared back, waving off his partner. "I *said* it's *my* turn." He turned back to her, too-crimson blood dripping slowly down his chin. "I'm really going to enjoy myself, bitch." The black stains on his skin writhed as he approached her.

"Your friend doesn't look very happy about that."

She wasn't sure where the words came from other than the fact that she was scrambling for time, for a plan, for John to wake back up and—

"I have no need of friends. Or lovers." He shot her a caustic look as he extended his hand. A freakish tendril of black magic emerged.

"Sebastian," the other creature said, his tone full of warning. "This isn't the plan."

"Shut up," Sebastian said with a glare at his companion. The ebony tendril snapped in impatience.

Oh fuck. She was so screwed.

A startled shriek emerged from her throat when a bolt of emerald magic seized the monster by the neck and yanked him to the floor.

"John!" *Thank God.*

Then she looked again. Her savior wasn't John. He was still

bleeding on the floor. She raced over and felt for his pulse again, thankful that it seemed less thready than before. "Wake up."

John didn't move, and her eyes were drawn to the man who'd stopped the monster from hurting her. Inky, barbed strands tangled with glowing, green magic. He moved like a shadow, dodging, engaging the attackers before a flick of his wrist turned Sebastian's companion to dust.

The fight intensified, and she gasped when the black magic made contact with her rescuer's skin, cutting deeply. He stumbled.

She *had* to help him.

But how? Her hands clenched in indecision and a twinge of pain in her cut palm reminded her that she still gripped the sword.

Pieces began clicking into place in her mind. The monster had died when she'd stabbed him in the heart. She held a sword. She'd just shove it—

But what if it didn't work? What if—

Another bolt of ebony magic slashed at their rescuer, making the decision for her.

Rushing forward, she was horrified by the amount of blood pouring down the man's sleeve, but she couldn't focus on that or the smell or the dust choking her, stinging her eyes. Sebastian had pinned her rescuer to the floor, and he raised his arm in what Daughtry instinctively knew was a killing blow.

Without thinking, she plunged the sword into Sebastian's back. Her eyelids closed as the blade penetrated.

Ashes.

Everywhere.

"Who's the cowboy, John?" the man asked as he regained his feet.

She froze, lids flying open, dust in her lungs, her throat, her—

Everything in the room went still at the beauty of his emerald eyes. They held a fury of emotion that was quickly locked behind a cold sheet of icy control when he saw her staring, mouth agape.

Shaken, she turned away and wiped her hands on her jeans. "Yipee ki-yay, motherfucker," she muttered, feeling like an action hero as she spat out the sickening remains of the monsters.

Then she cursed inwardly as her head spun.

A hero didn't faint after the bad guy got his comeuppance.

But that was precisely what her body was threatening.

Her adrenaline abruptly dropped off, leaving her muscles quivering and weak. She stumbled, put her hand against the wall. She needed to sit down.

"Daughtry!" John's voice was rough. Relief flooded her when she saw him shove himself to his feet. His balance wavered as he strode toward her.

"Good timing," she said. Her legs gave out and darkness seized her.

SEVEN

SHE CAME to in the back of an SUV, voices arguing loud enough to wake the dead. She grimaced as the terse words pinged painfully around her mind.

"Daughtry." John's voice was relieved. "You're awake."

The man who'd saved them was driving. His chilling emerald eyes met hers in the rearview, instantly making her feel like some ridiculous, delicate damsel in distress who'd needed saving.

She snorted.

Who was she kidding? She *had* needed saving. Those monsters were—

She pulled her gaze away from the mirror to whisper to John. "Sorry I lost it back there."

The driver snorted, and her spine stiffened. She'd dealt with enough today to warrant passing out, thank her very much.

"Yes, you did." John gripped her hand when she looked at him with question in her eyes. It was almost as if he'd reassured her for the thoughts in her mind rather than what she'd said aloud. "You also did good," he murmured.

She shook her head. "I was . . . I don't know. Lucky? What were those things?"

"They were—"

A cough cut off John's words.

"Let's get somewhere safe first." He didn't give her a chance to respond, peppering her with questions as he examined her injuries, a grimace marring his forehead as he palpated what she assumed was going to be a large goose egg on her forehead. "Anything hurting too badly?" he asked softly when he was done, frowning as he ran his fingers lightly over her cut palm.

"Me? I'm fine." She squeezed his arm. "I'm more worried about you. How's your head?" She winced when she saw the large black bruise on his temple, the skin only fragilely scabbed over.

"It's nothing," he said with a shrug, then straightened. "I need to do something." His hands came up to her cheeks, holding her in place. She was struck with how intimate a pose it was, especially with green eyes staring at her from the driver's seat.

John's fingertips tugged her closer. "Come here." He spoke quietly into her ear, and she shivered. "Look at me." Obliging, she was struck by the intensity in his gaze, by the warmth of his body next to hers. He was shelter, safety, kindness.

He pressed a kiss to her forehead, gentle and sweet. She could have almost sworn that she heard John's voice in her mind —*I never should have left you*—but the words faded as every hair on her body stood on end.

Magic balled in his palms, electric blue, before crawling across his body. The vines of power encased him from head to toe.

Daughtry gasped, her jaw dropping open. John placed his fingers on her temples and with a soft command the strands of magic unwound from his body, intertwining over hers. There was something about every inch of her being covered in him, in his essence, his power, that undid her.

"Amazing," she breathed, running a hand down her arm, blue sparks alighting on her fingertips. "What is it?"

The magic settled. "A ward," he said. Another masculine murmur made the strands of power invisible. But she could still feel them, like the softest brush of velvet against her skin. "To protect you."

That sounded an awful lot like a promise, and she wondered what she could possibly have done to deserve such a thing. People didn't put themselves in harm's way for others, not without a reason. Definitely not just because they were friends.

Grabbing her shoulders, he tugged her to his chest, held her tight for a long moment.

And even though she was defensive and skeptical and unsure, Daughtry let John hold her. She clung to the comfort he offered, overwhelmed by the sense of hope that was bubbling inside of her. Her heart felt lighter, her shoulders less stiff, and for a long moment, she was aware of nothing more than the synchrony of their breath, the beats of their hearts. Maybe everything would be okay. Maybe he could use the magic to fix her mind and she wouldn't have visions and—

A cough from the front row broke the spell.

She jumped, slipping from the embrace to slid over into her own seat. John let her go, but he laced his fingers through hers after she'd buckled her seat belt.

"What were they?" she asked to keep herself on track. "And where are we going? I need to . . . ." She trailed off, stopping herself from saying she needed to go back and get her things from the apartment. There was nothing left for her there and plus, what if she went back and there were more of those monsters?

Her gaze slid forward of its own volition, drawn to the man in the front seat.

Their eyes met, clashed. Daughtry fought the urge to recoil at the blind fury within his expression. Tearing her stare away, she waited for an answer. And still, she had to almost physically push away the urge to glance back. Her body was finely tuned to the driver's every movement. She wanted to ask his name, find out what made him tick.

Ridiculous.

She'd barely even seen his face. And yet—

No. She shook her head as she realized that neither of the men had answered her. "Why did they attack us?"

"We'll talk about that later," John said.

"Seriously?" she snapped when he didn't anything else. "You can't just come into my life after all this time and—"

"Don't get your panties in a bunch, cowgirl," the driver said, all too easily drawing her focus. "You don't need to know."

Daughtry fumed, barely controlling the urge to reach up and throttle him. "*Need* to know? Th-those monsters destroyed my apartment! I was nearly killed!"

"Yes, you were," John said, his blunt words somehow calming. "We would have died, or worse, if not for Cody's arrival." He leaned closer, his shoulder hard and warm against her skin. "I'll tell you everything when we get you someplace safe."

She gave him a hard look. "You'll answer my questions?"

A half-smile tipped his lips. "Every one."

"You've got to be kidding me!" Daughtry whispered furiously, less than thirty minutes later. "You can't leave me here with *him.*"

Not quietly enough, apparently, because Cody glared from

his spot on the recliner of the hotel room they'd checked into. "If I'd wanted you dead, cowgirl, I wouldn't have gotten this—" He gestured to the bruise on his cheekbone, the bandage on his arm. "—saving you."

Saving her. She snorted. Yeah right. She felt like pointing out that *she'd* actually been the one doing most of her own rescuing.

The silent version of Cody was much more palatable.

"Hurry up, John," he continued while she struggled to swallow her retorts. "Get permission to bring in the tartlet. Hulu's releasing another episode of"—he named a popular show —"at nine."

Okay, that was enough. Not the show part, but the tartlet part. She was not—

But as she opened her mouth to respond, John beat her to the punch. He wrapped his hand around Cody's throat, their faces mere centimeters apart.

"You will treat her with respect," John gritted out.

They stared at one another and for a heartbeat she was tempted to intervene, to stop them from breaking each other's jaws, if it came to that, but she had the feeling it wouldn't. John appeared furious while Cody seemed relaxed, despite the fingers gripping his neck.

He hadn't seemed so tall, so muscled at her apartment. But he was actually only a few inches shorter than John and slightly leaner—more soccer player than weightlifter. The light streaming through the hotel windows brought out the shades of platinum, brown, and strawberry that made up his rusty-blond hair. His nose was almost sharp, his lips the perfect mix of lush and masculine. Combined with the way he carried himself, the straight proudness of his shoulders, the almost liquid move-ments of his body—well, suffice to say that the Greek gods had nothing on him.

Cody looked over at her then, a strange expression on his face, before turning his attention back to the man holding him by the throat. "Fine," he ground out.

John peeled away his hand from Cody's neck and walked over to her. His fingers grasped her arm, warmth flooding into her from the vision-free contact.

"How long will you be?"

"I just need to debrief and get transport." He cupped her cheek. "I'll be back soon."

"We'll be fine." Daughtry intended to ignore the mass of menacing muscle choking up the perfectly nice hotel room.

John eye's twinkled as he looked at her in a way that said he could see right through her. Sliding a phone into her pocket, he opened the door. "My number's in there. Lock up."

With a sigh she threw on the deadbolt then turned to face her glowering companion.

Cody, his lips quirked in a half-smirk, looked back. He raised an eyebrow—even that was condescending. It made her want to take off her shoe and throw it at him.

Rolling her eyes at her idiocy, she kept her sneakers where they belonged and escaped into the bathroom.

"Yikes," she muttered, getting an up-close view of herself in the mirror. Between the dust, blood, and her absolutely out-of-control hair, it was amazing that the hotel manager had let her through the doors. Her hoodie was completely shredded so she tossed it in the trash, then undressed the rest of the way and hopped in the shower to wash off the dirt and blood from the attack.

Her arms hadn't fared too well from the explosion and subsequent flying debris, but at least none of the cuts were deep. Her head was another story. It ached, pulsing to the beat of her heart. "Would it be too much to ask for one of those alpha males to have caught me before I hit the ground?" she muttered.

At least the thick denim of her jeans seemed to have protected her legs.

Grimacing, she scrubbed the dust and slivers of wood from her aching body. After stepping from the shower she managed to scrounge a few Band-Aids from the courtesy toiletries provided by the hotel. Then she tore a hand towel into strips, using them to bandage her injured palm.

Her clothes were still dirty when she dressed again but at least her body was clean. Brushing her hands down her tank top, she decided that she'd stalled long enough.

When she walked back into the bedroom, Cody didn't bother to acknowledge her presence. She bristled before noticing that every muscle in his body was tense and alert.

"What is it?" she asked, afraid she'd actually get an answer for once.

Emerald eyes met hers for the barest second. "We might have company."

"What?" Rushing to the window, she tripped.

Cody cursed as he grabbed her arm. The action wrenched her shoulder, the cuts on her skin burning, but at least he'd stopped her from face-planting.

"Thanks," she said with begrudging gratitude.

A nod, his thumb brushing softly across the sensitive skin at the back of her biceps. His fingers had a slight roughness to them that made her shiver.

The motion made him blink, the hostility in his eyes roaring back to life and glared at her, tossing her arm away from him. "Be careful for fuck's sake." He turned his back on her to stare out the window, cursing again as he extracted his cell. It was at his ear in a moment and he was speaking into it in the next. "Too late," he snarled, grabbing her arm again. "Fine. Meet you there."

Hanging up, he hustled her out of the room and through the door for the stairs. "Hurry," he muttered, yanking her forward.

"Short legs," she grumbled, already panting from the pace he'd set. Their feet were loud on the metal treads until he pulled her to a stop. She opened her mouth to ask why, but the heavy sound of their pursuers' feet answered her.

Her heart sank and even Cody looked grim. Hauling her up into his arms, he flew down the remaining floors, out into the parking lot, to their SUV.

He barely paused as he flung her into the passenger's seat then rounded the car, hopped into the driver's side, and they screeched out the parking lot. Not a moment too soon, either. The door to the garage crashed open, more of those monsters pouring out of the stairwell.

She cringed back into her seat as the full force of their menace slammed into her.

"Why? How?" She could only manage single word questions. Her heart felt ready to pound out of her chest. "What?"

Cody's hands clenched on the wheel, his knuckles standing out sharply against his tan skin. He shrugged. "It appears we have a leak. Let's hope it's not John."

"What do you mean?" He couldn't actually think John would—

He glanced over at her, the frost in his gaze snapping her mouth closed. "Save your questions for someone who cares. We have a plane to catch."

What the fuck was happening?

EIGHT

DAUGHTRY HAD SPENT the last three-quarters of an hour alternating between worry for John and trying to ignore the compulsion to talk to the man next to her.

It didn't make any sense.

Cody didn't like her. He'd made that quite clear with his multitude of snotty comments, with his disdainful glares, but her body was shouting at her to forget all that.

Big deal, he was attractive. So was John. And a hundred other hunky guys in Hollywood for that matter. So what, he made her lady parts stand up and take notice. She was done with jerky guys.

She stifled a sigh. If only she could get her body onboard with her brain, because her body had apparently taken a trip down Delusional Lane.

"What are you doing?" she asked when he pulled off on a dark exit.

"We need to lose the car," Cody said with a sneer. "It's too obvious."

"And how do you propose we do that?" She took in their nearly deserted surroundings.

He didn't respond—surprise there, really—as he navigated the road that was more gravel than paved. The SUV stopped, the edge of the lake's shore peeking out from within the patchy brush.

Daughtry followed him out of the car.

"Wait there," he said, stooping to pick something up before pointing to a tree about twenty feet away.

Her jaw went slack as he wedged a stick between the seat and gas pedal. Engine revving and tires squealing, the SUV bucked like a pissed-off stallion.

He slid to the ground and released the brake.

The car shot forward.

The door slammed closed an inch from his head, but Cody didn't so much as flinch. His eyes were on the vehicle, which was tearing a respectable path through the underbrush.

Daughtry jumped at a sudden booming crash. A splash followed, with it the heavy slapping sound of water beating against the shoreline. Then everything went quiet. Bobbing headlights illuminated ripples in the navy-colored waters.

"Wh—?" The SUV's lights flickered out. She glanced around, half-expecting another car to appear out of nowhere.

Cody stood erect, a wicked grin on his face, while she was almost hyperventilating in her efforts to push out a full sentence. After another deep breath, she tried again. "What the hell was *that?*"

He shrugged. "*That* is far more efficient that just abandoning the car on the side of the road." He turned away and began picking his way through the undergrowth. "Plus, impound fees are a bitch."

She chuckled, amused despite herself and left wondering where the jerk from two minutes ago had gone.

"Let's go, cowgirl," he called, almost out of sight.

She hurried to catch up. It was already dusk, and she didn't want to be lost in the woods after dark. At least he had a flashlight. She watched the stream of light bounce with each of his strides.

"Hurry up. We've got a lot of ground to cover," he said. "That is, unless you're too precious to walk a couple of miles."

Ah. The jerk had returned.

Daughtry mashed her lips together—biting back her retort in the interest of a speedy journey—and followed. The ground was barely visible through the thick grass, and her progress was loud, the cracking of twigs and crunching of leaves beneath her sneakers echoing through the otherwise quiet woods. Cody, easily a foot taller and a hundred pounds heavier, was almost silent.

It only took a few minutes to regret leaving her hoodie in the hotel bathroom. The sleeves might have been mangled, but it would have been a heck of a lot warmer than her tank top. Especially with the temperature dropping as night descended.

"Here."

She looked up from the hand thrust in her direction into Cody's eyes. Her heart skipped a beat, every nerve at attention and completely focused on him . . . or rather, on the breathless way he made her feel. Mentally, she shook herself, knowing it was delusion talking, or adrenaline letting down or—

"Here," he said again, and she realized that she'd been staring at him stupidly as her eyes roved his body.

Fuck it all, she really needed to get a grip.

Jerkily, she grabbed the jacket, a hint of pine tickling her nose as she pulled it on. She inhaled, savoring the tangy scent of the forest around them, letting the smell relax her. The outdoors had always been her happy place. But then she realized the notes of pine weren't from the trees, but rather from Cody, all the more concentrated as she tugged up the hood. She inhaled deeply, felt her lips curve in satisfaction and—

Apparently, she was turning into a bloodhound.

When, aside from B.O. or bad breath, had she started noticing the way men smelled?

Daughtry sucked in another breath before she could stop herself and scowled. She'd never even liked the scent of pine. What the hell was wrong with her?

Oh, yeah. Near death experiences. That was what. And she had a knack for being attracted to men who treated her like shit and—*enough*. Halting that line of thinking in its tracks, she turned her attention outward. This walk was the perfect opportunity for her to gain some actual answers.

"Who attacked us?" she asked, thinking it an easy question to start with.

Cody's back stiffened as he glared at her over his shoulder.

She stared back, challenging and recalcitrant.

A muscle twitched in his jaw, but he answered. "They're called Dalshie."

Just the name sent a sliver of fear down her spine. Swallowing, Daughtry forced herself to keep her pace even. "Yal-shay?" The word felt foreign on her tongue, and, concentrating on the pronunciation, she tripped.

She caught herself on Cody's shoulder. "They're not human, right?" He tensed, and her fingers clenched, unwillingly intoxicated by the steely muscles separated only by a thin layer of cotton.

Cody turned, his flashlight blinding her as he pulled himself from her grip. "They're bad guys, okay? Now do you think you can restrain your annoying urge for questions for ten minutes? I'm trying not to get us killed."

Embarrassingly, Daughtry felt her eyes well up with tears. She was frustrated, on edge from the attacks, and neck-deep in something she didn't understand. She wanted to threaten Cody.

To demand information. But what would she do if he got frustrated enough to cut his losses and leave?

She was homeless. Broke. Pursued by freakish monsters that wanted to kill her. Oh, and maybe rape her first.

Blinking, she looked away, staring at the tree trunks in an effort to get herself under control. She wasn't weak, didn't cry at the slightest provocation. But her life had been spinning out of control for months, and after today, she was hanging on to it with the barest grip.

Cody sighed. "Christ, what now?" He reached over, grabbed her chin. His gaze clouded at what he saw there.

"Nothing," she said, pulling away. She didn't need his sympathy. "Let's go." Grabbing the flashlight from his hand, she started forward.

"Dammit!"

Her body jerked at his outburst, her fingers going limp. The light fell to the ground, her shoulders curling in on themselves in self-preservation. Damn Jimmy. He'd made her this way. No. Damn *her*. She'd let him.

Cody's face went blank at her reaction. He stepped closer, cautiously pushing into her space. A hand threaded through her hair, his slightly roughened fingertips brushing the skin of her nape. His next words were faint. "It's not you."

Daughtry rolled her eyes. Seriously?

He made a sound in his throat that could have been disgust and tilted her head so that she was forced to meet his gaze. What she saw there threatened to undermine all the defenses she'd put in place against him.

"It's true," he said. "I'm . . . not fit for human consumption."

Her gaze drifted to neck and for the first time, she saw the scar. It began on the left side of his face, at jaw-level, and continued down and around from ear to ear.

Tentatively, she reached forward, tracing the old wound

with a finger. Cody sucked in a breath, and her pulse soared when she realized that she didn't fear the contact.

He was safe. Like John—

John.

Guilt tore through her. Daughtry stepped back, pulling out of Cody's grip, using the distance to center herself. She was playing in the forest, tracing scars and focusing on lips and John was—

In danger.

They all were.

She should be focusing on making sure they *all* made it to safety. Especially when it was John who had come for her, fought for her, used his magic to protect her. Swallowing hard, she attempted to focus on her task at hand, but watching her hair as it slid through Cody's fingers, feeling the slight tug against her scalp as it caught on his calloused palms made her imagine other things.

Like trailing the strands across bare skin—

No.

She scooped up the flashlight and began walking.

The overgrown branches caught on her clothes as she gathered her anger around her like a shield. Cody was a jerk, plain and simple. And plus, she didn't need any man distracting her, not John, or Cody, or *hell*, not even one of the celebrity Chris's.

But most especially not hot-and-cold, disturbingly attractive Cody.

He caught up to her easily. "You okay, cowgirl?" This time the word came out more as an endearment than a slight, and she had to force away the little blip of pleasure that resulted.

That wasn't going to work. She couldn't risk him weaseling past her defenses.

She needed to distance herself from him. Fast, before—

Fortunately for her, she knew the surest way to irritate Cody was to interrogate him.

"Where are we going? Where's John? Why did the Dalshie attack me?" She sucked in a breath and asked the next question, even though it was a little stupid and very obvious, "Is magic real?"

Cody's head snapped back under the onslaught of inquiry, his expression bewildered. A thread of guilt wrapped itself around her heart, but she determinedly opened her mouth to continue her inquisition.

Understanding dawned in his eyes as his face reverted to the cold mask from earlier. When he spoke, the words were razor-edged with annoyance.

"Airport. On his way. Hell, if I know. And, yes, obviously."

Daughtry blinked, half-surprised that he'd actually answered her questions.

Cody's half-smirk turned full. "Cat got your tongue, cowgirl?"

"Don't be condescending," she snapped back.

"Then don't ask idiotic questions."

"There's no such thing as a stupid question." She crossed her arms before realizing how juvenile that looked. With a sigh, she let them fall to her sides.

A beat of silence passed as they glared at one another. Then her anger faded, passing as abruptly as it had come on. "Fine," she said. "Let's keep moving."

"Fine," Cody agreed, snatching up the flashlight as he pushed past her. She followed because, well, she had no other choice.

As Daughtry walked, regret sunk in. She'd hurt his feelings. She shouldn't care, but, unfortunately, and despite truly heroic efforts to pretend otherwise, she did.

Maybe it was a flaw in her personality. Maybe she was

destined to only be attracted to jerks. Sighing, she forced herself to face the truth. It wasn't all their fault. Someone could take advantage only if permitted.

Trouble was, after all the allowances she'd made with Jimmy, the endless apologies and concessions, she just couldn't take the risk. What if one apology led to a dozen? A hundred? More?

So she said nothing. Just watched Cody's stiff shoulders, his gait even and fluid despite his obvious anger. The silence between them grew more uncomfortable with every step. In the quiet of the woods, she was suddenly aware of how alone she was.

Well, she'd gotten the distance she'd wanted.

But it didn't feel as good she'd imagined.

NINE

IT WASN'T TOO MUCH LONGER before the airport lights came into focus.

"Thank God," Daughtry muttered, ignoring Cody when he raised a sardonic brow. So what if she was tiring? Her head ached, the cut on her hand throbbed, and she was panting from the rapid pace he'd set.

It wasn't like she'd known she'd needed to train to run for her life.

Where was John? She could really use him as a buffer between her and Cody. With each step, the tension between them had increased. Now it was stifling, a veritable cloud to push through. Something was going to have to give soon.

Hopefully it wouldn't be her head from her shoulders.

Cody stopped, his skin lightly glistening from sweat, but not even out of breath. He put a hand on her arm, pressed her back against a tree. She gladly took the break, trying to ignore the way the exertion had increased his scent. Pine mingled with the salty breeze of the ocean.

Turning away, he pulled out his phone and put it up to his ear. "It's me." Cody spoke as he paced, the tension in his shoulders making it seem like he carried a heavy burden. "Done." He locked the phone's screen and slipped it into his pocket before turning to face her.

The moment stretched as they stared at each other, Cody's eyes intense and filled with desire. Except the desire wasn't sexual, it was more like a wish to continue the cease-fire. To not be adversaries.

Uncomfortable with the ferocious need that notion evoked, she cleared her throat and looked away.

After a moment, Cody spoke. "Ready?"

She nodded and followed him across the tarmac. They approached a hangar on the far end of the airport that had seen better days. Harsh fluorescent floodlights showed that its exterior had once been bright white, though now it was a dingy grey. Black scum stuck to its eaves, eating its way down the tin sides in odd-looking patterns that could have been their own Rorschach test. A large acrylic *E* hung sideways near the roofline.

Cody began to speak as prickles of fear raised goose bumps on her arms. "John's just inside—" He broke off with a curse and shoved her toward the heavy iron door. She turned back, saw there were two figures running toward them. "Get inside," he snapped, his body a physical shield between her and the intruders. A gun appeared from somewhere beneath his shirt and a wicked-looking knife from the holster strapped to his thigh. "I'm going to kill him," he growled. "Why did he have to open his big mouth?"

She stood frozen, eyeing the weapons as the pressure under her skin increased, rising to the almost suffocating levels it had been at her apartment. Unable to stop herself, she peeked around Cody's broad shoulders and saw two Dalshie.

Fuck.

One of them held his hand up, conjuring a black ball of

power. This time, there were no taunts, no delays. He threw the glittering orb.

Her heart jumped into her throat, and she flinched back.

"Fucking moron talked," he said, deflecting the darkness with a casual brush of his hand. "I told him not to, but of course, he didn't listen."

"John wouldn't have—" She bit back the rest of her sentence when another strand of black snapped in their direction. Did Cody honestly think that John would have betrayed them to the enemy?

"Go," Cody said again and when she didn't immediately move, he added, tone hard, "John didn't betray us. *Now* get inside."

She blinked, wondering if she'd spoken her thoughts aloud.

His green eyes snapped to hers for a moment before returning his attention to the enemy. More Dalshie appeared, black magic crackling above their palms. "I was going to get us out before we tried to find the traitor who'd set us up. But no, he has to be *trusting* and follow all the procedures by going through the Council. And now look where that's got us."

An emerald strand of magic flew from Cody's palm and hit a Dalshie in the chest. The monster exploded into ashes. "John should know better than anyone that enemies can come from anywhere," he muttered, more to himself than to her.

Cody glanced back and startled when he realized she still stood there. "Fuck, woman. *Go.* John needs to get his ass out here and help me." This time he didn't wait for her to go on her own, he wrenched open the door and shoved her into the hangar.

The heavy metal panel clanged closed behind her, leaving her in a pitch-black cavern. She scrabbled for the handle, unable to see a thing.

What if there were more of them inside?

What if she was trapped in the dark?

Her heart thudded, sweat broke out on her spine.

"John?" she called softly.

Something or someone hit the building, and she gasped, the sound from the impact reverberating through the metal shell, making her eyes water.

Swallowing her fear and knowing that Cody needed help, not a pathetic weakling who was afraid of the dark, she raised her voice. "John?"

"Freeze!"

A light flashed on, and she blinked as her eyes adjusted.

John stood on the other side of the hangar. "Daughtry?" he asked lowering his hands—one with a flashlight, the other holding a gun—and striding over. "Where's Cody?"

She wanted to launch herself into his arms, she was so happy to see him, but Cody was fighting those monsters alone. "Outside. There are more of them."

John was still for a moment, his eyes unfocused. His lips moved, and she realized he was counting. "Ten recents, two elders. Damn. Where are they coming from?" He met her eyes, saw the question there. "I'll explain later." He shoved her into a corner. "Stay here." Then he was gone, and she was alone in the pitch-black hangar.

She sat waiting, her anxiety skyrocketing.

Distantly, she knew she was hyperventilating, that she'd pass out if she didn't slow her breathing. But the intensity of the feeling kept her on knife's edge. It felt like insects were crawling on the underside of her skin. And the sensation was increasing, smothering her.

No. She couldn't take another minute of cowering in the corner.

It was a struggle to make it to her feet, but she did and, eyes having finally adjusted, located the exit. She pushed through—

Holy mother of God.

Ash coated the air. More than a half-dozen bodies littered the ground, some flecking away to dust rapidly, others disintegrating more slowly. It looked like a set from some post-apocalyptic thriller.

John's head shot up as she emerged, and he hurried over to her. He looked terrible. His skin was a sickly white color, sweat dripped down his temples.

"Are you okay?" he asked, wrapping an arm around her waist and supporting her weight, despite looking to be the more likely of the pair to keel over.

"Great," she said despite her aching head.

"What happened?" John pulled her to a stop, gently touched her arm.

She glanced down, surprised to see marks there. It must have been from when Cody had stopped her from falling in the hotel room.

"Why do you have bruises in the shape of—?" His face went scary as he turned to Cody. "What the fuck did you do to her?"

Cody made his way over to them, glanced at the discolored splotches, and dismissed them with a shrug. "She's clumsy."

"You—" John was infuriated, but she cut him off. There was no time for this.

"He helped me."

Those navy eyes met her own and the anger in them waned. Nodding, he led her inside, and she watched Cody check the plane with the flashlight.

A bare minute later he crossed back over to them, tapping the light in his palm.

"Ready?" John asked.

Cody nodded before hopping up the small flight of stairs to board the plane. She helped John, who still appeared weak, ascend. "Are you okay?"

"Peachy," he said with a quirk of his lips.

She smiled back. Everything was going to be all right.

"Get strapped in. We're leaving now," Cody said, entering the cockpit. The metal rolling door that made up the front of the hangar rose noisily.

Daughtry surveyed the cabin as she took a seat near the wings. She knew that particular location made for the smoothest ride. Though it probably wouldn't matter. Their chances of crashing in this type of plane were high.

Dammit. She really hated flying.

She tried to think of something, *anything,* besides crashing to the ground in a giant fireball. So she focused on the expensive elegance of the plane.

The black leather covering the seats was silky, and a series of crystal chandeliers—yes, *really*—illuminated the aisle. The plane itself was a good size. Daughtry counted room for at least twenty. Maybe its safety rating was better than those single-engine puddle-jumpers.

Her attention was diverted when a swathe of gooseflesh covered her arms.

"John?" she called, not completely understanding the sudden edge to her emotions, but knowing it didn't bode well.

He held perfectly still for a moment, eyes unfocused and searching, before hurling himself for the door.

"Cody! Get her out of here!" he shouted, bounding down the stairs.

"John!" she called, unbuckling her belt and following. By the time she made it to the exit, he had already reached the ground.

"Where are you going?" she yelled after him.

John froze, then turned and cleared the steps in a leap. His heavy bulk tackled her to the carpet.

"Stop," she said.

"Duck!" He shoved her head down as a shot of power sizzled

over their heads. It hit the other side of the cabin, making the wallpaper bubble and blacken. The pungent smell of smoldering glue burned her nose.

John stood, shooting a bolt of blue magic across the hangar. It sliced the Dalshie across its neck, turning it to ash. Without pause, he hauled her to her feet, shoved her into the cockpit, and buckled her restraints.

"Go." He gave the order to Cody, who didn't appear happy to be on the receiving end.

John cut off his protests with a terse shake of his head.

"I'll delay them." He held Cody's stare, and they had a silent conversation. Finally, Cody nodded in acquiescence.

John turned to leave.

She caught his hand. "No. You're hurt." The action of the last few minutes had paled his face further, deepening the lines around his eyes and mouth. "You look exhausted."

"She's right, man," Cody interjected. "Between the ward and the others, you're tapped out."

"I have more in me," John said. "And they're closing in. We can't let them track us." He glanced at Cody. "You know that." John looked down at her. "I'll be okay. I'll meet you there." He squeezed her shoulder. "I won't disappear this time."

Blinking her eyes to hold back the tears that made her feel weak and stupid, she nodded. "Promise?"

He nodded before focusing over her shoulder. "Take care of her."

Then he was gone.

Cody was silent as he rapidly checked gauges and flipped switches. The jolt from the stairs slamming closed reverberated through the plane.

"Hang on," he said, hitting something that made the plane's engines roar to life.

As the plane vibrated beneath her, Daughtry saw a flash of light out of the corner of her eye. She leaned forward in her chair, cursing the restraints as she tried to see. Her heart jumped into her throat.

Four Dalshie stepped out of the shadows. They slid through the open hangar door and tried to surround John, who had shifted his position so the metal wall was at his back.

Magic started flying.

Black, barbed strands shot toward him. He managed to deflect them, to send a few electric blue ones in return.

But there were too many.

"Stop!" She fumbled at the maze of belts holding her in place. "He needs help."

"Sorry, cowgirl, no can do." The plane began to idle forward. "I promised John, and he means a hell of a lot more to me than you do."

"Not if he's dead, he doesn't." Cody's logic didn't even make sense. "We have to help him. He could die!"

The runway was ahead of them, the hangar to the side, John's blue bursts of magic illuminating the darkened space. Her neck craned as she tried to keep him in sight.

The vice grip on her lungs eased. Maybe her premonition had been wrong. John was standing amongst another sea of bodies, all of his attackers slain.

It was false hope.

More Dalshie appeared out of thin air. They hurled ropes of power, and the menace of the magic prickled her skin, even as her distance from it steadily increased.

John cut down one. Then another.

It only took a moment for the momentum to shift.

One of the ebony bolts struck him in his chest and knocked him to his knees.

"Cody. Please wait. John is—" She broke off.

"I know." Cody's voice was grim. The plane sped up. "But we need to get you safe. He wanted that."

A final blast of magic collided with John's head, and he fell to the ground.

Runway markers whipped by. The plane began to lift into the sky.

The last image Daughtry had was of John's prone body sprawled on the cold concrete.

Then the entire scene became nothing more than a blip in her vision as the plane shot into the sky.

TEN

"DAMMIT," Cody muttered, rubbing his fist across his eyes. "Fuck!" This time he shouted and slammed his fist against the dashboard.

Daughtry jumped, only the restraints keeping her in her seat.

Blood welled up on his damaged knuckles, the bright red drawing her attention. It gathered on his flesh, pooling without dripping over.

She watched, the drama of the last quarter-hour forgotten, as the blood froze in place. It slid back into the wound, and his skin reknit itself.

As if it itched, Cody brushed the offending limb across his thigh.

Her gaze was frozen on his hand, the rapid healing reminding her of the Dalshie from the apartment. *What if he was one of them?*

"I'm not."

"I know," she said, knowing that truth as certainly as she knew the sky was blue.

The Dalshie might have the appearance of a human,

creeping ink stains and red gazes aside, but their cruelty was evidenced in their eyes, in their malicious smiles.

"Oh. I guess I just—"

Her eyes shot to Cody's, saw frustration and something she wanted to pretend wasn't compassion in their depths. But she couldn't handle someone being nice to her right then, only barely holding it together as it was. John had come back for her, had risked his life and now—

"Can he do that?" Her voice sounded weak, tinged with pathetic hope. Maybe if John could heal himself, he'd be okay.

Cody's face hardened. "Hell no."

She blinked at the harsh response then mentally shrugged. Well, she hadn't wanted nice.

And at least the tears that had been threatening had gone away.

After a moment of silence, Cody cleared his throat. She looked over at him, surprised by the awkward expression on his face. A little of the tension in her gut eased at the unconscious admission.

He broke eye contact and stared back out the windshield. "John's alive, you know."

A flurry of emotions slid through her mind. Confusion, fragile hope, frustration, curiosity. She could sense Cody watching her carefully, the pine and salt of his scent clogging the air.

Eventually she swallowed, her throat tight. "How do you know?" She concentrated on the row of gauges in front of her. Maybe if she looked at them hard enough, they would make sense.

Cody sat back. "I can still see his ward on you. You're untouchable until it's gone."

"Untouchable?"

Cody looked uncomfortable and only mildly irritated at her questions. Progress.

"His ward shields your mind. You're basically Bubble-Girl."

Her mind flashed to the back seat of the SUV, to the indigo magic wrapping her from head to toe. Magic she could still feel like a balm against her skin.

John had promised to protect her.

Her heart squeezed with equal parts guilt and gratitude when she realized that he had indeed done just that.

"But how does it work?" she asked. "Is that why I haven't had any visions?"

"John's powerful. His ward will stop you from having them. Until it wears off." Cody paused. "Or has cause to break."

Break?

The hairs on the back of her neck rose. Her fingers cramped as they clenched on her thighs. "Break, how?"

One of the gauges beeped, drawing Cody's attention.

But she needed an answer. Her heart raced. Not knowing was suffocating her.

"What do you mean *break?*" she asked again.

Cody gripped the controls, the cut that already looked days old standing out sharply against the olive color of his skin.

Another chime.

Daughtry wished he would just answer her. He couldn't be insinuating what she thought he was. She couldn't be the barometer for knowing when John died.

No. The pressure of that was already unbearable.

She opened her mouth to do something. To say something.

"Goddammit, Daughtry!" Cody pulled a lever and punched at a button before looking at her, his emerald eyes frigid with cold. "Break, as in dead. The ward will dissolve if he dies. Now. Shut. *Up.* I'm trying not to crash this fucking plane."

Her mouth opened and closed a few times, doing a poor

impersonation of a gaping fish. Then, eyes welling in frustration, in despair and hopelessness, she looked out the window, concentrating on the panoramic views. The softly rolling brown hills were dotted with dark green gatherings of oak trees.

It should have been gorgeous, comforting even, because it was home. Instead it was blurry from the watery lenses of her tears.

Daughtry rubbed her eyes, dashing away the stupid wetness.

Cody spoke then, using a cautious voice that made it seem like he regretted the outburst. "Hey." He attempted a smile, but it just looked painful. "At least you won't get any visions."

No visions. That's what she wanted, right? But what would be the price? The ward had weakened John and now—

"Why did he do it?"

Cody was silent for a long moment. When he finally spoke, his voice had more warmth in it than she'd heard up until that point. "Why does John do anything? He's a Boy Scout, the person who always does the right thing. No matter the sacrifice."

Like traveling two thousand miles to let another man's fiancé know that the person she'd thought she'd be spending the rest of her life with had run off with someone else. Even though they'd never met.

Like sacrificing himself—

"But what's in it for him?"

Cody chuckled, a sound that held more sadness than amusement. "Never been able to figure that out for myself. Unfathomable really, because people don't just do things for nothing."

Hearing those words, which she'd so often thought herself, echoed by Cody sent a wave of cold over her. Did she really want to spend her life wondering about everyone else's motivations? Or did she want to take control over her own future?

Daughtry took in the world outside the cockpit as she

contemplated the notion. The hills had given way to a flat valley littered with small family farms. From this altitude, the homes looked like toys, the cows and horses simple flecks of color.

It was beautiful, but it didn't distract her from the thought blaring across her mind, the hurtful notion that might as well have been a billboard with neon flashing lights.

What made her worthy of such a sacrifice?

Nothing concrete came to mind. She was just an average girl with worse-than-average luck. Not particularly pretty, her auburn hair made her skin look pale, almost porcelain, and she was small, doll-like. No one wanted to date a doll.

At least nobody who wasn't a pervert.

The only thing unique about her were her eyes. They were violet. Not a facsimile of blue that appeared purple. No, brilliant violet, a shade that she'd never seen on anyone else.

Daughtry was starting to think it was the magic. The color of her eyes and the intensity of the blue and green shades that made up John's and Cody's seemed to support that.

It made her wonder again about what John had been trying to tell her before they'd been attacked. He'd said something about her real parents, about her being kidnapped. Was it possible that she had someone out there who cared about her? Someone who could . . . love her?

Her heart swelled, the potential intoxicating. She actually had to force herself to close off that part of her mind and focus on the task ahead. First, she needed to deal with the Dalshie.

That meant she needed some real answers.

"Where are we going?"

Cody jumped like he'd forgotten her presence. He turned, regarding her with a raised eyebrow.

"What's the plan?" she pressed.

"Plan?"

Swallowing against the force of his scowl, she forged on.

"Yes. Plan. It's a four-letter word, can be a noun or a verb. Though in this case, I want it to be a noun, so I can understand *what the fuck are we doing.*"

"Well, thanks to the Boy Scout, I'm now in charge of getting you to the Colony. Lucky me." His tone was bitter, but there was an emotion hiding underneath. Something about Daughtry apparently made him furious.

She had cringed back into the seat before she remembered herself. It was past time to buck up. No more allowing Cody to intimidate her, no matter how good he was at drudging up bad memories.

"Yes, lucky you," she said, doing her best to imitate his icy tone. She fumbled with the restraints for a long moment before finding their release. "I'll be in the back."

She turned to leave.

"Hey."

She hesitated and their eyes connected, his clouding with irritation, hers probably revealing how pathetically attracted to him she was. Stupid. As in, *she* was stupid. Sighing, she nibbled at the corner of her mouth and mentally shook her head at herself.

His gaze dropped to her mouth, staying there for so long that she almost wished he would just kiss her.

Maybe then she could get over herself.

But as his eyes came back up, she noticed something else— fury and disgust.

Her heart sank. Earlier in the day, she'd been thinking about John, about the past, the present, how she'd once hoped they had a chance at a future. Now that same man had sacrificed himself and she was already dreaming about kissing someone else.

No wonder Cody was disgusted. She could barely stand the thoughts going through her head.

She spun, scrambled toward the door to the cabin.

"What's the matter, cowgirl?"

She stopped, looked over her shoulder.

"I'm not pretty enough? Girls like you aren't usually that picky."

Her jaw dropped. A thousand sharp retorts were on the tip of her tongue.

How dare he say such a thing?

She opened her mouth to yell. To hurt him back. Then stopped.

Did he know how close to the truth he had hit?

It hadn't even been twenty-four hours since she'd considered whoring herself—

She dropped her eyes to the floor and exited the cockpit. Her bubble of rage had burst. Feet dragging, exhaustion sinking in, she walked down the aisle toward the bathroom. The crystal chandeliers jingled, throwing little rainbows across the plush beige carpet.

She stepped inside and closed the door. Since her legs were shaking, she plunked herself on the closed toilet. Her head rested against the wallpaper as she tried to steady her emotions. It didn't matter if what Cody had insinuated had almost been the truth. She hadn't gone through with it.

But it still made her feel dirty.

"John," she said, eyes burning. "Why would you risk your life for me? I'm nothing."

The rumbling of the plane's engines was her only answer.

Daughtry remained where she was, welcoming the numbness that was steadily filling her. It was better than crying. Eventually she grabbed a towel, wet it, and used the cool cloth to sooth her hot cheeks.

"Enough," she told herself in the mirror.

The bandage on her hand had come loose, disheveled by her

frantic exertions at the airport. But the bleeding wasn't bad. With the first-aid kit from beneath the sink, it only took a moment to set everything to rights. As she packed the supplies away, she gave herself a pep talk. Of course she was worried about John, concerned about the colony-place Cody had mentioned he was taking her, and freaked the hell out about the Dalshie.

And yes, Cody may be an asshole, but she needed him. She couldn't allow him to push her buttons.

Daughtry snorted. Easy in theory. In practice, not so much.

Exiting the bathroom, she selected a chair at random. The tenuous hope she'd felt had vanished. She was all alone with the exception of a goose egg the size of Kansas and a surly companion who was eyeing her like he couldn't wait to throw her out the emergency exit.

Waving at the hunk of blond-haired, emerald-eyed muscle currently glaring at her from the cockpit, she curled into the armchair, buckled herself in, and settled down to sleep.

ELEVEN

A SHARP DROP snapped her out of her dreams. Daughtry sat up, or rather, tried to. Altitude didn't allow her the time as another dip nearly pulled her out of her seat. A blanket she didn't remember grabbing fluttered into the aisle.

They had problems.

The major one being that they were thirty thousand feet in the air and flopping around like overcooked pasta.

Stupid John.

She didn't mean that, of course. But if she hadn't trusted him so much, she would have never gotten on the single-engine death machine in the first place. And now she was going to burn to death or be ripped into a million pieces on impact.

"We have two engines," Cody said, rather unhelpfully. "Plus the force will probably break your neck before you have the chance to burn to a crisp—" A curse broke off the rest of his patronizing comment as the plane dropped again.

Fear didn't allow her to snap back. She sat frozen, fingers clutching at the black leather.

Eventually, no more swearing drifted back, and the plane began to fly steadily. She relaxed with a sigh, turning her gaze to the window. They were descending, had almost passed through the cloud cover.

"Fine," she said to herself. "We're fine."

They dropped again and the image of every plane crash she had ever seen on television flashed through her mind. She saw twisted pieces of metal speared into grassy hills, steel logos of airlines shattered into a thousand pieces as easily as a plate dropped on the kitchen floor.

Lightning snapped.

She gasped, clutching at the seat. It was dark, the flashes of electricity the only illumination of her surroundings.

Each burst of light gave another frightening image: the ground coming up too fast, a backlit picture of crops nearly bent over themselves, their tops creepily bowing against the dirt; a fallow field looking very much like a cemetery with its graves already dug; a cloud of unnatural blackness that made every hair on her body prickle uneasily.

The aircraft lurched, throwing her roughly. She cried out from the pain of the seatbelt biting into her side.

Pushing herself upward, she looked ahead and saw Cody spot-lit at the controls. His shoulders were hunched forward, every muscle tense as he struggled to land the plane.

Her ears popped.

The plane rocked dangerously from side to side.

She looked out the window. Only a few feet separated them from the ground.

There was an oppressive moment where gravity yanked them down and the air tried futilely to keep the plane aloft.

A bone-jarring bump.

The airplane swerved before Cody got it going relatively straight. She released a breath when they didn't explode into flames. He'd done it!

"Fuck!"

Her eyes flew forward. The plane was careening ahead at breakneck speed, and it didn't take an oracle to recognize that they were on a collision course with the bank of trees forming a windbreak between two fields.

"Get up here!" Cody shouted.

She heard him, but didn't understand the order. What difference was it going to make?

"Daughtry!" Cody turned, the scar on his neck blatantly obvious. "If you want to save your ass. Get. Up. Here!"

It took forever for her to unbuckle her seatbelt, to stumble the few steps to the cockpit. Then Cody grabbed her hand and time ran in warp speed. A blast of pain made her knees buckle as he punched through the ward protecting her mind and she would have fallen if not for his arm around her waist. His mind penetrated hers—delving into her brain—as he wrenched magic she hadn't even known she possessed from deep within its depths.

Her spine and arms tingled as tendrils of that magic left her body via her palms.

There was something dark, almost alluring, about the power he'd pulled from her. She wanted more, *needed* more—

The plane jarred.

She stumbled, gripping the back of the chair and blinking to clear her vision.

Hundreds of threads of their power, hers a brilliant purple and Cody's an emerald green, were intertwined. The magic shot forward, bursting through the glass of the windshield like an elephant tearing through a tissue. It pressed backward along the sides of plane to form a parachute.

She could feel the threads pushing them, slowing them.

It wasn't enough.

"Cody." It was a plea. Funny that she was desperate to live

now when she'd wasted an entire year of her life wallowing in self-pity.

"I've got you." His words hit her in the stomach, shredding her to pieces even as he reached deeper into her mind. He siphoned off every bit of her magic, leaving her empty, weak.

The plane jerked and slowed.

The force of the deceleration stole her stability. She scrabbled against the floor, a huge push propelling her straight toward the windshield. Cody's arm locked around her hips, the strong limb the only thing that kept her in the aircraft. The screech of metal against the ground was piercing. Her ears burned and her fingers ached from clenching into fists.

But her eyes stayed open.

God, how she wished she could close them. The trees came closer. Glass crunched. Wind roared. Finally, *finally*, they shuddered to a stop. The engines rumbled, vibrating the plane roughly before Cody turned them off. The residual heat made their metal parts click loudly. The sound resonated in her body. The noise dwindled, slower and slower, just like her settling heartbeat.

Cody let go of her waist, slumping in his chair, exhausted.

Daughtry didn't dare move an inch. Her eyes locked on the tree branch that was casually sitting less than a foot from her forehead. If Cody hadn't grabbed her—

She clung to the back of his chair when her legs wobbled. She didn't even want to think about it.

Brushing hair out of her eyes, she stepped back from the offending piece of wood.

Cody heaved a deep breath before unbuckling his seatbelt and standing.

His emerald eyes dared her to freak out. What he didn't know was that she was made of sterner stuff.

Refusing to look away, she raised an eyebrow, speaking with

infinitely more aplomb than she felt, "Guess we're walking from here?" *Take that patronizing look and shove it up—*

She could have sworn that Cody's lips almost twitched. "We'd better move," he told her. "I'll call someone I can trust, and see if we can get a ride."

He'd volunteered information?

Daughtry felt her mouth fall open, and then Cody did smile. It transformed the harsh lines of his face into something boyish, almost innocent.

Why he didn't share that smile more often? The asshole routine had to be exhausting.

Why the hell did she care anyway?

Nerves. Or maybe leftover adrenaline from nearly being speared by a tree.

She told her conscience, the one that was pointedly reminding her that Cody had just saved her life, to shut the hell up. So what if he had streaks of goodness? He was still an ass—

He leaned into her, crowding her against the wall.

Her breath caught when his lips paused barely a hairsbreadth from hers, the heat in his emerald eyes almost undoing her. A blush crept into her cheeks.

He pressed closer.

At the last second, he turned his face away to reach behind her shoulder.

The cabinet made a quiet, humiliating *snick* as it slid open.

He withdrew a backpack and exited the cockpit. Daughtry closed her eyes and thumped her head back against the cabinet, clinging to that feeling—the one that made her feel like she was despicable and gross—knowing she needed to wield it like a weapon. She couldn't waste her time on someone who so easily made her feel bad about herself.

"I am not weak," she whispered to herself. "I have *some* self-respect—"

"Let's go, cowgirl," Cody said. He popped his head back into the cockpit, grassy-green irises framed by one quirked eyebrow. "We need to move."

"That nickname better not stick," she muttered.

He hopped down the stairs, not sparing her a look back as she hurried after him, head aching, legs like Jell-O. As she moved, her muscles warmed, and her movements began to steady. But there was something off about her recovery. It was too fast. She focused on the part of her mind from which Cody had commandeered her power. It was a pulsing presence in the back of her brain that grew brighter and stronger with each passing moment. She could feel it, watch it, but couldn't actually touch it.

Concentrating, she tugged at the ball of magic, but nothing happened. There was a barrier, a glass wall around that part of her mind, and no matter how she struggled she couldn't get to it.

Her magic was inaccessible.

The violet sphere grew, expanding, distinguishing itself into a yarn-like ball of entangled threads.

A sudden gust of wind lifted her ponytail, raising goose bumps, pulling her out of her self-evaluation.

She blinked, following Cody as he pushed through the crops, the tall stalks of corn only coming to the middle of his chest. She, on the other hand, they towered over, nearly obscuring the clear, blue sky.

Something niggled her mind.

Hadn't it just been dark?

Daughtry stopped, pushed a stalk out of the way, and looked up. All traces of the storm that had just knocked their plane out of the sky were gone. In fact, there wasn't a cloud in sight.

Some sixth sense deep within her mind had her hurrying to catch up with Cody. Something wasn't right.

As she rushed forward, the silk sprouting from the ears of

corn stuck to her hair and shoulders. It tickled the backs of her arms, her neck, making it feel like she was covered in ants. The feeling persisted even after she brushed them away. She actually had to shove her hands into her pockets to prevent herself from scratching.

Glancing up, she saw Cody reach the end of the field and increased her pace, unexplained anxiety turning her walk into almost a sprint.

As she neared him, some of the tension left her body. He would protect her.

He opened his mouth, probably to say something sufficiently mean to keep up his prickly exterior, then closed it and glared, not speaking until she was just a few feet away.

"What are you doing?" The question was brusque enough to make her want to snap back. He gestured at her arms, at the red scratch lines marring her skin.

"It's nothing," she said, feeling abruptly ridiculous for running after him like a pathetic schoolgirl. Shrugging, she couldn't resist the urge to rub her neck, to try and get all of the pestering silk off. "The corn got stuck in my hair."

He handcuffed both of her wrists in one hand then turned her. His free hand flipped up her ponytail to examine the abrasions on her nape, calloused fingertips gentle as they traced the skin there. A rush of heat that had nothing to do with nerves or magic shot through her.

But when the warmth faded, the disconcerting feeling of ants running under her skin persisted.

She stepped away, fisting her hands, focusing on the pain of her nails biting into her palms to stop herself from reaching up and scratching.

Looking up, she saw Cody studying her with a fierce expression. His jaw was tight, his eyes hot and liquid.

The corn surrounding them suddenly became fascinating.

But only for a moment because she still couldn't get rid of the itching. She glanced over at Cody and he seemed calm. She needed to chill. He was the expert. If there was any danger, he'd be clued into it.

Eventually, she gave in, trying to scratch the prickling away. Of course, that only made the crawling feeling worse.

Cody, whose stride was quickly overtaking her own, looked at her hard. Then his eyes widened.

"Shit! Come on." He grabbed her hand and began to run.

"What is it?"

His power surged into her brain, surrounding her. The creeping feeling dissipated, but she felt little relief. There was panic in his power, palpable enough that it took her breath away.

"Dalshie."

Daughtry stumbled for a few steps before regaining her stride. She watched her feet as he towed her forward, doing her best to keep up. Concentrating on not breaking an ankle meant she couldn't spare any attention to fear what was behind them.

Cody seemed frightened enough for both of them. His emotions hammered at her skin, almost bruising in their intensity.

He pulled out his cell phone and barked into it. "Dante. We have a problem." A pause as the voice on the other end spoke. "No! Keep it quiet. Where's the closest one?"

Pinning the phone between his ear and shoulder, he tugged them further into the crop. Corn whipped her in the face.

"Got it," he finally said, hanging up and stuffing the phone into his pocket. "This way."

They exited from between the stalks and hustled over a thin stretch of dirt that ran along the boundary of the field. For a moment, she thought they would seek cover in the stand of trees forming the next break.

Instead, once they reached the far side of the rise, Cody pulled her to the left. Running parallel, he scanned the landscape.

"Hurry up," he ordered, jerking her along behind him. He veered, the sudden change in direction almost wrenching her arm out of its socket.

By now, she was barely standing. Her breathing so rapid that she couldn't get enough oxygen into her lungs, let alone ask Cody what the hell was going on.

He stopped and bent toward the ground. His fingers felt the dirt in a methodical grid pattern below a strange purple flower.

"What . . . are . . . you... looking . . . for?" She deserved a medal just for getting the words out.

He ignored her, leaning forward and scooping up a handful of dirt. It exposed a small circular hole about the size of his fist. Producing a small knife from his pocket, Cody sliced his palm, guiding the drops of blood into the niche. Then he plucked the flower and stepped back. A quick movement shoved her behind him.

"Don't move an inch," he said, the commanding tone annoying enough to relieve some of her anxiety. That, and he wasn't even breathing hard.

Bastard.

But then her cursing of his cardio abilities disappeared because—

The hillside split open.

Literally split in half, dirt shifting, flowers and weeds spreading to the sides to reveal a hole, not much bigger than Cody could fit through.

A gust of air shot by, stopping about hundred feet behind them and obliterating their tracks. Then the wind curved, forming a new set of footprints to make it look like they had entered the next field.

Not giving her another second to admire his handiwork, Cody shoved her into the hole and climbed in behind her.

Their legs tangled. Their heads collided with a *crack*.

It was clear that the space had been created for one. But before she could suggest another option, the wind flew backward, dragging earth with it to recreate the seal around the crawl space.

Darkness.

TWELVE

IT WAS PITCH BLACK, the tight quarters and lack of light smothering.

Daughtry's mouth went dry as old anxiety welled up.

Panic made her want to flail her arms and legs, to scratch at the dark walls. Her hands cramped with the urge to claw at the earthen surface until she could see again.

But none of that would help.

She forced her body to stay still and focused on the sound of Cody's steady breathing. Inhale. Exhale. Inhale—

"Why are you hyperventilating?"

So much for not panicking. Even the frigid Cody sounded concerned.

"I-I d-don't like—" Breathing deeply, she pushed the memory away, concentrating on the thin stream of air blowing across her face. This wasn't that small, dark hole again. There was plenty of oxygen. Cody wasn't Jimmy, and this wasn't punishment for some perceived slight.

"I don't like small spaces, okay?" Her tone was harsh, but that was fine with her. She had enough emotional baggage without drawing up years-old bullshit.

"Whatever."

Daughtry clenched her teeth tightly together, wishing she could just get over it. But every time she was in a small, enclosed space, she remembered the panic of having been locked in the trunk and the laughter of her friends as she'd torn at the metal in a frantic effort to escape. And the fear. The bone-deep, soul-shattering fear.

By the time they'd let her out, she'd been near-comatose, her fingernails worn down to bloody quicks. She'd always been leery of tight, dark places, but that little bit of fun had propelled her into full-blown claustrophobia.

Cody grunted when her shoe connected with his stomach. Even though it was dark, and she couldn't see his face, she knew that he just wanted her to hold still. Logically, she knew that she wanted that too.

Closing her eyes to block out the suffocating blackness, she forced herself to stop, to breathe.

Never mind her fears. There was certainly a rational reason for being in this godforsaken hole.

Daughtry tucked her legs underneath her, and leaned back against the earthen wall—futile attempts to make herself as small as possible. Cody hadn't complained, hadn't said a single word actually, but he could use the space more.

"What are we doing here?" she whispered. Her eyes were beginning to adjust to the lack of light, and she could just make out Cody's form. He didn't look comfortable. His arms were folded across his chest as he lay on his back with one shoulder propped against the opposite wall.

Still, there was more room inside than she would have thought, given the size of the hole they'd entered. Her heart rate relaxed marginally. The space was maybe four feet wide and seven feet long, though the ceiling was low. Cody's head would almost touch if he sat up.

"Talk normal," he snapped. "We're safe here from the Dalshie. The LexTals will have already sent a recovery team."

Ignoring the *Stop Talking Now* billboard that he'd thrown up, she asked her question anyway. "What's a LexTal?"

Cody sighed, was quiet for so long that she thought he wouldn't answer. But finally he did. "We're the constables of the Rengalla."

"You're a cop?" She squinted to try to discern his expression in the dark light. She'd never liked cops. They were pushy and arrogant, just like—

"Not exactly."

Daughtry sighed both at the interruption to her thoughts and the non-answers.

"They'll be here soon."

She waited for him to say more. He didn't. That was his version of reassurance?

"So we just sit here and wait?"

"Yup," he said, unfolding his arms, propping himself on one elbow. "What's under the bandage?"

Blinking at the change in topic, her fingers found the small injury on her hand. She'd forgotten all about it.

"It's fine."

"That's not what I asked." Looking up, Daughtry was startled to find that he'd shifted, was way too close.

Glaring, she crossed her arms. "You don't exactly answer any of my questions, Mr. High-and-Mighty."

Plus, he didn't need yet another reason to think of her as weak and pathetic.

In one fluid movement, he closed the space between them. His expression was furious but his fingers gentle. He wrapped a hand around her wrist, tilting it as he peeled off the bandage.

She hissed when air hit the abraded skin, drawing the attention of those piercing green eyes that saw too much.

Their gazes connected, held. Time stretched—

"It's not bad," he said, neatly pocketing the bandage and sitting back.

"Yeah. That's what I said, remember?" She pulled her knees into her chest, feeling a brief ping of guilt at her tone. He *was* risking his life for her, after all.

But bitchy was good.

It meant she'd get him to leave her alone before she did something crazy and started caring what he thought.

He gave her a smirk, the flash of his white teeth easily discernible as her eyes had grown used to the dim light. "I remember."

She opened her mouth to retort then thought of something frightening. "Is John's ward still in place?" *God, what if—?* Anxiety swelled into her lungs, and she clutched at the denim of her jeans, the fabric rough, almost biting under her fingers.

Cody stretched his legs out, but she could feel the weight of his stare. She remembered how he'd punched through the barrier in her mind to help land the plane.

Had that hurt John? Or maybe Cody had been able to break through because John was de—

"Yes."

The knot of dread released.

"Missing the Boy Scout?" Cody raised a brow. "You'll just have to hold your own hand, cowgirl."

"John's my friend." Had been her only friend when her life had gone to pieces.

Cody snorted. "John is never *just friends* with women." His eyes raked over her body, cold, assessing. "Especially not one like you."

Asshole.

Especially because John had never given her any indication

of wanting something more with. Once upon a time, she'd imagined that, of course, but . . . no. It wasn't like that between them.

"No witty comeback? You're usually good for a laugh or two."

No doubt at her expense. She glared then leaned against the wall and started counting the roots penetrating the ceiling. Better monotonous tallying than conversing with a freaking porcupine.

The hole itself was one of the oddest things she'd ever seen. Roots intertwined, massing across the ceiling but the dirt walls were smooth. It was as if someone had physically spread the earth, taking care to leave it as undisturbed as possible. She had the feeling that as soon as they left, the soil would flow back together, eliminating any traces the hole had ever existed.

What if it decided to close up when they were inside?

For a moment, the memory of being trapped in the trunk swelled, and she had to swallow down the sudden burn of panic at the back of her throat.

Cody sat up, interrupting her thoughts. "Hey," he said, extending an arm toward her.

She glanced at him then turned away, trying to convince herself it wasn't concern on his face, almost wishing for another patronizing quirk of an eyebrow or lips. Compassion was too kind a balm against the rawness of her anxiety.

He sighed and lay back, but she found that she couldn't look away.

A cough brought her to her senses.

"Eyes up here," he said, tapping his temple, trademark smirk in place. "That is, unless you see something you like?"

"You mean you'll make an exception for a woman like me?" she snapped, angry at him, at herself for being attracted to him. She turned her back on him. "I could only be so lucky."

"I didn't know you had a preference."

Her heart skipped a beat, the reminder of her mistakes too recent to be anything but painful, but then she lifted her chin and glared over at him. "Fuck. Off."

His eyes narrowed in challenge, in anger. The atmosphere shifted, tightening, thickening enough to send a tantalizing chill down her spine.

For a moment she stayed frozen, wanting to take it back.

Cody wasn't a man she should be pushing. He was dangerous, his words sharp and cutting and . . . she wanted to brush her fingers across his forehead, smooth his scowl away.

See? Dangerous.

"Why is it like this?" she blurted.

His fingers had been drifting toward her arm, but her question made him pull them back. "It's—" He broke off. "It's nothing. It *means* nothing."

"Nothing," she repeated. That one word was hot splinters under her fingernails.

"Yes. Nothing. *This* doesn't matter."

"Please," she said. Her chest tightened, ready for the next blow. "Pl—" *Please just stop.* His words shouldn't hurt her. She barely knew him. But each dismissal, each flare of anger, cut her a little deeper.

Fingers that were slightly rough gripped her wrist, traced patterns on the sensitive skin there. Gooseflesh broke out in their wake.

"What, cowgirl? Tell me."

Her mouth was dry, her tongue paralyzed. What was she supposed to say?

"If you can," he added in his voice of velvet and sandpaper. It was sensual, sexy . . . except for the edge of contempt.

A bucket of cold water couldn't have been more effective in dousing the sexual haze around her mind. How the hell did he know what she was thinking? She *knew* she hadn't spoken aloud that time. Narrowing her eyes as something obvious occurred to her, she asked, "Are you a telepath?"

His laughter made her want to wipe the smirk right off his face. "No, cowgirl, that's John's job."

John was telepathic?

Her stomach clenched. He'd heard . . . too many things for her to recount. But it did make everything click into place. Why he knew about the visions. How he'd known when she'd been upset. But damn, why hadn't he told her?

"Don't worry. Boy Scout won't be hearing any more of your smutty thoughts. His ward protects you from everything. Mind reads, visions . . ." Cody paused. ". . . X-rated fantasies."

She yanked her arm. The damned man held firm.

"Since when is admiring a slice of prime meat a crime?" she snapped. "Men do it all the time. Does it hurt your sensitive ego? Or maybe"—she lowered her gaze to his crotch—"your parts don't match your exterior."

He raised that freaking eyebrow, and there wasn't one hint of anger in his eyes. For her, there was only cold contempt. "And what? I'm just supposed to believe you're appreciating the view?"

God, she wanted to punch him.

"You could try," he said with a smirk.

"Then how?" How did he know her thoughts?

"I'm observant. And you're easy . . . to read."

That little gem of censure snapped the last thread of Daughtry's temper. "Fuck you."

She dared him with her eyes to say something else. He wasn't a telepath, had said the ward would protect her. He shouldn't know what she was thinking. So maybe he was a liar in addition to a total jerk. This time when she pulled away, he let her go, and thankfully, they both shut their mouths. She went back to counting roots and Cody continued his brooding.

A few minutes later, the question that had been pinging around in her mind snuck into the silence before she had a chance to stop it. "Are you an incubus?" God knew that his personality was close enough to a demon's that it could have been a real possibility.

Plus, magical sexual prowess would give her an excuse for the insane attraction.

His face was a representation of total bewilderment. "No. Why?" The question was terse, like he hated the fact he'd been curious enough about the inner workings of her mind to ask.

She blushed, scarlet heat blossoming across her cheekbones, but didn't answer. *Of course* he wasn't a mythical sex demon. The problem was hers. Her prolific skill at being attracted to men who were absolutely wrong for her.

"You going to answer me?"

She giggled. "It's just that—" Another laugh bubbled up. She was losing it. "—you know, you and me . . ." She gestured wildly at the pair of them. ". . . and the, you know, the—" A flailing hand motioned to their respective parts. Giving in, the hysterics shook her torso and tears poured down her cheeks. She'd never known where her breaking point was. Today she'd found it. The Dalshie. Magic. Visions. John and Cody and her crazy, roller-coaster emotions.

Not that much really. Just her life turned upside down and torn to shreds.

"What's the matter?"

She tried to motion that she would be okay in a minute but wasn't sure he got the message. Not that it mattered. She was too far gone to care. And when he reached for her legs and pulled them onto his lap, she was so disconcerted that she let him. Those fingers pulled off her shoes, slipping under her boring white cotton socks with the sureness of a confident male. They were efficient, able to remove bandages or panties with equal aplomb.

And judging by how slowly he inched her socks down, she had the feeling that he was a savor-er when it came to opening Christmas presents.

Suddenly, she wasn't laughing anymore.

Her heart pounded in what had to be an unsafe rhythm. "You're trying to distract me," she said. Her voice wasn't breathless. It wasn't. *Really*.

"I'm not trying." The *"I'm succeeding"* went unspoken, but she still wanted to deny it.

She pressed her lips together to stop a sigh of pleasure from escaping. "Overconfident much?" He chuckled and started rubbing her aching feet. "You didn't answer my question."

He glanced up, eyes questioning.

"Well? Are you one?" she asked, and he looked so flustered that it was almost worth her idiocy.

Pink tinged his ears. "I'm not. I'm—" He struggled for a moment to say something intelligible before she finally gave in and giggled.

He glared, the intensity in those grassy depths shifting, abruptly focusing on her. Intoxicating her. Then he did something with his fingers that made her brain stop processing altogether.

Leaning her head back, she relaxed. This was comfort, pure and simple. It was . . . wonderful—and kind?—of Cody to distract her. That thought brought the tension back. She couldn't let herself be swept up in two minutes of surface niceness. As if the situation weren't complicated enough. She didn't need to start liking Cody.

And whose basis for appreciating another person began with their foot massage abilities?

Cody's hands paused on her calves before reaching up to clasp the back of her knees. He rubbed the sensitive skin there through the rough denim of her jeans. Then he leaned in, extending his hand toward the cut on her palm. She didn't stop him. Not even when sparks of emerald shot out of his fingertips. The magic fluttered toward her, connecting with her skin, making it tingle and itch.

"What was that?" she asked when the magic petered out and he'd lowered his hand.

She looked down. The cut was gone.

Cody looked shocked. Hopeful. Nervous. Then his eyes traveled down to her mouth. Molten. He leaned in again, and she panicked at the expression on his face. He was determined, aroused . . . furious. His hands came up and gripped her waist tightly. Rapid breaths puffed against her lips, teasing.

"Don't."

It took him a minute to release her, like he was almost too far gone to recognize what she was doing. But then he *did* let her go, giving her as much space as possible.

Which was all of six inches. And even that was too far for her traitorous, turned-on body.

Dammit.

She closed her eyes and thumped her head back against the wall. Anger and frustration radiated off him, beating against her skin in hot, pulsing waves, and she wrapped her arms around her waist, attempting to protect her body from the scalding emotions. She wasn't sure if Cody was irritated that he'd given into the weakness of kissing her or pissed because she'd thrown up a red light.

None of that mattered.

She snatched up her socks and shoes, wrestling them on and cramming herself into the smallest ball possible, praying that sleep would take over to pass the time.

But Cody couldn't make it that easy.

"Why?"

Why, what? She wanted to snap back, except, even as she opened her mouth to do so, she caught a thread of vulnerability in his expression. Her heart unclenched, and despite the barriers she'd erected, she felt herself softening toward him.

"John."

He was out there, in danger, and they were—

Cody's posture changed in an instant. "What?" he snapped, anger making the questions sharp as blades. "Little rich girl is too good for me? Only got eyes for the guy in the Colony with the most money?"

Her response was just as cutting, her wounds from his assumptions raw and deep. "Fuck you." She turned her back on him. "You don't know a single thing about me."

"I know that your jeans cost more money than most people make in a year."

She looked down at her jeans, now torn and stained with dirt. They *were* expensive. But they and one shirt were the only clothes she'd taken from her parents' house when she'd left a year ago.

Trust him to misjudge her for one yard of dyed denim.

"Like I said, you don't know anything about me."

"Then why don't you explain it to me?"

He probably expected some sob story about how the poor little rich girl had it so bad while her butler hand-fed her caviar, and her maid gave her a pedicure.

"Why do you even care?" she asked.

That stopped him. The anger slid from his face, and she saw that blip of vulnerability again.

"I don't know," he said.

Her heart squeezed. She was a total sap. Yet she felt like she had to give him something. An answer, no matter how superficial. "My life changed a lot when the visions started."

Changed, if she could call ruining the relationship with her parents changed. Or going from living in a fancy mansion with everything she could want at her fingertips to not being able to afford a crappy apartment in the worst part of town. Not to mention losing everyone she'd ever called a friend.

She couldn't work without seeing death. Couldn't get food from a fast food place without risking a vision. Initially, she'd tried therapy and medication, had researched her condition until her hands had been littered with papercuts.

And still hadn't found a solution besides psychosis.

Daughtry had cut off contact when her parents had threatened to commit her, packing a small bag of clothes and taking off. The small savings she'd had in her personal account hadn't lasted long, even with pawning the clothes.

Hence the eviction notice.

And *that* was enough of her mental pity party.

"The last year has been tough, but I'm fine now." There. That sounded better.

"Year?" His face wore a strange expression.

It gave her a moment of pause. Was she abnormal even amongst those with magic?

"Yeah," she said. "That's when the visions started. After—" She stopped. She couldn't believe she'd almost gone there.

He pounced on the weakness. "After what?"

"Never mind." Daughtry wished she hadn't said anything at all. She wasn't supposed to be thinking about Jimmy. How she'd lost an integral part of herself in their relationship. How she'd surrendered her confidence and then he'd left her for the girl in Germany. Pathetic.

Cody reached over, grabbed her chin, and forced her to look

into his eyes. They were narrowed, like he was ready to call bullshit on her entire story. "After what?"

She wrenched her face away. Fury fueled her response and it was so much like her pre-Jimmy self that she felt the truth settle deep in her soul. She was coming back. The last few years were over and though she'd been weak, that course wasn't her future.

"After my fiancé broke up with me two days before our wedding and didn't have the balls to tell me himself." She poked him in the chest. "Do you know who told me? Who stayed with me while I dealt with all the insinuations that it was somehow my fault from his parents and mine?"

Her voice faltered, and she withdrew her hand, clenching it tightly to her chest as if the pressure might heal the festering wound in her heart.

"Do you know who held me when I finally cried?" she asked in a pathetic whisper. The memory of the events sapped her strength. She'd been strong up until that point. Up until she'd gotten the check from Jimmy's parents. Until they'd made her feel like a paid whore.

The worst was that they couldn't have predicted the future any better.

She bit her lip. She wouldn't cry. Not over that. But in that moment, with Cody looking at her with a mixture of disbelief and pity on his face, the shame was unbearable.

"Hey," he said, swiping away a traitorous tear that was escaping down her cheek. "I'm sure your parents don't blame you."

She laughed. Its bitterness hurting even her own ears. "I'd call bullshit on that. I haven't seen them since right after the visions started. They had almost been out of money. Again." And counting on the influx from Jimmy's family to set them afloat. They'd been so hostile when she'd refused to cash the check. "The only person who stuck by my side was John."

Then he'd gone.

Daughtry closed her eyes, ignoring the weakness of the wet tears trailing down her cheeks.

THIRTEEN

ANTS CRAWLED up the toes of Daughtry's shoes, over her laces and under her jeans. The teeny black insects made their way up her spine, crossing her neck to congregate in her hair.

She woke on a gasp, bolting straight upright, running her fingers frantically along her skin to check for bugs.

"They're gone."

"Wh-what?" With an exhale, she looked around, the realization of where she was finally hitting her. "The Dalshie?"

Cody shrugged as if to say, *"Who else?"* Then he closed his eyes and turned away. But she wasn't so lucky as to have that peaceful blanket of blackness pass the time for her.

No.

Fear had her in its stranglehold. How were a few inches of dirt supposed to protect them from the Dalshie? Why weren't the LexTals there yet? Weren't cops supposed to be the first responders.

It couldn't be safe for them to be this close to the crash site.

Maybe they weren't coming.

Oh God. She should have never agreed to this.

She bit her lip, refusing to break down again, to let Cody see her as weak. Then she laughed at her own ridiculousness. It wasn't like he could think any worse of her.

He put his hand on her shoulder, and she jumped.

"What's wrong?" he asked.

Her jaw fell open. His question was soft, quiet, and without a trace of loathing or condescension. *Oh no.* That wouldn't do. She brushed his hand aside. "Don't worry. I promise I won't freak out again."

Cody had such a look of relief on his face that she laughed. Except now—shit—the laughing was turning into crying. She turned her head away, brushing at her cheeks, trying to halt the flow. But that was about as easy as putting her finger in the proverbial damn.

"Dammit," she muttered. She hated that she was so emotional. It was just like her to get bogged down mentally when there was a slew of way-more-important things to do.

His arms went around her and held her tight as she sobbed into his shirt.

It was stupid to soak up his warm strength, pathetic that she was crying on the shoulder of a man who couldn't stand her, but still she couldn't bring herself to pull away as he stroked his soothing hand across her hair.

"Shh. It's okay. You're safe," he said.

After an eternity, Daughtry managed to wrench herself from his embrace.

A twinge of guilt made her stomach clench when she saw the huge wet stain on the shoulder of Cody's shirt, but she ignored it and wiped her nose on her shoulder. *Gross.* She had to be a mess with puffy eyes and a splotchy face.

"It's true, then," he said, breaking into her embarrassed silence.

Confused, she looked up. "What's true?"

"'You are so ugly when you cry.'" He waited like he expected her to laugh at the punchline.

Except, she'd only really heard the word *ugly*.

Her cheeks went hot, but not in shame. "What are you talking about?" She poked a finger against his chest. "Do you get off insulting women when they're vulnerable?"

"What? No!" Cody scrambled, his mouth opening and closing a few times before he managed to push words out. "You're not. It's a line from a movie. I was making a joke. Shit, I didn't—"

Relief flowed through her.

His explanation shouldn't have mattered, but it did. She *wanted* him to think she was pretty. Shaking off her insecurities, she gave him a watery smile, "Oh. I remember that one. That's actually sort of funny."

He raised a brow at the last, but at least the tension between them had broken.

In the silence that followed she wanted to say something, yet found herself unable to find the right words. Damn him for being sweet, for trying to make her feel better. She was trying not to like him. When he didn't say anything else, she couldn't resist teasing him. "I didn't take you for a chick-flick man. Please tell me you and the guys cuddle up on the couch with a bowl of popcorn and watch *Pride and Prejudice*."

His face flushed just a little, making her think she might actually have hit close to the mark.

Then he surprised her by saying, "Come on! That movie is golden."

"You're an Austen fan?"

"No," he said, rolling his eyes. "*Bridesmaids*. And it is *not* a chick flick. I do *not* watch girl movies. My favorite part is . . ." he added, giving her a full-blown smile that hit her straight in the gut as he named the single grossest scene in the film.

She snorted. Figured he'd liked that part. "No! That's way more disgusting than funny," she said. "Typical guy move for you to like that one."

"Typical girl move for you to have *Pride and Prejudice* be the first movie that pops into your mind."

Daughtry lifted a finger. "First, because it's a classic. Second"—she did a chef's kiss—"we have both the Colin Firth *and* Matthew Macfadyen to choose from." She smiled at the glazed look in his eyes. "I don't know if I love the pond scene or the scene in the rain more."

His brows dragged together. "Do you have an obsession with water?"

A laugh slid from her lips. "No. But I do like seeing men in wet clothes."

"Wet T-shirt contest?" His green eyes twinkled.

"Or the eighteen-century approximation of them." She grinned at him. "There are whole Facebook groups devoted to the gloriousness that is Colin and Matthew and a running debate about which version is better." She lifted one shoulder in a half-hearted shrug. "I know it's tough, but I'd take either one."

"You're very charitable."

They both laughed and finally her actions caught up with her mind.

Was she actually bantering with him? A little whisper of pleasure expanded in her chest as the camaraderie between them began to blossom. Who knew the prickliness was hiding an actual sense of humor?

"Okay, then what about—?"

Suddenly, Daughtry was aware of exactly how close her lips were to Cody's.

He finished his thought and paused, waiting for her to laugh, but all she could do was stare. Mentally, she was inside a car perched halfway off a cliff, frozen, instinctively knowing that her next move would either free her or send her plummeting.

Clarity danced across Cody's eyes, but he remained still.

Daughtry.

It was the shadow of a thought—almost a plea—and gone so quickly she could have imagined it. Except, there was the soft whisper of Cody's mind against hers, full of concern and not disdain as she would have expected.

Maybe he didn't hate her.

A corner of her mind screamed at her to pull away. To remember all the reasons she'd been spouting to keep her distance. Cody was not the kind of guy she should be with. It shouted at her to remember John. He was the man she should be drawn to, but where John was merely warmth, Cody was molten. It was like comparing a hot water bottle to the sun.

John was comfortable and safe. A friend. Cody was a risk, one that threatened to make her feel real, dangerous things.

Before her life turned upside down, her reaction would have been a no-brainer.

Run.

Today she was tired of fighting it.

She kissed him.

He stayed frozen for a second, as if he had been certain she would reject him. Then he transformed into a flurry of activity. His hands tangled in her hair as his tongue swept across her mouth, parting her lips to delve deeply inside. She moaned. One of his thighs slipped between hers, and she arched back, the pressure a pleasant pain.

"Cody." It was a plea, and she squirmed, wanting more, needing every bit of him.

He pulled her closer and cursed as his elbow collided with the wall behind him. "Dammit. I need—"

He rolled to his back, pulling her with him. She ended up

sprawled across him, the ceiling pressing along her back so that she was plastered against the wide expanse of his chest. His muscles were hard against her breasts, but she didn't mind in the least.

In fact, she couldn't get enough of him. She pressed her nose to his neck, inhaled his wholly masculine scent. It was addictive. She wanted to linger, to rub against his body until the smell of him was imbedded into her pores.

But Cody wasn't patient. He grabbed her face, stealing her lips again.

Finally she broke away, gasping for air. She pressed a row of careful kisses all along his scar, as if her mouth might somehow erase the reminder of the grievous injury. He shivered and pulled her face back up. His hands went to her hips, and he started to move her, as if to flip her onto her back. She gave a little cry of pain when her hair snagged on a root in the ceiling.

"No," she said when he began to push her away, attempting to slide out from beneath her. They'd started this—

"Why is this damned hole so small?" she asked as she reached up to claw at her hair until it came loose then finished rolling to her back. Her every nerve was on fire for him. There was no stopping.

"It's only made for one person. Just enough room to lie down and sit up." Cody's voice was husky, his words quiet. His heavy weight pressed her down into the earthen floor, making it hard for her to concentrate. "There was nowhere else."

"It's fine," she said. And like *this* it was.

The sensation of his body holding her in place heady. Forget claustrophobia. If this were what she could expect being trapped with him, she would sign up every time.

Cody nipped at her lips, and, when she returned the favor, the salty taste of the ocean teased her tongue. His hand slid under her shirt—

"Ooof!"

She grunted as she found herself shoved back, the air abruptly icy against her skin. By the time she got her wits about her and straightened her shirt, Daughtry realized that Cody was kneeling, his muscular form shielding her as much as possible.

An opening about the size of a porthole had appeared in the front of the cubby, spotlighting the space around them and blinding her in the process.

"What do we have here?" came a teasing voice, no doubt taking in the displaced clothing, the mussed hair.

She tried to lean around Cody and see their interrupter for herself, but he put his arm back, held her behind him. Still, judging by his body language—tense but not homicidal—she decided that the man must be one of the rescue party.

Thank God they'd been interrupted before they'd done something insane.

The thought was pushed away from her mind as quickly as it had come, knowing that it was fear and the old Daughtry who had spoken. She'd been well aware of what she'd been doing.

The best kiss of her life.

She leaned around Cody to introduce herself to their rescuer, who said his name was Tyler. As she took him in, amusement flickered in his surprisingly blue eyes. Shaking his hand, she smiled in return. He wasn't exactly a trial to look at.

Cody growled, shifting his body to separate them.

She rolled her eyes. *Really?*

A smirk broke out on Tyler's face. He opened his mouth—

"Just get us out of here already," Cody said with a snarl. "Daughtry is claustrophobic."

A blush stained her cheeks, and she glared at Cody's back. Was he going to list her faults for the world?

"That's not what I meant," he muttered. "Hurry up," he said louder.

Tyler obliged, pale blue strands of magic bursting from his palms, looking bright against his caramel skin. The tendrils crawled along the hillside, peeling back the earth, enlarging the hole enough so that they could exit.

Cody shot out and regained his feet in one smooth movement. He paused just long enough to aid her rather ungraceful exit. Once she was steady, he dropped her hand like it was a stick of lit dynamite and took off down the road, not bothering to make sure she was with him. Apparently, the Dalshie no longer worried him. Or maybe he was pawning his problem off onto someone else.

That thought hurt more than it probably should have.

He approached a group of four men stationed down the divide and spoke a few terse words. Then he hopped into the waiting SUV.

She'd just witnessed the return of Cody's frigid exterior.

Daughtry sighed. That moment in the cubby, those few minutes of connection, were gone. He would be right back to the acerbic, untouchable man who had come to her rescue at the apartment.

It was surprising how sad that made her feel.

FOURTEEN

TYLER CLEARED HIS THROAT, drawing Daughtry's gaze. He smiled and put up a hand to gesture her forward.

Warm. Innocent. He almost made her feel tainted, standing in his shadow. Then he winked at her. She smiled. Okay, maybe he wasn't quite *so* innocent. She started to ask him where they were going, but the words stopped mid-flow as she glanced at the blue strands hanging in the air.

His magic was *incredible*. With a mere wave of his hand, strands of blue closed the hole, running over the dirt and grass, encouraging it to knit itself back together. The little purple flower even reappeared, waving like a friendly flag.

"Ready?" he asked, grabbing her hand and pulling her toward the waiting SUV.

At the contact she froze, barely resisting the urge to yank her hand away. She waited for nausea, for a vision, for any sign that her screwed-up skills of foresight were about to be put to use.

But nothing happened.

She released a breath she didn't know she'd been holding.

John's ward really worked. Then her heart knotted. John had said he would protect her. He had. And now he was—

Swallowing the guilt away to deal with her later, she forced a smile at Tyler, who was looking down at her with a concerned expression.

"Sorry," she murmured, forcing her feet to move.

The LexTals had come to rescue them. They would do the same for John.

She had to believe that.

She stumbled, but Tyler caught her easily before placing her back on her feet. He was strong, despite the lack of bulging muscles.

At least one good thing came of her klutziness: Tyler's hands on her waist caused nothing more than a feeling of neutral gratitude. After her reaction to Cody, she half-expected every male to turn her into a nymphomaniac.

The waiting SUV had looked far less intimidating from a distance. Up close it was an absolutely monster, lifted so its running board was practically at her chest. Huge tires adorned blacked-out rims, and the windows were tinted so dark that the president could have been inside.

If she had been asked to describe it, she would've skipped over bulletproof and gone straight to rocket-proof. The entire package screamed government.

Or drug dealer. Or mafia.

"Nice, isn't it?" Tyler said proudly, rubbing the SUV's side like it was a dog. "This little baby is tricked out. You could run over a grenade, and it would keep on trucking. Only the best for the LexTals."

She raised a brow.

Tyler shrugged. "What can I say? We're bad-ass." Without giving her time to digest that bit of information, he opened the door and shoved her in. "Go on. Check it out."

Daughtry looked up, right into Cody's eyes.

The cold within them took her breath away. Then his gaze shifted down to her hips, where Tyler's hands still rested from helping her in.

"It didn't take you long," he said, ice in every syllable.

She felt a surge of pain at his words but refused to let him know how much they'd wounded her. "Well, you're the one who ran away."

A flicker of annoyance crossed his face. "Good thing, apparently."

"Jealous much?"

His jaw dropped open, his expression like she'd clocked him upside the head with a two-by-four.

"Not hardly," he muttered, turning to stare out the window.

Tyler slid in next to her, slamming the door hard enough to rattle her teeth. Which earned him a glare from Cody that raised the hairs on the back of her neck by proxy. Good. Maybe he'd torment someone else for a change.

Rolling the tension from her shoulders, she noticed the two men sitting behind her in the third row.

Twins, she thought, thinking that the world was lucky to have a matching set. One of them met her gaze and winked, flashing a deliciously dangerous smile.

The remaining doors opened and closed, startling Daughtry into looking forward as the last two men hopped into the front seats. One with long blond hair was driving, the other, with his closely cropped black locks and hazel eyes, looked remarkably like the two in the back.

Not twins, triplets, Daughtry realized. And all annoyingly attractive. She frowned. She was going to get a complex being around so many good-looking men.

Still, her inner teenage girl wanted to squeal and clap her

hands. Or drop a pencil for one of them to bend over and pick up.

Cody sighed and crossed his arms.

Her temper boiled over. *Really?* Was it such a trial that he couldn't stand to even sit next to her? "Are you upset that I stole your virtue, Mr. High-and-Mighty?" she said, ignoring the burst of laughter from the back seat. "I thought you were—"

He whirled and focused the full measure of his glare on her. "You thought wrong." Then he snapped his mouth shut and returned his stare to the window.

She almost reached out and shook him. How dare he? He *had* to feel the same way.

Or did he?

It's not like you're some beauty, the darkness taunted. *You're barely passable and Jimmy always said you were cold in bed.*

Righteous anger flooded her, and it was an emotion she hadn't known she possessed. In fact . . . when she studied it closer, it almost felt like it wasn't even hers. As though someone were feeling the emotion on her behalf. But that made no sense. How could someone else's feeling get in her head?

And plus, she had no champion there.

"If you liked the hillside, you're going to like this," Tyler said, drawing her attention.

The anger faded. If the emotion hadn't been so strong, so unlike what she normally felt, she might have forgotten about it. But as it was, the notion weaseled its way into her mind and stayed there like an annoying flashing billboard telling her that she was missing something.

Tyler wouldn't be deterred, however, and he pointed her gaze behind them. The two men in the back, with martyred looks, shifted to the side.

Her eyes widened as she watched, thoroughly impressed,

the tread marks vanishing even as they appeared. "I made them myself, the tires that is, they—"

"Oh, give it a rest, Tyler," the man in the front passenger seat interrupted.

Agreement filled in from all around her.

"Hey. Come on! It's awesome!" Tyler retorted, and the men were off, tossing and receiving good-natured ribs.

Daughtry listened to them tease each other, even though it was tempting to start peppering them with questions. Odds were that one of them might help her find the answers she sought, but there was something comforting about listening to them. She even felt a spark of humor as Tyler continued his shameless flirting. It was enough to lift the nervousness, and the hurt, from the forefront of her mind.

Flirt or no, she got the impression that Tyler enjoyed the prospect of pushing Cody's buttons more than pursuing something with her.

He was both genuine and completely harmless.

And damn if his flirting didn't make her feel good.

Eventually, the teasing broke down, and Tyler stage-whispered in her ear, "I know you're new to the Colony, but I'm an excellent tour guide. I'd be happy to give you some . . . one-on-one lessons." His smiled widened when Cody shot him a hostile look. "Innocent, of course. Just to get you up to speed."

When she laughed, every man simultaneously groaned.

The driver twisted around and chided kindly, "Don't encourage him." He was beautiful with stunning grey eyes, but still her body—her *soul*—was painfully aware of only the man next to her.

Trying to force the traitorous feelings aside, she snuck a glance at Cody. He appeared like he was ready to reach over her and throttle Tyler. Then one of the triplets piped up from the back seat and his eyes flared with jealousy, which made no sense at all.

"As far as I can see, no one's made a claim," the triplet taunted, shooting her a wink.

She snorted. Claim? Not hardly.

"I'd be more than happy to provide some . . . tutoring," he added.

"Fuck off, Morgan," Cody said through clenched teeth.

"I'm not Morgan," the triplet said to Cody, while giving her a look of such devilment that she chuckled.

"Don't try to bullshit me," Cody retorted. "Your games may work on your mommy, but they don't with me."

The triplet groaned and ran his hand through his hair. "How can you always tell?"

"Easy," Cody said. "You're the ugly one."

"Fuck you," Morgan retorted, even as he laughed alongside Tyler and his brother. Then he winked at her again. "The offer stands, sweetheart," he said. "Anyone who can get that one so riled up is worth my time."

Daughtry rolled her eyes as the guys chuckled but otherwise remained quiet. How did exchanging insults always result in laughter? Or punches, she supposed. Because it had seemed very close to that for a moment.

Men were weird.

Yet, some of the tension in her heart loosened.

The LexTals had made her feel more welcome in two minutes than she had her entire life.

As the teasing broke down into individual segments of conversation, she took in the scenery outside the windows. The cornfields had given way to lush greenery. Trees and wildflowers filled the shoulder of the road, so different from the plain brown grass that filled the roadways that time of year in California.

"Where are we?" she murmured, more to herself, not expecting an actual answer.

"Kentucky," the driver answered.

Her eyes flew up, and he smiled at her in the rearview.

"Yes, really."

"But—"

"You didn't expect it to look like this."

"Um." She paused, trying to search for a polite response. In the end, she settled on "No."

"The Colony is on the border between Kentucky and Tennessee," he said. "There's a stretch of national forest there. We've managed to secure some of the inlets for our use."

"Dante means commandeered," Tyler whispered.

"But can't someone stumble onto it?" she asked. "Wouldn't they see the magic? Why aren't there YouTube videos of the Dalshie or you guys using your powers?"

"Glamor," Dante said, like that was supposed to make everything clear.

She glanced at Tyler questioningly. "You'll see when we get there," he told her. "But to the average person, the Colony doesn't exactly look like a place you'd want to spend a lot of time at if you didn't have to. Plus we have patrols, a shield. Those things are very effective at keeping people out."

"And the videos?"

"Did anyone ever see you pull a vision?" he countered.

Her mouth fell open. How did everyone know she could do that?

Tyler smiled at her expression. "You're well known at the Colony, Daughtry. Your parents, you—" He broke off when Cody cleared his throat. After a moment, he said, "There aren't many people who can do what you do."

"Oh." She sucked in a breath and tried to ask the next question as if her heart weren't stampeding in her chest.

"What happened to my parents? John said I'd been kidnapped."

Tyler glanced over her shoulder at Cody, and she bristled.

"It's *my* life. Not his. Tell *me*."

"I don't know if—"

Dante spoke then, in a no-nonsense tone that had her spine stiffening and her stomach clenching. "Your parents were killed by the Dalshie and you were taken—"

"Dante," Cody interrupted, his tone like ice.

"It's common knowledge, Cody," Morgan said from the back seat. "And it's not like we didn't search for her."

His words went over Daughtry like a bucket of ice water.

She hadn't realized how much she'd been hoping for her parents to be alive and waiting for her at the Colony until Dante had told her differently. *Stupid.* But, dammit, she'd wished there might be two more people in the world who cared about her. Bring her grand total up to three. So yeah, stupid. She was stupid to have hoped. Throat tightening, she swallowed roughly. Pushing away the yearning for there to be someone waiting for her with open arms, someone to love her unconditionally—

That wasn't going to happen.

Tyler touched her shoulder. "You're sort of famous because you have the visions, at least for a Rengalla. One of us—a person who can do magic," he added at what was probably a confused expression on her face. "Normal humans can't see or do magic, which is why there are no YouTube videos of us floating about on the Internet."

"Not of magic, anyway," the triplet sitting next to Morgan said. "Me, on the other hand—"

"Shut it, Monroe," Tyler said. "No one cares that you saved that kitten from the tree."

"It was a *cliff*. And that's not what I meant—"

"Well, Daughtry definitely doesn't want to see your foray into porn," Morgan chimed in.

Unbelievably, she smiled. Especially when Monroe started to tell his brother where to stick it.

She tuned out the conversation around her, letting the information she'd gained wash over her, trying her best to absorb all of it.

If she were being honest, she'd always felt a little different. Yes, the visions hadn't started until the prior year, but there'd been other signs that she wasn't like everyone else. An inclination here, a premonition there. None crystal clear, but feelings and impressions. Like being able predict when her teacher had been about to give a pop quiz or knowing that her parents had been waiting up, so she'd needed to sneak through the back door.

But nothing had been like the visions.

They were movies in her mind and the premonitions she'd felt growing up were nothing like that. Instead, they were more like strange feelings here or there that guided her choices.

Like she had a guardian angel, but only in her mind.

But she'd learned quickly to keep that thought to herself. One, other kids thought she was crazy if she mentioned angels, and two, talking a quiz or surprise assignment before it happened only brought too many questions, both from the students *and* teachers. She'd always felt like there was something she should have been able to do but couldn't—as though she had a phantom limb or something.

And now Daughtry knew what it was.

Magic.

If she hadn't just lived what she lived, she would have thought it insane.

Instead, she was en route to some magical conclave and left wondering what would it have been like to grow up with these men? Amongst magic? What could she do today if she could access the pulsing orb of power in her mind?

Maybe she would have been able to prevent the visions, to form something like John's ward. It was infuriating that she'd been left so vulnerable, that she'd harmed others when it had been preventable.

Because of the Dalshie? Or her kidnappers? She didn't understand how the two were related. Were they even sure she was the girl who'd been kidnapped? But then again, how many people could there be in the world, that had visions like her and purple eyes?

It was just—

She knew the people who'd raised her weren't the same as the monsters who'd pursued her. What she didn't understand was how or why they'd taken her. It wasn't like they'd tried to get her to do magic. If anything, they'd tried to convince her she was completely normal and that the visions weren't real when they'd come on. They weren't using her for her abilities, not that she knew how to harness them. But *if* someone had wanted her for her magic, shouldn't they have come for her sooner?

She tried to wrap her mind around it all, but only one thing was clear: she needed to understand her magic, needed to learn to use it to protect herself and others.

She needed to stop the visions.

Permanently.

Closing her eyes, she pushed away the sense of impossibility. Uncertainty awaited her at the Colony—she had absolutely no clue what her future would bring—but for right now, she just wanted to sit back in her seat and bundle up in the LexTals' playful banter.

FIFTEEN

VIBRATION BELOW DAUGHTRY'S cheek woke her, the faint smell of pine and sea salt tickled her nose. Her eyes flew open and she found herself plastered against Cody's softly rumbling chest.

She blinked firmly. Opened again. Nope, still there.

Crap. She should move. Really.

But instead of pulling away, she closed her eyes and soaked up Cody for just one more second. It was nice to feel protected, and while she certainly wasn't the burden he wanted, she could pretend. The SUV turned, and she opened her eyes again. The reverberation of Cody's soft snoring ceased.

She forced herself put some distance between them, knowing he didn't want her in his space. And she was right. The moment she began to pull away, Cody dropped his arms and leaned away from her.

A flash of hurt had her clamping her arms around her stomach, the feeling familiar, painful.

Why did no one want her?

She was a passing distraction. Nothing more.

Cody shifted next to her, leaning his shoulders back against the seat. His arm pressed briefly against hers. It was just a brush of contact, the gentle touch most certainly accidental, yet it stopped her self-loathing tirade in its tracks.

Closing her eyes, she willed herself to stay strong. This was a good thing. Her life was going to get better, especially if she could learn to control the visions. Plus, being surrounded by people who'd grown up using the same magic that was locked inside her brain, seemed like a damned good place to start with that.

Feeling marginally better, she glanced up. The light streaming through the windows was faint, leaving the cabin dimly illuminated. What time was it? She squinted to read the dash clock and saw it was only early evening.

Weird. She glanced back to the windows. They were an opaque black that got darker the harder she stared.

Confused, she turned to Cody, but he was doing an admirable job of ignoring her, looking out the jet-black window like he could see the landscape beyond.

She shifted her gaze to Tyler.

"Spell," he said. "The harder you look the less you can see. We're getting close to the Colony. You won't be able to discern much until you're cleared by the Council."

She nodded, impressed by the sheer scope of the magic that the Rengalla could wield. If she could learn one tenth of it—

"Can the Dalshie control storms?"

If the question came out of left field, Tyler didn't react with surprise. "No. They can't control elemental magic. Only we can."

"Oh."

"Why are you ask—?"

But Morgan interrupted Tyler's question with a comment about patrols.

She was left to her thoughts.

Which was a good thing because the pieces in her head that weren't adding up. Somehow the Dalshie had discovered their location. Several times. Then there was the storm that had brought down the plane.

If what Tyler had said about controlling the weather was true . . .

It just seemed like too much of a coincidence that the storm had been natural. They'd been targeted, brought down, and then the bad weather had disappeared. Like magic—

Suddenly, she remembered what Cody had said about a mole.

Was she putting herself into more danger by going to the Colony?

That thought had come a few days too late. She'd boarded the plane and the SUV, for that matter, and now the next stop was the Rengalla stronghold. Not a helpful thought at this point of her journey. Besides, where else was she going to go?

A while later, the SUV tilted like they were moving downhill. Pretty soon they slowed, the air changing, becoming almost thick.

It was difficult to take a full breath. Claustrophobia reared its ugly head.

Panicked, she turned back to Tyler, but his eyes were closed. The triplets too. Cody was awake, but his chilly facade was in place, so she couldn't ask him.

Not that she wanted to. She could handle her unreasonable fear by herself. Clenching her hands together, she concentrated on the sharp pain of her nails biting into her palms.

She jumped when Cody reached over and grabbed her fists. Gently, he separated them, his touch softening even further when he brushed his fingers along the indented skin of her palms. The small hurts disappeared with a tiny shower of green sparks.

Finally, the air relaxed—that was the only way she could think to describe it. One second the overwhelming pressure was there, and the next it was gone. She could breathe again but was abruptly aware that Cody still held her hand.

He traced the crescent of skin between her thumb and forefinger, and a curl of heat coiled in her stomach. She was frozen, not daring to move for risk of breaking the spell.

A sharp turn threw her against Cody's chest.

His arms came up to steady her.

When she risked a glance at his face, she saw him glaring accusingly at Dante. Following his stare, she found grey eyes gazing back in the rearview. Those mischievous irises twinkled and when Dante noticed her attention, he winked.

She joined Cody in his glaring. *Intervening busybody.*

Dante chuckled as he threw the SUV into park then yelled, "Up and at 'em, boys—"

"And girl," she couldn't help interjecting.

He turned. "And girl," he said. "We debrief in thirty. Hit the showers. You all smell." He gave her a raised brow that dared her to retort.

Daughtry shrugged in reply. After the large amount of running and small amount of bathing she'd done in the last couple of days, she probably did stink.

Dante smiled, a small quirk of his lips that had one side of his mouth curling higher than the other. "Cody, get Daughtry to the infirmary."

"But—" Cody broke off, his protest lost, as Dante and the crew all but disappeared.

She was alone with Cody again. She firmly told her tripping heart to cooperate.

"I can find my own way," she said, not wanting to be his burden any longer.

He snorted. "Not likely." Without another word, he opened

his own door, slid out, and extended a hand to help her exit. "With my luck, you'd probably stumble into the armory and blow up the place."

She pulled her hand away and crossed her arms. "Not possible."

"With you, cowgirl, I think anything is possible." He paused, and she had the strangest notion that maybe his words weren't the jibe she'd first taken them for. "Let's go."

Daughtry followed but couldn't help asking, "Is there really an armory?" She didn't know what to make of that. Had she stumbled onto some sort of domestic terrorist group?

A half-smirk graced Cody's lips. "Yup. When you're at war, you need weapons." He was quiet for a beat, no doubt taking in her wide eyes. "We also have bathrooms and Band-Aids."

She opened her mouth.

"Don't."

"What—?" She frowned.

"No more questions," he said then gave her a smile that took the sting from his rebuke.

Her lips curved down into a scowl, but she was amused despite herself. "Fine." She'd just ask John. Her stomach turned. If she ever saw him again.

No, dammit. They would find a way to get him home.

Sighing, she shook off the guilt and looked around.

There wasn't much to see. The underground parking structure could have been in any mall, university, or movie theater. Wide cylindrical pillars at regular intervals supported the low ceiling. Caged fluorescent lighting did little aside from illuminating the oil-stained and cracked concrete.

The only thing differentiating it from the typical parking garage was the lack of peeling paint declaring what section they were in.

"This way." Cody held a rusted steel door open, and she

balked at the glare on his face. *What the hell?* This guy had more mood swings than a PMS-ing teenager.

She brushed by him and walked up the short flight of stairs. They opened up onto a pavilion in front of a . . . decrepit office building?

The squat grey structure was about five stories tall and could have been relocated from any 1970's business complex. Dowdy orange-peel stucco covered its walls, broken only by bland steel-framed windows. Double glass doors opened automatically as Cody approached. She hesitated at the threshold, suddenly reticent to follow when he continued down the dark hallway.

Her pause was warranted. If the parking structure had been dirty and the exterior of this building dated, the inside was the worst of both worlds. Grime covered the floor, stained the worn industrial carpeting in huge discolored splotches. The track fluorescent lighting added to the slimy feeling, highlighting poorly patched holes and a slew of fingerprints.

At least the earth of the cubby had been just that. She could handle getting dirty, but questionable body fluids? Not so much.

"Hey, soldier," a slender brunette called, rising from a small metal desk. The woman was tall, thin, and stuck her chest out almost obscenely in Cody's direction.

"Mags." To his credit, Cody's eyes remained above neck-level. He ushered Daughtry forward. "This one's with me." The pair exchanged a few words about patrols.

A flicker of something caught her attention. She turned, wiggled out of Cody's grasp, and squinted at the beige walls. Nothing but poorly patched holes and boring brown paint. She waited, but when the brightness didn't reappear, she shrugged. Her brain must be fuzzy.

Still looking around at her shabby surroundings, she couldn't help but be disappointed. Given the plush elegance of the plane they'd so casually abandoned in the field, she'd expected more luxury.

"If you're done admiring the decor, we might actually make it to a place where we can shower."

At Cody's words, her mind went to a bad, *bad* place.

She glanced away, cheeks heating.

"What I meant was—" He gave an uncomfortable cough, and Daughtry knew he was imagining the same things she was. *Hot water.* "What I meant was just . . ." *Soapy hands. Slick skin.* " . . . just . . . *hurry up.*"

He whirled around and continued walking.

Daughtry smiled. *He was cute when he was embarrassed.*

Had she actually just thought that?

The man was over six feet and a solid block of muscle. He was tough, gorgeous. But cute? No.

That line of thinking was dangerous.

She gave herself a mental slap. She'd been head-over-heels in love before and all it had gotten her was dumped days before her wedding, disgraced by her parents, and saddled with an ability that made her worse than any serial killer.

No more. She had to protect herself and her fragile, love-seeking heart.

But she was so intent on her thoughts that she almost bumped into Cody. He halted her by grabbing her shoulders and for just a second, they were chest to chest. Heat blossomed, his eyes warmed.

An unknown force drawing her in, she leaned up. He tilted his head down. Their mouths were a hairsbreadth apart—

A door slammed in the distance and they both jumped, shooting apart.

Cursing, he turned, long legs eating up the length of dirty carpet. She wanted to call him back, except her feet felt encased in concrete.

A sharp slice of pain in her mind made her eyes water.

She cried out as she took another step forward, and her legs gave out, tumbling her to the carpeting. It was surprisingly soft, despite its worn appearance. But there wasn't time to concentrate on the thread count. Her brain felt like it was going to explode. A bubble of energy welled up then compressed, stealing her breath, and for one scary moment, Daughtry thought she might suffocate.

There was a *snap*, as quick and stinging as the pop of a rubber band.

She was vulnerable, exposed.

"Fuck," Cody said softly, reappearing and kneeling by her elbow.

She knew without asking what had happened.

The ward was gone.

John was dead.

SIXTEEN

SHE WOKE ON A SCREAM.

Strong arms held her, stilled her thrashing. "It's okay, cowgirl." Pine inundated her, and her eyes flashed open. "Shh. It's okay."

"Cody?" She blinked, clearing her vision enough that she could finally see him.

He looked terrible. His hair was a mess, like he'd repeatedly thrust his hands through it, and there were heavy, purple circles staining the skin below his lashes. Concern softened his features.

She could almost pretend that he was worried about her.

"Where's John?" she croaked. Her throat felt like she'd swallowed a flamethrower.

Cody's face hardened.

The last hours hit her with the force of a Mack Truck.

The pain of the ward bursting. Not being able to breathe. Cody yelling for help. Then hands, so many hands.

And death. Over and over.

One in childbirth. A few in old age. Then so many—a truly horrific amount—at the hands of the Dalshie.

There was no doubt of the war that Cody spoke of.

"Hey. Hey!" Cody grabbed her shoulders, shook her. "Stay with me."

She shrugged him off, only half-realizing that throughout it all, his touch had been—and still was—safe. Why?

Why him?

"Don't touch me!" She shoved away from him, sliding over on the bed, heart pounding, throat feeling as though it had been scoured raw. The visions whirled in her mind, viscous images that made her want to scream. She curled her legs underneath her and leaned back against the headboard. "It's not—*I'm* not safe," she explained, knowing that her actions had hurt him.

She forced her eyes to open, a feeble attempt to shove away the torrent of images swirling through her mind. She'd had so much hope that these people would help her.

Cody grabbed her hand.

She felt that old fear swell up, and a cold sweat broke out over her skin as she tried to retract it.

"Look at me." He tilted her chin up, forcing her to meet his familiar emerald eyes. "It's safe now."

She yanked her hand away and laughed coldly. "Bullshit. You people are supposed to be safe! You know *magic!*" She shoved her hair out of her eyes and threw back the thin comforter. "Instead, what did I get? Visions! I could get plenty of that at home! I shouldn't have come. I should—"

"You would have already been dead." He was calm, his words coolly logical.

That stopped her self-righteous rant. Yes. There was that.

"You're one of us people, you know."

She shrugged her shoulders. For all the good it had done her. "John never said anything—"

"Dammit," Cody growled, and she jumped. "It's just like

John to do this. Think with his cock. Start a project and not finish it. Now I'm left picking up the pieces."

"Don't talk about him like that!" Daughtry shouted, her anger swelling. John was—

No. Even in her mind she couldn't get the words out. "He didn't have time."

"He had an entire year!" Cody stood in front of her, glowering. "He could have gone back to you sooner. Told you something! He knew where you were. He could have brought you here!"

"He knew?"

Oh God. Her legs went weak at the thought. John had known and he'd left her anyway.

Cody winced. "John suspected. He even told Dante where you were, just in case something happened on his deployment." Cody's voice went a little softer. "But he wanted to be the one to talk to you. To ease you into it."

Ease? She closed her eyes and swallowed hard against the rage and pain. There was nothing easy about the visions, about dealing with them, about screwing with other people's futures.

"He thought leaving me alone and vulnerable was the way to do that?"

"No, it's not that," Cody said. "John didn't realize that you were having visions, wasn't even one-hundred-percent sure that you *were* Rengalla until he went back." Cody sighed. "He said your mind felt different, altered. He wanted to investigate."

"Different how?"

"Too ordered, too contained. Minds are full of chaos." Cody's shoulders dropped. "But then, as he was preparing to go see you, Dante saw your picture, and the truth came out. You look just like your mother. John couldn't have known that because he'd never met her. But Dante and I—"

She opened her mouth, but Cody waved her off.

"John was supposed to bring you back. To keep you safe." Cody turned away with a curse, muttering under his breath. "Now this becomes my problem. My responsibility. Just what I need."

"Well, thank you very much, but I don't need you," she snapped, slipping from the bed and finding her footing despite her spinning head. "But I don't want anything from you."

Cody snorted, the derisive gaze he shot over his shoulder cutting her to the quick. "Women like you always have ulterior motives."

"Women. Like. Me?" Her words were as sharp, as frigid as icicles.

Pun or not, the asshole was treading on thin ice.

He spun to face her, regarding her with open hostility. "You know damn well what I mean."

Daughtry exploded, the pain and embarrassment of the last year too much to bear. "Who? *Whores?* Gold-diggers? Hopeless, lonely damsels in distress?" She grabbed her sneakers from the floor and shoved her feet into them. No matter that she was all of those things. She didn't need someone to rub it in her face.

Cody froze, his eyes widened in shock. He opened his mouth.

"No!" she said, cutting him off. "I already know how unworthy I am." She took a breath and spoke quietly, "But better unworthy and a work in progress than a paid-off Stepford wife."

She strode to a door, opened it, and found a closet. Damn. Fate never helped her make a poignant exit.

"Stop."

Yeah, no. She cracked another door. Double damn. Bathroom.

"I said *stop.*"

She snorted. Did he seriously think that would work? Like

he could say sit, and she would obey like a wriggling puppy? Been there, done that, and that was humiliation enough.

Her hand closed on the last knob. Suddenly Cody was there, surrounding her, overwhelming her.

His lips slammed down over hers, and she gasped. Taking advantage of her open mouth, he slipped in his tongue.

For a second, she let him kiss her. Then she remembered his cold words. His insinuations and something snapped.

Ripping away, she shoved against his chest with every ounce of strength she possessed. "How dare you? What right—?" She shook her head, lungs heaving. "Stay the fuck away from me."

This time Cody let her go, but just before the door closed, she heard him say something. It might have been, *"Like hell."*

Daughtry hurried down the hall, hoping to avoid contact with anyone.

She didn't get her wish.

Tyler strolled around the corner, whistling to himself. He took one look at her before grimacing.

"He bungled it that badly, huh?"

"I don't know what you're talking about." Her eyes dropped to her scuffed sneakers.

Tyler stepped forward, arms extended like he meant to pull her into a hug.

She shrunk back instinctively.

"Hey." He put his hands up, "I'm safe. I promise."

"Forgive me if I don't believe you." She didn't like how cold her voice sounded.

"Walk with me." Tyler made a show of tucking his hands into his pockets before he inclined his head down the hall. "I'm shielded. All the LexTals are taught to shield constantly. You can't get a vision from me."

"Then why did every damn touch bring another vision of—" She broke off and took a shaky breath. "It's not safe for me to see.

If I do something to alter the person's end, it gets worse. I can't risk it." She looked up, meeting his gaze. "I can't have any more stain on my soul."

A look crossed Tyler's face, part pity, part anger. "You shouldn't even have to be dealing with this. You should already know how to control them."

"Control?" Funny how that single word buoyed her heart, made all of her anger and helplessness disappear. "There's a way to control them?"

"God, yes." Tyler reached for her and this time she let him wrap an arm around her shoulders. "You don't have to live like this. All of the Oracles have always been able to control their foresight. You just need training."

Her throat went dry, her knees weak. "Please tell me that you're not just saying that to make me feel better." She squeezed his hand before pulling away. This was too much contact too soon. Her voice dropped to a whisper. "Please tell me that I might not have to worry about touching someone. Please—"

"Daughtry." Tyler stepped in front of her, forcing her to stop. The expression on his face begged her to judge his sincerity. "It's true."

Relief flowed through her, fast and heady, and she smiled. "Okay, then." There was a beat of quiet then she asked, "When can I start?"

"Now." Tyler grinned, the warmth of it as pure as sunshine. "Let's go find Dante." He turned and led her down a corridor.

As they walked, she was reminded again of the disparity between her current surroundings and the plane and SUV. It just seemed unfathomable that people who could afford crystal chandeliers and silk wallpaper on an airplane lived in a place with stained carpeting and fluorescent lighting.

She snorted, remembering the hovel that had been Jimmy's

room in his parents' mansion. Yet his car had been pristine. This was probably just another case of men and their toys.

"What are you smirking about?" Tyler glanced at her, and she realized how much taller and bigger he was than she. Next to Cody, he had seemed juvenile, almost boyish. But there was more to him, an awareness in his eyes that one might miss if they focused only on the laughing exterior.

It made him dangerous.

Focusing on the spoken conversation rather than the one in her head, she told him her observations.

He laughed so hard that tears streamed down his cheeks. "Please . . ." He swiped his face with the back of his hand. ". . . oh God, please tell me you told Cody that."

She frowned.

Tyler slung an arm around her shoulders and squeezed.

Enjoying the comfort despite herself, she let him.

"I'm not making fun of you, honest. You wouldn't believe how many times he's said the same thing. I swear you guys are perfect for each other."

Daughtry's jaw fell open. "You're wrong." She wondered why it hurt to say the next words. "Th-there's nothing between us."

"Who're you trying to convince, sweetheart?" Tyler's question wasn't hostile, but he held her stare, not letting her get away without acknowledging the truth. "Don't let the ice fool you. Cody understands what you're going through more than anyone else here."

"How could he? Anyway, it's not like that. He doesn't — Not with a girl like—" She shook her head. "Just . . . not me."

At her words, the lightness in Tyler's face disappeared. "What did he say?"

"Forget it. He didn't say anything." Tyler snorted, but she

ignored him and started walking again. Not so subtly, she changed the subject. "Where's Dante's office?"

For a moment, she didn't think Tyler would let it go. But after another long moment he blew out a breath and pointed to a door down the hall. "I'll let you escape for now, but I'm going to kick Cody's ass later."

She opened her mouth to protest then shrugged. That was so not her problem, even though her disloyal heart clenched at the thought of Cody hurt. Shaking her head at herself, she forced him from her mind. She had far more pressing things to deal with.

Tyler had stopped and was knocking at a beige door.

"Come in," a voice called.

Tyler opened the door, gestured for her to precede him. Once inside, she found another nondescript room. The desk was plain and covered in papers. Unlike the hall, there weren't any harsh fluorescent lights, just a single desk lamp with a green glass shade. Annoyingly, it was the same color as Cody's eyes.

"Daughtry." Dante set aside some papers and stood. "How are you feeling?"

Well, this was embarrassing. Everyone knew she was some sort of freak, damaged by a simple touch. She forced a smile. "Great. Thanks for asking." The gratitude came out almost as an admonishment. She winced.

Dante looked at her, the lightest of frowns marring the skin between his brows.

The silence went on a second too long. "So." He cleared his throat. "What did you need? I figured you'd want a few more hours to rest after your ordeal."

Ordeal. That was a far more pleasant word than what had actually happened. She'd had about a dozen visions before she'd been able to extricate herself from the so-called helpful hands of the infirmary staff. After so much exposure, her mind had been ping-ponging visions around so rapidly she'd passed out.

Some of that had faded, but she wouldn't be ready to sleep and let her dreams regurgitate the graphic images any time soon.

"Rest is overrated," she said, and the frown between Dante's eyebrows deepened. Well, *damn*. Discussing her emotional baggage wasn't where she wanted this conversation to go.

"Have a seat."

She obliged, dropping into a wooden chair.

"Now tell me why you're here."

"The Dalshie. They—"

Dante interrupted her. "I know about the attacks. What I want to know is why you came. What you expect to do here at the Colony."

She hesitated, at a loss. How could she know that? "I don't understand."

Grey eyes were piercing in their intensity. "Are you here for training, or do you want someone to guard you? Do you need money?" The last question was spoken with chilling logic, and she felt Tyler shift position to stand protectively behind her left shoulder.

Dante looked over her head, his next comments more to Tyler than her.

"John said you'd lost your job." An attempt to justify the insulting words.

But she couldn't really blame him for the question. He probably had a lot of open hands to deal with. Still, something in her stomach tightened. So much for a fresh start. Not even one full day, and someone had accused her of wanting a handout.

"The only thing I want is to learn to protect myself."

Dante's forehead smoothed. He offered her a half-smile, genuine interest sliding into his eyes. "I wouldn't have it any other way. When do you want to get started?"

"How about now?" She'd show him her intentions.

Tyler laughed. "Told you you'd like her, boss-man."

Dante didn't respond, just stared at Daughtry as she clenched and unclenched her hands. She needed to learn how to control the visions, to protect herself and those around her. "I can make an appointment and come back later," she said, though that was the last thing she wanted to do.

"Now is fine." Dante addressed Tyler. "Come back in a half-hour so you can escort Daughtry back to her rooms."

A half-hour? She was going to be pissed if she'd suffered this long for something that could be learned in thirty minutes.

"Got it," Tyler said. He paused, waiting until she met his eyes. "You okay?"

The words melted the last fragments of ice from her encounter with Cody. She nodded. "Thanks."

The sound of the door closing seemed very loud in the quiet of the room.

She waited for Dante to say something. To do something. But he seemed content to ignore her and shuffle some papers. Finally, he tapped them on the desk and set them on top of a precarious pile on one corner. There seemed to be a great many of said piles all around the small office.

"Are you telepathic, too?" she asked.

"Just a touch. Not like John," he said then seemed to catch his mistake. His face sobered. "I have a far less exciting ability." He circled the desk and leaned a hip against it. "I can bore you with that later. Ready?"

She swallowed her dread and nodded.

Dante's fingertips came up. He rested them on her temples exactly as John's had during the car ride that seemed like an eternity ago.

"Close your eyes."

She let them slide shut.

"Imagine your mind as a house. Tell me when you're there."

Daughtry pictured the little cottage she'd lived in for one summer. It had been before middle-of-the-night moves, before pretentious luxury and thousand-dollar-a-plate dinners, and before the visions.

The house had cobblestone siding, and light had flooded through its numerous windows, illuminating little motes of dust. The sun-kissed wooden floors had been warm under her bare feet.

"There," she whispered, hating to burst the peaceful memory.

"Okay," Dante said, voice quieting to match hers. "Now, open the front door."

It was honey-colored oak and heavy. The black hardware made it look like it belonged in a medieval castle. Turning the worn knob, she hauled it open.

She felt, more than saw, Dante enter her mind.

"Can you hear me?" he asked.

"Yes," she answered aloud, not sure if he'd hear her otherwise.

"Okay, I'm just going to . . ." She could feel him tramping about in her mind, his mental footsteps loud enough to make her eyes water. *Strange.* He touched something that made her gasp in pain.

"Close the door, Daughtry. Right now."

Panicked by the seriousness of his tone, she slammed the heavy door closed, and mentally threw the lock. Then she opened her eyes.

Dante's face was set in hard lines.

"Wh-what is it?"

He sat down in the chair opposite her, the leather creaking loudly. "Someone has been in your mind."

"What does that mean?" she asked. "H-how could you

know?"

Dante scrubbed a hand over his face. "There are triggers in your mind, like a trap has been set. I don't want to risk setting it off."

She clenched her hands together. "But how?"

"Everyone has a specific mental signature. If you looked into my mind, you'd see my own brain's fingerprint, for a lack of a better word, but also traces of my teachers, my family, of anyone who might have been close enough to be beneath my shield." He leaned back against the desk. "Even if the interference might not seem obvious from the outside, anyone looking will always be able to see the footprints of those who've gone before."

"Who?" Or more importantly, why? She took a breath and tried to slow her racing heart. "What did they do?"

"I can't tell exactly. It's wired to do something, but minds and telepathy aren't my specialty." He sighed. "I don't want to trigger it and risk hurting you. It doesn't make any sense. It doesn't feel like anything I've sensed before . . ." Breaking eye contact, he tapped his lips as if deep in thought.

The silence lengthened, Daughtry's mind turning inward, trying to see the mysterious fingerprints or mental signature or footprints. But she couldn't see anything and the longer the quiet went on, the more frustrated she became.

Finally she couldn't take it any longer and blurted, "Then at least tell me who I can talk to. Who can go into my mind and help me untangle the trap or control the visions or—"

"I can only think of one person," Dante said. She narrowed her eyes at his too-innocent expression.

"Tell me." *Please don't let her suspicions be right.*

Dante's voice was muffled, the pulse in her ears deafening. "Cody."

Seriously?

SEVENTEEN

"YOU CAN'T BE SERIOUS."

Dante just shot Daughtry a look.

"Why would he help me? Cody said he wasn't telepathic."

"He's not."

Dear God, and she'd thought Cody was infuriating. "Then why?"

"I'll let him explain that."

She opened her mouth to protest, but he kept speaking. "Just suffice to say that he's the best person now that Jo—"

A sound of dismay slipped past her lips.

At her noise, Dante stopped. Then he leaned down and touched her shoulder.

She forced herself to stay still. A vision would be ample punishment for her sins.

"It's not your fault."

"Funny how it feels like it is."

"You know that John knew? About your powers?"

"Cody mentioned something about that," she said, and her voice sounded bitter, even to her own ears. Why hadn't John said anything sooner? They might have—

Dante sighed and squatted next to her. "He thought your mind was too pat, too clean. But he never felt any magic."

"How is that possible?"

"I don't know. But I'll damn sure be looking into it." He hesitated. "For what it's worth, Daughtry, I am sorry."

"Why?" she asked. "It's not like you kicked me and my family out. I was kidnapped."

Dante shook his head. "John described you, mentioned your hair, your eyes. I should have put the pieces together, demanded to see a picture."

"So you blame yourself because of a description that could have encompassed a large chunk of the female population?"

"I should have known."

"You couldn't have."

Dante sighed and stood. "I know. But *you* need to know that you're family. You're not alone anymore."

As he went back to his paperwork, she thought about what he'd said. About the potential that she might have people who cared for her here. Allies, friends. It was a tempting prospect.

One she was almost afraid to believe might come true.

When Tyler returned at the appointed time, she was barely aware of his presence.

They walked down the empty halls in silence. But, of course, that couldn't last.

"You've really got him on edge, you know?" She knew without question the *him* to whom Tyler was referring.

"I know." She'd felt that edge.

Tyler sighed. "Normally I stand back and watch the fireworks, but I think you might be the best thing that could happen to him. He's so controlled, so robotic he's almost cold. It's good to see him show some emotion."

"I wish that emotion wasn't at my expense."

Tyler grimaced. "You still want me to kick his ass?"

"No." She laughed. "Not yet anyway."

"Good. Do me a favor and think about what I said. Once you get past his bark, there's not much bite."

She nodded, partly to shut him up and partly because she had the feeling that Tyler might be right.

But how could Tyler think they would be good together? Yes, they were attracted to each. Yes, their chemistry was explosive. Mentos meet Diet Coke, and all that, but they couldn't exchange more than a few sentences without coming to insults.

Now she had to *talk* to him? Ask him for help?

The fates must really be laughing at her.

She walked for a little longer before she realized that she didn't know something important. "Is anyone ever going to tell me what a LexTal is?"

Tyler hesitated in his stride and glanced over at her. "You mean, you don't know?"

She pointed to herself. "Newbie here. Cody said you guys are constables?" Whatever that meant. "My Rengalla knowledge is slim. I know I can manipulate how a person dies. That you guys can do some pretty spectacular things with dirt and bolt-holes, and I know . . ." She paused as she thought. "Yup, that's pretty much the extent of it."

Tyler shook his head. "I guess that's true. It's just strange to come across one of us who doesn't know who we are or what we do."

"Which is *what* exactly?"

"Besides bad-asses?"

"Yes," she said with a sigh. "Besides that."

"Well, we are constables. Basically mall cops on steroids." He grinned at her expression. "I'm joking. We're part of the military of the Rengalla. The best part, the most elite, well trained. The best looking—"

She rolled her eyes. "I get it. So you're like the marines or something?"

"More like the SEALs," he said. "We don't really patrol the base—well, there is one rotation here, but the rest of them are at the other Rengallan bases or deployments for missions to seek and destroy Dalshie who are preying on humans."

That sounded exceedingly dangerous. "Was John . . .?" The past tense made her eyes sting.

Tyler nodded. "He was. One of the best."

"Who else?"

"Cody, of course. And the triplets, Morgan, Monroe, Mason. Dante. Me. And we have two new recruits, but don't bother learning their names. They probably won't last."

"Is the training that hard?"

"Harder than you can imagine."

"Oh." She could imagine a lot, but didn't say that. "So there are more of us?" she asked instead.

"Of course. The Colony is the biggest with several hundred of us here, but there are a few smaller settlements around the world."

"Wow."

"If I had a nickel for every time a girl said that to me," Tyler drawled as he stopped near a door. He swept into a bow. "Your room, milady."

"You're ridiculous. You know that, right?"

"The girls also say that all the time." He grinned, placing his hand on a panel next to the door. The lock clicked, and he chucked her under the chin. "Get some rest." He ushered her into the room before saying goodbye.

Outside the window, the sky was dark, filling the room with shadows. She didn't feel the least bit tired after recovering from the ordeal of the ward breaking, but one glance at the clock showed her it was obscenely early in the morning.

Nothing to do then, but wait.

She sat on the edge of the bed then wrinkled her nose. Okay, then. Shower first, then wait. Opening the door she'd tried to storm out of earlier, she strode into the bathroom and turned on the water. She might as well do something productive if sleep was out of reach.

Her hands found the hem of her grimy top and started to pull it up. Then she noticed the many bottles of shampoos and soaps on the counter and tucked into the shower cubbies. Maybe she could wash her shirt in the sink. She pulled it and her bra off, and set them both on the counter. Now if she could just find some towels . . .

"What are you doing?"

Shrieking, she bolted upright and promptly banged her head on the underside of the cabinet she'd been scouring.

"Shit. I'm sorry." Cody's voice was concerned, if still slightly scolding. "What's with you and head injuries?"

Placing his hand on the back of her neck, he guided her head down and out of the vanity, rubbing the knot already forming on her scalp.

He spun her around. "Look at me." Studying her eyes must have brought whatever result he was looking for, because he nodded. Then he looked down. And kept looking.

She followed his stare with her own. "Oh my God." Scrambling out of his arms, she reached for the towel she'd spotted.

It was a flipping washrag, but she gathered it to her breasts anyway. "Turn around!"

He complied but took his time in doing so, his eyes molten and tempting. Stopping that train of thought at the station, she snatched up her shirt and threw it on.

"What are you doing?" She crossed her arms over her chest, not liking the heated look he was sending that particular body part. Not that her nipples seemed to mind. They'd beaded into tight little points, making her braless state quite obvious.

"I asked you first." A charming smile graced his plump lips. "You're in my room."

"What?" Now that he'd said that, she could smell him all around her: the salty tang of the sea, the slightly bitter mark of pine. So the room she'd awoken in before her meeting with Dante wasn't a random one. She had slept in—

Cody's bed. A flame of arousal shot through her.

Something unreadable flashed across his face before his expression locked down. "It's not even five o'clock in the morning."

"Yes." She turned away and splashed water on her face. "Why did Tyler tell me this is my room?"

She searched her memory as she waited for him to respond, teasing out flashes of the evening before. She remembered Cody intervening at the infirmary. How she'd found safety in his arms —a layer of ocean and tangy pine—covering, protecting her. He'd—*oh*—ignored the doctor's protests and had carried her out of the hospital. But she didn't remember telling him to take her to his room or to let her sleep in his bed.

"I wouldn't let them put you anywhere else." He might as well have crossed his arms for how defiant that sentence was.

Well, screw that.

"I wasn't aware you were in charge of me. I seem to remember you saying quite clearly I was a responsibility you didn't want." She glared at him. Where did he get off demanding to protect her then ridiculing her when he'd shouldered the responsibility himself?

"I don't recall *needing* your permission."

Permission?

Daughtry opened her mouth to retort then snapped it shut again. She needed to ask him for help with her mind. It would probably be better if she didn't burn all her bridges in one fell swoop.

"You're safe here," he said.

She snorted in response. *Maybe physically, but this animosity isn't good for either of them.*

Sighing, she turned off the shower and walked back into the bedroom.

"Is there somewhere else I can stay?" She needed space to think.

Cody shook his head. "You stay here."

Irritated at the caveman speak, she started for the door on unsteady legs. Damn, her head really hurt.

When she wobbled, Cody grabbed her arm, his palm burning against her bare skin. The intensity of him, of her body's reaction to him, snapped Daughtry back into reality. "Stop that."

It came out harsher than she'd intended. But why did a simple touch from him incite such a fierce reaction?

Cody dropped her arm and stepped back.

Not that, she wanted to say. She wanted to tell him to keep holding her but stop making her body react like one of those cartoon thermometers, the mercury rising and rising until the top blew off.

And honestly? She was annoyed at herself. At him. Annoyed that, despite everything that had passed between them, she still wanted his arms around her. That she *wanted* his comfort.

What does that make you? the darkness taunted. *A whore, scrounging after bits of affection, that's what.*

A cold sweat broke out over her body, but she swallowed against the pain that notion brought.

"I need to ask you something." She shoved her bangs off her sticky forehead.

"What?"

She turned away, sucking in a deep breath before trailing her fingers over the old desk along one wall of the small room.

"Dante looked into my mind." It felt weird to try to put the conversation into words, but she explained the experience—the evidence that her mind had been tampered with. "He said that you might be able to help."

Cody snorted.

Her eyes flashed up and the anger in his gaze made her take a step back.

"Did he put you up to this? Play a trick on the guy whose powers don't work right?" He started pacing and she strained to hear his quiet ranting. "Always trying to get me . . . not safe . . . moron."

After his grumbling seemed to defer solely to name calling, she intervened. "Dante didn't put me up to anything."

Cody faced her, his expression carefully placid, except his eyes were hopeful. Cautiously hopeful.

She recognized the careful optimism because she'd felt it so often before. It would be so easy to expose that vulnerability, to crush the fragile expectation. But despite Dante appearing to have an ulterior motive at referring her to Cody, she didn't think it was malicious. His words, his concern, had been too sincere for that.

"He seemed to think you could do it because he couldn't."

Emotion flared across Cody's expression before he battened down the hatches. Had he really thought his boss, his friend, had set him up to fail?

"Okay," he said finally, the single word relaxing the ball of tension in her stomach. "Sit and let me take a look." He perched her on the edge of the bed and knelt before her.

His hands were just rising to rest on her head when there

was a knock. Cody cursed, taking a breath before rising to answer it.

He came back bearing a duffle bag. "You need to get changed. The Council wants to talk to you in an hour."

Didn't that sound foreboding? "The Council?" she asked.

"Just as it sounds," he said. "The people you don't want to piss off." He tucked the duffle into her hand, and she rose. "Suz brought you some clothes."

"Okay." Daughtry crossed into the bathroom, heart racing at the prospect of meeting those who might decide her fate. "You'll look into my mind later?"

He nodded.

"Thank you."

She started to close the door.

"Hey, cowgirl?" Her eyes met his. "I'm sorry I was such an ass earlier. I didn't mean to imply—" He looked awkward apologizing, and she had the impression that it wasn't something that he did often.

"Forget about it." She forced a smile. "I already have."

He looked so relieved that she didn't feel guilty about lying. Well-practiced or not, apologies were a dime a dozen.

Actions were the only things that she trusted. And Cody's were so all-over-the-place that she didn't know what to think.

Give him another chance, her conscience said. *He'll come around.*

She sighed. Only time would tell if that were true.

EIGHTEEN

SHE EMERGED clean from the shower and very thankful for the clothes from Suz. It had taken until she'd been midway through the second shampoo, but Daughtry had eventually remembered the doctor.

In and out of consciousness at the time, the shouted words had been muffled through a fog of nausea and fatigue. But she'd heard the doctor's concern, her frustration at being unable to help.

Daughtry pushed aside the memory and zipped up the bag.

In the end, Suz had found a way to be helpful.

Very helpful, she thought with a snort, applying deodorant after removing a Post-it with a smiley face. Point taken. The last few days had been hell on her grooming habits.

Shoving her bangs out of her eyes, she returned to the bedroom. Cody was on his cell.

He'd changed and now wore a black shirt that made the green in his eyes stand out sharply against his tan skin. Her eyes trailed down, and she sighed. The way the man carried off a pair of jeans should have been illegal.

Her body said yum. Her heart and mind were undecided.

"Ready?" he asked as she was tying on the pair of sneakers she'd found in the bag.

She shrugged. "Sure." As they walked to the door, she found herself asking, "Why did Tyler say you'd understand my situation better than anyone?"

Cody went motionless. "Goddamn him," he muttered so quietly that she had to strain to hear it. "Don't worry about it," he said louder. The *"just drop it"* was left unsaid. He whirled away and grasped the handle.

Daughtry should have abided the unspoken order, but something screamed in her she had to know. That it was critical. And God knew *he'd* pushed *her* plenty.

She grabbed his arm, halting his movement.

A piece of her hair escaped her ponytail and brushed the exposed skin on his arm. He jumped like it had burned him. Then he faced her, eyes hot and muscles tense. He rubbed the lock of hair between his fingers, face softening as he tucked it behind her ear.

His mouth was close to hers, his breath hot against her lips. She gasped, her fingers tightening on his bicep. Cody bent even closer, until the hard planes of his chest brushed her breasts. He was going to kiss her—

He tore his arm from her grasp and was across the room in a movement so fast her mind could barely process it.

She followed him slowly, trying not to spook him.

Her hand returned to his bicep, the bare skin there almost feverish. As she leaned close, he sucked in a breath. Her own breathing wasn't particularly steady either.

"Daughtry." It was a warning.

She didn't listen, just tilted closer. "Why, Cody?"

The answer, when it came, seemed torn out of him. "Because I was like you." He brushed past her. "Time to go." He wrenched open the door.

She pushed in front of him and closed it.

"How?"

"I didn't grow up here."

He sidestepped, and if he hadn't looked so panicked, she would have smiled at his efforts to try and leave without actually touching her.

"Were you kidnapped too?"

"Not exactly."

"You and that phrase," she muttered. Cody glanced up, finally met her eyes. "So tell me *what exactly*."

"I grew up in the human world."

A sudden burst of anguish hit her straight in the gut. It felt like it had come from Cody. But that was crazy. She shook it off. "Did you have human parents?" Like her?

"No."

There was such agony in that one word that she wanted to grab him and pull him into her embrace. As if the contact would cure him. But she didn't. "Then"—her next words were almost a whisper—"*were* you kidnapped?"

He laughed, a jagged sound—broken shards of glass against her soul.

"What happened?" she said. "You can tell me."

At her words—her sympathy—anger shadowed his face. But Daughtry couldn't let it take him.

Moving slowly, she reached up and cupped his cheek. She half-expected Cody to slap her hand away, to demand she leave him alone.

He didn't. For a moment he even closed his eyes, leaning into her touch. Then, as if he realized he'd almost given into her comfort, they flashed open, and he wrenched his head away.

"Cody," she whispered, her hands coming up again to cradle his face in her palms. Her thumb traced absently over the top of his scar. "Tell me."

"My parents abandoned me because I was a Null." He sighed and held up a hand when she would have questioned him further. He extricated himself and leaned back against the wall. Some of the tension in his frame eased, like the space made it easier for him to think about his past.

"I didn't have magic as a child. My parents opted to dump me in a human orphanage rather than keep me with them." The sentences were monotone. Bare facts recited.

She frowned both at the tone and the words. "But your magic. I've seen it. It's—"

"Uncontrollable. Dangerous. Unreliable." He turned his head away. "I'm a menace in the field. A liability." She could almost see the quotation marks. That was something he'd heard many times over.

A small seed of something grew in her heart. Affection, perhaps more. But she wasn't ready to admit it, even to herself.

Instead, she said the only thing she could think of. "You saved my life. I'd take that kind of liability any day." She reached over and clasped his hand. "Thank you." She rose on tiptoe to press a kiss against his cheek. "For telling me."

He'd trusted her enough to share the truth, to expose his vulnerable underbelly, and that filled her heart, bolstering the hope in her soul. Jimmy would have never done that, never attempted to put them on equal footing. She wanted desperately to believe that Cody could be different but knew it was going to take her time to truly trust him.

She stepped back.

Cody, seemingly ill content with her putting distance between them, swooped down and took her lips.

A blaze of heat roared through her.

They were two crests of a wave meeting in perfect harmony, every touch amplified until she was standing in the middle of a maelstrom of stroking fingers and dueling caresses. She wanted

Cody to hold her, to never let her go. It could have been hours or minutes before he released her, but she lingered, breasts pressing against the hard planes of his chest as she tried to catch her breath.

He rested his forehead against hers.

"We need to go," she whispered. *No.* They needed to stay. God, how they needed to stay.

"Yes," he said. "We do." He backed away, sucked in a breath and she watched, dismayed, as his face hardened to granite. How much ice he would layer on to make up for what he'd shared?

When Cody reached for the door handle this time, Daughtry forced herself to let him go.

She followed in his wake, well able to understand his war between vulnerability and desire. Sharing memories rather kept in the past? Uncomfortable. Ignoring the draw between them? Impossible.

Great. Now she sounded like a credit card commercial.

Still, Cody talking about his history, opening his soul and exposing his pain, was far more frightening because it softened the barriers around her heart. Even now, it made her want to yank him to a stop and hug him until the agony of the past eased its grip. Then hunt down his parents and curse them for hurting him so thoroughly.

Regardless, she recognized that Cody needed a little space to pull himself together. She could give that to him and maybe the distance would give her a chance to forget the pain she'd felt from his earlier words.

Turning the corner, she was almost bulldozed by Tyler. He took one look at what must have been mussed hair and swollen lips and pulled her to a halt. Cody paused, but she nodded for him to continue on.

Tyler leaned in, whispering as he pulled out a small makeup

bag. "From Suz. She thought you might like a little war paint before facing the Council."

Daughtry laughed. She owed the other woman big time. Last thing she wanted was to appear before the people in charge looking like a strung-out college student. She could use all of the armor she could get.

"She must be more psychologist than doctor," Daughtry said, having Tyler hold the bag as she flicked open a compact and fixed her hair. A little powder hid the stubble marks, and gloss disguised her swollen lips.

She looked . . . neutral. Together.

"I could kiss you, Tyler." Her fingers zipped the bag closed, and she gave the man she was fast considering a friend a hug. It felt good to initiate the contact.

Tyler smirked as he hugged her back. "Ah, the goddess known as Daughtry, I knew you wouldn't be able to resist me for long." He tugged her arm. "This way."

As they walked, she craned her neck, wondering where Cody had gone, before chastising herself. It didn't matter. It shouldn't matter. But when she caught the faintest hint of salt and pine, something inside of her relaxed. He wasn't far.

"Penny for your thoughts?" Tyler asked, eyes serious.

He was almost too insightful and gave her a wide smile when she told him as much.

She rolled her eyes. Still, she couldn't help teasing him. "Plus, you would need way more than a penny to get what's bouncing around in here." At the rate thoughts were whipping through her mind, she'd mow Tyler down the moment she unloaded.

He winked. "I'm always prepared." Then he held up a twenty, and she laughed again, his warm sunshine of a chuckle joining in with hers.

"Fine. I'll let you keep your confidence. This time."

They walked through the maze of hallways in pleasant silence, their path fading into her memory.

"How can you find your way? Every hall looks the same." Beige. Brown. Cream. Blah. Boring.

He smiled, gave an ambiguous wave. "It will all be explained soon."

"'These aren't the droids you're looking for,'" she replied with an equally cheesy pass of her palm.

He looked at her blankly.

Really?

"It's from a movie. Maybe you've heard of it? *Star Wars*."

Tyler shook his head even as Cody's voice warmed her from head to toe. He came to stand very close to her, the heat from his chest intense against her spine. His amused words brushed her ear. "I can't believe you actually rendered him speechless."

Her stomach clenched with desire, because, while serious Cody was hot, this playful side was sexy.

"That may actually be the first time in history," he said, resting his hand on her hip.

Sucking in a breath in an attempt to mute her reaction, she jumped when Morgan pushed past Tyler and through the door they'd stopped in front of. "Yeah. Even when he was a baby, his mother couldn't get him to shut up."

"I had colic, dick," Tyler responded, following and punching Morgan on the shoulder.

Morgan shoved him off and gave him the finger.

"After you," Cody said, drawing her attention. His voice was husky, and she could tell the closeness had affected him too. Desire rose, and she would have forgotten they were in a public venue had Tyler not chosen that moment to intervene.

"Come on, Dee," he called. "I've got a seat saved for you." He patted the chair next to him.

The space itself was extremely masculine, about the size of

a standard conference room and adorned in dark leather and deep cherry wood. A large table was shoved to one side, surrounded by comfortable-looking office chairs. Monitors filled the opposite wall.

Most of the men had electronic tablets open, but Dante was proudly old-fashioned with a pad of paper and pen. He gestured at her to come in, to take the seat next to him.

He wore a simple grey T-shirt and black cargos. There was some sort of crest with a bird and Latin writing above his heart, but it was too small for Daughtry to discern it clearly. The rest of the men at the tables wore the same shirt, albeit in different variations of white to black, and either cargos or jeans. Since she recognized all but two of them, she assumed this was the de facto uniform of the LexTals.

And that the two nervous-looking youngsters at the end were the new recruits.

A few of the chairs were empty. Had one of them belonged to John? She could easily imagine him amongst all the mahogany and leather. The thought made her eyes sting, guilt at his sacrifice pouring through her all over again, and she hastily studied the wall of blank monitors, trying to get her emotions back under control.

"Look, they swivel *and* recline."

An unwilling smile curved her lips as Tyler demonstrated the merits of said chair. He seemed to have a knack for rescuing her from her pain.

Just as she took her seat, the door opened, and a group that she assumed was the Council entered. She was unsurprised to the find they were composed predominantly of men who looked to be in their mid-fifties or older. There were plenty of softened stomachs poorly hidden beneath bland dress shirts and slacks, and more than one receding hairline. Pale beige and white were the favored colors amongst the six men. She wondered if their opinions were as vanilla as their clothes.

There was *one* surprise, however.

A woman with a clear air of authority approached the table and sat down at its head. Her hair was a shock of red, though minus the curls and freckles that usually accompanied the color.

She pinned Daughtry with a stare that made her feel like she was being judged within an inch of her life, and when the woman transferred that gaze to Cody, Daughtry was relieved.

The woman smiled at him, a small, intimate quirk of the lips. Daughtry could almost hear her thinking, "*So this is the pathetic twit who is responsible for all of the theatrics?*"

"Caroline," Cody warned.

The woman raised a perfectly groomed eyebrow in response.

Daughtry hated her instantly.

"She'll need to be tested." Caroline's words were perfectly polite, but they still sent a shiver down Daughtry's spine.

Cody's face changed in an instant. Anger gathered his expression into a fearsome frown, but when he went to protest, Dante beat him to the punch. "Caroline, a simple mind-read will do. John and I both vetted her already. Testing isn't our normal protocol." The words were laced with disapproval.

"She may be Dalshie."

"She's not—"

Caroline ignored Dante's protest and nodded to the man sitting on her right.

Cody growled—literally growled—and Daughtry had the feeling he would have been across the table in a second had she not placed her hand on his leg. She gave it a light squeeze and shook her head.

"It's okay," she whispered.

"It is not," he snarled back.

Caroline's eyes rounded, whether with surprise or anger, Daughtry wasn't sure.

"Fine. You have a problem, Cody? Then you do it."

He was protesting before Caroline finished speaking. Even Dante and some of the Council chimed in.

"I haven't had time to prepare—"

"Caroline. This is an unnecessary risk—"

"Council-head—"

"It's not safe—"

"Enough! I am the Council-head, and I say Cody does it!" Her voice boomed around the room, quieting the sudden uproar of voices. She met the eyes of each of the men on the Council. "Anyone have a problem with that?"

Silence, tense enough to smother, followed her words.

Daughtry glanced around, and a wave of cold spread through her body. The LexTals were perched tensely in their chairs, ready to intervene at the slightest indication.

Cody's face was pale.

She pressed her hand against his chest and felt the rapid beat of his pulse under her palm. There was no reason for her to be the cause of all of this dissension.

"Please, Cody. It'll be okay."

There were a few snorts from the peanut gallery at Daughtry's comment, but they were silenced with a glare from Caroline.

Even Cody muttered, chest rumbling against her palm as he spoke, "It won't."

"How is this different from before?" she asked. Why was he suddenly unwilling to help her?

"It's a *lot* different." He thrust a hand through his hair and pulled her away from the circus of the table. "Before, I was just going to observe, look, then come up with a plan. Caroline wants me to combine our powers. It could be dangerous."

"But didn't you do that on the plane?"

His fingers clenched into fists. "Yes. But this isn't an emergency, Daughtry. We would have died had I not risked mixing our magic on the plane. This test is unnecessary."

She rested her hand on his elbow. "I trust you," she said. He was a man who, despite all his blustering, had protected her. Fought for her. "You won't hurt me." She believed that. He wouldn't harm her physically. Emotionally on the other hand—

No. This was definitely *not* the time to think about that.

He opened his mouth to say something, but Caroline didn't give him the time to delay any further.

"Continue." She gave him a hard look. "Or Thomas will." The skinny blond glued to her right shoulder, nodded in solidarity.

Cody looked at her, and she inclined her head in agreement. Sighing, he placed his fingertips on her temples. She swallowed roughly She might have agreed to this but still dreaded the thought of him in her mind. Would it hurt, like on the plane? Would he see the awful things she'd done?

Still, it wasn't like she had a say in the matter. Someone was going to read her mind, whether she liked it or not. But—

Shit. What if she had another vision?

Would Cody have to drop his shields to conduct the test? She started to ask—

Too late. He was already sliding through her consciousness.

It would be okay, she tried to convince herself. Nothing had happened with Dante.

He slipped into her mind and she imagined him turning the handle, carefully pushing open the front door. Cody was gentle as he moved deeper, yet her mind still fought to keep him out. It was almost too intimate, a real struggle to relax and let him in. But when he did finally pass through the barriers and touch the magic deep inside her brain, it was absolute ecstasy.

His mind was a perfect fit against her own.

Except—

Nausea welled up, threatening to overwhelm her. "Stop," she gasped.

It eclipsed Cody's presence in her mind, blinding her to everything except the panic of the forthcoming vision.

She didn't see the wave of his power until it was too late.

There was no time to react.

The magic crashed into her.

NINETEEN

THE REVERBERATION from the impact knocked Daughtry flat on her back.

Something pulled taut in her mind.

It hurt.

Nausea raised to a crescendo before fading away. "Oh God," she groaned, laying her head back.

Cool hands touched her forehead. She knew without opening her eyes that it was Cody.

"Are you all right?"

She peeled an eyelid back, squinted against the bright lights.

"Please tell me you're okay," he said.

"I'm fine," she muttered, suddenly aware of the crowd of LexTals surrounding them. At Cody's obvious concern, there was a round of raised eyebrows and smug looks.

Lucky for them, he'd missed the exchange.

She leveraged her elbows beneath her and managed to sit up. Her brain throbbed like she'd just passed through the most painful portion of the world's worst headache. "I'm perfectly fine," she said again when Cody didn't look convinced.

He opened his mouth to say something, but Dante shoved

him aside to check on her. The glare Cody gave his boss made Daughtry happy she wasn't on its receiving end.

"Let's get you to the infirmary." Dante bent to lift her.

"No." She scooted out of reach. She'd had enough of that place. "I'm not going."

"I think—"

She cut him off with a shake of her head. "I'm okay. I swear."

Dante looked at Cody, seemingly searching for an ally.

"Don't even start," she said. It was an order to both men. "I'm not some weak thing who needs to be carted off for every bonk on the head."

She stood—unassisted—and dusted herself off.

The pull in her consciousness had only gotten stronger, and she wanted to get the meeting over with so she could examine it. It was as if a piece of her mind had been swapped out with someone else's.

Daughtry had her suspicions as to whom it belonged.

Maybe it wouldn't be a big deal.

She snorted. When had life ever been easy? She turned to Dante. "So is that all you need—?"

An immense pressure bore down on her mind. The air thickened. Goose bumps popped up on her arms.

Her hands clutched at her temples, clawing at her skull, desperate for relief from the vice-like grip. It felt like she was stuck in a blender, whirling blades tearing at her mind.

Shouts echoed through the room. Someone grabbed her arms and held them still at her sides.

Cody.

That was her last coherent thought. Her mind shrank back, hiding in the deepest corner as it tried to avoid the power's barbed edges.

Daughtry opened her mouth to speak, but the pressure was expanding, snaking down, blocking her throat.

She fell to her knees as she watched the room go to chaos. Several of the LexTals ran and tackled the tall man with limp blond hair to the ground.

They shouted at him to stop, to release his hold on the magic.

He didn't.

The noose around her neck grew tighter.

"Stop, Thomas!" Cody shouted, dropping to his knees in front of Daughtry. "Do *something*, Caroline!"

He gripped her arms so tightly that it was painful, but the small hurt was the only thing keeping her grounded. If he let go, the power would overwhelm her. She'd disappear.

"Don't . . . let . . . go . . ." she managed to gasp out.

"I won't." His lips pressed into a grim line as he watched Tyler and the triplets struggle to contain Thomas. "Just hang on."

Black spots formed in front of her eyes. She watched a blurry version of Caroline approach the man, tendrils of green magic flying out of her palms.

The pressure didn't abate.

Daughtry closed her eyes.

When she opened them again, all the magic in the room had become visible. Green from Caroline, blue from Tyler, grey from Dante. Brown and gold intertwined from Morgan. It was a vibrant rainbow of colors that threatened to distract her.

She looked down and saw the net of black strands wrapped tightly around her body.

It was instinctive.

Power tore out of her mind. It flowed down her immobilized arms and out her fingertips in bright purple sparks.

The particles pulled themselves into thick strands that flew at Thomas, who still had his magic wrapped around her torso.

Catching him by surprise, the fibers around her relaxed enough that she could take a full breath.

Oxygen hit her blood in a heady rush.

New power launched itself at Daughtry, but Cody was there. He blocked her with his body, and the black strands hit a wall of translucent green magic before bouncing off to disappear into thin air.

Dante walked over to the struggling mass of bodies surrounding Thomas.

"Fuck this."

His arm reared back, and he punched Thomas right in the face.

As Thomas slumped into unconsciousness, the rest of the magic dissipated.

There was a strange moment inside Daughtry's mind as she struggled to focus on what was happening around her. Her powers called to her, distracting her as an unnatural joy welled up in her mind, encouraging her to reach for her magic again. The exultation was as intoxicating as those bottles of vodka had been back in her old freezer. But even more potent, more addictive.

Then as abruptly as everything had begun—the magic, the odd temptation—snapped back into that locked compartment of her mind.

She glanced at the surrounding faces. The warriors were grim, the Council members calculating. Thomas lay on the floor, face down, with Dante looming over him. Caroline stood next to them, her hair almost in flames from her fury.

"How long has he been betraying us?" Morgan asked. "How long has he had access to the Council's meetings and records?"

Caroline bit out the words. "Months. Maybe close to a year." She glanced at Dante, raising a brow. "He's the mole you've been trying to ferret out? An effective technique using the girl."

"We'd never use—" Dante said, but Daughtry didn't hear the rest of the statement as Cody started running his hands over her body.

"I'm fine," she told him. He began to protest but stopped when Caroline turned to face them.

The expression on her face gave Daughtry a chill, which was ironic, considering she'd just nearly died.

"Nice, Dee," Tyler said, from behind her shoulder. "Impressive, with not having used your powers before."

She nodded, pushing to her feet as Caroline crossed the room.

The din had begun to rise as the men started talking amongst themselves, but now it went silent again. Caroline stood in front of her and raised her hands. They hovered next to Daughtry's head, an inch away from touching.

Would the Rengalla ever get tired of screwing with her head?

Daughtry glanced over her shoulder to Cody, who nodded in approval, though his face was serious.

He stepped forward. "She's just going to take a look. See if she can find out what's been done to your mind. She'll be careful." The last was said like an order.

They locked stares until Cody spoke again. "Right, Caroline?"

The Council-head nodded, if one could call the smallest tip of her head a nod.

"This is the final matter to attend to," Caroline said. "I promise," she added when Daughtry narrowed her eyes.

The words Caroline spoke were the correct ones, but the tone was off. There was something about her that made every nerve in Daughtry's body stand up and take notice.

And not in a good way.

"But Dante said only Cody could do it," she blurted. She really didn't want Caroline in her mind.

At that, Caroline raised a condescending brow. "He did, huh?" She turned to Dante and gave him a look that made it clear they would be having a long discussion later.

"He would be the best"—Dante shrugged, unperturbed by the Council-head's anger—"and you know it."

"I think one example of the unpredictable nature of Cody's gifts per day is more than enough," Caroline said.

Daughtry bristled. It wasn't Cody's fault, and really, was it possible for the other woman to be more of a bitch?

"If my *brother* will consent," Caroline added. "I can continue."

Brother? Apparently Daughtry was wrong. More bitchiness actually was possible. This scorn, the cold contempt, was how Caroline treated her *family?* But that was beside the point, so she shoved all of that away and inclined her head to accept the procedure. Might as well rip off the Band-Aid and get it over with.

Soft fingers grazed her temples before winding into her hair to find her scalp.

There was no warning.

Their minds clashed, painful and familiar at the same time. Yet there was none of the comfort or intimacy she'd felt with Cody.

"Ah," Caroline said. "Only a few rudimentary blocks. I'll remove them." She took a great inhale, then—

Pain.

A flash of white-hot lightening shot through her mind and body. She gasped. Then the pain receded, flashed away as quickly as it had come, and images sped through her brain—

An old Victorian house, painted in a palate of garish

colors, was surrounded by the quintessential white picket fence. The brass numbers 4, 7, 8, 0, were hammered into the doorframe. Then she was on the other side of the oak panel, its ancient brass knocker echoing loudly through its thick planks.

She watched her younger self run to the door, her tiny fingers closing on the handle. The knob turned, and there was a surge of energy. Her miniature body flew backward, slamming into the wall awkwardly, before sliding to the floor in a heap. Her lips parted to call out for help. But before she could complete the hail, four Dalshie entered through the open doorway, as horrific and evil as the ones she'd seen while on the run.

One of them casually flicked a glance in her direction, but she was barely conscious, observing them blearily through swollen eyes. They dismissed her with a sneer, two heading down the hall to the kitchen, the other two climbing the stairs.

She tried to move, to lift her broken body and warn her mother. The mother whose voice she could just barely hear singing along with the radio.

A scream echoed through the house.

Too late.

There was the crash of a plate hitting the ground as power surged, sending painful prickles across Daughtry's skin, raising every hair on her body.

The sickening thud of a limp body hit the ground.

Masculine footsteps raced down the hall above her head. Another rush of magic. A deep voice, her father's, echoed down the stairs shouting for Daughtry and her mother to get out.

That was impossible.

Unconsciousness came for her young mind. The last

thing she remembered was the delicious smell of
cinnamon and sugar from her mother's snickerdoodles.
The cookies had turned to charcoal by the time she'd
woken up, staring straight into her father's sightless
eyes—

The vision cut off, and she was hauled back into the real world. Caroline's fingers gripped her scalp brutally, causing tears to leak out of her eyes.

"Let go," she demanded.

Caroline gave her a hostile look before stepping away.

She glared right back.

Caroline turned her gaze on Cody.

"You've bonded." It was said with incredulity, with loathing, her rage a palpable force.

The room went silent as every occupant gaped at Daughtry and Cody.

"Bonded?" she asked. "What does that mean?" Hope welled up in her soul, even though she couldn't begin to comprehend all of the undercurrents present.

Caroline was angry. Dante unsurprised. Everyone else openly stared, expressions ranging from shock to unrestrained happiness.

Well, that was mainly Tyler.

Ignoring the gawkers, she focused on the only person who mattered. Cody's breathing had accelerated, his pupils dilated wide with panic.

"Impossible," he said, the word like ice.

That single adjective speared her heart, tearing it to shreds.

But why? It was a rejection from a man she barely knew, for a connection she didn't understand.

Caroline spoke, her words angry barbs. "Have any odd feelings, lately?"

Cody opened his mouth to protest.

"Don't bullshit me, brother. I know you saw that vision. Your minds are linked. Permanently."

Daughtry reeled back, looking to Cody for some semblance of an explanation. "What does Caroline mean?" she asked.

His teeth snapped together. He glanced at the ceiling, the floor, everywhere but where she wanted him to look: at her.

Frustration warred with hurt.

Was it the bond itself that was so bad, or was it *her*?

Dante stepped closer, interjecting himself into the conversation. "It's all there, Cody. The possessiveness, the protectiveness. Christ, the bond is strong enough that I can see it with the slightest bit of magic."

Cody's entire body tensed, his lips ground out into a flat line. It was clear that he wanted to deny the statements. Eventually, he let out a sigh, and the rigidity in his muscles relaxed minutely. He glanced at Dante. "You knew?" The words were soft, hopeless.

Dante nodded, and Cody's shoulders slumped. His chin bobbed down to his chest.

Daughtry had the feeling it was as much of an agreement as she'd ever get.

"It's there, Cody. You can't go back now," Tyler said, coming up behind her and squeezing her shoulder.

Cody looked at Tyler, at Dante, and *finally* Daughtry, dread evident in his expression. That look—the desperation to get away from her, to not be tied to her in any way—was another jab in a lifetime of hurts. "There has to be a way to break it," he said. "It's happened before."

Dante was shaking his head before Cody finished speaking. "Of course, a bond has to be nurtured to survive, but it doesn't just disintegrate because you've got cold feet. You can't hide your feelings from it."

Tyler wrapped an arm around her waist, ignoring the sudden hostility in Cody's eyes. She leaned into his touch, feeling a sliver of her hurts disappear off into space.

"The bond knows you care," Tyler said, fixing her and Cody with a penetrating stare. "You *both* care."

She nodded despite the urge to lash out, to protect herself. She couldn't deny that she felt something for Cody.

His next words shattered that fragile thread of possibility.

"No," he said, frost in every word. "*No*. I don't feel anything. She doesn't mean *anything*."

Her heart deflated, and tears welled in her eyes. She felt the sting of his rejection down to her very soul, in the tightening of her skin, the flush of her cheeks, the way her chest squeezed painfully. She wanted to speak, was desperate to say something to hurt him back, but her throat was too tight, her tongue too dry.

There was a long, tense pause where no one said anything. She could hear every rustle of fabric, every crinkle of paper.

Stupid. So *fucking* stupid.

She'd thought they'd begun building something. That this bond, whatever it was, would be something good to add to that. But even as Daughtry thought of the pain she was feeling, she couldn't shut off the fondness she felt for the frigid, unyielding, endearing man in front of her.

It didn't mean she was a glutton for punishment, though.

She wasn't going to throw herself at someone who didn't want her. Been there, done that.

In the lull, the uncomfortable silence of shattered hopes, Morgan came over and began to discuss what to do with the unconscious Thomas sprawled across the rug at their feet.

The distraction gave her the moments she needed to pull herself together, to blink back the tears and swallow down the pain.

"Good plan. Go and deal with it," Dante said finally, giving Thomas's senseless form a push with his boot. He grabbed her arm and led her back to her chair. "I just have a few more questions." His voice dropped, the next words for her ears only. "Hang in there just a bit longer."

She nodded.

Dante looked over her shoulder, his voice going hard. "Caroline, you want to sit in for this?"

Caroline declined, self-importance in every syllable, and departed, her assorted crew of underlings following on her heels.

With some of the audience gone, Daughtry could breathe a little easier. She took advantage of Dante getting settled with a clean sheet of paper and a pen to divert the attention to someone other than herself.

"You know they make computers for a reason," she said.

Dante groaned but flashed her a grin. "Not you, too. You young ones are always going on about technology, but do you know what the best invention is?"

She shook her head, a smile emerging in spite of everything.

"The ballpoint pen. It—"

Tyler dropped into the chair on her other side and pretended to bang his head on the table. "No! Don't get him started." He gave her a wink that made her feel better by millimeters. "Just because Dante was alive during quills and inkwells doesn't mean we need to give up our iPads."

Daughtry laughed until the point of Tyler's joke hit home. She glanced between him and Dante. "You're not seriously—"

Tyler interrupted, a huge smirk on his face. "Yes, *seriously*. He's really that old. Ancient, one might say—"

"Tyler," Dante warned, cutting him off. "I wasn't aware how remiss your education was, Daughtry." Education? Did he think she'd been home-schooled in spell-casting? Taken a remedial college course in fortune-telling? "We'll remedy that as soon as possible," he said, ignoring what was probably a very irritated expression on her face.

Dante didn't give her much time to think about how a magical education might be conducted before he began peppering her with questions. *Who were the people who raised her? Where had she lived? How long had she been having the visions?*

They should have been easy to answer, but they weren't. At least, not now that she knew the parents she'd grown up with weren't her biological ones.

She'd been raised by kidnappers instead of the slightly indifferent mother and father she'd always believed. And no wonder they couldn't be bothered to see her as more than a meal ticket. They'd probably been compensated to keep her. It didn't take much to realize that people who'd been paid to take care of a child didn't make good parents.

"You probably know more about my childhood than I do," she pointed out. "I didn't even know I was different until I came here. Did my real parents live at the Colony?"

"For a while," Dante said. "But they preferred the country. Your mother liked the isolation."

Daughtry's heart squeezed as she recognized the need to decrease the chance of visions. But did that mean her mother could see death too? Had she needed distance to control her powers?

Dante was staring at her as she digested the information. "Was she like me . . . ?"

He nodded. "She was an Oracle. Her visions were different, however. Where yours are based on the person you're touching, your mother's were always related to the Rengalla's future." He gave her a moment to process that. "What about your visions?" he asked. "Cody said you've only been having them for a year."

"Yes," she said. "After Jimmy. I thought I was going insane when they started." She risked a glance up, embarrassed that the visions had so easily destroyed her life. Her eyes skipped right past Dante to fall onto Cody.

Cody broke off his discussion with one of the triplets, either Monroe or Mason—she had seen Morgan enough to recognize that he kept his hair slightly longer than his brothers—and stared at her. She could feel his sympathy along the connection between their minds.

God, even *that* hurt. Did he enjoy tormenting her? Pretending to care about her only to make a public declaration of the opposite?

It was difficult to speak with Cody's gaze focused on her, the weight of it heavy and intense. "I—they just started one day. John was gone. I was alone. I didn't know what was happening. I touched the guy at the drive-through, and my head was full of death. Then I saw the story online the next day, and it was the same as what I'd seen. I didn't—I couldn't stop . . ."

She trailed off, chest heaving, the horror of those initial visions weighing on her.

"Slow down, Dee. It's okay. You're safe here." Tyler touched her arm. She took a deep breath and attempted to steady her pulse.

Dante didn't say anything for a moment, just studied her face with a small frown between his brows, but his next question was softer, less inquisitional. "That wasn't the first time you'd noticed you were different, was it?"

She shook her head. "But being able to know when there would be a pop quiz or whether a movie would be bad wasn't exactly something I thought of as magic. Good instincts, maybe. The power to manipulate the future? Not so much."

"Hmm. It's possible that the trauma of your . . ." Dante said, and she watched his hand move across the piece of paper as he made notes ". . . broken engagement." He said the words so carefully that she knew John had told him his part in it.

Great. More of her drama spread around.

But she knew John hadn't meant it like that. He'd been looking out for her, protecting her. Which had gotten him kill—

She closed her eyes.

Dante went quiet for a bit, the only noise the scratch of his pen on the notebook. Unwillingly, she tuned into Cody's conversation.

". . . John."

John? She shifted, straining to hear.

"Nothing . . . blood and ash . . . his swords . . ."

Swords? The hope that had bubbled up as a result of eavesdropping evaporated.

He wouldn't have left them behind.

"It's possible that the emotional trauma fractured the initial block on your powers," Dante said, drawing her back into what had become a one-sided discussion. He tapped his chin as he spoke. "The manipulation is—*was*—clear, but the blocks could have also just degraded with time. That type of shielding requires periodic refreshing. That may have caused your magic to leak sporadically if they weren't consistent in putting on new ones . . ."

And he was off and running again.

She shivered. The notion that someone had been messing with her mind was frightening. But even scarier was the idea of her childhood without those shields. Would she have glimpsed her classmates' deaths? Her teachers'?

Could the manipulation have been some sort of misguided gift?

Not that it made a difference now. With the ward gone and the blocks in her mind erased, she was left vulnerable in a brand-new way. She needed to learn to protect herself, to create something similar to John's ward or the shielding the LexTals were trained to hold.

"Who do you think made the blocks?" she asked. "Or why?"

"Now those are the important questions. And the ones, I'm afraid, that I don't have the answers to." Dante paused, tapped his pen to his chin. "I'd like you to study with Francis. He's our best shot at figuring out who made the blocks in your mind and he can also teach you to shield."

"That will prevent the visions?"

Dante nodded. "It should. Francis has been training and studying with Oracles for the last few centuries. If anyone knows how, it's him." He picked up his pen again and made some notes on the paper.

Something occurred to her then. Maybe the easiest way for her to help people would be to stop the visions altogether. No futures to screw up. She could even break the bond. No magic meant she wouldn't force the strange connection on Cody.

Her gut clenched at the notion of not using her powers again.

But she couldn't miss what she didn't really know. Right?

"Do you think Francis could block my powers completely?"

Dante gave her a peculiar look even as Cody whirled around and strode over, opening his mouth. He spoke before Cody could. "Perhaps." He gave her a glance that was so perceptive it was uncomfortable. "If that's what you wanted."

"No—" Cody said, and she shot him a glare fierce enough to snap his mouth closed.

"Hot and cold much?" she snapped. Why was he bothering to pretend to care about her future? But the truth was, she wasn't sure what she wanted. In the past, she'd dreamt of having her powers stripped away. No visions meant she'd be free to live. Yet the little glimpses of magic, the intoxicating feel of helping Cody land the plane, of protecting herself here against

Thomas. Those moments made her feel fully alive for the first time in her life, like she was finally using every part of her brain.

There had to be more to her powers than just seeing death, right? And now that she'd gotten a glimpse of the possibilities, could she live without trying?

Cody touched her arm. She wanted to shove him away, curse him for daring to interject himself into her life. But when he inclined his head to the far side of the room, she followed.

When they'd reached a quiet corner, he rounded on her. "You can't give up your powers."

"Why not?" Why were they even having this discussion? Maybe he wanted to fuck her, but Cody had made it quite obvious he didn't give a damn about her otherwise.

"That's not fair. You don't know how I feel."

Her mouth dropped open. "You just can't—"

"—*order me around,*" she finished mentally.

He crossed his arms. "If you're being unreasonable, I can and I will. Daughtry, I didn't mean before as you took it—"

"You do realize you just rebutted my thoughts and not my words."

There it was.

The panic. The absolute terror at being attached to her.

"Thought so." Swallowing her hurt, she went to stand by Tyler. At least *he* seemed to have her back. He glared darkly at Cody.

For a moment, she felt Cody's confusion, even understood how overwhelmed he was.

Because she felt the same.

Still, that didn't mean she kept putting him through the wringer.

Self-respect had been pretty low for the past year, but it was trending upward. She wouldn't let someone, or her own idiocy, draw her back down the slope of hating herself.

Yes, it would have been nice if she and Cody could have figured out the meaning and consequences of this strange bond together. But it wasn't meant to be.

Lesson number one thousand on why she should only rely on herself.

"Daughtry," Cody began, his tone conciliatory.

It only opened the wound further. He didn't want her. Why didn't he just leave her alone?

"Cody," Dante called, drawing his attention. *Thank God.* "I'd like you to take tomorrow's patrol on the north side. We have a hole to fill."

"I can't," he said, walking back over to Dante.

Daughtry didn't process anything further. All she knew was that she couldn't take one more insult—visual, spoken, or otherwise. The door swung open quietly, and she slipped out, not stopping for anything, and definitely not when Cody called out her name.

She allowed herself to get lost in the endless sea of beige.

TWENTY

DAUGHTRY RAN until her legs felt ready to collapse. Then she kept walking until she hit a dead end, her sneakers squeaking to a stop. That's when she realized everything was wrong. She spun in a circle, opened and closed her eyes, but nothing changed.

Where the walls, carpeting, ceiling, and even doors had been a blah-brown before, now they were a rainbow of colors.

Huge, almost-three-dimensional murals covered the surface of the walls. The track fluorescent lighting had been replaced with twinkling crystal chandeliers, and beneath her feet the dingy industrial carpeting had been swapped for hardwood floors in a mouth-watering chocolate color. She bent to run her fingers across the polished surface—smooth as glass without a scratch in sight. The effort it would take to keep it clean made her shudder.

Completing her rotation, she regarded the dead end again. Except, it wasn't actually a dead end. The doorknob was almost unnoticeable it blended so well into the panel's depiction of the night sky and she couldn't resist the urge to touch, to trail her hand along the stars, a buzz of power trailing up her arm at the contact. The brightly glowing constellations flickered. Her fingers went to the handle, but before she could turn it, she noticed that her magic was collecting on the walls.

"What—?" A broad purple streak marred the door. She whirled around, and the line followed her path.

Her focus dashing from side to side as she tried to take in every pattern, Daughtry walked back the way she had come. Every hallway had a unique design. Some looked intentional, like the images had been created by the occupant of a room. Others could have been accidental, a Jackson Pollack of power as their stripes and dots overlapped and flew off in every direction.

Her purple contribution was in different shades. It grew brighter as she paused next to the walls, but farther down the hall it had faded, becoming more lavender than violet.

Daughtry placed her hand against a depiction of a waterfall beating against treacherous-looking rocks and felt the buzz of magic again. It reminded her of rubbing a balloon against the carpet and then holding it up to her head. The static electricity would make her hair stand on end, attracting different pieces as the balloon moved. The hundreds of tiny strands of magic being drawn to the walls was like that, only more intense.

The Colony was powered by magic.

She smiled, the little kid in her taking joy in the simplicity of it. "The future of energy," she murmured, thinking that power companies would kill to get their hands on that secret.

Retracting her hand, she continued walking, the draw of her magic linking her to each picture along the way. Maybe that was why, despite Cody and the bond, she felt so centered at the Colony. Her contribution was tangible, and something more—

She belonged. Her powers fit here.

Curiosity eventually drew her back to the door, the opportunity to investigate too tempting to pass up. Turning the knob, she pushed through and gasped. Dense foliage created a veritable jungle, and when she turned her eyes upward, she saw the garden was open-air. Stars glimmered in the distance, the smallest sliver of the moon just barely visible above the horizon. How long had she spent in those corridors?

No wonder her feet hurt. And how freaking big was the Colony that she'd walked for hours without encountering another soul?

Or maybe no one had cared enough to come after her.

Pushing that stupid thought aside, she moved onto the path. It was well worn and easy to follow, despite the dim light. Meandering along it eventually led her to a small circle lined with seating. A few strategically placed lights tucked into the foliage gave the cluster of benches a romantic, candlelit appearance.

Romantic. Just perfect.

The notion made her want to curse, to give up on finding her personal slice of peace and leave. Except the space was too pretty, too peaceful.

Frustrated and annoyed at the persistent niggle in the back of her mind that represented Cody, she paced. She couldn't even get away from him in her own brain.

"Ridiculous, arrogant jerk."

An outdoor storage chest was tucked behind the circle of benches, and she crossed to it. Frustration had her yanking a cashmere blanket and pillow from within its depths and Daughtry forced herself to take a deep breath, to gentle her grip on the delicate fabric.

The bench she picked to sprawl out on was hard beneath her back, but the blanket was soft as silk as it covered her from neck to toes. Settled, her eyes were drawn to the deep midnight sky, its stars coldly beautiful.

Just like Cody.

A jab of pain caused her to suck in a breath before she pushed further thought of him aside. It was smarter, *safer* to hold on to her shield of anger.

No more tears. Not for him.

Plus, it was better to find out now, before her feelings grew.

Except her traitorous body remembered the feel of his mouth against her own, the heat of his chest scalding her breasts, the way his hands had gripped her hips.

Sighing, she wrenched her throbbing body under control and purposely emptied her mind, watching the moon as it crawled across the sky, the small sliver dim enough that she could make out several constellations. As tiredness began to tug at her, she closed her eyes. The quiet, the stillness of the empty space was wonderful, and her mind was lulled by the peaceful-ness. Her thoughts drifted about, too relaxed to focus on anything in particular. The delicate scent of jasmine, the soft rustling of leaves tickling her ears, the quiet *hoot* of an owl in the distance, the feel of the soft throw against her exposed skin.

That there was such a sanctuary in the middle of the corri-dors, command centers, and, most exhausting, the *politics* really was, "Amazing."

"Yes, you are."

She bolted upright, the blanket falling to the ground.

"Somehow I knew you'd be here," he said.

Daughtry sprinted across the clearing . . . straight into John's arms.

She hugged him hard and heard his quick intake of breath. Dropping her hold, she jumped back. "Oh my God! How are you—?" She held her arms out to the side, unsure what to do.

"Daughtry?" came another male voice, slightly muffled from the bushes.

She stiffened.

John whipped around, a wide smile on his face. He limped

toward the exterior of the circle as they waited for Cody to emerge from the path.

When Cody did, he faltered. "John?"

John strode over and pulled him in for a brief hug. "Thanks, man. You got her here safe. I owe you."

Cody's arms hung limply at his sides for a moment. Then one came up to pat John tentatively on his back.

When the two men parted, Cody looked miserable, which improved Daughtry's mood immensely. The tingle in the back of her mind sharpened as she felt Cody's turmoil.

Not going there, she reminded herself. Instead, she focused on the sudden buoyancy of her heart. John was here. He was alive.

It was a miracle.

Cody glared at her. She glared back.

"What's the—?" John asked.

Just then, Tyler poked his head around the corner and looked straight at her. "Everything okay here?"

She shrugged in response. In what world would she be okay?

"We need to talk," Cody muttered. He spoke close to her ear, his breath causing her to shiver. Just that quickly her anger was back.

"I think you've said enough," she gritted out before walking toward John.

Tyler was peppering him with questions without giving him a chance to answer. When he paused for some much-needed oxygen, John looked over at her and rolled his eyes.

She smiled back, shocked, relieved, and, if she were being completely honest, guilty. Because the way John was looking at her in that moment was decidedly *not* friendly. Instead, he was looking at her like a woman . . . a woman he wanted.

But then Tyler was talking again. "Hey, no offense, dude,

but you look like you could use Suz."

Daughtry chuckled at first, thinking Tyler was being his usual unfiltered self, until she saw that he spoke the truth. John was a mess, covered in dirt, his clothing torn and bloody.

She and Cody spoke at the same time, in consensus for once.

"We need to get you to the infirmary—"

"Yes, you need to see Suz—"

Tyler nodded in agreement.

John protested, "I need to talk to Dante first. Suz can wait."

"No, it can't." Cody's voice was sharp. The smile slipped off John's face.

Daughtry reached for John's hand, intent on hauling him to Suz if she had to. But just before her fingers reached his, Cody lunged toward her and batted her hand away. The movement knocked her to the ground.

"What the hell!" John shouted, reaching over as if to help her up.

"No!" Cody and Tyler yelled.

"Show me your palms," Cody said, his voice quieter but no less firm. When John hesitated, Cody added, "Now."

John's hands were clenched tightly into fists, his arms stiff at his sides. "You think—? How could you think that I'm one of them?"

"Then clear it up for me." Cody's eyes glittered with anger. "You know the procedure. Hold. Them. Up."

"Just show us, man," Tyler said. "Then we can all go."

Daughtry didn't miss how Tyler and Cody had stepped forward, subtly positioning themselves between her and John as she got to her feet.

"What's going on? Why do they need to see your palms?" She addressed John since neither of her two bodyguards would look at her.

"They think I'm one of them!" John burst out. Hurt and indignation warred on his face.

"But why? Oh—" It was obvious now that she thought about it.

Folding her arms across her chest, she gave a hard look to each of the three men. "For God's sake, John! I know you're not Dalshie. Just show them your damn palms so we can get out of here."

All three men stared at her like she'd started glowing green, but no one moved.

She stamped her foot. "Seriously John, just open up those hands. Tyler"—he turned toward her with wide eyes—"call Dante and have him meet us at the infirmary." When none of them moved, she clapped her hands, finally startling the men into action. "Hurry up."

Tyler whipped out his phone and pushed a button. In a few seconds, he was speaking in rapid succession. She gave John a hurry-up gesture and, bewilderingly, he held up his palms.

Daughtry nodded at Cody to inspect what looked to her to be stain-free hands. "Good?"

He nodded.

She could feel his annoyance, his impatience, his hunger—

Pushing the traitorous thoughts away, she grabbed John's hand and hauled him forward, only slowing when she guiltily realized he was limping.

So maybe she was going a little bit overboard.

"You think?" Cody asked. The sarcasm in his voice was really unnecessary. She could feel it crystal-clear in her mind.

He slipped past her and held open the door.

Annoying man. Good manners or not.

When they exited the gardens, John pulled her close to his side. After all the worry, being near him should have been wonderful, but John's actions just made her feel uncomfortable.

Especially with Cody shooting daggers at them over his shoulder.

"I was so worried about you." John spoke quietly into her ear, his breath whispering across her neck.

"M-me too," she stammered out, untucking herself. She needed a little distance. "When the ward failed, I thought . . ."

John squeezed her arm. "I know. It's okay. I'm just glad you're here. Safe."

"What happened?" She was almost afraid to ask.

John looked at her, his normally kind eyes haunted. "It was close."

"But John—" She bit her lip, forced herself to stop. Every muscle in his body was tense, exhaustion pouring off him. Now wasn't the time. Instead, she swallowed her questions and tried to make her voice sound upbeat. "Well you're here now, and that's all that matters."

"I'm not so sure," he replied, blue eyes haunted.

They walked the rest of the way to the infirmary in tense silence, not even the mosaic of murals adorning the walls providing her a distraction. All she saw was a blur of color as she worried about John and Cody, the Council, her powers . . .

Since Tyler had called ahead, Suz was there waiting. The moment John passed through the door, the doctor had his arm in a vice-grip and hustled him into the adjacent room. Dante, who'd also been waiting, followed them.

They'd been summarily dismissed, but Daughtry couldn't bring herself to leave, so she plunked her butt down in a chair. She withheld a sigh—barely—when Cody, not Tyler, sat next to her.

She glared at a smirking Tyler, who met her eyes and mouthed, *"Have fun."*

"Traitor," she muttered. He shrugged, leaning against the

opposite wall and feigning focus on a magazine with the newest celebutante on it.

"Everyone told you not to encourage him."

She looked at Cody in confusion. A million responses to that ran through her head, but she settled on the truth. "I have no idea what you are talking about."

"Tyler." A thread of humor tickled her mind as Cody tilted his head in the other man's direction. "He's an idiot."

"Yeah, *obviously*," she snapped, annoyed at herself, at Cody, at the depth of her attraction to the man. Even as hurt and furious as she was with him, a portion of her mind urged her to move closer.

"Hey!" Tyler protested.

They both ignored him.

"It's time we talked." The sentence should have been a request, but it came out more like an order. Which was why she bristled like an angry porcupine.

"No," she said coldly. "It's time for you to shut your mouth and leave me the fuck alone."

As soon as the words passed her lips, she closed her eyes in embarrassment. She was acting like a pouty teenager, made worse when an eavesdropping Tyler let out a long "ooooh" from across the room.

She opened her mouth to apologize, only to be interrupted by Suz and Dante, the latter of which who nodded to the room before taking up post at the opposite wall. Suz looked to Daughtry, then Cody, whose face was frightening in its anger. "You can go in now." She paused. "As long as you both behave."

Cody shot out of his seat and was through the door in a flash.

Daughtry followed at a more sedate pace, stopping to thank Suz for all of her help with the meeting.

"Glad I could do something." There was frustration in the

doctor's chocolate-brown eyes. "That was some scary stuff, after the ward broke."

"Yeah."

Suz reached out then stopped and fisted her hands. "I'm not shielded."

Crap. Daughtry forced herself to not react, to not take a step back. "I'd better learn quick, then."

"You and me both," the doctor said with a sigh. "I'm not a fan of not being able to touch my patients."

"It's not your fault. But I do appreciate the *war paint*. And the deodorant."

Suz chuckled, and a genuine smile split Daughtry's lips. It had been too long since she'd been in the position to make friends, but found she liked the other woman.

"Come see me when you have time. I need to rope in another assistant." Suz pushed back her heavy mane of caramel hair.

"Will do." Daughtry dropped her voice. "Thanks." It would be nice to have something to do besides pining after Cody and worrying about her lot in life.

She entered John's room and breathed a sigh of relief when she that he looked so much better. A large bandage covered a good chunk of his forehead, and his arms were covered in bruises, but they were already fading to yellow.

"You're pale," she said, perching herself on the edge of the bed.

Exhaustion was written in the lines of his face. "I'm fine. Suz wants me to stay the night, but I'll be good to go by morning." He cupped her cheek in his palm, and it took everything Daughtry had not to pull away. His touch just didn't feel right.

He frowned, but she hurried to speak so that he couldn't ask her what was wrong.

"Good . . " She stopped, having run out of steam after the

single word, unsure of what to say next. Cody didn't help. He stood silently in the corner while she talked, or rather, tried to find something safe to discuss.

Rising, delaying, she slid a chair next to the bed.

At least she could stay and keep him company.

Tick. Tick. The clock clicked loudly in the background. The legs of the chair screeched on the floor when she sat down.

John was the one to break the awkward lull. "Cody, can you take Daughtry back to her room?" She started to protest, but John cut her off. "I can see the circles under your eyes. You're exhausted. You need a full night's sleep and you're not going to get that here."

"But—"

"Go. Really. I'll still be here in the morning."

Cody grasped her arm and nodded to the door. She considered arguing but relented in the end, figuring John could also use some rest and her carrying on wouldn't help that.

"Let. Go," she gritted between clenched teeth once they'd said goodbye and were back into the waiting area.

Cody didn't.

Instead, he hustled her past Tyler and Dante, who were discussing something in serious tones in the hall.

"We need to talk," he said again once they were alone.

Her feet slid to a stop, the exhaustion from the past several days threatening to overtake her. She was tired, emotional. Sure, Cody seemed to be feeling guilty for acting like such a jerk, but that was in this moment. Tomorrow he'd be distant again. Or worse, he'd be mean.

She couldn't deal with the rollercoaster of his emotions.

"Not tonight, okay? Please—Can we just talk about this tomorrow?"

For once, he didn't argue with her. Just held her arm and led her to bed.

The last thing she remembered was Cody covering her with a blanket as he whispered, "You need me, you call."

With that promise, she fell headlong into sleep.

———

SHE WOKE A FEW HOURS LATER, still tired but alert. A pang of something—longing, dammit—hit her when she realized the scent surrounding her wasn't Cody's. As in, she hadn't slept in Cody's bed. Earlier she'd been too exhausted to notice the difference.

Now she looked around and wondered why he'd put her there. Was he trying to grant her the space she'd wanted? Or maybe he'd tired of her as quickly as Jimmy had.

"Don't be an idiot," she muttered, and padded to the bathroom, determined to put herself in some semblance of order. "What—?" She opened the door, peeked back out into the bedroom, shock making her jaw drop. Much like the corridors, the quarters had been given a steroid dose of luxury. The space had expanded, and the furnishings, while still bachelor, were expensive.

Heavy ivory wallpaper covered the walls, the bed was sandwiched by bronze sconces. In fact, the only thing that seemed out of sorts was the mustard-yellow Bruins comforter.

The duffel bag of clothes from the previous day was sitting on a large leather chair, and so she crossed to it, pulling out a pair of jeans and a simple blue T-shirt. Once dressed, she brushed her teeth and hair then exited the room.

Content to focus on the murals adorning the walls, she let the path lead her where it may. The sheer volume and variety of the magical paintings was spectacular. She wondered how anyone was able to go about their business without stopping and admiring them. Case in point, Daughtry was so enraptured by the illustration of turquoise-and-white-tipped waves crashing into a death's bed of sharp, pointy rocks that she didn't see the child until it was too late.

They collided, a stack of papers fluttering through the air. Colored pencils ripped free from their box and scattered. The sound of the thin shafts of wood hitting the floor collided with the noises accompanying the images pouring through her reeling mind—

Click. Click. Click.
Dog's nails on hardwood floor—

She braced one hand against the wall as the nausea accompanying the vision swept through her—

The dog was an overweight collie. She trailed it as it
walked through a house, its claws echoing on the wood.
A streak of color caught her eye, and she noticed the path
of crimson paw prints. The dog stepped on one, causing
the stain to break apart, to flutter through the air like
flecks of ash.
She followed the dog, almost gagged at the smell.
Death.
The boy sat in a chair beside a large bed. His parents lay
dead on the floor, the gunshot wounds on their foreheads
almost fake-looking, like a bad Halloween costume. But
the boy's eyes were still tinged with life.
The dog glided up to the boy and nuzzled at his hand. He
fell slowly to the ground. His gunshot wound, which had
been invisible before, became evident. Blood spread
generously along his back—

"Sorry," her partner in the collision said, halting the movie playing in her mind. He was no more than seven or eight, with a shock of white-blond hair.

When he smiled at her, a fistful of papers and pencils clutched in both hands, she noticed an endearing gap between his two front teeth.

"S'okay," she forced across her still-numb lips when he looked at her for a response.

He smiled again then tore off down the hall, his sneakers making a squealing sound when he took the corner too fast.

Daughtry stumbled backward, falling against the wall as the nausea and images became too much. But then . . . a wave of magic surrounded her mind. Entwined strands of violet and emerald burst outward to coat her skin like liquid mercury. She watched in frozen amazement, afraid to move, afraid to touch the strange covering. Eventually the temptation was too much to resist. She trailed her fingers down her arm, sparks of power rising, fluttering about her hands.

The magic disappeared, sinking into her skin like a set of invisible armor.

Had that even happened?

The fatigue washing over her seemed to speak to the affirmative.

She was still leaning against the wall when voices came around the corner. Recognizing the source of one of them, she scanned her surroundings for a hole to crawl in or for the floor to open up and swallow her whole.

"Too late," she muttered under her breath.

". . . messed up as always," Cody said, apparently in answer to someone's question. "They surged, showed me some kid dying."

Her breath caught in her throat. Cody could see her visions?

Daughtry might be pissed at him but there was no way she'd subject him to the horrors of her mind.

"I'll go, Morgan," he was saying. "I don't need a babysitter."

"Just following orders, my friend," Morgan said. "Your powers may be unusual, but you've never had foresight before."

"Unusual." A snort. "That's a new one. My magic—"

His shoulders appeared before his face, and for a moment he didn't notice her. Then his smile slipped away. In fact, it happened so abruptly that it would have been comical if it hadn't been in reaction to seeing *her*.

"Excuse me," she said, pushing past them.

Cody's hand on her shoulder stilled her movements.

"I trust that I can release him into your care, Daughtry?" Morgan asked with a smirk. "This one skirts the infirmary so often that Dante requires him to have an escort."

"Go away," Cody snapped as he turned her to face him.

Morgan's words took a moment to penetrate, but when they did she stopped struggling against Cody's grasp and asked, "What happened? Are you okay?"

Had the vision harmed him somehow?

"And *that's* my cue to leave," Morgan said, though no one was listening.

"I should ask the same," Cody said as he grabbed up her hand. "Whose vision did you see?"

Her gaze fell to the floor.

Cody was there, crushing her against his chest. "Hey," he whispered. "It'll be okay." In his arms, with words of comfort in her ear, it was tempting, so fucking tempting, to let him take the burden. But then she remembered everything that had been said on both their ends.

"No," she said, pushing him away. "Please no. Just leave me alone."

The last thing she felt, before sprinting the other way, was a pulse of agony in the part of her mind devoted to Cody.

But she couldn't stop. She couldn't risk her heart again.

TWENTY-ONE

DAUGHTRY HAD ONLY RUN a few seconds before she felt Cody, his presence in her mind growing until it enveloped her. She threw a look over her shoulder and met his fierce emerald eyes. "I mean it. Leave me alone."

"I'm not leaving until we talk."

Her mouth fell open. His voice in her head was so much clearer than just the day before.

"I know," he said aloud, keeping up with her rapid strides without issue. "The bond is growing. Strengthening." He said the last as if he were chewing on a lemon.

Great. "Whatever."

"You know—"

"I *don't* know, actually, but I can't wait for you to tell me." She glared.

He raked a hand through golden locks. "God, you're difficult sometimes."

That was his idea of an apology?

"I'm trying!" He took a deep breath. "I was with Dante this morning."

"And?"

"And . . . he helped me see that I need to level with you if this is going to work." He looked at her, and she could see, could *feel* the uncertainty within him.

"It doesn't *have* to work." She didn't want to be tied to someone who didn't want her. "We don't *have* to be anything."

He pulled her to a stop and gripped her chin in his hand.

She writhed, attempting to yank her head out of his grasp, but the idiot caveman held firm.

"That's bullshit, and we both know it. Not because of the bond," he added before she could protest further. "We could both ignore the attraction if being together didn't feel so right. Bond or no bond, I like you and want to see where this takes us." He released her jaw to caress her cheek with the back of his fingers. "And that—" He shook his head. "I haven't let myself care about anyone in so long that I'm . . ."

Terrified.

Yeah, she knew the feeling. Her anger drained away. "I'm scared too."

A breath hissed out between his lips, and he dropped his hands.

She waited for him to say something and when he didn't, she started walking, partly so she didn't pressure him for a response, and partly because the nervous energy at his lack of one made it impossible for her to stay still.

He followed her. They strode side-by-side not touching, awkwardness raging.

She wanted to say *something* to ease the growing tension, but she'd put herself out there as far as she was willing. So instead, she just continuing walking, an empty robotic motion that did nothing to solve their problems and did everything to make things more strained.

"I've been such an asshole," he said, finally breaking the

silence. His shoulders slumped as he thrust a hand through his hair.

That was what she'd been waiting for?

She could have said that ten minutes before. A snort escaped, and he glared down at her. She shrugged in response. It wasn't like she was going to deny what was obviously the truth.

A begrudging smile quirked his lips. "You know what I like about you, cowgirl?"

Another shrug. Until that moment, she would have said he didn't like a single thing.

"You never let my bullshit slide."

A laugh snuck out of her. Pausing, she turned to look at him. "Somehow I doubt you actually like that."

"You'd be surprised," he said, stopping too and scooping up her hand. He pressed a kiss to her palm. "I really *am* sorry."

He sounded like he'd been chewing on glass.

"How'd that feel coming out?"

"About as good as it sounded, I imagine." He pinned her in place with his stare. "But seriously, will you give me a chance to explain?"

She weighed his words, judged his sincerity against the bond. With their connection, it was easy to see that he meant what he said. "Okay. But—"

He'd started to smile, but it faded with her words.

"—I'm going to need some information. I have so many questions. I don't know what I'm doing. I hardly know where to begin." She paused, sucking in a breath. "I need to know *everything*." What she was, what it meant to be a Rengalla. She needed to know her place.

She needed to belong.

His eyes were serious. "I'll answer what I can and help you find out the rest."

Hope bubbled within her. "That's all I ask. I can do the rest."

His lips curved up causing her heart to lighten even further, until it almost felt buoyant. She swallowed against the ensuing panic, forcing down the need to do something to temper that hope.

"Okay," he said.

She'd give this a chance. Her best chance.

"Now, let's get you to Suz. You're not dying under my watch."

A burst of amusement and tenderness along the bond embraced her as they made their way to the infirmary.

Cody visiting the doctor was just as bad as Morgan had made it seem. He squirmed the entire time he was seated on the paper-covered table, one foot twitching, his fists clenching and opening on his thighs.

"I can only go as fast as I can," Suz told him. Her eyes unfocused as chocolate-colored strands of magic emerged from her palms. They crawled over Cody, examining him from head to toe.

"What are you doing?" Daughtry asked, curiosity warring with concern.

"Checking his vitals," the doctor said. "My specialty is the body. I can heal, but I can also see how an organ is functioning."

Cody sighed.

Suz smiled. "And this guy's heart and lungs are functioning normally." She glanced down at the six feet of impatient male in front of her. "Along with everything else, it seems. Should I torment you by checking your power levels, too? Or maybe a blood draw? I know how much you love needles."

"No." It was a grumble that made Daughtry smile as she processed the information. Cody—aside from an unfounded fear of needles—was in perfect health.

"Good," Suz said. "Eat something nutritious and take the rest of the day off. You too," the doctor added to Daughtry. "Make sure she rests," she told Cody.

Daughtry's lips twitched. Suz was smart. Now he wouldn't object. He might not want to take the time for himself, but he'd definitely seize the chance to order Daughtry around.

He snorted as the doctor said her goodbyes and left.

"Come on," he told her once they'd left the infirmary. "I can feel your hunger. Did you skip breakfast?" Emerald eyes narrowed. "Again?"

A bolt of emotion shot through her—fear and wistfulness, all in one. If, through the bond, he knew when she was hungry, knew that she tended to skip the meal all together, what else did he know? "I wasn't hungry," she said stiffly, though . . . she looked closer at their connection and found it was concern driving his questions, not irritation or frustration.

That warmed a part of her she'd thought permanently frozen.

"Well," he said gently. "You are now."

"Yeah. Can you do something about that?"

One half of his mouth tipped up. "Yes, I can."

Less than ten minutes later they were seated across from one another at a table in the cafeteria, both pushing around mostly uneaten, yet perfectly tasty, chicken piccata. Finally giving in and placing down her fork on the swirling-blue-granite tabletop, she settled back in her seat and looked around.

The room resembled one of the fancy buffets where she'd eaten with her parents in Vegas once. Except there were no sneeze-guards, the carpeting was decidedly less red, and it had way fewer gold-encrusted accents.

Instead of gaudy, the cafeteria was a study of neutrals, all pale blues, warm beiges and dark chocolate.

A *clink* of metal against china had her glancing across the table.

Cody had also given up the pretense of eating. He stared at her, unblinking. Outwardly he seemed calm, but along the bond, his thoughts were foggy, whirling like a miniature tornado.

Hers were probably no different.

Her mind began to settle as she remembered all of the nice things he'd said and done. How he'd saved her life—

You helped, the darkness reminded.

How he'd comforted her. Taken care of her when the ward broke. Shielded her from his toolbag of a sister—

He called you a whore!

"Did you mean it?"

Head jerking at her words, he met her eyes. "Mean what?"

"That I was, you know, a—" She shook her head. She couldn't do this right now. Not with everything so raw. "Forget it."

With a stifled sigh, she picked up her fork and knife and preceded to cut her chicken into even smaller bites. She also deliberately ignored Cody entering her mind, the feel of him teasing out the meaning of her question from the knotted ball that was her thoughts.

Some part of her *had* to know.

"No," he said and the constriction on her lungs eased. At least, until he spoke again.

The piece she'd been chewing turned to sawdust. She kept her gaze glued to her plate.

"Honesty, right?"

She nodded without looking up.

"I thought you were unreliable, flighty. That's John's typical choice."

"He didn't choose me," she muttered. "He left."

"But he came back."

Her eyes met his, slid away. "Once upon a time, I hoped

that things with John might be . . . something." Her fingers traced a nonsensical pattern on the table. "But I don't think we were ever meant to be. What I feel with you—"

She broke off, avoiding his stare as she gulped from her crystal goblet.

"I know," he murmured. "I *know*."

Eyes on the table, she nodded. It was a relief to know he felt . . . if not the same then at least, he knew what was between them.

Silence for one long moment before he spoke again.

"I saw how you reacted when I said that." His mind pulsed in hers, his regret a dagger to her brain. "I didn't realize what it meant to you. I just . . . seized the opportunity to keep you at a distance." To alienate her. To *hurt* her.

"You *didn't* realize?"

Cody swallowed convulsively. "At the meeting yesterday. When my powers surged and hit your mind, I-I saw a lot."

"A lot," she repeated, her voice sounding dead even to her own ears. "*The visions? The drinking? The bar and Weasel Face? Jimmy?*"

Cody nodded, acknowledging the unspoken questions with a minute movement of his head.

Her eyes shut in embarrassment. Pathetic. *She* was nothing more than a lonely broke girl, pursued by freakish enemies. Alone—

"No, not alone," Cody said. "Not anymore."

She wanted to believe him, to fall into the picture he was painting.

He spoke again, eager now. "There are people here who knew your real parents. People who remember you as a child. This is a place to learn. To build a family."

Nice words. Except—

"That's worked for *you*?" Daughtry had seen him interact

with Caroline and knew she'd struck a nerve with the question, but she didn't have it in her to let it go.

She'd born witness to the fact that Cody was well liked amongst his peers—he couldn't walk down a hall without someone smiling or saying hello—but she could also feel the careful distance he'd placed between himself and the rest of the Rengalla. He might be equal parts friendly and helpful, but he didn't let anyone see the *real* him.

The only reason she even knew about the façade was because she could see the truth of it directly in his mind.

"We have problems here," he said. "Same as anywhere." His eyes pleaded at her to drop it, but she had to know.

"Was your sister in the orphanage with you?"

His expression locked down and she instinctively knew he'd been pushed far enough. But she didn't stop. She *couldn't*.

"Do you have that perfect family life you're painting? Sunday dinners and family holidays?"

He shook his head, lips ground into a firm line.

"No?" she said. "I didn't think so. So why would it be different for me?" She clenched her hands into fists. "Everyone keeps saying this is a place for me to build a new life, to finally have a real family, but the truth is I don't fit in here. I'm not a LexTal, don't know anything about magic or our history. My parents are"—a shake of her head—"I have no one."

His face was absolutely frigid, not a lick of emotion in his expression and Daughtry braced herself for the cold slice of his anger.

Instead, she got, "How about we skip the empty promises and discuss the life-altering mental bond instead?"

It might have been sad, but that single question brought her a boatload of hope.

Maybe they could move on together?

And so she grabbed onto the lifeline and smirked up at him.

"You have a big ego, don't you?"

Cody's expression relaxed, a twinkle in his eyes now that she was playing along.

But he didn't deny the ego part. "You must think a lot of yourself."

He snorted.

"Okay then, I'll listen to the bonding stuff, but I need you to do something for me."

"Besides answering all of your questions?"

Her lips twitched. "Yes," she said, picking a random piece of lint off her linen napkin. "I want you to teach me about my magic. How I have it, how I use it. I mean, what are the limits? Are we talking space exploration and time travel? Or cleaning *Fantasia*-style?" She paused, added in a quiet voice. "I also need to learn how to shield."

"I can do most of that," he said softly. "Or find someone to help with it, if I can't. As for shielding . . ." He tilted his chair back so the two front legs hovered off the floor and was silent for long enough that she thought he'd refuse outright. Finally, he nodded. ". . . I think can do that too, but you have to understand there's a risk involved."

Her heart swelled. "I'll be careful, I promise. I'll follow all of your instructions—"

"Christ, Daughtry." His chair plunked to the floor and he stood. Helping her out of her seat with a hand under her elbow, he said, "You're not a risk to me."

"I don't understand."

"How could you not?" He sighed, clenching his free hand into a fist. "Remember the meeting? I'm dangerous to you. My powers could flare again, and this time I might actually hurt you. Permanently."

With that, she had the sense that they finally were getting somewhere.

He'd been trying to keep her safe.

A sliver of ice fell away from her heart.

"I trust you."

It was the truth. As their bond strengthened, it gave her peeks into his soul and with every one she understood him a little better. He had tried to push her away to protect her from himself. Even if that meant she'd hate him in the end.

Cody's voice was a little rough when he spoke again, hinting at the emotions locked deep within his soul. "I can feel that you do."

They stared at each other for a long moment.

"Okay," he eventually said. "Let's go back to my quarters."

"And start shielding."

There was that grudging nod again.

"Cody," she said, finally knowing what to say to help him understand. She wasn't pushing this because she wanted something from him—well, she *did*, she supposed, just not for the reasons he thought. "I need it so I can protect myself." She touched his arm. "If you've seen all that I think you've seen, then you know. I *have* to control them."

His face clouded, anger palpable across the bond. "I hate that you have to deal with this."

"So why can you hear me more than I can hear you?"

"I've been hearing you longer." He grimaced, taking her hand and leading her forward. "Even though I didn't want to believe it. I think because your powers were blocked, you couldn't sense me the same way."

"But I could feel you sometimes. When you were really angry or turned on—"

Cody snorted. "No doubt, that's been most of the time."

Her face grew hot, and when she shrugged in answer, he laughed.

As they walked, she realized that this was right. Being

together felt natural. Like they were two faces of a coin. Or two sides of a sandwich.

"You're the peanut butter to my jelly?"

"I heard that at a wedding once. I thought it was sweet. What?" she said, defensive when he smirked. "It's not like I said it aloud. You can't make fun of me for the thoughts you cherry-pick out of my mind."

One brow lifted. "I never would have pegged you for a romantic."

"Right back at you, Prince Charming." She poked him in the shoulder. "Don't think that I've forgotten your hidden chick-flick addiction."

He rolled his eyes, but she felt a little blip of nervousness in his mind. "Should we discuss the bond?"

She sensed that he'd thrown up the question to distract her, but still pounced on it like a dog on a bone. She had *all* the questions. "Yes"—her stare locked with his—"I'll let you change the subject. *This* time. But I'm watching you."

"That's what I'm afraid of," he muttered. "Okay, so proximity grows the bond." A squeeze of her hand. "Some more time together means we'll be able to hear more, feel more."

"But *how* did we bond? When did it happen, exactly?"

He was quiet for a moment. "I think we would have bonded completely when we mixed our powers on the plane, if your powers weren't blocked. From what I understand, it's not an instantaneous connection. Not like you lay eyes on another person and *bam*, you're bonded."

"Then *how* is it?"

"It's like . . . your magic knows it needs to be with the other person's, yearns for it, but it takes mixing to actually engage. You're drawn to one another, a physical pull, a mental tug." He shrugged. "At least that's what it felt like to me. I wanted to be near you, touch you, link my powers with yours."

"I wanted you, too."

"I know. I could feel it." One corner of his mouth tipped up. "Which made it a hell of a lot harder for me to stay away from you."

Daughtry didn't know how to take that. "Is that such a bad thing?"

Cody stopped and hauled her close to him. "God, no. But cowgirl, you're *you* and I'm *me*. You deserve someone who—"

Relief slammed into her as she finally began to understand. He thought himself as unworthy. Which pissed her off. He kept telling her *she* was valuable, that she could have a place here, yet he didn't believe the same for himself. "Shut up. Enough of this beating yourself up. We're bonded. We ride it out. The end."

His expression transformed from bewilderment to approval. Admiration trickled across the bond, wrapping itself around her heart. "You're pretty incredible, you know that?"

For once Daughtry didn't shake off the compliment. Instead, she took her own advice, accepted the words and simply said, "Thank you." Then asked, "So if not the plane, then when?"

"During the meeting. After Caroline removed the blocks, my magic surged, mixed with yours. That's when I knew for sure."

Those damn blocks kept coming up. She sighed in frustration, wishing she knew who'd put them in place and why. If she understood then maybe—

"Anything else I should know?" she asked, cutting off the circling thoughts.

"That's pretty much the extent of my knowledge."

"Seriously?"

Cody shrugged "It's been so long since there's been a new bond that I don't have a lot of information on it."

"How about another bonded couple?"

"That's just it. There aren't any." He paused. "Well, that's not entirely true, Dante thinks there might be one alive, but they're getting near a millennium. They're not big on technology, so it might take a while to track them down."

"Wait," she said, putting the millennium thing on hold to deal with later. "How long since there's been a new bond?"

"Almost five hundred years. And yes, Rengalla can live almost indefinitely." He gently closed her mouth, which had gaped open. "We're hard to kill. Not exactly immortal, but we don't really get sick, and we heal faster than humans. Usually, our magic begins to decline at about a millennia-and-a–half, and then we just fade away."

Unless the Dalshie get them first. "But why haven't there been any more bonds?"

Cody shrugged. "I don't know. The elders don't talk about it." He guided her to the right, around a corner of bisecting hallways. "All I know is that most people bonded before then. Now it doesn't happen."

Something about the sudden disappearance tweaked her mind. It didn't make sense that everyone would casually accept the loss of something that had once been so prevalent in their society. How could they dismiss it so easily?

She shook her head, not understanding, but setting it aside to deal with later. There were so many other things that she needed to know first.

"What about our magic? How does it work?" she asked. "Are were born with it? Inherit it? Drink a magic elixir? Maybe the blood of virgins?"

"I'm sensing a trend here," Cody said with a smirk.

"And what is that?"

"That you watch too many bad movies."

She shrugged. "The Internet is my friend." It was safer than a crowd, and life as a whole was heck of a lot less lonely when she could get lost in a world different from her own.

A wave of sympathy spread to her side of the bond, but when Cody spoke, his voice was carefully neutral. "Most Rengalla come into their powers between five and eight years of age."

"Most?"

"Some never do."

Daughtry caught the word *Null* floating around his subconscious and remembered it from their previous conversation.

"I take it you were different."

"Yes." The word wasn't terse exactly, more just . . . final, as if he'd reached his threshold on the topic.

Since she'd pushed him so much already, she decided to drop it.

There was a lull in the conversation. She took in the walls around them, starting to recognize of few of the murals.

That made the corridors easier for her to navigate.

"Rengalla use elemental magic," he said.

Her eyes flew up to his, surprised that he'd volunteered information without her asking. "Like earth, wind, and fire?"

His lips twitched at her deliberate but nerdy reference to the band. "Something like that. Except it's earth, air, water, and fire."

"But how do you control them?"

"How do you breathe?" He shrugged. "It's instinctive. At least that's what I hear. My powers are inconsistent. As a Null, I shouldn't even have them."

"So why *do* you?"

Daughtry started to take back the question when she realized how harsh it sounded, but Cody waved her off.

"No clue. Nobody else has been able to figure that out either. I didn't get them until I was in my twenties, when I almost die—" He broke off, but something in their bond pull taut, as though another piece of their minds was connecting, deepening. But when she reached out for Cody across the link, she found herself unable to make it across. It was like trying to swim against a really strong current.

"You going to elaborate on that?" she asked after a moment of struggling.

"Not today."

A sigh escaped her. "You know, for people who live centuries, you guys sure leave a lot of unanswered questions."

"That's the problem with individuality, with genetics, and unique DNA." Cody smiled. "We're not all the same and neither is our magic. There's a scale of power, though usually families have similar strengths. In my case, however, I happen to be at the opposite end of that from my sister and the rest of my family."

She took that in for a moment, remembering the strength it had taken for Cody to fight off the Dalshie, to land the plane. How powerful was Caroline if she was on the other end of the scale? "They're stronger than you?"

"Yes," Cody said with a laugh. "Caroline even more so than my father. Which is why she succeeded him as the Council-head. That position goes to the most powerful Rengalla."

She shook her head at that notion. The sheer force and forti-tude it had taken to stop them from crash-landing in the field was incredible. If Caroline was that much stronger . . .

Cody paused outside his door, placing his hand on the lock panel. He opened it after the *click*, and she followed him inside. The scent hit her straight in the gut. Daughtry took a long inhale, catching just the faintest whiff of sawdust.

Which reminded her of John. "Oh," she said, the urgency in her tone making Cody freeze in place. "We need to talk to John about—"

Cody had just started nodding when they heard, "Talk to me about what?"

TWENTY-TWO

JOHN STRODE through an adjoining door she hadn't even known was there.

Daughtry paused on the threshold and caught a glimpse of the yellow Bruins quilt she'd slept under the previous night. Well, this was weird. She'd once thought that she and John might be . . . something. Which hadn't worked out, obviously, but standing between these two men now, straddling the line between their respective rooms, and she realized how strange the situation was.

"Um, so . . ." she said.

"What did you want to talk to me—?" John asked but didn't finish the question because his eyes widened, and he changed to a different one. "Has someone taught you to shield?"

"No." She and Cody both spoke at the same time.

He frowned, his dark-blond eyebrows furrowing into deep grooves.

"I can't sense you at all. Maybe I should—" He extended a palm.

"Wait." She cut him off, retreated back a pace. "I need to talk to you."

"Okay." John smiled, even though he must have been taken aback by the abruptness of her tone. "Step into my office." He waved a hand toward the adjoining door.

Cody stepped close, leaned down to whisper. "Cowgirl—"

"No," she said. "I . . . I need to make sure he's okay with this. With us. I don't know. It's stupid, I guess since we never were anything concrete—" A shake of her head. "But I feel like I owe him an explanation anyway."

Daughtry could feel the war within Cody.

"He came back for me," she said. He'd sacrificed himself, had protected her. She needed to make sure he was okay.

Cody nodded. "You need me, you call," he said with a tap to his temple.

She walked into John's room, closed the door behind her.

"What is it?" John asked again, placing his free hand on top of her arm. His touch was comforting but didn't raise any of the heat of Cody's. Just another example of something that might have been but never would be.

Cody was different.

She was different with Cody.

Leaning back against the door, she sucked in a deep breath, unsure how to explain what had happened since she'd seen John last. She wanted to know what had happened at the airport, how he'd gotten home, and even though she wanted to ask him what he knew about her parents, her powers, and what the bond meant, she was more concerned about him. Was he still hurting? How could she help him for a change?

He'd been her rock and now she wanted to return the favor.

John chose that moment to look at her. *Really* look at her. The slightly unfocused gaze in his blue eyes told her he was accessing his magic. "What the hell is that?"

The absolute lack of emotion in his voice made her every

hair stand on end. Forcing herself to lock her knees, she said, "Um, I guess . . . Cody and I bonded."

"Are you fucking kidding me?" He dropped her arm, stepped back.

There was emotion in his words now, a red-hot fury that had her shifting nervously from foot to foot.

"I'm sorry," she said quickly, thinking his mind might be going someplace dark, might be thinking they'd betrayed his sacrifice. But the bond was so far away from that, it was almost comical. She and Cody had fought its urges until the end . . . and then they'd still fought it. Now . . . well, she also knew—and this was selfish, but the truth—because having truly felt the bond, she knew she wouldn't give it up without a struggle. There were bound to be learning curves and set-backs, but she knew in her heart of hearts that the bond was something good and valuable and she was keeping it. "Neither of us meant for this to happen—" She broke off, studied the toes of her sneakers. "I'd always thought you and I might . . . be *something*. But with Cody, it's different. We—"

"Stop." One sharp word that had her shoulders stiffening.

She waited for him to rage at her. To accuse her of being a whore, for not saving herself for him, for any of the other numerous things Jimmy used to yell. What Daughtry *wasn't* prepared for was the shattering pain that crept into his eyes, the hurt he was trying, but unable, to hide.

John turned away from her, crossed the room, and punched his fist against the wall, the sheetrock giving way with a burst of dust and paper. Then he went still and silent.

She watched the cloud of white powder disperse until it disappeared altogether.

She felt more than heard Cody rise from his bed at the disturbance. *"I'm fine,"* she told him, hoping he could hear her. After a long moment, she sensed him deciding to stay where he was. Still the force of his protectiveness was palpable. It warmed her like nothing else had ever done.

Gathering that feeling, she used it to shore her strength and focused back on the man in front of her.

"I'm—"

He put up a hand, and she stopped speaking. Then turned to face her, eyes searching hers for something. When he spoke, his voice was so kind that it tore open a gaping hole in her soul. She'd hurt him. She hadn't meant to, but she'd still wounded him deeply.

Dammit, why hadn't she—

"It's not your fault," he said. "It's not even *his* fault."

John shoved a hand through his hair as he shot a dirty look to the shared wall of his and Cody's quarters. "I *wish* I could blame him. I should have known you weren't in my cards. You are way too good for me."

"That's not true."

"It is, Dee," he said. "You're so damned strong, but have this light inside of you, this softness, despite everything you've been through." He sighed. "I wanted to be a part of that."

"But, you and I . . . We never . . ." Her words trailed off into nothing.

He smiled. It was a sad version of his usual one. "That's where I fucked up," he said. "I should have—" A beat, a shake of his head as he cut off his words. "You're too good for him, too." He walked over and grabbed her hand, his eyes intense. "If he ever does *anything* to hurt you, know that I will tear him limb from limb."

Her throat went tight. "I'm sorry."

"I am too, but let's be thankful that this happened now"—his thumb traced her cheekbone—"before anything happened with us."

She decided it would have been easier if John was furious.

This calmness, the affectionate acceptance was harder to swallow. Suddenly, all the emotions of the last week swelled up within her and she once again found herself sobbing on John's shoulder.

He rubbed his hand up and down her back. "What can I do?"

Daughtry sputtered. He'd come for her when Jimmy had left then he'd come back when he'd found out about her past. He'd fought and bled for her, then accepted he was going to die to get her and Cody safety. So the idea of him doing *anything* else for her tore her heart to shreds. He'd done so much and . . . she'd hurt him.

She rose on tiptoe to press a soft kiss against his lips before returning her forehead to his shoulder.

"You are worthy of someone who feels as much for you as I do for Cody." A weight lifted off her chest as she finally spoke her inner feelings aloud. "You deserve better than me."

John snorted, but she squeezed his arm and continued, "None of this makes sense. It was all too fast, too sudden, but it feels right . . . here." She pulled back, pressed her hand against his heart. "It's right, no matter how much I wish things might have been different or slower."

He gently peeled her hand off his chest. "I understand . . ." He paused, lips curving just the slightest bit. "But it'll probably make things easier if you don't touch me."

Daughtry forced a smile and stepped back. "No problem."

"You're something special, Dee."

She scoffed. "I've taken up with your best friend. Stop being so nice. You have *carte blanche* to be as mean to me as you want."

His mouth tipped up further as he walked over to examine the hole in the wall. The result made him curse under his breath.

"No, seriously," she added when he didn't say anything. "Give it a try. Take thirty seconds to be an asshole, and it'll make you feel better. It's Girl Code."

He crossed to her and reached out as if to push back her unruly bangs. But his hand stopped just short of touching her. "Your hair looks ridiculous."

"Feeble attempt," she said. "Still, I'll take it." She lingered, unsure of what to say next.

John solved the problem for her. "You'd better go."

"Okay." She turned to leave.

"Daughtry?"

She stopped.

"That shield around you, from the bond?"

She nodded.

"It's the most powerful one I've ever seen."

The words washed over her. "It is?"

"Yes."

"The vision," she murmured, remembering how her magic had swelled in its aftermath. At the time she'd been too disoriented to understand it.

"You had another vision? God, I'm sorry."

"It's okay. If it means that I'm . . ." What? Safe? Protected? It was okay that she had foreseen a child's horrible death, so long as she gained *something*? A wave of self-loathing rolled over her, weighing her down. God, she was a terrible person. She swallowed and forced the words out. At least she could reassure John. "I'm fine. Really. Almost good, even."

His expression said what he thought of that sentence, but his next words took her by surprise. "I'm being deployed in a week."

The news hit her straight in the gut. She didn't want him to leave. "Why John? Why do you go?"

"I'll tell you some other time," he said. "Or maybe Cody will.

That's how we met." He closed the distance between them and squeezed her shoulders. "Don't feel guilty. This happened for a reason. Now go," he added. "Bother someone else with your interminable questions."

She left, a miserable smile on her lips. Guilt for hurting John, for feeling good about the results of the vision, add in the attraction to Cody, how vulnerable he made her feel, her heart flayed open and unprotected, plus all the changes and upset and confusion about her powers and the bond . . . and she was a mess. But Cody was at her side before the door fully shut, his arms banding around her as he rubbed soft circles on her back.

Tears welled up, but Daughtry fought them back.

She'd shed enough in the past few days.

After a long moment, Cody released her and stepped back and even that little bit of distance made her feel cold and vulnerable.

"I'm not good enough for you," he whispered. "You should be with someone better, someone—"

"Now, I see why you two are friends," she quipped. Both good men, both thinking they were unworthy, but Daughtry knew a little about feeling unworthy herself and so she closed the gap between them, wrapped her arms tightly around his waist. "Don't push me away, Cody. Please." *Not now. I need you.*

He stroked a single calloused finger down her cheek, his motions steady, but the panic in his mind a growing force. "Ah, Daughtry. If it's upsetting you this much . . . I ca—"

"Before you say you can't, will you at least hear me out?" She waited until he nodded before continuing. "We didn't ask for this, but you and I both know there's something here." Relief flooded her when he nodded again. "It's like you said before. Being together is right, almost effortless when we don't fight it." Then she said something she would have not been capable of even one week—hell, one *day*—before. "We deserve to pursue this."

However it ended.

And God help her if it ended badly because Cody was connected to her in a way no other man had ever been. If they didn't work out—

She would survive. No matter what, she would survive.

Daughtry inhaled deeply, let it out slowly. Yes, she would.

But she might not survive this silence.

She wished he would say something. She focused on the small space of her mind devoted solely to Cody, and though she could hear him thinking, she wasn't able to discern anything tangible. Thoughts flashed through too quickly for her to keep track.

"I—" she began.

His lips found hers.

A torrent of power flowed through them, as though a door between their minds had been flung wide open. She fell through that gateway, the intensity, the intimacy of their connection equal parts frightening and fulfilling. Their minds were interwoven on a most basic level, strands of violet and emerald magic tangling together.

"I'd give this a hundred chances," he said into her mind, *"Even if you always destroyed me in the end."*

The softly spoken words threatened to break her heart. They'd each been through so much. How would they ever be able to trust each other?

He kissed her again. *"Let's start by trusting in this."*

Then there were no more thoughts. They communicated their fears, their desires, with hands and mouths and tongues.

TWENTY-THREE

"MORE," Daughtry said the next day.

Cody smirked. "If I kiss you again, we'll never get out of here."

"Fine." She mock-frowned but released the grip she had on his hair as she bent down to tie her shoes. How he was still standing after a full night of patrols was beyond her. But she was excited about their breakfast date.

"Okay, fine. Just one more."

He stole her lips again, and she fell into the bond. Their connection, their mingled magic, was more intimate than if they'd both been naked. But it was also comfortable, which surprised her. Given her past relationship, she wouldn't have expected to be at ease with Cody. He was so much bigger and stronger and yet their mental connection meant he was just as emotionally vulnerable as her.

That gave her the confidence to keep moving forward.

"Do you have to be bonded to have children?" she asked when he let her have a moment to breathe.

Cody froze at her question then pulled back to look intently into her eyes.

"No," he said, a boatload of caution in those two letters.

"I mean, I've seen kids around," she began. "I just . . . I wondered if the bond was needed to . . . um . . ." Daughtry paused, feeling more and more ridiculous the longer she spoke. Of course the bond wasn't required to procreate, she'd seen loads of kids in the Colony and they'd already told her that a bond hadn't happened for hundreds of years. She was an idi—

"Do you—?" Cody started to ask then broke off with a shake of his head.

"Do I what?" she asked. A moment later, her cheeks went hot as she read the full question in his mind. "Oh. I—" She bit her lip. "Yes. I want kids at some point. You?" She was shocked at how important Cody's answer was.

When her visions had been out of control, she hadn't dared to even consider. But the Rengalla had brought her hope. She did want children.

In the future.

Cody smiled. "I never wanted them before." A breath caught in her throat. *"But now that I have you, my mind is full of glimpses of what it could be like. A little mahogany-haired girl with my green eyes, a blond boy with violet irises. I want—"* He laced his fingers with hers. "I want so many things I'd never thought possible before."

Her heart swelled. She squeezed his hand. "Me too." A pause. "So about what I asked—"

"You and your questions." He laughed. "I haven't completely answered the first one, have I?

She shook her head and smiled.

"The bond's purpose seems to be more about creating stronger magic than procreation. When powers are mixed, their strength increases almost exponentially," Cody said. "Remember how difficult it was to let me in when I was trying to read your mind before the bond?"

Daughtry nodded. "Yes. It was almost like my body was repelling your magic."

"Exactly," he said. "But now that we have the connection, our powers are mixed all the time."

He stepped forward, close enough that she had to tip her head up to maintain eye contact.

"According to the historical accounts Dante gave me, if we could harness the mixture, just a little of the *bond magic* would be stronger than anyone here at the Colony."

"That sounds . . . powerful." And dangerous.

"I imagine it would be," he told her, his hands squeezing her hips gently. "Not that I can figure it out. Our powers are combined in our minds, but not outside our bodies. I can't even touch the bond."

Hmm. Daughtry closed her eyes and studied the strands of emerald and violet linking them together. But when she went to try to pull them closer, they were slippery. She couldn't grasp them.

It was strange, almost—

Cody stepped back then, and she peeled open her lids, taking note of the seriousness of his expression. His mind had shifted, no longer playful, and the swirling mass of feelings churning along his end of the bond made her desperate to erase the frown lines from around his lips.

"Enough questions," she said in a rough approximation of his voice.

His eyes crinkled at the corners, but he didn't manage a smile.

She could sense him in her mind, the connection somehow both overwhelming and faintly present. It reminded her of one of those hidden object pictures—a swirling mass of ink, a vicious swath of color. But look at it sideways, tilt her head just right, and the picture slammed into the forefront of her mind. The bond was like that. A *buzz* in the background and then with the slightest bit of concentration Cody's thoughts would smash into her with the equivalent force of a Mack truck.

"What are you holding back?" she asked, not sure if she was referring to his past or the bond. She sat in the chair at his desk, curling her legs underneath her, leaning forward to try and get comfortable on the hard wood.

His eyes lowered, and she realized they'd locked on the deep *V* of her shirt. She bit her lip, feeling both shy and sexy to have distracted him so efficiently with such a small peek-a-boo of flesh.

"It's a mental link," he said finally, shaking himself visibly and sinking down onto the edge of the bed. His voice was husky, even raspier than normal. "It's . . ."

She looked at him with a raised brow and barely withheld smile. "You were saying?" She trailed a hand down her neck, brushing away a nonexistent strand of hair. Was this actually working?

He swallowed, then cleared his throat, staring at the wall of books. "Sorry . . . uh . . . so . . . it shouldn't have happened. Not with my powers anyway."

"But what about your powers? Because they're inconsistent? Or for some other reason?" She crossed her arms, laughing to herself when he cursed under his breath. She'd need to be more careful with her body language if she wanted to actually finish a discussion. Yet the stupid game—her juvenile attempts at seduction and his reactions to them—made her feel powerful.

"Fine, have your '*I am woman, hear me roar*' moment, but know I won't be responsible for my actions." His voice held a tempting amount of promise, and she had to press her lips together to stop an invitation from leaving her lips.

Of course. He felt her struggle.

He chuckled. "See? I'm not the only horn dog here."

An incredulous look before she burst out laughing. *"Horn dog?* Who says that? How old are you? A hundred?"

The tips of his ears pinked.

Well, that was interesting.

She strode to the bed and sat next to him. "How old?"

"Only ninety-four."

Her face or the bond must have registered her surprise because he froze, his expression the placid mask that she'd come to recognize as bracing himself. Daughtry rolled her eyes because really? She was going to forgive him for everything he'd said, but get hung up on his age?

"That young?" she said, affecting casualness. "Are there any medications I should know about? Something for high blood pressure or maybe erectile dysfunction?"

With a snort, he interlaced his hand with hers, brushed it against the hard length of him. "We both know *that* isn't the issue."

She smirked. "Uh-huh. Sure." Her fingers twitched, wanting to explore that part of him very closely, but also knowing this wasn't the time. They needed to slow down, to learn each other, and so she kept her hand laced with his, just slid them from his lap and rested them on the comforter.

"I'm fairly young by our standards," he said and at her raised brow added, "Our history isn't very exciting. We've lived both separate of and intertwined with human culture, depending on the attitude of the time. We've been shamans, sorcerers, witches, gypsies, even sideshow acts."

"That sounds pretty exciting," she told him, the image of Cody walking a tightrope with a top hat popping into her head.

He rolled his eyes. "It had always been the choice of each Rengalla. Some had always lived here at the Colony. Some have chosen to be separate."

"But how did we get magic in the first place?" she asked.

"Did someone just wake up one day and they were able to shoot colored strands out of his palms?"

His lips quirked. "Not exactly. A few of the elders have talked about four ancestors, each who were able to control one of the four different elements. They fu—" Cody broke off, his cheeks darkening just the slightest bit.

"Got frisky?" she supplied with a smirk.

"Yes. Basically," he said. "Through interbreeding, most of the Rengalla are able to control all four elements. Though we typically have an affinity only for one of them. That's the first tier of magic, the one you'll learn how to control first."

"And the Dalshie?" she asked. "What can they do?"

All laughter faded from his eyes, lips pressing tightly together. "Their only strength comes from their ability to cause harm, to create pain. They can't control the elements. They can only maim. Or kill."

She remembered the malice coming off those black barbed strands of magic, how it had sliced so easily through John's and Cody's skin. "How do they exist?"

"They exist because of us."

Her eyes widened. "But how? Why?"

"Our powers can be very tempting, but they can also be misused, and once that taint exists, it transforms a Rengalla into a Dalshie." He sighed. "We'd always been able to control the Dalshie, hunted them down ruthlessly. We protected the innocent against them—human and Rengalla alike—until . . . everything changed."

Goose bumps rose on her arms at the cold, dead look in his eyes. "During the second World War, the Dalshie made their first move in centuries. They teamed up with a mortal and corrupted many pure souls. The result was that millions died, including most of us."

"But . . . you can't mean . . ." Her mind spun as the information finally penetrated the fog around her brain. She wanted to deny it, but she could feel Cody's anguish at the truth. "They—? Hitler?"

He nodded. "All of those experiments weren't really his. He was simply a drone the Dalshie created, a front for all of the evil and corruption."

"So he was innocent?" she asked, sliding closer, pressed her thigh to his. Daughtry found she craved the contact, needed his comfort.

"God, no," he said. "The Dalshie couldn't have used him so effectively if he wasn't evil down to his core. But they magnified that darkness in him, exploited it to their advantage." He put his hand on her knee and squeezed gently. "They wanted their own army of disposable drones and they tried everything from gene manipulation to injecting their blood into humans in order to create the perfect magical soldiers."

"Did it work?"

"No. The only thing they succeeded at was harming innocents." He cleared his throat roughly. "And even though we fought the Dalshie, millions still died."

The sheer amount of suffering the people in those camps had been through made her throat tight. And Cody had seen that horror firsthand. She felt the stranglehold of those images in his memory. "But you won in the end."

"Yes." *But at what cost?* He met her gaze as the words drifted across the bond. "We don't consider it victory because, ultimately, it's our greatest failure, the thing we measure our actions today against. We waffled, were too slow to act. As a result, we lost most of our people and failed all of those innocents." His voice hardened. "The LexTals won't let it happen again."

He rose off the bed and squatted next to her knees. "For the most part, the Dalshie have stopped their attacks on humans, but the Rengalla are still on their radar. We have spent the better part of the last half-century fending off attacks, rebuilding, while the Dalshie have gotten stronger, larger. We lose more of our number to them every year. The Colony and a few smaller settlements are all that's left."

"You're hunted." It was meant to be a question, but she already knew the answer.

"Yes, and that's not all. The magic they use is perverted."

"How?"

He extracted his hand then used it to spread her fingers. "Magic done in harm corrupts your soul." He tapped a finger in the center of her palm. "It begins here." He traced along the skin of her wrist, up to her shoulder, and she shivered, not in pleasure this time, but in fear. "It travels up the arms and with each inch it consumes, more of you is lost." Cool fingers tapped her temple and above her breast. "Once it infects your brain and heart, the only thing that's left is a black shell, cold and immoral."

"Is there a cure?" Her voice was neutral, but she felt chilled to the bone.

"No. Just a slow, excruciating death. The person they once were is gone, replaced by someone with no morality. No conscience." He paused before continuing. "The only thing to do when someone is infected is . . . euthanasia. A blade through their heart, separate their head from their body, and they're dust. Anything less and..."

Daughtry remembered the sight of rancid flesh knitting itself together and let out a shaky breath. "But the ones from the apartment, they looked—"

"Human," he finished for her. "At least for a little while. The Dalshie can glamour most of the stains until they use their magic. Then the glamour falls away, and the infection shows."

"So I have to wait for them to use their powers?" That seemed extremely stupid.

"Yes and no. There are other ways. But the glamour never works here." He touched the center of her palm again. "Always look here."

DAUGHTRY WOKE the next morning feeling both rested and restless. They'd spent the day together, first a breakfast date, then together in his rooms while she read, and he caught up on sleep. Later, they'd taken a walk through the gardens then eaten an early dinner before Cody had left to run another patrol.

While it had been nice to spend such a normal day together, to keep building their connection, she was also getting antsy. She needed to find Francis, the teacher Dante had recommended.

It was time she started learning how to use her magic.

But honestly? The notion scared her. There were so many variables and things to learn and . . . what if she did something wrong—

Well, she couldn't just lay in bed all day eating bonbons, she had to do *something*.

Suz's invitation popped into her head. Maybe she could try that?

Coward.

Well, maybe. But at a least it was a start, right?

Sighing, she rolled to her side, slipped from the bed, and then did an amusing impersonation of an elephant on roller skates. Apparently, Cody hadn't been gone the entire time she'd been sleeping, because as she slid off the mattress after her first full night's sleep in however many nights, she almost stepped on him.

He was tucked against the side of the bed with only an old sweatshirt for a pillow. He'd slept in his jeans and T-shirt.

She looked to the mess of blankets on the bed and the two pillows indented from her head and winced. She'd been sprawled spread-eagle in the center not too long ago, and yet he was sleeping on the floor, after having spent the night protecting her and the rest of the Colony. After extracting the quilt from the bed, she tucked it over him, then dressed and hurried out of his quarters so not to wake him.

It didn't take long to make her way to the infirmary. But once there, her hand on the door handle, she hesitated.

"Don't be a coward," she muttered, squaring her shoulders and pushing through. She asked the young teenager working the desk for Suz. Before she could blink, the girl grabbed her hand and hustled her down the hallway with all the efficiency of a worker bee.

And Daughtry felt nothing.

Not a twitch of nausea or the smallest flare of an image. She relaxed.

The interaction gave her the courage she needed as she stood, deposited like a bag of mail in front of Suz. "I'm here for my orders, Captain."

The doctor laughed, its throaty nature matching her outwardly sexy appearance, and clapped her hands together. "Good. I was hoping you'd come. There's a list for you on the counter."

Daughtry walked over to the spot Suz had pointed then picked up the paper bearing small, cramped print that filled the front and back and every inch of the margins.

"When you finish that, I have more."

"No problem," she said, deciphering the first few tasks and pocketing the note. "But I might not be ready for that until sometime next century."

Suz snorted, walking over before hesitating, hand a few inches about Daughtry's shoulder.

She grabbed it, squeezed lightly. "I'm safe now," she told the doctor, hoping that her theory would continue to prove true. "The bond is protecting me."

A relived breath. "I'm so glad."

"Me, too." Daughtry started opening cabinets. "Now get back to work, I hear my boss is a real taskmaster."

Suz snorted. "You'll do just fine here, Daughtry." She sat her desk, opened a thick file, and focused her attention on her computer.

The next few hours passed rapidly. Suz was very patient, so by the time Daughtry had finished a few items, she had a decent idea of where things were. She was refilling a bin of gauze, thinking that being Suz's glorified gopher wasn't a bad gig, when the doctor called her over.

She hurried across the room to where a little boy sat on an exam table. There was large gash on his thigh. His mother looked frighteningly pale.

"Here," Daughtry said, grabbing the mom's arm to settle her into a chair. "Sit down." She turned to Suz and saw the doctor was struggling to get the boy to stay still.

Coaxing the child to lie back, she asked, "What's your name?"

"Donovan," came the squeaking voice, his nervous eyes darting down toward Suz.

Daughtry steeled herself—this touch would not bring a vision, it *wouldn't*—and brushed her hand across his forehead.

A breath she hadn't realized she'd been holding slipped between her lips. No nausea. No images. Perhaps it would hit later, but she didn't think so. The bond was protecting her.

"Donovan," she said. "You look like a big boy—"

"I am!" he interrupted.

"Okay, but are you big enough to count to thirty?"

"I can count to fifty. No, a hundred!"

Daughtry chuckled as she spared a glance for Donovan's mom, who was starting to look more amused than pale. "Okay then. Let's hear it."

"One, two . . ."

The strands of Suz's magic descended onto the wound, knitting the layers of skin and muscle back together. By the time Donovan had reached twenty-five, the cut had been closed, when he'd reached sixty, the wound that already looked days old had been bandaged, and by ninety-five, Suz had tucked a glass of orange juice and a package of crackers into his mom's hand.

"One hundred!"

"Great job," she told him. Then before she could hesitate, could worry, she gave him a hug. He hugged her back for a heartbeat then squirmed and pulled away, but damn, did it make her feel good. Every touch that was safe felt like a gift she'd never expected to receive.

"You have a knack for this," Suz said after they'd gone.

She shrugged. "I don't know anything about first aid. I've never even taken a CPR class."

"Regardless," Suz said, balling up her gloves and chucking them into the hazardous-waste bin. "You're good with people."

Funny how she never expected to hear that again.

THE DOOR SLAMMED BEHIND DAUGHTRY, but she hardly noticed. Her mind was on—where else? Cody.

Her lips tingled every time she thought about the scalding kiss he'd stolen on the threshold hours ago. She'd stared dumbly after him, his heavy boots silent on the floor, until he'd disappeared around the corner.

"Go back to sleep," he'd thought, smugness in every word.

If only it had been that easy. She'd lain frustrated, tangled in sheets that smelled of him, until finally a fitful rest had taken her. She'd woken missing him. Even the bond felt muted, his distance from her too large for her to glean more than that he was safe.

Probably a good thing, given the smutty direction of her thoughts.

But it was far from helpful in her current condition. She was buzzing with energy that had no outlet.

Sighing, she walked down the hall and turned in the direction of the gardens. Maybe she could walk off her restlessness.

"Daughtry." The skin on her nape prickled at the voice, and she looked up into eyes so similar to Cody's.

"Caroline," she responded politely, even as her insides churned with anxiety.

"I was hoping to find you," the Council-head said. "I have some . . . tools that might be useful for you. Come with me."

Daughtry immediately wanted to rebuke the order, and it was most definitely an order, but for Cody's sake, she obliged. "Sure, thank you."

Caroline led the way through the corridors, not saying a word to relieve the silence, her chin high enough to top the tallest skyscraper.

Excellent communication skills. Must be a family trait.

"Come."

Caroline paused at a door. A man stood in front of it, feet spread, gaze scanning. He wasn't wearing a LexTal uniform, but his posture and the concise movement with which he opened the door marked him as part of the Rengallan military.

She trailed Caroline into the room and was blown away by the wealth present. The space was absolutely inundated with it.

"Oh, wow," she said, unable to hold back the sentiment.

Here was the opulence that matched the private jet. Vaulted ceilings with beautiful chocolate woodwork drew her eyes upward. Huge canvases hung along one wall, illuminated with gallery-quality lighting. Expensive wallpaper had her itching to run her fingers along its silky width. The desk was exquisite. A gorgeous mahogany, it was a testament to craftsmanship with its fluting and rosettes.

"Gaudy, isn't it?"

She faced Caroline and attempted to keep the disbelief off her face. The space was exquisite. She struggled for a moment to find a proper response. Eventually, she settled on, "It's not to your taste?"

Caroline gave a decidedly unladylike snort before indicating a door.

"*This* is more to my liking," Caroline said, sinking into a chair on a sigh.

The room was smaller, still decorated in equally expensive furnishings, but it was like having been transported into another world. Except, Caroline's sanctuary was modern, cold and devoid of any comfort.

The molded acrylic chair Daughtry perched on felt at once too flimsy to hold her weight and torturous to her spine. Worse, it had probably cost as much as the wooden versions in the other office. Then there was the visual jar between the clinically white walls and olive-green accents.

Frankly, it took a minute for her eyes to adjust.

Which is why she started when she realized they weren't alone in the room.

An older man stood across from her. He appeared to be in his mid-fifties but who knew how old that translated to in Rengallan years? Silver shadowed the hair at his temples. He was tall, in good shape, but lean and under-muscled.

This was a politician, not a warrior.

He belonged in the other room.

"Oh, excuse me," she said when he looked at her, his eyes flicking to her seated position. She stood to offer her hand. He gave it a perfunctory squeeze and continued standing. It was obvious he was familiar with the bear traps that were Caroline's chairs.

"Let me get to the point," Caroline said, forcing the conversation back to her.

Yes, let's, Daughtry just barely resisted saying. Excess energy was still bunched below her skin. She wanted to be as far away from the pretentious woman as possible.

"Alexander would like to mentor you." Caroline indicated the older man, her face expectant.

Why would he want to do that? "Oh?" she asked.

Caroline's eyes narrowed. "Yes."

Daughtry waited for them to say something, to give a reason for the interest. To give her the truth—even if it was because they thought she might be a useful tool.

"What would mentoring entail?" she finally asked, unsure how to proceed in a conversation that felt filled with landmines.

"You need to learn to protect yourself. I can teach you," Alexander said.

Her bullshit detector was blaring.

"As for the unfortunate bonding," Alexander continued, "I think we might have found a way to disengage it. If Caroline could have access to your mind, she could lay a series of wards that would silence the connection without severing it. That way you won't lose your powers."

"What do you mean?"

A self-satisfied smirk creased Alexander's face. "I see. So Co —the *soldier* has been keeping secrets?"

Her stomach twisted.

"You need to listen very carefully," he said." The bond is dangerous. Especially with one like him."

"Dangerous in what way?" That pushed her doubt away. Cody had *always* protected her.

"Cody's powers are unpredictable," Alexander said, his voice so coldly calculating that she wanted to snap at him to tell the truth. "He's useless to you."

"He's a Null," Caroline chimed in.

"Was," Daughtry said.

"Pardon me?"

"He *was* a Null," she said, "I've seen his powers. He saved me."

"A simple coincidence is all," Caroline said, "If you aligned with our interests, we could protect you from him. Help you achieve a status—"

"Okay, well, thank you for the offer," Daughtry said, cutting off the hard sell before it got a full head of steam. She'd probably pay the price later for the slight to Caroline's ego, but she couldn't stand another minute of listening to the two of them insult Cody.

She could only see into one person's heart and it held none of the calculating malice that these two had filled the room with.

So, yeah, she'd take Cody. Every single day of the week.

"I'll consider your offer," she promised when it looked as though they'd protest. "Thank you." Her eyes focused on the table. " Are those for me?"

"Yes," Alexander said.

She lifted one of the books, saw it wasn't light reading, but rather, a textbook. "Thank you. I'm looking forward to reading them." With that, she had the pleasure of watching Alexander sputter for a second before his calm mask slid back into place. She tucked the books under her arm and turned for the door.

"It was my pleasure," Alexander said, recovering his manners. "I hope that you'll take me up on my services. I think I have a great deal to teach you."

She nodded. Teach her? Not so much. More likely, he wanted to mold her into a drone who obeyed his every wish.

"In fact"—she paused in her beeline for the door—"I taught your mother."

That was almost tempting enough to make her want to talk to them further. She'd actually hesitated, her foot hovering above the white marble tile, when Cody burst into the room.

"What the hell are you doing, father?" he said, frost in every word, every line of his body.

Her mouth fell open. But now that she looked, she saw the same firm jaw, the nose, the eyes. Except that Alexander's were a muted green—sage rather than emerald.

"Cody," Caroline warned.

"No." He shot his sister a glare that would have frozen lava. "How dare you do this?"

She laughed, and there was something very wrong about it. "How *dare* I? How dare *you* risk her? She's the greatest asset that's come our way since—"

"Risk her?" he growled. "I've done everything I could to protect her and I will continue to do so."

Caroline lifted one brow. "And will you use your *magic* to do so?"

Cody's face blanched.

"Enough," Alexander said, his voice soft but authoritative enough to silence the squabbling siblings. "Charles, leave. We have a discussion to continue."

Daughtry had to physically stop her mouth from falling open. "*Charles?*" she asked across the bond.

He gave a mental shrug, anger still pulsing along their connection, but she felt just the tiniest bit of humor enter his mind at her inquiry. "*What can I say? My parents like royal names.*"

Fitting, she supposed given the size of his and Caroline's egos.

Shaking her head, she put her hand on Cody's arm and squeezed. *"Let's go."*

"I *will* think about it," she said to Alexander and Caroline, feeling like she had to say something, or they wouldn't let her leave.

"Think about what?" Cody asked, concern flying across the bond.

"Tell you later," she thought. *"I have more questions."*

"Shocker."

They'd just entered the hallway when Alexander caught up to them.

"Daughtry." He didn't look at Cody, didn't even bother to acknowledge his son's presence.

The leash on her temper finally broke.

"I—"

"You bastard!" she hissed. "Do you think that I would ever accept anything from you when you don't even support your own son?" Purple sparks shot out of her fingertips, her power a roiling mass in her mind.

"Easy, cowgirl."

She took a breath, forcing herself to calm down. "I have no interest in anything from you." She shoved the precious text-books into his arms, not wanting any ties with the asshole who'd dumped Cody in an orphanage because he hadn't had magic.

Alexander straightened, lips pressed into a firm line. After shooting her a steely glare, he whirled away and stomped down the hall.

Her hands cramped with anger. Her magic was *right* there, and it would be so easy to—

"No fireballs indoors. Dante gets really pissed if we scratch the floor." Cody squeezed her shoulder, and she sighed, the hostility at Alexander easing somewhat at the contact.

"I'm sorry," she said. "I shouldn't have said that. Did I make things worse for you?"

A shrug. "There's not much you could say to them that I haven't."

She seriously doubted that.

"I had hoped that Caroline would turn out differently," he said, sadness in his voice. "But she's changed since she became Council-head."

Daughtry wanted to rail at the worthless beings that were Cody's sister and father, but she could feel how tired he was.

"Let's go back to the room. You've been up all night."

"I'm not tired." He paused and fixed her with a look that made her breathing hitch. "Come here."

"Lies," she said but smiled and stepped into his arms. "You know, I've decided that all of the bad hype about in-laws is true."

Cody rolled his eyes, but his amusement was a soft coating over her skin. She soaked it in, feeling as though they had weathered their first storm as a couple.

"Why did they say the bond was dangerous?" she asked a moment later, after they'd continued walking.

He went stiff as a statue, his sudden panic tearing along their connection.

Or maybe the storm was just beginning.

TWENTY-FOUR

"WHAT DID THEY SAY?" Cody asked, caution in every syllable.

"Basically what you told me." Except for the losing-her-powers thing.

He pulled away to pace, untamed power in every step. She was once again aware of his sheer size, his strength.

Daughtry wondered if she would ever be as resilient. She certainly wasn't that strong.

"You underestimate yourself, cowgirl," he said with a tug on the end of her ponytail.

"Pot, meet kettle," she said, knowing that he didn't see himself the way she did. Shame from his childhood was a hot lance buried deep, the residual waves of pain muted, yet still uncomfortable, along their connection.

"So?" she asked when he didn't immediately answer. "The bond?"

Cody sighed. "If either of us is with anyone else, we die."

What?

Cody was great, but was she ready to spend her life with

him? On pain of death? She knew that she cared about him, but—

Stop. Listen.

Blowing out a breath, she forced herself to calm down. She was learning that with Cody sometimes it was what he *didn't* say that was more important. "What do you mean, die?"

"We'll live a human lifespan."

Relief flooded her senses. She was okay with only being on this earth for eighty-something years.

"That doesn't seem so bad."

He thrust a hand through his hair. "I'm sorry. I'm doing a crap job of explaining this. The reality is, if we don't stay together, foster our bond, we lose our powers. No extended life. No magic. No longer Rengalla, we become human."

Daughtry sucked in a breath. That was what she'd wanted all along, right? But now that it was in front of her, she remembered how using her powers made her feel complete. If she lost her magic, would it feel like an entire chunk of herself was missing?

Yes. She was sure of it. Even more, now that she could connect with her powers. She opened her hand and watched as a flutter of purple sparks hovered above her palm. When the blocked had been in place, she hadn't understood, but with her magic free, she could feel it with every breath, every heartbeat. It interlaced with her soul, bound so tightly that to excise it would be excruciating.

Could she do *that* to Cody?

The part of her that wanted to never again experience a vision screamed *yes, she could.* The rest of her knew that the reason the visions were so terrible in the first place was because of the helplessness she'd felt.

It wasn't about the gruesome pictures. *No.* Her sorrow was

because she couldn't do a damn thing for the people whose deaths she'd seen.

Though the risk was that she might get more visions, her hope was that learning to harness her powers would bring her more joy than agony. That with her magic, she might finally be able to control them, that she could be vision-free unless she chose differently. Because if she *could* control them, maybe she could use them to help someone.

And she found she wanted that more.

A chance to help people . . . a chance at a future with Cody.

Finally, she understood why he'd been so upset at the possibility of the bond. He'd been abandoned by the most important people in his life and he was now dependent on her.

She met his gaze, almost afraid of what she'd find. Would he be angry that she was tempted to give up her powers? Infuriated that he was stuck with her if he wanted to keep his?

But instead of resentment, she found compassion. Understanding.

That hurt more than anything. He expected her to take the out. To sacrifice a part of his soul for her own peace of mind.

The reality was so obvious that it could have slapped her upside the head.

After all of her blustering about distance and her desperation to keep her heart safe, she'd sacrifice her vision-free future in a heartbeat. If it meant she saved the man who was linked so completely with her soul further pain, it wouldn't even *be* a sacrifice.

Was that what it meant to love?

It was too soon to know. But what she *did* know was that the price of this choice wasn't her freedom or her happiness. Cody wouldn't condemn her decision either way.

That gave her the strength to do what needed to be done.

"So, that's it then," she said.

Cody straightened his spine. "It's fine. I can cope with being human. I'll be—"

She slung her arms around his neck and pulled his face down so it was a hairsbreadth away from hers. "Never, Cody." Her hands slid around to cradle his face, his scar rough against her palm. "We'll figure this out."

He nodded in answer to her statement, but she could sense his shock. He'd apparently been certain she would take the chance to jump back into her old life, free of the burden of her visions.

A week, hell, a few days ago, she might have done it. But things were different now.

His surprise had her making a silent promise to herself—she would not abandon him. They would find some way to make the bond work.

No matter what.

A burst of tenderness surrounded her even as he pulled away to lean back against the wall. His mind was a maelstrom of words and emotions. "*Null.*" "*Failure,*" rattled along the bond.

After a few minutes, she realized that he probably needed some space to come to terms. He'd been dreading this conversation because he'd thought the inevitable conclusion was that she'd leave him, that he'd lose his magic, his home and the non-biological family he'd built.

"Please don't go."

A softly spoken plea, as if his brain couldn't believe his mouth had let the request out. His fingers grabbed hers, and he pulled her against his chest.

"Stay. Please, just stay."

Always.

"Daughtry?" he said after a long moment, one arm wrapped around her shoulders, his other hand sliding smoothly through her hair.

"Yes?" she said, feeling a little vulnerable, hoping that he'd say something meaningful.

"Thanks."

Not exactly the soul-inspiring poetry I've been waiting for.

The tips of his ears turned pink as he caught her thought. The awkwardness between them broke, and he smiled. "Sorry, I'll pull out my Lothario handbooks and study up." He looked at her, finally meeting her eyes. "But, seriously, please stay."

"I'm not going anywhere," she said, but couldn't help adding, "So *you have more than one handbook?*"

"*I'm not going to live that one down, am I?*"

"Nope."

"Great—" He was still talking when she slanted her mouth against his, but he recovered quickly, clutching her closer on a groan, shoving his tongue into her mouth, his—

"Get a room!"

They jumped apart like teenagers caught making out in the closet.

"*Not far from the truth,*" Cody thought with a smile, pressing his lips to hers once more.

"My eyes," Tyler groaned. "Dear God. My *eyes.*"

"Shut up, Tyler!" they both shouted.

He gave them a wave over his shoulder before disappearing around the corner.

"Guess we should find someplace else," she said, cheeks hot.

"*I know just the place.*"

"THIS WASN'T WHAT I EXPECTED," Daughtry whispered, her mouth close to Cody's ear.

She turned her attention back to the group of children sitting in a makeshift circle of stools. The different heights of logs turned on their ends provided efficient, but maybe not comfortable chairs.

"Just watch and listen," Cody said.

Straining her ears, she tuned into the discussion the instructor was leading.

"Who can tell me how to assure your magic is used in balance?"

A girl's hand shot up.

The teacher nodded for her to answer.

"You must only use magic for good and unselfish reasons," the girl said. It was a dutiful recitation.

"Good." The instructor nodded. "What else?"

A boy with shaggy hair hiding his eyes said, "For defense."

"Yes. How about to help others? Or to . . ."

She turned to Cody. "What kind of class is this?"

"We call it Primary," he said. "This is where children learn first to control the elements. Once that's mastered, they move on to Secondary."

She watched the kids wriggle on their logs. "What's Secondary?"

"Putting two of the elements together. Like teleportation or healing. Weather control," he said.

A wave of giddiness made her smile. *This* is what she'd been dying to learn.

"You'll be able to do this too. Watch."

"Okay, children," the instructor said. "Close your eyes, focus, and when you're ready, show me."

She bit her lip as each of the kids held out their hands. When a ball of flame burst out of the first palm, she gasped, drawing the attention of the teacher. He met her eyes then pointed to his side.

She glanced at Cody, who nodded encouragingly, then feeling as though she was taking a trip to the principal's office, she stepped out of the shadows and walked across the clearing.

By the time she arrived, small spheres of flame sat above every child's palm. Each was a unique color: a pale blue, a muddied green, even one gorgeous amber globe that reminded her of whiskey, interwoven with threads of brown and gold.

"Good," the instructor said. "Now release the magic."

The balls blinked out of existence. She squinted against the sudden loss of color in the air.

"That will be all."

The kids gathered up their books and backpacks and scurried off, barely sparing her and Cody, who'd trailed her, a second glance.

When the clearing was empty, Cody finally spoke. "Francis, this is Daughtry."

So *this* was the man Dante had wanted her to study with.

Francis, whose pale blue eyes reminded her of the cloudless sky, nodded in recognition as he extended his palm. A flash of embarrassment slid across his face, and he pulled it back. "Oh, excuse me."

Daughtry grabbed his hand before it retracted all the way to his side and shook it firmly. "The bond shields me."

Eyebrows raised. "Really? How interesting." Scholarly interest flared to life on his face. Yet his expression was different from the calculating ones that had belonged to Caroline and Alexander.

He tapped the side of his head and asked, "May I look?"

"Sure," she said with a shrug.

His blue eyes unfocused and Daughtry could feel the tickle of his magic on her skin, though she couldn't see it. There were no colored strands bursting from his palms, just a change in the atmosphere, a pulse of power in the air.

She ran a hand down her arm, able to feel the sparks from his magic on her fingertips.

Francis smiled at her obvious shock. "A secondary skill is all. I can bend light. The magic is still there, just not visible." The tickling of his powers cut off as he dusted his hands on his pants. "It does have its uses. Gathering gossip, for one."

Her mouth dropped open. "You mean, you can—?" She gasped when he disappeared before her eyes.

"Yes, I can disappear. Or make it seem like I have," he said.

Whirling with a laugh, she saw that Francis had moved behind her and was visible again.

"That is so cool."

"Yes," Cody thought, his amusement sliding across the bond.

"So what can I do for you two young folks?" Francis asked, his gaze drifting between them. "I can see the bond is strong. Your shield as well."

Cody nodded. "I was hoping you could teach Daughtry to use her magic."

"I'd be delighted." Francis looked at her. "Why don't you have a seat? I have a few minutes before my next class." To Cody he said, "Shoo now, but close. Daughtry will call you when we're done."

"You okay?" Cody rested his hand on her shoulder, the touch casual yet reassuring.

"Yeah, I'm good," she thought. *"And Cody? Thanks."*

"Anything you need." He disappeared into the trees. "Cowgirl? You need me. You call." Then he was gone, the distance between them increasing until it muted the bond to a faint buzz.

Daughtry glanced up to find Francis smiling at her. "Were you communicating along the bond that entire time?"

A flush filled her cheeks. "Sorry if I was rude. We're still getting used to it." Plus, when Cody talked to her, the rest of the world just up and disappeared.

"Not at all," Francis said. "I just found it rather fascinating. Both of you had the most pleasant expressions on your faces."

She forced a smile. Now she had to worry about making funny mental-talking faces?

Francis gestured to a log. "Why don't you tell me what you know about magic?"

Studying his pale blue eyes, which were framed by a few tasteful wrinkles at their corners, she waited to see some sign of derision or disdain. Instead, he just looked curious.

"Honestly?"

He nodded.

"Hardly anything. I didn't even know magic really existed until John came for me."

Francis rubbed his long fingers across his chin. "Well that, my dear, can be easily remedied. Learning magic is the easy part. Control? Now not everyone can do that."

"You mean the Dalshie."

"Quick and bright." He tilted his head to the side. "No wonder Cody is so enamored with you. Yes, the Dalshie exist simply because they have violated our first, and most important tenet: Do no harm."

"Do no harm?" The buoyant feeling within her burst, leaving her stiff and frozen. She'd already violated that rule. Too many times.

Her face must have displayed her turmoil because Francis reached across the gap to pat her knee. "It's the intent that matters."

Which didn't make her feel better.

Last time she'd checked, ignorance didn't let a person off the hook when it came to culpability.

"With Oracles," Francis said, "that is often hard to discern. Your burden may be a little heavier than the rest of us, I'm sorry

to say, my dear. You have to walk the fine line between interven-
tion and leaving well-enough alone."

"I don't understand." He was talking like there was something good about her seeing people's deaths. "Every time I've
tried to help, the . . . outcome was worse. More violent. More—"
She looked away from the sympathy in his expression. "It was
just worse."

"I think the blocks were responsible for that."

There they were again, those fucking blocks. "How can you
be sure?"

"I can't be," Francis said, his tone carefully bland. "We won't
know until you try again."

Her blood ran cold. *Try?* No, what he meant was for her to
jump from a plane with the equivalent of no parachute. Already
her single success had driven her to make a dozen attempts she
would have never risked. He wasn't giving her a plan for
success. He was proposing she hope right back into Russian
roulette and Daughtry wouldn't do that again.

"I won't." She wouldn't be responsible for more pain, more
death and suffering.

"I understand."

"No," she gritted out. "You *don't.*"

Francis stared at her for a long moment before nodding.
"No, of course I couldn't."

She gripped the sides of her log, holding tight to the sensation of the bark biting into her palms. It took a while for her to
calm down enough to continue their discussion. "Tell me more
about intent," she said when she had.

Francis nodded. She could almost see him pull on his
professor cap, he spoke so confidently. "Take the average
Rengalla and assume they want a gold ring. They could use
their earth skills to locate and extract the ore and their fire abili-

ties to mold that gold into the design they want. Or they could make themselves invisible and steal it."

She grimaced. She'd reduced him to children's lessons about the Golden Rule.

He smiled at the look on her face and shoved himself to his feet. "Walk with me."

Rising to follow him, she took comfort in the rustling of the leaves, the soft grinding of dirt beneath her sneakers. The air was crisp, slightly cool even though the sun was out.

"The difference isn't always so clear cut," he said once they were on the path, encased in the trees. "A healer might invent an antibiotic to combat illness in humans. It might help countless people, or it might give way to an antibiotic-resistant bacteria that kills many more. Does that make the scientist evil?"

"No, of course not," she said. "They couldn't have predicted that outcome."

"Exactly. It doesn't make them evil, it makes them *normal*. Good isn't always a straight line from *A* to *B*. The same is true of foresight."

He stooped and picked a flower from a bush, then twirled it in his fingers. "Rengalla aren't gods, aren't immune to arrogance and deceit. We certainly make our share of mistakes. But Oracles aren't any different. Only, instead of antibiotic-resistant bacteria, you're surrounded with futures."

She shook her head. "But I hurt people. I screwed with their lives. I *killed* them."

Francis sighed, giving her a look that this was an argument he'd heard many times before. He nodded at her to continue down the path. "And I will never be able to convince you otherwise. The burden of relieving your guilt is on your own shoulders.

"I don't expect—I mean, I don't need—" What? Redemption?

Absolution? Maybe she didn't *need* them, but good God she wanted them.

He tucked the flower behind her ear. "Think about it this way. Here, this plant is harmless, but introduce it halfway across the world, and it could decimate the local ecosystem. The same is true with the darkness of your magic. Let it take root, and it festers, grows until it has eclipsed everything in its path." He placed a hand over his heart. "What separates us from the Dalshie is here. Love, compassion, concern."

"But how am I better than the Dalshie? I've done harm."

"Ah, so you *did* intend to hurt them?"

"No, of course not! But—"

Francis cut off her words with a slicing motion of his hand. "No equivocations. If you were to go out and deliberately pull someone's vision and then alter it to harm them, that would be different." He nodded to himself, as if he'd made a decision. "I told you that Oracles are unique."

She withstood the urge to roll her eyes. Unique was one way to describe it. But, still, she did her best to absorb Francis's words as they continued to meander along the path.

"Your powers are closely intertwined with the present and past, with the future and fate," Francis said. "That makes finding balance tricky. You must find the key."

She frowned. "The key? To what?"

"It's the piece of a vision that you can alter and still keep the elements balanced. The place to where you can shift the fulcrum of the scales of the future without making a person's death worse."

His words gave her so much hope that she could almost feel it bubbling up within her veins. "But what does the key look like?"

"Each Oracle's key is different."

Her emotions settled. "So I'm not looking for a sparkling golden key, then?" Of course, it wouldn't be that easy.

Francis smiled. "I'm afraid not. But I do have access to the Journals. They're the personal accounts of all of the Oracles in recent history, including your mother's."

"My mother had journals?" Her hands itched to get ahold of them.

A nod. "All of the Oracles kept them. Because there have always been so few of you, they found it was a helpful way to pass along knowledge."

"Like a Google Drive of Oracle information."

"I'm not too old to know that reference," he said, teasing her. "But no, they're the Oracles' individual experiences—what their visions were, how they controlled them, what measures they took when altering them. Because they are personal and every Oracle is different, you may not be able to directly apply them to your own powers, but they should give you a good starting point."

Her heart skipped a beat. That was all she could hope for.

"I'll send them to your rooms tomorrow, along with a few other books I think will be useful," he said. "For now, I'd like you to start with a simple exercise: make a flame appear in your hand."

"What the kids were doing?"

Francis chuckled at her tone and guided her around a turn. She saw the clearing straight ahead of them, just through a narrow stand of trees. "Yes. It *is* a beginner exercise. But control of fire is something all Rengalla can do, in varying degrees, of course. However, Oracles tend to have an affinity for that element."

Affinity sounded a lot like a pyromaniac.

But if he said to practice then . . . "How do I do it?"

"Focus on your magic. Will the fire into existence."

"That's it?"

He grinned as they both stepped back into the sunshine. "That, my dear, is why magic isn't for the faint of heart. Find a quiet space and give it a try."

There was that word again. *Try.* As if all she had to do was make an attempt.

In this, at least, she would. "I'll work on it."

A group of teenagers burst into the clearing, increasing the noise level exponentially. Seeing her dismissal as imminent, Daughtry thanked to him then crossed through the now-crowded space to the same path Cody had taken. The bond strengthened, became more finite as she got closer to him.

"*Cody?*"

He appeared a heartbeat later, face smooth, eyes happy, until they drifted to her ear. He frowned, his hand moving like lightning to snatch the flower there. He held it between his fingers like a bag of dog poop.

His side of the bond was clouded, twisted, as if he warred with himself. "What's the matter?" she asked, distracted. She was anxious to get started on the exercise.

"Why did he give you this?"

She shrugged. "I guess he was being sweet." If being gifted with a potential invasive species was sweet.

The bond iced over. "No one else is allowed to give you flowers." He glared. "*You shouldn't have accepted it*".

"*Allowed?*" Annoyance won out over her preoccupation. "Cool it, Mr. High-and-Mighty. It's not like you've been lining up to give them to me. Why shouldn't I enjoy it when someone else does?"

Cody opened his mouth to retort.

"Let's go," she said, so not wanting to have the discussion.

The bond buzzed angrily in her ears. This was beyond possessive. It was ridiculous.

"You're the one who wanted me to talk to him," she muttered.

"Not give you flowers." He shortened his strides to accommodate her shorter legs, even as his anger battered at the connection in her mind.

Daughtry snatched the flower out of his hand, threw it on the ground, and crushed it below her foot. "Happy?" She pointed to the smashed stem and petals. "That means nothing to me, beyond it's pretty to look at. This"—her finger jabbed him in the chest—"means more. Controlling. Hot-headed. Misogynist." She'd been so sure that he was different. But this reaction, so out of proportion for such a small thing, reminded her too much of Jimmy.

Cody's face sobered. "Daughtry, that's not what I meant. It's a stupid flower."

"Exactly."

She turned, her eyes burning with unshed tears, and strode away.

TWENTY-FIVE

"OF ALL THE PIG-HEADED--"

"Daughtry," Suz said.

She looked over, still balefully watching the bond for any signs of Cody's pursuit. So far, he hadn't moved except to depart the gardens and go to his quarters.

Alternating between raring for a fight and wanting to apologize, she wasn't sure if she wanted him to or not.

"Daughtry," Suz said again. "He's a man."

"Hmph." That much was clear at least. "So maybe I'm a little sensitive." She ignored Suz's snort. "But how dare he go all He-Man on me? Even if he's sincere in trying to help me. It reminds me too much of—"

She broke off and closed her mouth. She didn't want to think about Jimmy. About the person she'd been with him.

To keep the memories at bay, she scooped up Suz's list of things to do and studied it. Unfortunately she'd been so efficient there wasn't much left on it. Her eyes traveled around the smallest of the exam rooms that functioned as overflow for patients and Suz's office.

There had to be something for Daughtry to accomplish,

even if it was organizing Band-Aids. She'd just grabbed a cardboard box of supplies when Suz spoke again.

"Reminds you too much of whom?" she asked. Her face was carefully placid, but her eyes were a mix of concern and pity.

The pity, at least, irritated her enough that she didn't feel like a slobbering pile of weakness. "It doesn't matter anymore."

"The hell it doesn't," Suz said with a penetrating stare. "Tell me. Now. Who do I need to kill?"

Annoyed at Suz's persistence, Daughtry glared.

But the truth was, she *did* want to tell someone. If only so the past would no longer have that hold on her.

"My former fiancé."

Her friend let out a breath that was equal parts sympathy and relief.

"Jimmy was an idiot—a cruel idiot—but one nonetheless." Even now, the memories made her palms sweat.

Suz patted the space next to her on the exam table and Daughtry hopped up, settling herself on the crinkling paper. She wiped her hands on her pants, stared down at the dark wash of her jeans.

"I've always been afraid of small, dark spaces." A flash of her in the pitch-black, legs flailing uselessly against the metal frame of Jimmy's Beamer. "Kids — and my ex-fiancé could certainly have been considered one—being as they typically are, thought to cure me of it by tying me up and leaving me in the trunk of a car." Tears welled. She forced them back. "It didn't work. I'll just leave it at that."

Her subsequent lack of pride was worse.

"A year later, our parents encouraged us to date. I was too embarrassed to say anything, too afraid to be ostracized from the cool kids, too scared of disappointing my folks." Clenching her fist, she banged it on her thigh. "I allowed someone to abuse me and just took it."

She'd let it go much further: reporting to him where she'd been, wearing only a certain brand of clothes, having sex before she'd felt ready.

In the past she'd been too much of a coward to stand up for herself, but that wasn't going to happen again. She tore a strip of paper off the roll covering the exam table and crumpled it into a ball. If she kept her hands moving, she could almost pretend the words coming out of her mouth were part of someone else's story instead of her own.

"Some sick part of me agreed that it made sense for us to be together. That Jimmy—his parents' money—was a good catch. My own parents would finally be accepted into the group they'd been vying for, finally have the money they claimed they needed."

They'd been beyond disappointed when the engagement had broken.

But it had been a good thing, because, with John's help, she'd drifted back into herself. Out of Jimmy's control, it was like a spell had broken. Daughtry could see clearly, breathe fully for the first time in ages.

Freedom had been good for her.

But then he parents had confronted her, demanded she go back, or at the very least cash the check Jimmy's parents had sent. She'd refused, of course, and had finally been on her way to making a decent life for herself when the visions struck.

"At the time it did it made sense," she said, pushing off the table. She wanted Suz to understand that the girl who'd put herself through that was different than the woman Daughtry was now. "It seemed like a good match."

"For whom?" Suz stood and gripped Daughtry's shoulders. Her voice was filled with venom. "Certainly not you. Not with someone so cruel. Not just for money."

Daughtry shook her head. "No, not for me." She stared at the bold amethyst wall, packed with bright white cabinetry, and said into the silence, "I'm sure there are a fair number of arranged marriages, or at least *matches,* here."

The Rengalla seemed aristocratically heavy. Surely, they had their own customs for marrying off their progeny.

"We have many problems. But I count myself lucky that it's frowned upon to marry for something other than love." Suz grimaced. "A millennium is too long to live without devotion and passion. And we don't do divorce. We seek to resolve our problems with discussion." She rolled her eyes, indicating what she thought of such methods. "Oodles and oodles of talking."

The laugh that burst out of Daughtry surprised her.

"Which is probably why I haven't married yet," Suz said and gave her a light squeeze on her shoulder. "Give your relationship with Cody a chance. I'd be more worried if you *weren't* arguing. At least this means that you both care enough to fight."

With that, Suz rubbed her hands together. "Now, enough *talking*. Help me organize the new shipment of supplies and then I have some charts that need to be transcribed."

"CODY?" Daughtry called, later that night as she walked through the door to his rooms. Wary green eyes shot to hers, but he obligingly put down the pen he'd been writing with. "I'm sorry," she said. "I shouldn't have reacted—"

A wave of relief crashed into her through the bond. "No," he said. "It was my fault. I wasn't trying to control you. I just—"

"*It's okay.*"

He winced. "It's not. I saw enough of that asshole in your memories to know better. I—" A sharp breath. "Every time I'm apart from you, my emotions get all twisted up. I don't know if it's the bond messing with me or just my own idiotic self." He closed the distance between them. "Regardless, I was jealous and stupid, and it won't happen again."

Her heart thumped. "It's okay," she said again. "And, really, I understand. I feel the same way." She cupped his cheek. "Truly, you're about as different from Jimmy as humanly possible."

"Thank you for understanding."

She nodded.

They were quiet for a long stretch before Cody spoke, "It's late and I'm off patrol tonight. I'll find somewhere else to crash."

It took her a minute to understand what he was saying, to realize that this was the first night they'd be together at bedtime. *Bed.* Her cheeks heated. So far, they'd avoided the whole sleeping-together topic because she'd either been unconscious or Cody had been doing his LexTal duties.

He picked up a duffle bag he must have packed earlier. "I'll see you in the morning."

Her body wanted him to stay, to strip her naked and lick her like a lollipop, but her body was also somewhat ahead of her heart. Still, there was some middle ground to be found. She nudged him toward the chair. "Sit down and *turn around.*"

Cody rotated so his back was to her.

She stripped off everything except her panties and tank top then slid under the covers. The cool cotton smelled like him, and his presence just a few feet away made her stomach clench. There was something exhilarating about lying in Cody's bed almost naked, his mind brushing against hers, his masculine presence a cloud that filled the room.

It was oppressive. It was awesome. She'd never been more aroused.

And frightened.

Jimmy had used sex as a weapon, had wielded it to slice away her confidence. Before him she'd been comfortable in her own skin. Now she felt insecure. Still, she could read Cody's mind. His intention to let her set the pace of their intimate relationship was as clear as a billboard.

He wouldn't force her.

That gave her confidence. Hope that one day she'd be able to shed the emotional baggage of her relationship with Jimmy.

Her voice shook a little, but she kept speaking anyway. "That chair doesn't look very comfortable."

Cody had stepped out of his shoes even before her lips fully managed the sentence. A half-smirk softened the hard line of his scar as he slid under the covers, fully dressed aside from his boots, and still trying to put her at ease. The ball of fear in her gut loosened.

"It is more comfortable than the floor, however," he said.

"You should know I'm horrible at sex," she blurted. Cody went motionless, several feet of space between them, and she found herself scooting toward him.

He burst out laughing. "You're kidding, right?"

"No," she said, her cheeks hot. "I'm just not good at it. It hurts, and Jimmy said—"

"Stop right there." He tucked a finger under her chin and forced her to meet his eyes. "That name doesn't get spoken in this bed." She might have bristled at the command in his tone if not for the relief coursing through her. "And you're not horrible at all," he said, "In fact, you're quite good at torturing me."

"What do you mean?" she asked, giving into the urge to get closer to him, wrapping her arms around his neck, nuzzling his shoulder.

He sucked in a breath of air and spoke through gritted teeth. "Seriously? You're being all sweet and cuddling, but all I can think is that your hand is exactly six inches above my—"

"Cody!" She hadn't noticed before, but the hard length of him was pressed against her thigh.

He shrugged, but his lips were twitching. "You're the most innocent temptress I've ever met."

The stiffness that had come into her shoulders without her even realizing it dissipated. Cody was a balm to past hurts. His attraction to her was obvious and she knew he wouldn't use it like a weapon. He'd cherish it, use it to make them stronger, to give them a chance—

"Possibilities," he thought, the words flowing like liquid courage across the bond. *"You make me feel as though the frozen fist that has for so long choked my heart could just melt away."*

"That's beautiful," she whispered and knew exactly what he meant.

Their connection took away the games. There could be no pouting, no pretending nothing was wrong without the other knowing, if not the truth, then at least the emotions behind their actions.

They made sense together.

The truth hit her like a baseball bat to the kidney. She loved him. But it was a tentative love, like the first buds of an apple tree.

With time, the leaves would unfurl, the flowers bloom, the bees come to pollinate. And perhaps it would be luck, or simply Mother Nature, but if they fed the connection, maybe it would one day bear a whole, ripe fruit.

A relationship that could nourish them both.

SHE STOOD outside John's door, her fist poised to knock. The same way it had been for the last five minutes. He was leaving the next day, taking Mason and both of the new recruits with him to investigate some suspicious activity outside Seattle.

Her stomach clenched at the thought of him in danger, that he might get injured again, that he might die.

That it might be her fault.

The door whipped open, and she jumped.

He stood there, slightly rumpled, stubble on his cheeks and his hair mussed. There was a smile on his lips, but his eyes held a little-boy vulnerability that made her feel awful all over again.

His face sobered. "No, don't do that." He reached forward, tugged her into his room, his arms. He wrapped her in a tight hug. "I'm fine, sweetheart."

"I—uh. It—"

"I'm not leaving because of what happened." John released her and crouched down a little so that he could meet her eyes.

His dark blue ones weren't ringed with soul-shattering pain or even anger.

Instead, it was acceptance that she saw in his gaze.

"This is my job," he said. "It's important. There are Rengalla who slip through the cracks. Kids whose parents live on the edges of our society or some who left by choice and have no way of getting back when they need. I have to go."

Daughtry sank onto his desk chair. "I understand." Her eyes flew up when he snorted. "I do! I just can't help but think—"

"That's it's because things didn't work out between us?"

Well, didn't that sound egotistical? She shrugged, a little annoyed at herself for thinking just that. She and John had only ever been a possibility and one that hadn't worked out. To have gotten herself all worked up when she should have known better—

He grinned. "I'll admit," he said. "That it will be easier to not see you and Cody together. But I'm over a hundred years old, Daughtry. I've had my heart broken before. I'll survive."

Her throat went tight. "*I* broke your heart?"

"God, sweetheart. *That's* what you heard?" He closed the

few feet of space between them and rested his hands on her shoulders. "How about dinged? And anyway, I'm trying to tell you that *I'm okay*." He paused, gazed into her eyes. "You're pretty incredible. But . . . it's not all about you."

That made her feel better, made the guilt she'd been carrying around about coming between John and Cody, by being the evil temptress—*ha!*—in this situation, go away, even as her ego took a little hit.

She *had* been making it all about her and *her* feelings. It was time to change that.

"You'll be careful?" she asked, standing.

He came to his feet, followed her to the door. "Always."

She slid her arms around him and gave him a quick squeeze. "John?"

"Yeah?"

"You're pretty incredible yourself."

TWENTY-SIX

"GOD, Suz," Daughtry said, slamming the textbook closed and setting it on the stack of more than a dozen of the same. Her study material was taking up more than one-half of the counter-space in Suz's office. "It might as well be gibberish." Or oversized paperweights.

"Well, Francis doesn't do things halfway."

"I can see that," she said, keeping her eyes on the teetering stack. "But tell that to the piles in my room."

She might not be so cranky if she could actually do the task Francis had set forth. So far, she hadn't succeeded in making any sign of a flame or fireball. No matter how easy it was supposed to have been.

Suz laughed, thumbed through the titles, held up one, *The History of the Rengalla 200 B.C. to 740 AD*. "From his choices, it appears he's trying to make you fall asleep."

Daughtry snickered. It was true. She *had* slept well the past few nights, helped by the heavy reading and the tentative peace between her and Cody.

Who, to her equal parts of longing and relief, had returned to his patrols.

It had been pleasant to be in bed next to him, except her body had vacillated so readily between aroused and relaxed that it hadn't brought the most restful night's sleep. She'd been unable to make the first move, and Cody was content with waiting until she was.

Hard to believe he could be so pushy in some things but perfectly patient in that way.

Not that his mind was waiting.

No, it kept conjuring up smutty images that nearly scalded their way across the bond. How was a girl supposed to concentrate with those pictures plastered to her skull?

"My smutty thoughts?"

The question brought a smile to her lips, and Suz sighed in disgust. Apparently, she got a certain look on her face when Cody was near. Which was often, since he'd been sneaking in to see her on a regular basis.

Her cheeks flushed when she remembered how he'd left her the last time—hair mussed, mouth red and swollen. It would have been obvious to anyone, let alone a doctor, what they'd been doing.

"Go on, then," Suz said. "But be here bright and early tomorrow."

Snagging a couple of the books, Daughtry hurried out into the hall. Cody tucked them under his arm and grabbed her hand.

His eyes narrowed. "When's the last time you ate?" he asked as he rifled through her memories of the day. She found that she didn't hate it when he checked up on her that way. Because it was concern and not possessiveness that drove him to do so. She rolled her eyes at herself. At this rate, she'd be better off just turning in her feminist card. "I ate when you brought me something."

He sighed in frustration. "You're lucky I'm here. That was ten hours ago."

"Oh," she said. "I hadn't noticed."

She and Suz had been busy cleaning up the results of a dodgeball game gone wrong. There'd been multiple skinned knees, one broken arm, and two black eyes. Then she'd tried to tackle the textbooks and summon fire.

"The day just slipped away."

Cody huffed, but Daughtry felt his annoyance fade away. *I'm glad you're settling in,* he said. "But promise me you'll eat."

"I promise," she muttered. *Thanks, Mom.*

"Because"—he ignored her quip, fixed her with a fierce look—"Be forewarned that if you don't do a better job of taking care of yourself, I'll pester you and Suz to death by showing up with three square meals and snacks for the both of you."

"God no, no that!" she said in mock-horror. "Not *snacks!*" She smirked because the truth was that his concern touched her. *Hey, He-Man?*

Yeah? he replied across the bond, his amusement at her awful nickname filling her, warming her all the way to her toes.

Thanks.

The amusement turned to affection as Cody wrapped his arms around and pulled her against his chest. She could hear the beat of his heart under her ear, the steady rhythm a comfort.

"Suz works too hard," she said when he'd released her, and they started walking again.

"She does. The infirmary is her baby." An unspoken blip along their connection revealed there was more to the story than a hard worker.

"What happened?"

"Doc will tell you in her own time."

"I hope so," she murmured. God knows, she'd blabbed to Suz enough about her own demons.

"Wait here," Cody said, leaving her in a small alcove outside the cafeteria. He returned a few minutes later, the textbooks replaced with a small bag, its contents clinking together as he hitched it onto his shoulder.

"Look! This one even has fish under the water." Daughtry pressed her finger to a mural of a river and showed him the salmon swimming their way upstream. Bright purple threads of her magic gathered in the spot, lingering for a moment before sliding away to nothing.

"Yes, very pretty . . ." He snagged her hand. "Let's go, cowgirl. I can feel your hunger."

She allowed him to drag her away. "Why do you keep calling me that?"

"Call you what?"

"Don't play coy." She pinched his hip.

Cody jumped then groaned. "I wish you hadn't found that spot."

She raised her brows, a silent admonishment to answer her question or she'd find his ticklish spot for a second time.

"I'd dare anyone who saw you launch yourself on that Dalshie's back, John's sword in your hand to call you anything different. You were fierce, your eyes flashing, and . . . just beautiful. I could call you something else. Shooter, maybe? Or Quick Draw?" He waggled his brows. "Slayer?"

She snorted. "No, I've decided I'm fine with cowgirl."

"Good," he said. "Because I've got a pair of boots and a hat—"

"Cody!"

He just laughed, and they walked in amiable silence. A few doors they passed bore a crest identical to the ones on Cody's and John's doors. At the top of the insignia was the Latin phrase *Lex Talionis* and below that, a falcon—or maybe an eagle—wore a crown of thorns as it clutched a branch in its talons.

"What does it mean?"

Cody was silent for a long moment. *"Relentless. Humility. Adversity. Honor."* He paused. *"Retribution."*

Daughtry understood the silent distinction. The Rengalla wouldn't kill for vengeance, wouldn't commit violence for the sake of violence. They protected the innocent.

And that very notion meant they would kill to do just that.

"Come on," he said and opened the door to the gardens. A few steps in, he slid off the trail, leading her down a small break in the foliage.

As he held a branch aside, her eyes were drawn to the way his muscles rippled under the thin cotton shirt he wore. He was so much stronger, more physically capable in ways she'd never be. That he could take her into his arms, throw her over his shoulder with little effort . . . that strength was intoxicating.

God. Anyone would think she was a love-struck teenager, the way she was drooling after him.

"Maybe lust-struck," Cody thought. *"And I'm no different. Christ, you're beautiful. Come here."* He'd plunked himself on a bench. *"No, wait. Don't. Or we'll never get around to eating."*

He opened the bag and pulled out the contents.

"Oh." She clamped a hand over her mouth. Cereal? Really? The man was adorable.

Cody's face fell, and she hurried to reassure him. "No. That wasn't laughter at you. It was happiness," she said. There was a definitely learning curve when trying to differentiate emotions across the bond, especially when several feelings came at once. She didn't want there to be any misunderstanding between them in this case. "It's the sweetest thing anyone has ever done for me."

A smirk tugged up his lips as he poured the cereal and milk into two bowls. "That's sad," he said, setting a package into her hands. "Happy anniversary."

"What?" Daughtry fumbled a little to keep from dropping it.

"It's our one-week anniversary." Her brow furrowed. They'd been together longer than that. "One week without a fight," he added.

She laughed until her sides hurt, and when she could breathe again, he closed his hands over hers. "Open it."

Her fingers tore off the wrapping paper to reveal a small velvet box. She opened it and a sigh escaped her. "Oh, Cody."

"Do you like it?"

"I love it."

He pulled out the necklace and drew her close to clasp it around her neck. Daughtry traced the charm with shaking fingers. "A violet?"

"Like your eyes." He pressed a kiss to her forehead. "And because this way I get to always give you flowers."

Tears filled her eyes, happy ones for a change.

A rogue one slipped down her cheek, and she swiped it away.

He thrust a bowl into her hands, the frantic effort of a man trying to prevent a woman from breaking down into sobs. "Eat. You're hungry."

The little round circles of corn were the best meal she'd ever eaten. Daughtry hadn't been lying when she'd told him it was the nicest thing anyone had ever done for her. Cody, for his part, was a study in soldiering as he ate, his gaze on their surroundings, scanning with a part of his mind that never seemed to turn off.

"What?" he asked, focusing the full force of his attention on her.

"Nothing." The clearing was dim, and what muted light snuck through gave Cody a golden hue, highlighting the green of his eyes, the blond of his hair. Finding that she couldn't resist, she reached forward to run a fingertip across one dappling of brightness on his chest.

His bowl made a clinking sound as he plunked it on the bench.

"What—?"

He took advantage of her confusion by pulling her into his lap, and stealing her lips in a blazing kiss. With a moan, she wrapped her arms tightly around his neck, pressed her body against his. When he slipped his tongue in between her lips, she nipped his playfully in response.

"*So fucking hot.*" He groaned across the bond.

"Mmm," she agreed, reveling in his taste of his mouth. It was slightly salty like the ocean and tart enough to make her want more. She moved closer, her lips frantic as they tried to reach every inch of him—his cheek, his jaw, his ear. He was her fix, and she needed all of him.

"Enough teasing," he groaned, grabbing her face, slanting their lips so he could devour her mouth fully.

His erection was rock-hard and pulsing where it sat snugly between her thighs and she couldn't stop herself from writhing against its steel length, from wanting so much more than a simple kiss.

"*Simple? I resent that,*" Cody thought, eavesdropping. He picked her up and placed her on the bench. Then he knelt on the ground to kiss her from a better angle. He took his time, making no movement to take it any further. Even when she reached forward and tried to pull him closer, he resisted.

She couldn't stop the frustrated noise from escaping her throat, the sharp words from her lips. "*I won't break, damn it!*"

He stopped and leaned back, hands resting on her thighs. He traced them up the outsides of her legs, down the insides, and the vibration of his fingers through her jeans had her cursing him under her breath. If she didn't get more—

"*Is there a problem?*"

"Yes." She resisted the urge to cross her arms, trying not to feel vulnerable. She knew he wanted her. But why did he keep going so slow? She was ready—

"You're the first."

"Your *first*?" she shrieked, mortification staining her cheeks crimson. "Oh my God. I'm so sorry. We'll take all the time you need!" She shoved herself out of his arms and staggered away, guilt tearing through her. Having had personal experience with being pressured, she knew what it was like. To be the one doing the pushing—she fisted her hands as guilt raced through her.

"All of the times I—" he broke off, probably catching a glimpse of her horror across the bond. "What are you talking about?" Clarity dawned on his face after a moment. "I'm not a virgin! Christ, cowgirl."

He was so outraged that her horror dissipated, hysterical giggles in its place.

"You—said—" she gasped as she gestured between the two of them. "I—you—the first!"

"The first woman I've *loved*! Not the first person I've had sex with." A curse as he shoved his hands through his hair, an adorable blush coloring his cheeks pink. He paused. "Dammit. I didn't mean to say that yet. Not that it matters, I guess," he muttered, "since you can read my mind."

Her laughter had halted at his declaration, hope and fear slamming into her. She'd loved before, and look where it had gotten her. But Cody was different. *They* were be different. So she shoved away the fear, concentrating instead on the joy his words had given her.

"Do you mean it?" she asked softly.

He strode over to her, frown fierce. "*Of course* I mean it. I wouldn't lie about something like that. I just don't want to force you to say—"

She slammed her mouth against his, swallowing the words whole.

When she finally broke away, they were both breathing hard.

"Cody, I—"

"Seriously, cowgirl, don't feel like you have to say anything back."

"I was just going to say—"

"No, don't say anything. Because then I'll feel like it's only in response to what I said and that I made—"

"Cody, stop."

He clamped his lips closed, tension radiating off him across the bond.

She smiled. "All I wanted to say was that you have a leaf in your hair."

"That's it!" But he was laughing as he grabbed her around the waist and tackled her to the ground. He cradled her against the fall with his arms before tickling his fingers across her waist. *"Where's your spot? Fair's fair."*

"I'll never tell," she gasped as she wriggled away from his hands, trying her best to fight back. Success was found when she discovered a new spot on his thigh.

In turn, he was relentless as he found the place behind her knee, his fingers teasing as they tickled, then serious as they traveled further north to find a place that wasn't ticklish at all.

Suddenly she wasn't laughing. Cody's hand pressed between her thighs and pleasure radiated out to all her limbs. They drank each other's mouths, the kiss long and slow and scorching. She felt crazed, ready to tear off her clothes. His too, if necessary.

But he'd sensed her fever pitch, and he slowed the kisses again, turning them soft, teasing.

She pulled away to catch her breath. He had her head spinning.

"How could you think that skill was from a virgin?" he teased even as he kept his distance from her.

She reached for him.

He took a surreptitious step back.

Not this again.

A plan struck her. "I don't know. I'm not quite convinced." She fluttered her lashes. "Want to have another go at persuading me? Or maybe I should find one of the triplets."

He lunged for her. She sat up and gave him a peck on the cheek before pulling away.

Done with the teasing, Daughtry ran. There would be no more build-up. The only thing she was stopping for was a nice, soft bed. Or chair. Or supply closet. Laughter bubbled out of her as she scurried quickly through the halls, aware of Cody on her heels. His predatory presence pulsed along the bond as he stalked her.

It was possible that she might have finally succeeded in breaking his control.

That should have made her nervous rather than excited.

It was almost tempting to stop and let him catch her. But then he'd probably find another way to delay things. Besides, she was almost there. She turned left. Excitement bubbled through her—her excess power staining the walls with a wide violet streak as she rushed by.

He was close, the beat of his arousal molten across the bond.

Daughtry rounded the corner. *"I'm coming for you, cowgirl."*

The mental voice raised goose bumps all over her body.

"I'm giving you two minutes. Then we'll—"

"You have to catch me first," she interrupted, sending an image of the pair of them in the shower. Hot, soapy hands running over his body, trailing down his abs.

"You'll pay for that."

She paused at a corner, chest heaving, trying to remember if the turn was left or right. Her knees almost buckled when Cody sent a much dirtier, much more R-rated version of her fantasy into her mind—

She was pinned against the shower wall, water pulsing against her breasts, teasing her nipples. He kissed his way up her legs, shoving them apart until his shoulders could fit between her thighs. His mouth descended—

"You're dangerous."

Left, she realized and ran down the hallway.

"You like it."

"Yes. Yes, I do," she murmured, feeling the bond strengthen as he got closer. *"I definitely will want a rain check on that one."*

There it was!

She dashed the last thirty feet, her hand just missing the lock panel as his body slammed into hers.

His chest was hard against her back, scorching when compared to the cold metal of the door. He kissed her nape, tracing burning lines across it before he flipped her around and hauled her up to his lips. Her hands came up to grab his shoulders and she encircled his waist with her legs, needing to get closer. He grabbed her ass, clutching her tight, grinding into her and causing them both to moan in pleasure.

Finally her brain screamed for oxygen. She tore her mouth away, breathless.

His head dropped to her shoulder, lips pressed against her throat.

"Please." She panted, nipples brushing against his chest, and thinking she might just die from the violence of her need.

"I couldn't stop," he said, his voice ragged, his hot breath raising gooseflesh on her skin. "Not even if you begged me too."

One of his hands wrapped tighter to support her ass, the other slammed against the sensor on the door. It opened after what felt like the two longest seconds of her life. Finally, they were inside, mouths fused together—tongues dueling. She shrieked when he tossed her onto the bed, but then he was on top of her, his eyes darkened by desire to a deep emerald.

"I love you," he said, and the sureness of his words trickled across the bond, solidifying his oath.

She froze.

There was a reason she hadn't said it before.

Her panic and desires were still tangled together in a heap of emotions.

What if she screwed this up?

He cupped her cheek, kissed her tenderly. *"Together,"* he *murmured. "We'll figure this out together."* His fingers brushed down her jaw, her neck, the outside of her ribs, then back up, but he stopped his teasing fingers just below her breasts. His breathing—*and hers*—was erratic, the pulse at the base of his neck jumping rapidly. "Fuck, you're sexy."

It hit her then. *She*, not some perfect, plastic–Barbie-doll version of herself, had caused him to feel that way. He wanted her as she was. That opened her lungs, allowed her to breathe. His gaze meandered down her body, eyeing her simple shirt and jeans like they were a corset and thigh-highs. Adoration assaulted her through the bond and the last piece of fear that Daughtry had been grappling with fell away. She could see, could *feel* his love with every beat of her heart.

When he leaned down to kiss her again, she stopped him, placing a finger across his mouth.

"Epiphany happening."

The bond prevented them from hiding anything from each other. If he was playing her, she'd know, but more than that, they were connected so deeply that she *knew* he wouldn't hurt her.

He nuzzled her neck. "Have I given you enough time to think?" His tongue darted out and caressed the spot where her throat met her shoulder.

"Yes." She slid her hands up to weave her fingers through the hair at the nape, inhaling his ocean and pine scent. "*You love me.*"

"Yes." He trailed a line of kisses along her throat.

"*We're meant for each other.*" She tugged his head toward her mouth, desperate for another kiss.

"Yes." He obliged.

"*Okay then.*"

He laughed.

"*Let's try not to screw it up, okay?*"

He laughed harder. "*Agreed, cowgirl.*" Then his tongue succeeded in distracting her.

Eventually he sat back onto his heels. Thinking he was going to stop again, she groaned in protest. It was short-lived, however. Only a brief rustle of fabric as he tore off his shirt then came back to press his hard chest against hers.

"Mmm."

His hands found the hem of her top. She reached down, hindering in her efforts to help him in removing the cumbersome layer.

Then, *finally.*

A rush of cool air was the only thing she felt before his hot mouth descended. Stubble scraped her skin in a pleasant sting and when he nibbled just above her hipbone, lights flashed behind her eyes. She barely noticed when he unsnapped the top of her jeans and slid them off. Her bra followed suit, torn off in the barest of a second to leave her clad only in her panties.

"Yours too," she said in a voice that was so husky she almost didn't recognize it.

His eyes were intense as he stood, drinking in every inch of her. His jeans fell to the floor, followed by his boxer briefs. Then he was back in bed, perched over her, forearms on either side of her head. Despite the need raging through her, despite his erection pressing against her hip, he gently eased the pace from frenzied to unhurried. Soft fingers pulled out her ponytail and ran through her hair, moving the strands off her face to fan out over the pillow. Those fingertips made a lackadaisical path down her neck and shoulders and traced a wide berth around her breasts before continuing down the plane of her stomach. He paused.

She looked up into his gaze, and her heart swelled so much that it threatened to burst from her chest. No one had ever looked at her like that.

Like she was the most important person in the universe.

"You are the most beautiful thing I've ever seen." The words were soft, nearly tear-inducing. He pressed his lips to hers in a sweet, perfect kiss. She cradled his cheek. Her vision slightly blurry, her heart full. For once, she could believe she might actually be worthy of such intense love.

"I'm glad," he teased. *"Maybe that means you'll stop fighting me over it."* His lips quirked and he coaxed a smile out of hers.

"Don't hold your breath," she teased back.

He snorted and the quiet moment was pushed aside.

"I want you," she said. *"Now,"* she ordered when he continued to press kisses against her torso. He ignored her, grinding his erection against her core, the thin material of her underwear doing nothing to block the delicious pressure. His fingers teased along their hem but resisted giving her what she wanted. Instead, he pumped his hard length between her thighs, each stroke teasing. The rhythm was maddening.

The hell with it.

The next time he leaned away, readying himself for the next torturous swipe, she pulled the crotch of her underwear to the side. And felt . . . nothing.

Her eyes flew up in shock. Cody knelt over her, a glistening of sweat across his chest, his abs rippling with strain.

But his face was calm. He raised a brow. "Losing patience?"

Before she could say anything, his fingers came to her hips. He tore the straps, yanked the material free, and tossed her ruined underwear somewhere in the vicinity of his clothes.

His jaw was tight, his teeth clenched, and his hips angled forward, hard seeking soft.

She moaned, every nerve in her body on fire, needing more.

He stroked forward, fitting himself between her legs, rubbing up and down but not where she needed him. Not *in*.

"Cody," she said. It was a plea, it was begging, but she didn't care. She wrapped her legs around his waist and dug her heels into his ass, trying desperately to get him where she wanted.

Curses erupted from his mouth. He pulled back—her legs came loose—head hanging, breaths coming in panting gasps.

"Dammit!" Emerald eyes glared at her, as desire and affection warred along the bond. *"I want to make it good for you."*

A different kind of war was going on in her mind until, finally, she relinquished her hard-fought control. *"Fine."* She crossed her arms. *"Do your worst."*

Yes, she may have been a little surly, but she was in desperate need of an orgasm.

"You'll get plenty of those, I promise."

"Fine. But I get to do you next time."

Cody quirked a brow and she blushed.

"Oh, shut up." She narrowed her eyes. *"You know what I mean."*

"Mmm-hmm." He rubbed his stubble on the underside of her breasts, sensitizing the skin there, teasing her nipples into tight beads. She fought not to grab his head, to make him do it again. But since he could read her mind, he obliged her anyway.

"I may have seen most of your memories, but I have no idea what kind of kinky fantasies you have rolling around in there." The words were slightly muffled from the meandering route of kisses he was placing around her chest.

"I—*ah*—"

He took one nipple into his mouth and sucked. "Yes?" He paused in his exploration then kissed his way over to her other breast.

"Nothing . . ." She gasped when he gave her neglected nipple the same treatment. "Weird. Strictly mission—*ah*—ary."

A bite to the hard, aching nub had her moaning in pleasure.

"We'll remedy that part at least." He moved his body down to crouch between her knees and cupped between her thighs.

She arched, writhing in impatience—thrusting against his hand. "Please." She didn't know what she wanted. A hundred different things. His fingers. His mouth. His c—

He slid two fingers inside her, easily finding a rhythm that had her grabbing the sheets. His thumb traced up and pressed against the bundle of nerves at the apex of her thighs.

"Fuck. Cody, I need—"

Withdrawing his hand, he bent to put his mouth on her, groan vibrating against her, raising goose bumps, heightening her pleasure.

Every muscle in her body tensed. She was so close.

He pressed his tongue firmly against her clit, plunging his fingers back inside, curling them forward.

"Oh fuck," she moaned.

Then she was over the edge, rivers of pleasure exploding through her, dragging her under, until she could barely feel her legs. *Hours later, it seemed,* she floated leisurely back to earth, languid, satisfied.

Cody was holding her, bringing her down, running his palms in circular patterns from her shoulders down to her hips. "Okay?"

She didn't deign that question with an answer. Instead, she reached down and wrapped her fingers around his hard length. *"Now, Cody."*

*He cursed, brushing her hands away, b*ut rose over her, his elbows on either side of her head. She was mesmerized by the way his biceps bulged, how a light sheen of sweat made his skin shine. One hand trailed down and stroked his cock.

Throwing his head back, Cody pumped into her palm. "Cowgirl—"

His words cut off when she slid down, mouth following the path of her hand. But she had just closed her lips over him when he gripped her shoulders and yanked her back up.

"Not today," he said, his breaths coming roughly.

She relented because she was right there with him, the throb between her legs back with a vengeance. Only one thing would soothe that ache, and it was pulsing quite determinedly against her thigh.

He bent, stole her lips in a blazing kiss.

"Now," she said when they came up for air.

He pressed forward, starting to slide into her, then pulled out and cursed. "Condom."

"Suz took care of me. I'm safe. I can't get pregnant." And since the Rengalla apparently didn't get STDs . . . "Hurry."

"Thank God," he said, obliging her and taking her body in a slow, excruciating thrust. He paused, hilt deep, to let her acclimatize.

When she tilted her hips, aching for more of him, desperate for him to move, needing him deeper, he groaned. "Cowgirl. Please God. Tell me you're with me."

"Yes. *Now*, Cody."

Finally, he moved, pulling out, thrusting in. Everything faded except for the press of his chest against hers, the feel of him inside of her, the stream of love showering her across the bond.

It was everything—and more—that she'd hoped it would be.

"I can't wait," he said, starting to slow.

"If you stop, I will kill you." She grabbed his ass and pulled him deeper.

That was enough to shatter his restraint. He slammed into her. The tension inside of her spiraled higher, higher until—

Their shouts mingled as they came.

When their breathing slowed, Cody rested his forehead against hers for a moment before sliding to the side and tucking her into his chest. "God, I love you."

Her heart had been shattered into a million pieces then glued effortlessly back together by this man, by his love, his protection, his care with her body and soul. Daughtry wanted to shout her love in return, to bare her soul to him so completely that nothing lay between them.

Except Cody was already drifting off, his eyes closed, his breathing steady, his mind quiet along the bond.

She rested her head across his chest.

His hands clenched in her hair then went limp as sleep stole him away.

"I love you too."

SHE WOKE a short time later to water running. Stretching, she groaned and snuggled into the mattress, enjoying the salty scent of Cody teasing her nose.

"Why aren't you in bed?" She was grouchy. He should be next to her.

The bathroom door opened, pouring light into the bedroom, spotlighting Cody's fabulous naked body. Her tongue went dry as he strolled over. The memory of his strong body pressed tightly against hers was enough to send a shiver down her spine. Good grief, the man was hot.

"Want to join me?" His palm rested on her hip, drawing the lower half of her body to quivering attention.

"*No.*" She pulled the blanket over her head, feeling vulnerable all over again. Not to mention like she'd been ridden hard and put up wet.

"*Mmm. Speaking of wet, I know what will make you feel better.*" An image of sudsy hands drifted to her mind and made her smile despite herself.

"*Payback?*" she asked, daring to peek her eyes out. Cody stood with his arms crossed, one eyebrow raised in humor.

"Maybe just a little." He stooped, drew her off the bed, and scooped her up into his arms in one smooth moment. "Okay, a lot."

She squealed, trying to wiggle from his grasp, but he held firm. The door to the bathroom closed with a *thunk*, the large space cramped with six-plus feet of strong, turned-on male.

Especially since Cody crowded her, pressing his chest against her back as she bent to brush her teeth and splash water on her face.

But she didn't push him away, sensing that he needed the physical contact as much as she. The bond was strong, a pulsing force that connected them soul to soul. Any separation was a physical ache.

Daughtry hoped that it would settle soon. The last thing she needed was to replace alcohol with Cody. She'd wasted too much time drowning her sorrows with booze and didn't need another addiction. No matter the sexy package.

"I have no problem with becoming your new vice," he murmured in her ear.

"You wouldn't," she thought across the bond since her mouth was full of toothpaste. The moment her toothbrush clinked to the granite, he swept her up then plunked her on the counter.

"Cold!" she screeched as he held her still.

"You're gorgeous," he said. "Sexy. Tough. Strong." He punctuated each adjective with a kiss on her cheek, her jaw, her bare shoulder.

Daughtry blushed but forced herself to accept the compliments without argument for a change. "Thank you."

She reached for him. He leaned back. *"Payback, remember?"*

His hands slid to her hips and he tugged her to the edge of the granite.

"Oh no. It's—" She moaned, clenching the counter as pressed his mouth to her.

Cody smiled into her mind. *"I thought you liked me playful. You said it was sexy."*

"I never—"

Then he did something that felt so good it should have been illegal. Their pleasure intertwined, each fueling the other's, and when she couldn't take it any longer, she yanked up hard on his shoulders. A shift of his hips was all it took. Then he was inside her, thrusting in a rhythm that skyrocketed them both over the edge.

Afterward, he pulled the door to the shower open and plunked her in the stream. His hands were gentle as he washed her.

Post-sex tenderness was something she'd never experienced before. Jimmy would finish and fall asleep. She'd slide out from underneath him before he could smother her.

"Another reason for me to kill him."

"Don't waste your energy. He doesn't matter. Not anymore."

Surprisingly, that was the truth.

Yay for personal growth and maturity.

Soon her eyes were drifting shut. She leaned back against his chest, her limbs heavy. The water creaked off, the shower door opened, and a towel that smelled wonderfully of Cody wrapped around her. She peeked to see him with his own towel slung haphazardly around his hips.

It was a pity she was ready to fall asleep on her feet.

She felt his smirk across the bond as he led her out of the bathroom and slipped one of his T-shirts over her head.

"Come on. Let me tuck you in. I have to go do my patrol."

"I don't know how you're still standing," she murmured.

"Neither do I," he said, pulling the covers up and over her. *"Bye, cowgirl. Remember, you need me, I'll be here."*

The words wrapped around her mind as he departed.

Then sleep had her in its iron grip.

TWENTY-SEVEN

ASPHYXIATION JOLTED Daughtry from her peaceful sleep.

She forced open her eyes, vision already marred with black spots. A heavy body secured her as efficiently to the mattress as restraints. Initially she froze, thinking it was Cody and there was a reason he wanted her to hold still.

There was a sudden rush of noise, an alarm blaring to life outside the door.

"*Cody?*" she called across the bond. A faint buzz was the only response.

Acrid breath bombarded her nose. A cold hand found the hem of her shirt, pulling it up to expose her nakedness. Her skin revolted, almost crawling away from her skeleton in its effort to avoid those rough fingers.

It wasn't Cody.

That was her last rational thought.

She fought, punching and scratching anything she could make contact with. Her legs scissored as she struggled to find purchase on the bed. Finally, she shoved with her hands and feet, bucking upward. The man pinning her flew off.

She bolted for the door.

That was when she realized there was more than one of them.

Another strong pair of arms grabbed her and threw her back onto the bed.

She screamed, but the sound was cut off in an instant.

A fucking pillow silenced her.

Eventually, the fabric was peeled back, replaced with one intruder's hand.

She was surrounded by Dalshie. How had they gotten past the patrols?

What if Cody was hurt?

"Cody?" she called, louder this time but her mental voice hit a wall, bouncing back and reverberating in her skull hard enough to hurt.

Fear for him had her struggling again, but she only got in a single punch to the Dalshie on top of her. He barely flinched before nodding at his assistants. "Hold her." It took scarcely a moment before she was secured, spread-eagle, on the bed, a Dalshie holding each limb in a biting grip.

"Cody!" This time she screamed across the bond, panic numbing the pain of her echoing shouts. If she could yell loud enough, she might break through the barrier, and then he would hear. He'd promised he'd be come for her if she needed him.

She only had to hold on a little longer.

Kicking her legs, she wriggled a foot free, gaining a glancing blow to her attacker's nose. *"I need you!"*

Her reward for that bit of defiance was a punch to her face. Her cheek split open, but she managed to get a scream—a good, bloodcurdling one—out before the hand clamped back over her mouth.

She reached frantically over the bond and . . . nothing. That sense of aloneness was almost worse than what was happening to her body. She'd gotten used to the comfort of the connection.

She was outnumbered. Abandoned.

No.

Cody, John, *somebody* would come. She just had to stay alive, to stay sane for a little longer.

The leader looked between her legs and licked his lips. "I'm going to enjoy this."

She watched, horrified, as he unbuttoned his pants. He cupped himself, exposing a rancid-smelling pair of testicles.

Wrenching her head away from the hand covering it, she lost the previous evening's dinner. It covered her arm, staining the sheet. And yet, even the acrid scent of her own vomit was better than that of the man in front of her.

"Mmm," he said cruelly. "I do love the smell of fear while I'm in bed." His face was a study in hard lines and what had probably once been a great deal of handsomeness. But the malice in his eyes, the black stain creeping up his solid jaw, across the bridge of his sharp nose, stole any beauty he might have once possessed. It made him more frightening than any monster she'd ever seen.

"Fuck off," she said.

"No, sweet, I intend to fuck *you*."

"Goddammit, Cody! Please!"

It was futile to fight, restrained as she was, but when the leader shifted, inching his hips closer to her, she freaked.

She kicked and lurched. And it was for nothing. Her captors held fast.

That final burst of energy faded, and she lay panting on the bed, sweat soaking the sheets.

Her attacker smiled. She was utterly helpless.

The feeling returned her to the past, back to the days where the only way to cope was eighty proof—

Fuck that.

"Cody!!!" She shouted across the bond, loud enough to burst

her eardrums and with as much magic as she could muster with her limited skills.

Yes!

It pierced the fog shrouding the bond.

But her relief was gone in an instant because reality hit, and the only thing she got in return was panic. Cody knew she was in danger. He was coming. She could feel his terror and . . . something that scared her more than her attackers. He was injured, badly.

Horror slammed into her from across the bond.

Whatever had been constricting it was fading. Not that it mattered.

Cody wouldn't get there in time.

She almost wished their connection would go back to being blocked. At least that way he wouldn't see what was going to happen next.

"You fucking bitch," the leader said. "You burned me." He leaned over and punched her in the face. Once. Twice. Unconsciousness threatened but remained elusive in the end.

Fate never gave her an easy out.

She tried to tamp down on her pain, her fear, wanting to prevent Cody from seeing as much as possible. But in the end, she was exhausted and weak and hurting too much to do anything more than make a passive attempt.

"Oh, look. She wants it," the Dalshie mocked, taking her limp, broken form as invitation. "Don't worry, sweet. I won't be gentle." He patted her face with a horrid black palm.

Deep down, buried in the darkest recesses of her mind, something snapped. The subsequent rush of her power was almost painful.

It was time to stop waiting for someone else to come and save her.

It was time to be her own champion.

This time when the Dalshie leaned over her, Daughtry didn't avert her eyes. She stared him down, putting every bit of her anger and raging disappointment into that glare. He'd said she'd burned him, *well*, she hoped this glare scalded him with its intensity, reduced him to fucking ash.

He recoiled in response then froze, his flaccid cock hanging out of his pants.

Maybe she wouldn't get free, but there was no way that she was going to lay there and let him pretend that she was enjoying it. He was going to have to look right into her hate-filled eyes.

Her power expanded further, undulating and jumping below her skin. It itched as it made its way down her spine and out her fingers and toes.

She arched as it exploded into the space around her.

Suddenly, the air was filled with a terrible smell, tangy and . . . burnt. It wasn't until those holding her limbs cried out and released her that she realized it was the smell of her attacker's smoldering flesh. She hadn't imagined it. She *was* burning them.

It was frightening. A bit horrifying. And wonderful.

The stench, the smoking skin didn't lessen her rage, especially when one of the Dalshie threw a sheet over her and held her down when she would have risen.

"Do it! I can't hold her much longer," he shouted. Smoke threaded through the air as the cotton began to catch fire.

Time stretched.

The Dalshie leader was on his knees on the mattress, the markings on his palms trailing like ink to blacken his wrists and fingers. His fly was down, the hideous member pointed directly at her.

It was hot in the room, and he wasn't immune to it. Sweat glistened on his brow. It dripped past his blond eyebrows, threatening to get into those awful red eyes.

She hoped it stung like a motherfucker.

There was a brief pressure between her thighs before the man recoiled.

A horrific scream ripped through the air and the smell of burning flesh magnified.

She watched him from opposing views. One saw him writhe in pain and reveled in delight. He'd gotten what he deserved. The other part was paralyzed, freaked the fuck out that she had the power to do such destructive things.

His penis turned to ash and flaked to the ground. The Dalshie on top of her gave up the pretense of pinning her and dragged his injured accomplice along with him toward the window.

She shoved herself to her feet and looked down. Brilliant violet flames covered her body.

The tinkling sound of breaking glass drew her attention. The Dalshie were fleeing.

Flames, sharp as a whip, shot from her palms.

But she was too late. They were gone.

She took a step toward the window. She wanted revenge. She wanted peace.

The twin parts of her fought, legs weakening as her internal battle raged on. Eventually, they gave way, sending her to the ground where she screamed until her ears and throat hurt, her soul still undecided if hysteria or unfulfilled fury drove it.

More fire poured from her. It was spreading, out of control.

There was a final blast of heat. She watched, disconnected, as it scorched the walls, the bed, the shelves, the books. Everything in the room was incinerated.

Horror at her actions won out.

The flames extinguished.

She fell to the ground on the brink of consciousness, vaguely aware of shouting, but numbly detached from reality.

Footsteps echoed across the floor, and voices inquired but

didn't manage to penetrate the veil of fog around her mind. She groaned and curled into a ball, clutching her head. Eventually, the voices stopped, and a blanket covered her.

But when unfamiliar arms began to lift her, she screamed.

Some part of her registered that she was yelling at someone who was trying to help her.

Too bad. No one was going to touch her.

"Leave her be for the moment. It'll do more harm than good to move her."

Daughtry breathed out in relief and closed her eyes, silently waiting. People spoke in the background, but she didn't comprehend the words.

The blanket itched.

It wasn't until the smell of pine needles and sea salt overpowered the rancid stench of burnt fabric and flesh that she relaxed. "I'm here," the voice said.

Cody. She was safe.

Blackness came.

TWENTY-EIGHT

IT FELT way too soon to be waking up, but the bright light shining in her eyes was impossible to ignore. Daughtry reached up, and someone caught her hand.

She tried to pull away. They held fast.

The Dalshie were back.

She fought. Cuffs clicked around her wrists and ankles.

Warm liquid—blood—pooled on the bed. It dripped down her forearms and calves as the restraints cut into her exposed skin.

Then she heard Cody's voice. It was muffled at first but became clearer when he burst into the room.

"Everyone get out!" he roared and despite the noise, she relaxed. "I told you I needed to be here for this! What the hell do you think you're doing?" She blinked a few more times to clear her vision. Cody was towering over a petite brunette in pale blue scrubs, and on his heels was Suz, looking equally pissed-off.

"She was having a night—"

"I don't give a fuck," Cody said, at the same time Suz said, "Get out."

The nurse bolted out the door, the rest of the staff following, heads down as if that might make them less noticeable to their combined wrath.

Suz placed a hand on Cody's shoulder and said something Daughtry couldn't hear.

He shook his head, pointing to the door.

Suz's spine went ramrod-stiff, but she left, giving Cody a pointed glance.

He turned and approached the bed in that careful way that someone would move toward a cornered animal.

It pissed her off.

At least that reaction was typical, she realized, coming a little closer to earth. Her breathing slowed, the sweat sheeting her body cooling her fevered skin.

"Cowgirl?" he asked tentatively.

The question was so soft that it barely reached her ears.

But her frustration at the cautious way he was treating her faded because she'd noticed the blood. The entire front of his shirt was soaked.

"Are you okay?" she asked, her voice raw.

He froze at her words and glanced down as if he'd just realized the sight he created. Striding over to the sink, he ripped off the stained cotton then tossed it in the hazardous-waste bin. He washed his hands and dug through the cupboards for a new shirt. When Cody turned, Daughtry took note of the large gash on his chest.

The red line was angry looking but healed over.

"*Are you okay?*" she asked again.

"*I'm* fine," he muttered, resuming his search through the cabinets and withdrawing a grey T-shirt along with a small plastic basin with wrapped supplies. His shoulders were tense as marble, his eyes locked on his task.

Daughtry wished he would look at her.

"Cody?"

He finally met her gaze, and the pain in his eyes stole her breath. He approached the bed, paused to set the supplies on a rolling tray, and pulled on the shirt. It had to be Tyler's. Broad cursive strokes spelled out *I'm with stupid,* and there was an arrow pointing up.

She stifled a chuckle, amazed that she could feel anything close to amusement. She should be feeling broken. Violated.

Instead, there was only relief that she'd protected herself in the end.

Her hand reached out for Cody's, a surge of terror surging through her at finding herself still restrained.

Okay, so maybe she wasn't entirely unscathed.

"*Shit*, I'm sorry." He leaned over and removed the cuffs. Then gently turned her wrists and ankles over, examining the wounds there. Steady hands removed the gauze and saline from the basin. He flushed and dried each wound before using his magic to heal them. But he didn't say anything, didn't touch her more than necessary. Good God, the tension in his body would have made granite look soft.

Green tendrils of his magic had wrapped around her wrist before she tried for a joke. "I look like a wannabe mummy."

Cody scowled. "I told those idiots to leave you alone." He was a ball of hostility, but she knew it wasn't directed at her. He was obviously mad at the staff and—she delved deeper into the bond—angry with himself. He thought he'd failed her by not protecting her.

"It's true," he said, every nuance of his speech carefully controlled. But she could sense the raging emotions behind the icy armor. "I did fail you."

"*No.*"

His jaw went rigid and she fought down the urge to argue further. It wouldn't change how he felt. Anyway, there was something Daughtry needed to ask. She sensed Cody examining the memory of the assault in her mind, knew the conflicted feelings she'd felt while using her magic were prominent in her thoughts.

"It felt like I was splitting in half," she said when he finally looked at her. "One part was thrilled by the pain I caused, the other was scared to death."

Her mind hadn't wanted vengeance, nothing honorable like what the LexTals dealt in. When she'd used her powers, the darkness inside her had wanted to destroy every Dalshie on the planet—screw whoever got in her way.

"Is that—?"

Normal?

She couldn't quite force out the entire question, but Cody understood, and his reaction frightened her. His face went pale, hands shaking just the slightest bit as he reached up to tuck a lock of her hair behind her ear. When he did speak, the chilling calmness of his tone alerted her to the seriousness of what had happened. "It's normal to feel separate from your magic at first. Even like it's controlling you instead of the other way around."

Releasing a slow breath, she lifted her chin. "But that's not the whole story, is it?"

A pause as the bond shuddered under the impact of his emotions. Then a soft, "No."

"So what *is*? What aren't you telling me?"

Then Daughtry *knew*.

"Oh my God. *That's* why, isn't it?" Her voice was hardly loud enough to reach her own ears, but Cody's frame went stiff.

The explanation had been right under her nose, amongst the textbooks Francis had provided her. In one there had been a discussion of the three levels of powers: Primary, Secondary, and Tertiary—what she had, the power of foresight.

"That's why there are no other Rengalla with Tertiary powers," she said.

There had been a paragraph in that text that had made the hairs on her nape stand on edge as she'd read it:

Foresight, and its many dangers, have proven to be most harmful to the Oracles of the past centuries. The risk of viewing present and future appear to have strongly negative effects on the Rengallan psyche.

Negative effects on the Rengallan psyche.

"They all turn into Dalshie, don't they?"

His head dipped the barest bit and the gesture reminded her of his earlier words: *"The only thing to do when someone is infected is... euthanasia."*

A chill swept through her, but she asked the next question anyway.

"My mother?"

He hesitated, the silence stifling her, and she swung her feet over the side of the bed, her body itching for movement.

"No." He gripped her arm. "She resisted. Which was probably why she—and you—became targets."

"But that's why it felt like I was being pulled in two." A cold ball of anxiety sat heavy in Daughtry's stomach. "If the darkness takes over, I turn into a Dalshie."

"It's not that simple."

She extricated herself from his hold, retreating from the concern in his eyes. "How? How could it *not* be that simple?" Maybe she should just give in now. Then he could put her out of her misery.

He grabbed her again, tilted her chin up to force her to look at him. "*You* of all people should know the future isn't set.

You've seen enough to understand that things can and do change."

"For the worse!" She drew back, pacing, and pissed off. "I've learned that things only get worse!"

She punched the wall. Yes, it was stupid, but it made her feel better. At least until the pain welled to the surface. "Son of a bitch," she grumbled, shaking out her aching fist.

Cody strode over, gripped her wrist.

His power washed over her hand in a sheen of green and the hurt disappeared in an instant. He crushed her to his chest, holding her tight when she would have fled. "What about the blonde in the bar? You made her life better."

He wanted her to have faith in the one good thing she'd done?

She'd tried that and it had gotten her nowhere.

"And what about what Francis told you?"

Yes, that damn key. Should she just experiment with innocents? Put people at risk so that she could understand her powers?

She wouldn't.

So far, the Journals hadn't been helpful, and Francis didn't know what it looked like. After screwing with visions for close to a year, she hadn't seen one thing that resembled a key.

He met her eyes. "But you have your full powers now. That gives you an edge."

She turned to the wall, tracing the textured surface with her gaze, and sighed. It didn't do any good for her to sit there and wallow in what-ifs. Her future would be what it was.

But that didn't mean that she'd risk others to have an easier path. She wouldn't do it, no matter how much she wanted to master her visions.

Still. Straightening her shoulders, she turned to face him. "I do have things the other Oracles didn't. You. The bond."

"Yes, you do." Cody closed the space between them, pressed a kiss to her forehead. "Let's get some sleep. We'll find somewhere to stay after we've both had some rest."

She nodded and grabbed the hand he extended her. "Cody?"

"Yes?"

"If it happens"—he swallowed—"promise me you'll be the one to do it?" To end her suffering before she hurt anyone.

He didn't answer.

"Promise me." *"Please."*

His emotions battered at the bond, but she felt him batten them down, and he was calm when he eventually answered. "I promise."

Relief flooded her. She didn't want to end up as one of those monsters, reveling in other people's pain.

"I won't let you fall, cowgirl."

She pushed aside her fears and grasped tight to the slender thread of hope he extended. It was fragile and cautious, but at least it existed.

Pausing his efforts to herd her to bed, she wrapped her arms around his waist and prayed to whatever gods were out there that it would be enough.

TWENTY-NINE

"I TORCHED THE *ENTIRE* ROOM?" Daughtry asked later that week, taking in the charred bookshelves, the blackened pillowcases. Flecks of ash had been kicked up when they'd entered, and she covered her itchy nose.

Cody turned to her, a half-smile on his lips. He shouldn't be amused. Not when she felt so awful. "I didn't believe it when Francis said you had an affinity with fire. I think you've successfully proved me wrong."

Her mouth dropped open. "How can you joke about this? I destroyed everything you own."

He stooped and picked up what looked to be the handle from her duffle bag of clothes. "Yours too, it looks like."

Feeling sick at the destruction she'd caused, she turned away.

Cody was there. He tilted her chin up. "It's just stuff. Plus," he added, releasing her. "There's this."

He opened the closet, and she saw that most of his clothes were unharmed. Those closest to the door looked to have some smoke damage, but his bevy of black T-shirts was untouched.

She leaned in to smell one, wanting his scent to mask the odor of destruction and terror wafting in from the bedroom.

The shirt slipped off the hanger, and she grabbed for it, knocking a box to the floor. It had looked innocuous.

It definitely wasn't.

DVDs crashed to the floor.

"Oh my god. It's true." Hands grabbed her from behind, almost succeeding in shooing her out of the room. No doubt he'd hide it someplace else.

She clapped a palm over her mouth to stifle a laugh and poked her free hand into those rock-hard abs, tickling him until she managed to extricate herself.

He cursed as she took in the haul.

Every Meryl Streep and Sandra Bullock movie from the past two decades sat at her feet. "*Love Actually?*" She held up the cover. "*Pride and Prejudice?* Hey! I thought that was cliché?" She collapsed, breaking down into giggles, the pile of movies sliding to the side. "*Dirty Dancing?* Seriously?"

"That's it," he muttered, voice ominously dark except for the swath of amusement coloring the bond. He hauled her up, sat her on an already-packed box, and kissed her forehead.

Something—longing, perhaps the slightest blip of arousal—spread through her. She leaned closer and pressed her lips against Cody's. Pleasure was there, but fear also.

The Dalshie had taken something precious from her. Yes, she'd saved herself from being raped but they'd violated her body, stolen her faith in Cody to protect her.

He'd promised he would be always be there for her—

No, he *had* been there. He'd come for her, been injured rushing to save her.

Yet, some part of her had retreated. It took time to rebuild unconditional trust.

"When you're better."

She jumped at the intimate contact of their minds. It was the first time he'd spoken across the bond since the Dalshie had come. He pulled back and looked at her hard. "But if you breathe a word of this to anyone—"

His communication across their connection buoyed her, made her feel more like herself than she had in days. She took a step toward the door. "I think I saw Tyler in the hall."

"Not a chance in hell."

"Fine," she said, not wanting to fight when she was just starting to get him back. "But I get to pick the next movie." *"And I need you to stop blaming yourself and start talking to me again."*

He opened his mouth to protest, but she interrupted. *"It hurts me, too,"* she said. It was painful to have their minds purposely separated.

He swallowed roughly. "Okay." *"Okay."* There was a beat of silence. *"I couldn't keep myself from doing it for much longer anyway."* He touched his heart then the spot above her own. "You're impossible to resist."

DAUGHTRY WAS BRUISED AND BATTERED. In agony.

Of its own volition, her mind slid along the bond and dipped into Cody's brain. He was ensnared in a nightmare. No, a *memory*—

She heard her frantic calls along the bond and watched him struggle to reach her.

"Hang on!" he screamed, hoping, praying that she could hear him.

The Dalshie attacking her weren't the only ones in the Colony. They clogged the corridors, attacking the inno-

cent, wreaking havoc. Pulsing lights made it difficult to discern friend from enemy. Sirens peeled, their echoes reverberating down every corridor.

A pack of rancid-smelling, red-eyed assholes stood directly between him and Daughtry.

He moved. He fought and ashes were all that remained when—flames.

He dropped to his knees, distracted by the sudden painful rush of Daughtry's powers. He didn't even see the whip of black magic con

necting, only felt the wave of agony seize his limbs—

Startling awake, Daughtry sat bolt upright and searched the room, almost expecting Dalshie to appear out of thin air. The sparse surroundings of their borrowed quarters pulled her back into reality.

A sound drew her attention. Cody lay next to her, body thrashing, chest coated with sweat.

"Cody!" She shook him. "Wake up!"

His eyes flashed open and he grabbed her, crushing her to his chest, stroking a hand down her spine.

She murmured in his ear, thankful that this time she could provide the comfort.

She sensed when he finally woke up, the jolt in his mind and body a visceral response.

He shoved her away and stood.

"I'm sorry—"

"*Stop it!*" She couldn't stand another moment of him beating himself up. *"I'm the one who put you at risk. If I hadn't used that much magic, it wouldn't have distracted you."* "You were injured," she said aloud, pointing at the thin pink line still marring his chest. "If you'd died, it would have been *my* fault."

"I wouldn't have."

"Cody." She waited until he looked at her. "Not even *you* can heal an artery fast enough to stop yourself from bleeding out."

"I can now."

"What are you talking about?"

He kicked the wall and thrust a hand through his hair.

Daughtry recoiled at the sharp burst of pain along their connection. *"The bond does nothing for you, but it does everything for me."*

When he turned back to her, his palm was open. A ball of flame floated above his skin. It spun then shot through the air to stop a few inches from her face. He closed his hand and the flame disappeared. When he opened it again, a sphere of water appeared, dancing over his fingers, rotating in mid-air.

"Do you see?"

Daughtry was starting to. "The bond makes your magic—"

"Reliable. Instinctive." He looked at her. "It gives me control." The ball of water evaporated. "It gives you nothing. Nothing except insight into my nightmares and an obligation to comfort me for them."

"But Cody, I get—"

He stooped and extracted a knife from the pile of his clothes on the floor. She instinctively flinched, but he was cutting himself, not her.

In horror, she watched the sharp blade penetrate the skin of his arm. It took only the slightest pressure to flay it to the bone.

"No," she whispered, feeling faint.

His arm was neatly dissected, the layers of dermis, muscle, and fat visible. But no blood. She could feel him keeping it within the walls of his veins and capillaries.

"I control it," he thought. *"I think, and my magic obeys. It cooperates. It doesn't swell up."* Between one heartbeat and the next, he let his powers flow. Green strands crawled across the

wound, sealing the cut, repairing the damage. His skin drew together, and the pink scar that remained was even more faint than the one marring his chest.

"I. Control. It," he said again. "I never thought—"

She stared at her own hands, littered with small white scars. To have Cody's gift, magic that could heal . . . The man she loved was able to help with a thought, and she was a murderer by proxy.

Shaking, she curled her legs up to her chest.

Cody crouched at her knees, and when she finally looked up, in control once more, his mind was apparently on a different topic.

"Did they—?"

She was surprised it had taken so long for him to ask. "No." But it had been too close. "I'm fine."

"Fine?" He vaulted to his feet like a jack-in-the-box. "You were beaten and almost raped, and you're fine?" He glared at her. "What a joke."

Unbidden, happiness welled in her chest. Cody was the gladiator in her corner, pissed off at the world for daring to hurt her. Or at her for minimizing her experiences. He might think that he'd failed her because he hadn't made it to her in time to rescue her, but Daughtry knew the truth. He'd never given up on her.

That meant more than anything. She—

"I love you," she said.

He froze.

She realized it was the first time he'd heard her say the words.

"I love you," she said again.

He shuddered, the bond vibrating under the force of his emotions. Possessiveness, adoration, and hope engulfed his mind. Along with a feral desire to lock her up in a padded room to keep her safe.

She smiled. "I won't consent to being locked permanently in my quarters. No matter how sexy you are when you go caveman."

"Well, you *are* mine." He stared at her, emerald eyes daring her to deny it.

She couldn't. She was his in a way no one else would ever be able to fully grasp. And he was hers right back.

"It would be a lot easier to protect you." *"And to not have to share you."*

"Right back at you," she said, not above possessiveness herself. "Also I get plenty from the bond. You. The shield."

He rolled his eyes. "That's a very long list."

"Cody!" She smacked him. "You know how important the shield is."

"Yes, I do." He stroked a finger down the *V* of her shirt, and she winced, wishing he hadn't noticed that. "What's this—? My God." He moved the cotton aside, exposing the skin beneath.

"I'm sorry. I ruined it." The necklace had turned to ash alongside everything else.

"Sorry?" Cody's fingers traced the raised mark. "Your skin is branded." Green sparks burst from his palm and hovered in the air above her chest.

"No! Don't heal it." She batted the magic away. "I like it." The violent flames might have destroyed the necklace and scarred her skin, but they had left behind an image given to her out of love.

"But it must have hurt—"

She snorted. "You make it sound like I'm breakable."

"You are." She was surprised at his vehemence.

That's when Daughtry finally got it.

He'd almost lost her. That was bound to make anyone a little crazy. She remembered her fear when she'd seen him drenched in blood. The way her heart had stuttered, her mouth gone dry.

"Thank you," she said.

He glanced at her in surprise. "For what?"

"For loving me back." She smiled. "And *for not throwing me off the plane like you wanted to.*"

His eyes filled with the smallest bit of humor. *"You heard that, huh?" he teased and* hugged her like the fragile, valuable object she was—

She stuck her tongue out at him.

He lifted one brow. "Misogynists need not apply?"

Daughtry laughed as he pulled her into bed. They lay in silence, each listening to the steady breathing of the other. She was just about to drift off when he spoke softly.

"My words will always be true." His magic tickled as it flowed across their bodies. It called hers forth, forming a delicate web of interwoven green and purple tendrils. "My heart will never waver."

Her eyes fluttered closed, the peaceful sensation of their entwined magic giving her the final push toward oblivion.

"My soul is forever yours."

"Promise?" she asked around a large yawn.

"Promise."

"I'm tired." She sighed.

"Then sleep," he told her. "I'm not going anywhere." Cody let her nestle in and find a comfortable spot before wrapping her in his arms. *"You need me, I'll be there."*

She smiled at the familiar words, at the sheer breadth of emotion fueling them.

Their relationship still had some healing to do, but for the first time since the attack she felt like they were on the right track.

THIRTY

"ALRIGHT, Dee. You've put it off long enough," Suz said the next week, plucking the container of bandages that Daughtry was restocking out of her hands.

"Put what off?" she asked, even though she already knew. The doctor had been pressing her to use her magic over the last few days. Daughtry—quite reasonably, she thought—was feeling a little gun-shy.

Torching a room and all its contents tended to do that to a girl.

"Don't bullshit me." Suz fixed her with a stare. "We finally have a lull from all the injuries from the attack, and this is a safe place to practice. So do it already."

Fear shot through her. What if the darkness took over? What if she turned?

Her soul was screaming caution, and she trusted it.

When she used her magic again, it would be under control, on her terms.

The pleasure she'd felt when she'd hurt the Dalshie had stuck with her. The cool burn of revenge, how it had frozen something inside of her, made her unfeeling, perhaps even inhuman, in her revelry of it.

She'd snapped back into herself. But it had been a brutal arrival, the horror of her actions acute.

Delighting in someone else's pain just didn't compute. Justice was fine. Protecting herself was acceptable. But feeling joy as she'd scorched the men, used the fire to raise roiling blisters upon their skin, to burn deeper through the layers of muscle and fat . . . that wasn't okay.

"You don't understand, Suz. It's—"

Cody stepped into Suz's office. Relief poured over her, letting her lungs release a breath she hadn't even realized she'd held. He wouldn't push her. He'd promised to never make her do something she was uncomfortable with.

"*Let's go,*" she said, heart beating fast at the near miss.

"*I think you should do it.*"

Her head popped up like one of those whack-a-mole games. "*You cannot be serious.*"

Cody, of all people, should understand her reticence. He saw into her mind, felt what she felt.

"*You've been avoiding using your powers.*"

That was true, but it was avoidance for good reason. The black magic was alluring. It would be easy to let her guard down, to allow it to infect her.

"*Now that you know the risk, you can avoid the darkness.*" He wrapped an arm around her shoulders and spoke softly into her ear. "It'll be okay. We're here. You're safe."

Some of the fight leaked out of her.

"We've got you covered," Suz chimed in. "Cody won't let anything bad happen."

That set aside a big slice of her fear. She *was* avoiding her magic, yes, but did she really plan on never using her powers again? Ever?

No.

She'd come here looking for a fresh start and wasn't going to let a little fear stop her from seizing it. Plus, as they'd pointed out, the safest place to try her magic was in the empty infirmary with Cody by her side. He could stop her if—

Nope. She wasn't even going to think that.

"Okay," she murmured. "Okay." A little firmer, as she wiped her sweaty palms on her thighs. She could do this, dammit.

Closing her eyes, the first thing she saw was the bond, a hearty weaving of emerald and violet linking her with Cody. Starting there, probing gently at the junction of where it rooted into her mind, she followed those tendrils, delving down into the deepest recesses of her brain.

Her powers burst to life.

Bright. Joyous. Tempting . . . *tainted.*

"No." She immediately dropped the link, the magic floating away into space, taking the urge for destruction alongside it. "I can't do it." She looked up, pleading at Cody and Suz. "Something's not right."

But they didn't understand. Their voices—one mental, one verbal—were loud against her pounding head.

"Don't give up, Daughtry."

"Cowgirl. Just tear off the Band-Aid and go."

"Stop!" she cried. Her magic called to her, writhing in her mind, pleading with her to call it forth. She shoved it down and met Cody's eyes. "Please *stop.*"

He didn't.

"Let go." His voice was cajoling. *"You can do this. Stop holding back."*

Damn right, she was.

But he was in her mind. Why couldn't he see the otherness inside her? The piece that was intrinsically wrong. It was boiling over with power, strong enough to make a dozen perfect spheres of flame. If only she would pull it forth and use it.

It was a risk Daughtry couldn't take.

Something slammed into her mind, and she cried out in pain. "What—?" She blinked back tears, dismayed.

"Protect yourself, cowgirl. Don't let me push you around."

That Cody would be so cruel after knowing her past hurt more than the physicality of the mental blow.

"Please, don't," she begged. And—fuck—she was *begging.*

At the next blow, her heart iced over and shattered so completely, so forcefully, that she knew she'd never retrieve all of the pieces. She had *never* been so devastated. Because this man, the person she'd handed her heart to on a goddamned silver platter, had just stomped on it.

She was too broken by her own stupidity, by Cody's cruelty, to stop him when he shoved his way into her mind.

He burrowed deep, the pressure increasing until she had to clutch at her temples.

By the time she retrieved her wits and tried to push him back, it was too late. The darkness in her mind rebelled.

It pounded against the barrier she'd erected, eager to get out, excited to cause harm.

"No!" She shoved him. Hard.

He seemed so shocked by the physical blow that he staggered back a few steps. His face went pale.

The mental assault stopped in the next heartbeat. "Shit, I'm sorry, cowgirl. I didn't know—"

It was too late.

Her mind triggered.

A flame popped to life in her palm. It was the size of a Hershey's Kiss but infinitely more deadly.

Goose bumps broke out on her arms and pleasure shivered down her spine. The thick barrier she'd erected to contain the darkness splintered as effortlessly as a shoji screen, the trickle of restrained magic transforming into a torrent of uncontrolled darkness.

The fire formed a perfect sphere before expanding. It began to fill the room, devouring oxygen so quickly that Daughtry—even in the grip of the alluring darkness—felt the strain of her lungs, the singeing of her hair and eyelashes.

"Do you see what you have done?" she cried out, her arms fully coated in the flames. It looked darker on the edges, the faintest hint of black intruding on the pure violet.

"Stop!" Cody commanded. As if it were that easy. As if she could just turn it off.

The fucking moron. He deserved this. They *both* deserved it.

Cody and Suz coughed, gasping for air.

The moisture in the room began to evaporate with a series of ominous hisses.

Everything slowed. Her lips felt parched, cracked. The light bulbs shattered, one by one. Plastic tubs melted into colorful blobs of uselessness.

And the power.

It slipped further from her grasp. It was out of control, angry that she dared to attempt to control it. It flew forward, along the . . . bond.

God no!

It was a plea, a prayer, the whisper of a thought. She hastily erected barriers along their connection, but no door, no shield could separate them.

"Cody!" Even in the flickering flames, Daughtry could see his eyes widen with sudden clarity as the blackness of her magic came for him.

An ebony cloud, it swarmed, swathing him head-to-toe in sick, malignant power.

THIRTY-ONE

A FLASH of bright light blinded her.

What she saw when she blinked the spots away was frightening and horrifying, hopeful and beautiful.

Cody was bathed in emerald light, a pearlescent shield of goodness. Wherever the darkness touched him, it just *poofed* out of existence until there was nothing in the room again except the two of them and Suz.

It was over.

Should she be relieved? Happy Cody and Suz weren't hurt? Thankful that the magic had stopped?

Probably.

But instead she was angry. Angrier than she'd ever been in her life.

The moment stretched in silence, all the room's occupants aware that they stood on a precipice, that the next words would decide which direction they'd fall.

Cody let out a breath. "It's—" he said then stopped. "I'm okay. The bond—"

"The bond!" she screamed, any restraint she'd had burned away by those tainted violet flames. "Fuck the bond. I saw it!

It's like you're a magnet for the blackness. It went straight for you."

She'd promised herself that she wouldn't risk others in her pursuit of magic.

And Cody was an *other*. An other that perhaps held more pull over her soul, but still an innocent. She wouldn't sacrifice him. No matter if he'd once been the most important person in her universe.

"Cowgirl."

She looked at him—just looked at him—and he cringed back.

What had shown in her gaze? Hurt and betrayal, certainly, but that shouldn't be a surprise after what he'd done. He'd wounded her, sliced her to her fucking core. And the realization that she'd left herself wide open, allowed him the luxury, was horrifying. Her past, her ex should have taught her better.

"Sweetheart," he said gently. "I'm okay. Everything's fine."

Air wouldn't move into her lungs. Her mind couldn't process. She needed space.

"Please, don't." Her hand went up and stopped him when he would have stepped closer. Her words sounded broken even to her own ears. Despair gave way as her anger finally boiled over. "*How* could you do that to me?"

She'd told him to stop. Begged him.

Daughtry felt vulnerable, more violated than the attempted rape, because it had been Cody who'd done it. Who'd pushed her past where she was comfortable.

He was just like Jimmy.

"*I'm not anything like him,*" he snapped, the words visceral, a sharp whip against her gut. He took a step forward. "Cowgirl, wait." His voice went soft, conciliatory.

The metal of the handle was cool beneath her hand. She bolted.

"Daughtry!"

The corridors were the key to her freedom, the gateway to a space for her to cope with the pain that was tearing her apart. It was only when she saw the wall of windows on the opposite side of the lobby that she was finally able to take a breath. The wide expanse of blue lake and green trees offered peace.

She started to push past the guard at the desk.

"Hey, wait," he said, rising from his chair.

She didn't have it in her to give an explanation. Her world was splintering. Cody was just like Jimmy, claiming he was pushing her for her own good but creating only more damage in his wake.

And Suz—

The doctor was her friend. Or so Daughtry had thought.

She changed directions, saw a door was in reach. She threw open the heavy oak, was relieved to find a set of stairs. Fuck it. She'd go out through the parking garage.

The vision hit just as her foot lifted to descend the first step.

Cody shouted in concern along the bond.

The images flowing through her mind were so horrifying that she didn't sense the person coming behind her until it was too late.

There was a sickening crunch, the snap of bone breaking as something hit her in the back of the head. The pain was so sudden, so severe, that she hardly felt the frigid bite of metal against her body as she tumbled down the flight of stairs.

Barely conscious, she caught a flicker of movement, a flash of blue and garbled words as someone yelled. Then nothing as unconsciousness carried her away.

SHE WOKE WITH A HARD, muscular body pressed against her.

Breathing in, she expected the scent of pine and salt and instead got a nose full of lemon. She forced open her eyes.

Tyler.

Where was she?

"Cody?" she thought across the bond. The name reverberated back, slamming into her mind, bringing tears to her eyes.

Blocked. Just like during the attack.

"Cody?" she tried again, quieter. The sharp bite of pain made her bite her lip.

The chest below her rumbled. Daughtry sat up in alarm as Tyler cleared his throat painfully and tried again, "You okay?"

His eyes were open but squinted against the minimal light, and he looked awful. Two black eyes and a large gash on his cheek competed with an obviously broken nose.

She shrugged then winced at the action. The entire right side of her body felt like someone had struck her with a sledgehammer. Her head throbbed in tune to silent techno music. "Fine. You? It looks bad." Her voice didn't waver. Much.

He chuckled, but it was a pathetic attempt. "Nah. These are just scratches. I told you, we LexTals are tough." He lifted his head, struggling against gravity for a moment. "Hey, give me a hand."

Swallowing, she reached over. The vision from the stairwell —the first time she'd ever had one about herself—was bright in her memory. With the bond blocked, was she vulnerable to more?

Her fingers brushed the warm mocha of Tyler's skin. She waited.

Nothing happened.

The tension in her stomach unknotted and she heaved him into a sitting position. He made it, just barely, sitting still for a moment, breathing slowly in and out. Pain marred his startling blue eyes.

"Hold still." His hand gripped hers. A stillness froze his body in place.

The hair on her arms prickled as strands of sky-blue magic emerged from his palms. It crawled close enough that she could feel its healing touch.

Daughtry let it come but was ready to lurch away at the merest hint of another vision.

The magic tickled where it made contact with her skin and the pain and stiffness in her side faded, dissipating steadily.

He let out a groan, his head flopping back. The magic disappeared.

"Not enough," he said, gasping. "It's all tied up in healing *me*." He slammed his fist on his thigh then recoiled at the pain. "Dammit! I'm sorry, Dee. I can feel you're hurting."

The discomfort in her side reared back. "It's okay," she said once she could talk without whimpering. "Thanks for trying."

The effort from using his magic seemed to catch up with Tyler. His skin went grey, and sweat broke out on his forehead. She coaxed him into stretching out flat on the stone floor, and cradled his head in her lap.

"Can you contact Mr. High-and-Mighty?" he asked a minute later.

Daughtry tried to smile at his use of her nickname for Cody, but it was a failed effort. Instead, she touched the bond, barely a graze. Her brain buzzed uncomfortably. Cody was alive, but she couldn't tell exactly where or how to breach that damned barrier. Not with her head already hurting so much.

"No," she said, shaking her head. "What happened? Where are we?"

Tyler's face turned thunderous. "Caroline happened. She's turned."

"What? Are you sure?"

He gave her a look.

"Okay, you're sure. But, why? Why go after me?"

"Dee, really? The Dalshie live for death."

"You can't put yourself at risk for me."

He looked at her dryly. "A little too late for that, don't you think?"

Ouch. She turned away and stared at the stone walls. They were covered in dirt and stained dark with something that looked suspiciously like blood.

Tyler put a hand on her knee. "That's not what I meant, sweetheart. I wouldn't let a stranger be taken without a fight, let alone you. I'm a LexTal."

She nodded, fingers reaching up to feel her scalp. Her hair was clumped together with dried blood, the skin raised, but at least there wasn't a giant hole in her skull as she'd half-expected.

"Are you positive she's infected?"

Tyler grimaced, pointing at his side. "Saw the mark myself. Right before her black magic broke half my ribs."

The sound of metal grinding against metal jarred them into reality. The wooden door on the far side of the room opened. A Dalshie entered, bucket in one hand and tray in the other. She dropped both on the floor before leaving and locking the cell.

"What are we going to do?" Daughtry whispered.

"Survive."

THIRTY-TWO

THE SMELL WAS the worst thing about that night. Well, that and the wait. Every noise set Daughtry's teeth on edge, her heart racing, her skin writhing as she kept waiting for something to happen.

It didn't.

Tyler was able to eventually heal her enough that she could hobble around the room. It was dark and a small torch provided only minimal lighting.

The first thing she did when she could walk was to investigate the objects the Dalshie had left on the floor.

Food and water. Or something that sort of resembled them.

It wasn't until Caroline actually strode into the room that Daughtry let go of the final piece of hope she'd held on to. Tyler *hadn't* been mistaken. No, she and the rest of the Rengalla had been betrayed by the person they'd trusted to lead them.

Cody's family had once again stabbed him in the back.

Caroline studied her and Tyler for a moment before turning to her entourage, her eyes roving over the half-dozen men. Eventually, she nodded to one.

He stepped forward to kneel at Caroline's feet.

She looked up at Daughtry. "Take his vision."

Daughtry swallowed back bile, the knot in her stomach tightening. No."

With a shrug, Caroline whipped out a knife and plunged it into the Dalshie's heart. He exploded into ash.

Daughtry jumped, an unwanted sound of surprise sneaking out of her lips. She tried to take a step forward, but Tyler grabbed her arm, his injured grip surprisingly strong.

"No," he whispered.

At Caroline's gesture, another guard stepped forward, moving like a drone to the queen bee. He had to know that death awaited him. When his knees hit the floor, Caroline met Daughtry's eyes again.

She shook her head mutely.

Another abrupt movement. The room coated in more ashes.

Caroline took it all in stride, her face alit with pleasure. She was as persistent a force as her brother. And she seemed to enjoy the opportunity to flaunt her cruelty.

"Thomas," she called, and this time Daughtry froze, seeing the familiar blond head detach itself from the rear of the pack. He walked into the faint light.

There was fear on his face, but his gait was steady.

"Show them your hand."

Thomas held up a palm. A black stain was present with creeping tendrils emanating outward. The infection wasn't new, and it crawled up his arm.

Tyler finally spoke. "He was clean. I saw it myself."

"Aw, Tyler. So naive." Caroline stepped toward them. "Do you not realize how powerful I am? I can make your weak minds believe anything." She smiled and it was freakish. Wrong.

"I'm the strongest telepath in the Colony. You can't manipulate me."

Caroline snorted. "I can make you see whatever I want. I

can make your body feel real pain." Her hand raised. Black strands shot forward and encased Tyler's torso.

Caroline's hand curled into a fist, and Tyler screamed, the sound horrible as it echoed off the stone walls.

"Stop it!" Daughtry yelled.

Caroline's green eyes finally met Daughtry's. Her fingers fell open.

Tyler fell to the ground, one long, pained gasp escaping him before he fell to unconsciousness.

"One more chance," she said to Daughtry.

"Never."

"As you wish." Caroline turned. "Take care of this," she told a guard as she paused in the doorway, looking over her shoulder, her lips twisted with sick humor. "And make it a slow lesson."

She departed with the remainder of the Dalshie.

The chosen guard stepped forward, withdrawing a long dagger from the holster on his back.

Daughtry flinched.

Except she wasn't the blade's focus.

The guard approached Thomas and calmly sliced off his thumb.

She screamed alongside him . . . and didn't stop as the guard demonstrated how much damage a Dalshie could sustain before death took them.

Tears burned tracks down her cheeks as she watched Thomas be tortured. Blood puddled on the floor, too dark, too crimson. Too much to be from one person, it seemed.

Her eyes were frozen open, her throat hoarse from her screaming protests. Thomas's magic prolonged his suffering. It bubbled up, healing the damage, giving the guard more to work with.

Finally, the dagger was plunged into Thomas's heart and he burst into ash.

Not bothering to brush away the dust from around his face, the guard nodded almost deferentially to Daughtry and left.

The puddles of blood remained.

TWO TABLES with an assortment of sharp and shiny objects sat to her right. A narrow plank of wood, iron shackles sunk into its rough surface, was perched at an angle, the top butting against the stone walls.

A Dalshie tore off the tattered remains of her stained T-shirt and jeans before strapping her to the wood.

It was rough against her bare skin.

But splinters in her ass were the last thing on her mind.

Caroline raised a hand and the manacles locked, their serrated edges biting painfully into Daughtry's ankles and wrists. She flexed against the points, gasping as they tightened further, and warm blood trickled down her arms.

So, fun fact, her restraints were the grown-up version of a Chinese finger puzzle.

"You can't resist the darkness," Caroline told her. "Let it in. It will guide you and together we can rule everything."

Her heart began to race, panic gripping her insides, but instead of giving into that, she lifted her chin and said, "This sounds like some weird Lord of the Rings shit that I'm definitely not into. I don't want to rule anything."

The last wasn't entirely true, her power definitely wanted out, wanted to consume and reign, but Daughtry knew the blackness inside her didn't speak with her.

It was a taint, plain and simple, and one she was desperate to ignore.

Caroline came closer, her breath hot on Daughtry's cheek.

"Oh, you will. Even now, the darkness calls to you. Listen to it. Follow the destiny that has been foretold for you."

She wanted to ask what destiny, but curiosity wasn't enough of a reason for her to encourage Caroline further. Instead, she shook her head and said, "I will never be what you want me to be."

Caroline's eyes flickered, their color shifting, darkening to a deeper green from her fury before her face shut down altogether. "You were always such a disappointment."

A flick of her fingers and a guard stepped forward.

Daughtry forced back a scream.

Because this Dalshie was rabid, his eyes cloudy and darting, spittle foaming at the corners of his mouth. His arms shone a glossy ebony in the torchlight, the stain covering his face like a freakish mask.

His hands fluttered over the table, black fingers waffling. She already knew what he'd choose. It was why she'd stumbled when the images had first poured through her mind at the Colony.

The hook.

Slightly larger than his fist, it curved around his hand. He traced it gently, almost a lover's caress, along the skin of her cheek.

She flinched as the metal traversed from her face down to her torso, the cold tip of the barb brushing her stomach, abrading as her skin resisted its knife-like edge. More pressure. Then a bee-sting of pain accompanied by a dribbling of blood. She swallowed a whimper, unable to look away from the bright red rivulet dripping down her naked skin.

Taunting her, the weapon returned to its tracing, drifting away from her stomach. If only she didn't know what was coming, Daughtry might have been able to relax, to suck in a much-needed breath of air. Already she was dizzy from the lack of oxygen, and nothing had even happened yet.

Caroline chuckled.

Her breathing was ragged and in time with the guard's pants of excitement. She watched as the hook meandered its way back to her torso.

And couldn't look away.

There was no more delay. The Dalshie pressed harder, and the hook finally found purchase in her abdomen. It tore skin, muscle, and fat alike. Agony burned through her like wildfire until—finally—her nerve endings shorted out.

The only thing left was a peculiar tugging.

It didn't hurt. Not any longer. Blood splashed out of the wound to warm her skin. And still, she watched, the contrast of that horrific black hand against the shiny silver metal of the hook keeping her attention ruthlessly focused. Then the shock snapped away, and she got angry, frustrated at her circumstances, at being captured and helpless, and her power raged to life. It ripped down her spine, into her limbs, filled her every cell.

The torrent of magic built, swelling.

Fury at her weakness fueled it, growing it to impossibly larger scales.

But she had no control over it, and it was consuming her, *changing* her. Darkness swamped through her veins, staining her from the inside out, violet becoming black.

Her body couldn't contain it.

The darkness burst through its confines and incinerated everything in its path.

The rabid guard disintegrated before her eyes. Then the hook. The weapons' table collapsed under the fury of her flames.

And still her magic kept building. Another guard fell, then two more.

Seeking revenge, her purple flames crawled toward Caroline, who stayed deliberately in place, smiling. That smile sent Daughtry over the edge. Her magic exploded, torching the room, straining to reach Caroline.

Familiar voices shouted for her to stop, but that wasn't something she was capable of any longer.

A flash of violet blinded her. She blinked against the brightness, and when she opened her eyes, the only things that remained in the room were ashes and charred corpses.

Still restrained, her gaze flitted over the bodies, searching, instinct telling her she needed to find him. The plank creaked and broke. It knocked her to her knees, her arms still strapped above her head.

She was cold, so damned cold.

And then, finally, she saw what she'd been looking for. A large body, its blond hair scorched and barely recognizable. A few scraps of dark jeans and a black T-shirt coated the remains. But Cody's emerald eyes were untouched, fixed open.

She'd done that to him. A scream tore through her lips—

DAUGHTRY WOKE ON A SHOUT, the images from the vision— the only one she'd ever had of her own future—fading from her mind.

"What happened?" Tyler asked. "What did you see?"

"It's over," she said, her voice rasping. "I can't do anything to stop it."

She shouldn't have slept, had known the risk. After a vision, her mind tended to regurgitate the gruesome scenes of foretelling. Between that and Thomas, her brain had plenty of fodder for nightmares.

"Bullshit," Tyler said, squeezing her arm. "We just have to stay alive long enough. The LexTals will come for us. *Cody* will come for you."

That's what she was afraid of.

Tyler placed a finger under her chin and forced her tear-clogged eyes to meet his own. "We have to fight."

She nodded, despite her dismay. Fight or not, she couldn't see how it would make a difference. But she wouldn't take that hope away from Tyler.

Even if they lost in the end.

Even if it would be easier to surrender.

THIRTY-THREE

A MINUTE, an hour, a day later, the door crashed open.

Two people were shoved into the cell. They—

Her parents?

"What?" she whispered. Daniel and Judith, her adopted parents, her kidnappers—whatever they were—stood surrounded by Dalshie. The fear in their expressions made some of the betrayal she'd felt as a result of their deception fade away.

Caroline cleared her throat, pulling Daughtry's gaze to hers. She moved into the center of the room, a pageant queen in front of her audience. Her deep red hair was darker, more mahogany in the dim light. She gestured in front of her, and Daniel and Judith lurched into position, almost tripping over themselves to obey the summons.

"Down."

They fell to their knees.

"Stay." Caroline smirked. "You like my pets?"

A sinking feeling gripped her. After discovering the truth, she'd contemplated her parents' involvement in her kidnapping, but never imagined it went this far. Was all of her childhood—

every kissed hurt, every goodnight hug, every unreasonable expectation she'd tried to fulfill—a lie?

"It's okay," Tyler whispered, coming alongside her.

"How is it *okay?*" she hissed back, horror and anger competing as her dominate emotion. She glared at Caroline. "Nice of you to partner with them. I hope you enjoyed all of the cheesy family photos."

"Partner?" Caroline scoffed. "I own them." A beat. "But I find myself in a particularly generous mood. I'll give the happy family a moment together. *Then* we'll see if you have the proper motivation."

She waited until the door slammed closed before turning to the two people in front of her. There were a dozen questions she wanted to ask but she had the feeling she wouldn't like the answers. Did she dare ruin the few good memories she possessed?

"Honey," her mother began.

That sentiment was a knife to the kidney because implied affection, something Daughtry was starting to see had been a complete and total fabrication. Tyler moved to stand behind her, halting her when she would have stepped back, giving her the strength to deal with this conversation.

"D–don't call me that." She'd been a fool to hope their feelings might have had an inkling of authenticity.

Judith's eyes filled with tears, and words poured out of her mouth like a broken dam. "She made us take you. It wasn't our fault. We didn't mind. After we lost . . . well, we'd always wanted a daughter."

Daughtry almost believed it, except for the fact that the woman in front of her had never shed a genuine tear in her life. "Why? So you could marry me off and use Jimmy's money?"

Judith's face changed in an instant. "Why couldn't you have just gone through with it? He"—she pointed at Daniel—"made us run. Said it was wrong to manipulate your mind. But she found us. And she stole him!" Judith took an accusing step forward. "Why couldn't you have just married Jimmy? That money was going to get our Thomas back."

If Daughtry had felt cold before, she was frozen now. Ice trickled through her veins, eliminating the small piece of hope she'd held close to her heart. She'd never been a child to be loved, instead only merely a means to an end.

Old anger welled up. "And later?" she asked. "When the Dalshie came to my apartment?"

Daniel finally spoke, his features stern. "When? What Dalshie?"

Judith interjected. "That was *always* the agreement," she said. "When you turned twenty-four, they were to have you. And I was supposed to get my Thomas back."

So she'd basically been the prized cow raised to slaughter. Her already-smudged rose-colored glasses about her childhood were getting dirtier by the moment.

Daniel looked as stunned by that news as Daughtry felt.

"What did you do?" he asked.

"I–I told them," Judith said. "But it was important. They said they'd bring Thomas home if I told them."

"You *sent* them to her?" The outraged words from Daniel did something to Daughtry's soul, loosening the hold the darkness had on her heart. His eyes were sad when they met hers. "I'm sorry. Christ, I'm so damn sorry, but none of that matters now. I have a lot of things to tell you and hardly any time." He glanced at the closed door.

"Then spit them out," she said, hurt and pissed at the same time. "And stand up, for God's sake."

His face went bright red in anger. *"I can't."*

He gestured to his knees, and she focused on the spot, a shot of pity cooling her fury. Now that she looked, she could see the strands of power wrapped around his legs, keeping him on the ground.

"Why me?"

The words slipped out, despite herself.

Daniel's expression clouded, something akin to guilt marring the usually placid features. "I don't know. Thomas—"

Daughtry closed her eyes when the name finally struck home. *Oh God.* "What did Thomas look like?"

"Blond hair. Blue eyes. 5′10″ and thin. A freckle on his right cheek . . ."

The air flew out of her, and her face must have revealed Thomas's fate because Judith burst into tears.

Daniel's shoulders curled in defeat.

"When?" he croaked out.

"Last night," she said.

Tyler squeezed her shoulder and she leaned back against his chest, soaking up his strength.

"W–was it bad?" her father asked.

Daughtry bit her lip and Daniel deflated, head bobbing in a silent expression of agony. That drew the last of her anger out of her. She couldn't fault them for what they'd done.

It had all been for their son.

A small piece of her shriveled up to nothing, knowing that she had no one who would make such a sacrifice for her. But she pushed it aside. This wasn't about her. This was about a boy who'd lost his childhood, who'd suffered a horrible and depraved death he hadn't deserved. Her parents, adopters, kidnappers, or somewhere in between weren't any more at fault than Thomas. Yes, they'd been cold and distant, but there had been glimpses of love and affection there. She had to believe those were genuine. *That* was what she'd hold on to.

Crossing the room to kneel in front of them, she asked, "How was Thomas a Dalshie? You're human."

Daniel looked up, eyes glassy with remembered pain. "We survived the experiments at Ravensbrück. We're not human. Not any longer."

"Impossible," Tyler said, and she jumped, not realizing he'd come so close. "None survived that concentration camp."

"*Some* did." Daniel's expression was challenging now. He opened his palm, every muscle in his body tensing, straining for a long moment. Then—

A cluster of sparks burst forth, the blackness that stained his hand, his wrist, emerging like a sick version of metamorphosis. Except instead of a caterpillar turning into a butterfly, the unblemished skin molted into an inhuman ebony carapace.

"How?" Tyler asked.

"Fate. Cruelty. Torture. What does it matter?" He pinned Tyler with a fierce glare, the magic disappearing. "There are more of us."

"The Forgotten," Tyler said, the words barely a whisper.

She glanced up at him. "What—?"

"I love you," Daniel said.

Her gaze jerked back down, surprised, but he had already turned away. He shared a brief look with Judith, who nodded slightly and straightened her shoulders. Struggling, muscles wrenching against the magic holding him in place, he rose to his feet.

Blood began to drip out of his nose.

He pulled a knife from somewhere—his thigh, his sleeve. She couldn't see. Then with a movement so fast that she couldn't track it, Daniel reached over and slid the knife across Judith's throat.

Blood gushed to the floor.

Judith's hand came up to press just above her heart, a peaceful smile curling her lips.

Daughtry stood frozen in shock. Daniel gently lowered his

wife to the floor and crossed her arms over her chest as though she were sleeping. A heartbeat later, her body began flecking away to ash, slower than a typical Dalshie, but disintegrating nonetheless.

"What?" Daughtry asked. "Why would you—?"

Daniel staggered to face her, tears glistening on his cheeks, glowing bright orange in the torchlight. "I'm sorry I wasn't the father you needed me to be."

He bent and drew the knife up along the inside of one wrist. Then the other. Blood poured onto the floor, and his legs buckled. The last words he spoke were choked out. "Stay . . . st–strong."

Footsteps thundered down the hall as Daniel's still-warm body began to crumble.

Caroline burst through the cell door, saw the carnage, and gestured to her guards. There was such obvious hatred in her expression that Daughtry had actually taken a step back before she caught herself.

"You idiots!" Caroline shouted. "Who searched them?"

No one answered.

"Who?" she screamed, black sparks shooting out of her fingers.

"Me." A guard stepped forward.

The bolt of magic had flown through the air and sliced through the Dalshie's neck before Daughtry had a chance to blink. He burst into ash.

Caroline went still, her magic banking, her words as sharp as the dagger that had killed Daniel and Judith. "Bring her."

Tyler grabbed Daughtry's arm and shoved her behind him. "You're not taking her anywhere."

Caroline's face grew even more frightening.

"Tyler," Daughtry warned, struggling to get around him.

"No," he whispered, then louder. "I won't let you hurt her."

"Who's going to stop me? You?" Caroline laughed and it held a hysterical edge to it that didn't sit well with Daughtry.

"Yes," he said. "You'll have to go through me first."

A genuine smile lit the other woman's face. Then her arm cracked like a whip, and a strand of black magic shot forth, wrapping itself around Tyler's torso.

He grunted but didn't cry out, even though Daughtry saw the barbed tendril was tearing through his shirt and cutting into his skin. Caroline raised her other arm, black sparks already bursting from her palm.

"No," Daughtry said, shoving herself between them. "I'll go."

Caroline raised a brow as black flames engulfed her body.

The strands around Tyler tightened. But this time he screamed.

"Stop."

Caroline didn't respond other than to squeeze her hand into a fist, causing Tyler to scream again.

Fuck it.

She launched herself at Caroline.

Daughtry tensed her body, preparing for an impact that didn't come.

A force halted her in midair.

"Stupid bitch," Caroline said, tightening the band of magic that had caught her around the waist just enough to steal her breath. "I'm more powerful than you. I could squash you like a bug. I won't stop because you order me to. I'll stop because I *want* to." She stepped closer and Daughtry could feel the cold burn of those flames. "I can make you do what I want, whenever I want. And I will. Until I'm done with you."

With a wave of her hand, the magic disappeared.

Daughtry hit the ground with a gasp then turned to look

over her shoulder. Tyler was free, pushed up onto his knees, a series of bloody cuts across his torso.

A guard came forward and jerked her to her feet. "No," she told Tyler when he moved to follow. *"It'll be okay,"* she mouthed and allowed the guard to lead her away. But when she passed through the door into another cell, she had to force herself to continue forward. *This* was the place. This was where the events from her vision would happen.

They brought her into the center of the room.

"Kneel." Yeah, no. That wasn't happening.

She glanced up, found Caroline's face mere inches from hers.

"I said *kneel.*"

She never saw the blow.

It knocked her to her knees and was followed by a series of punches and kicks to her injured side. Any hope of not crying out evaporated when Caroline's foot connected with her damaged ribs. Black magic wounds around her, burning terribly where it cut into her skin.

Eventually Caroline sighed and stepped back.

"Obey me tomorrow, and you might actually learn something," she said.

Daughtry didn't move, *couldn't* move, just collapsed flat on the ground and let unconsciousness come to take her away.

THIRTY-FOUR

A BUCKET of ice-cold water woke her.

She blinked it out of her eyes, barely resisting the urge to scramble back when she saw the Dalshie standing in front of her.

"Breakfast." A platter hit the ground at her feet, scattering its meager contents all over the filthy floor. The guard left and the *click* of the lock in the cell door resounded through the room.

She sighed, righted the tray, and turned to survey her surroundings.

"Tyler!" she said on a gasp.

He was chained to the wall, arms limp, feet dangling, but his blue eyes were bright and awake.

Hurrying to her feet—ignoring the fact that every part of her body was bruised and aching—she rushed over to him. Then stopped. She wasn't sure where to risk touching him. Every single inch of his body had been damaged.

"You okay?" The idiotic question slipped out. Of course he wasn't.

He smiled, but there was something off in it that made her stomach drop.

"Curiosity killed the Rengalla," he said, and his smile took on a genuine tinge.

She took a breath. "What happened?"

He just rolled his eyes. "Besides the obvious?" He nodded to his chained extremities. "Here's to hoping they let me down soon. Otherwise they're going to get a nasty surprise." He cut his eyes toward the bucket that had become their toilet.

She huffed a laugh, and when his eyes flicked over her shoulder, she didn't need the warning. Her skin was already prickling in awareness of the Dalshie at her back. Ignoring the asshole behind her, she tugged out her ponytail holder, wrangled her hair into some semblance of order, and straightened her shoulders. *Steady, now.*

"Her liege requires your presence."

Daughtry turned.

The Dalshie was in full glamour, as though a pretty face and some broad shoulders might be enough to sway her into being cooperative.

"Well, the *liege* can just kiss my ass," she muttered, though apparently, not quiet enough.

"Daughtry," Tyler said, warning in his tone.

The Dalshie's glamour flickered, his anger making the façade slip.

She pretended not to notice. "Unchain him."

The guard's eyes flashed red, his human charade fading completely at her insolence. But he surprised her by acquiescing and extending a palm, black strands of magic flying forward. The chain clanked loudly, unwound, and dropped Tyler to the floor.

"Thanks, I think," he muttered, shoving his elbows under him with a groan, levering himself off the ground. "Be careful."

He gave her a penetrating stare, eyes cautioning. *"Don't turn,"* they seemed to scream.

She nodded her understanding even as she wondered if it was a promise she could keep.

The guard preceded her down the hall, taking the lead through the twisting maze of corridors. On either side, the cells were empty of bodies, but not bodily fluids, and the too-crimson blood she recognized as belonging to the Dalshie puddled in the corridors.

Did they torture each other for fun?

She stumbled as she sidestepped one such mess, bumping into a cluster of crusted weapons laid haphazardly along one wall.

"Hurry up," her escort said with a snarl.

Acting on instinct, she palmed a small knife and when the guard turned away again, slipped it into the back of her pants, covering it with her shirt. Then she followed him through the door.

It was the room from her vision. Knives, hooks, and chains were spread on the wooden table. The familiar plank was already perched against one wall. Her mouth went dry and she struggled to swallow. So today was the day. She attempted to stay calm even as her mind ran through the vision over and over again, searching for the key, for some solution that wouldn't end in the decimation of everyone she cared about.

"Join us," Caroline said. She gestured to the spot in front of her, and it was all Daughtry could do to keep her feet moving.

"Caroline," she said by greeting, pleased that her voice was steady, despite her maelstrom of emotions. Terror warred with frustration, and the blackness of her magic was tempting, calling to her in a siren's song. It would be so easy to let it take over, to kill Caroline.

Or die trying, her conscience said. *Then you'd do nobody any good.*

The inner dialogue gave her the strength to shove the magic back.

"Don't fear, my dear," Caroline said. "You have such power. Most Oracles only see the future. You can control it. Yet you seek to squander the gift. You need to embrace it."

She needed time. Time to come up with a plan. Time for—

What exactly?

Daughtry didn't know, but every minute she wasn't using her magic meant she was safe another minute.

Caroline nodded to the Dalshie closest to her. "Pull his death and change it."

"No."

"Then your friend dies."

Daughtry's stomach clenched in horror, knowing she couldn't refuse and yet already recoiling against the nausea, the images soon to come. She leaned heavily against the nearest object, which happened to be the table containing Caroline's torture instruments. They clinked together, the reminder making her retch.

She couldn't do this, had to think of something else—

Calm, her conscience ordered.

Steadying her mind, she concentrated on the good she could do with her magic. The dark parts of her powers reveled in chaos. In pain. So she would focus on helping, not harming the guard. And maybe the infectious magic would leave her be.

Or maybe it wouldn't—

"Do it," Caroline ordered.

Closing her eyes, Daughtry released her hold on her powers.

Immediately, the light and dark battled as it flowed down her spine. Blackness tinged the edges of the purple strands emerging from her hands.

Easy. Slowly now.

Carefully, she removed the darkness as one might peel the skin from a clove of garlic, and locked it behind a closed door in her mind. It was instinctive, the door appearing before she'd even fully pictured it. Sparks alighted on her fingertips, gathering until they formed thick tendrils. She directed them across the room, and they snaked up the guard's shoe, wrapping around his ankle through his pants.

That was enough contact. A vision tore through her.

She struggled to slow the images, to not be inundated by the blood and violence. "Find the key," she said under her breath. Please let Francis be right—

The guard faced another Dalshie, their broadswords raised and ready to do violence. Snowbanks enclosed their battlefield, and crowds of Dalshie shouted.
The blades collided with a shower of sparks, a booming crash.
Snow had been cleared, but the ground was muddy, slick. Perspiration glistened on the fighters' bodies, giving their ebony skin a polished look. No glamours were necessary in this place.
Their red eyes met in anger. In fatigue. In fear.
Her guard took a single misstep, fell to one knee—and that quickly it was over.
The sword arced down and cleaved his head from his shoulders—

The stones were hard and cold under her knees when she resurfaced, struggling to catch her breath. At the end of the vision, she'd been in the man's body, had seen the sword come straight for her head. She'd felt the splintering pain as the blade had penetrated her skull.

Daughtry clutched her thighs, the bite of her nails through her jeans centering her. She was here. Alive.

For now.

"Not good enough," Caroline said.

"Wait!" Her throat was sore. Apparently, she'd screamed. "I'm not done."

The magic flowed out of her again, grasping the man's vision more easily this time around. She turned the death over and over in her head. There were a thousand details to notice, things that might normally have frightened her into dropping the vision or giving up, but Caroline's threat to Tyler forced Daughtry to ignore all of that.

Her mind kept going back to the moment when the guard slipped.

Dammit. All she could see were mud and sticks. *Sticks?* Why was that one pointed straight up? Its angle wasn't quite right, the placement almost unnatural.

She played the vision again, surprised that the nausea was gone. In its place was sheer determination. She had to save Tyler. But how?

Except . . . Caroline needed her, wanted her powers.

It was the only card Daughtry had left to play.

She let the vision drop. "Let him go."

Caroline laughed. "Do I need to remind you that you have no power here?"

Fuck that. Daughtry had a good chunk of the power. "Look, this will go easier if you do what I want. And you should know, I'll only cooperate if you let Tyler go. I'll pull as many deaths as you want, but not until you release him."

"No."

"Then what's my motivation, your *liege?*" She crossed her arms over her chest. "You'll kill me, kill *him*, the first chance you get. Let him go, and I'll do what you ask. If not, every bit of foresight you get out of me will have to be fought for."

"You say that like it's a bad thing."

She didn't respond, just held Caroline's eyes.

The room wasn't silent. She could hear the excited breathing of the guards, the soft footfalls of more Dalshie outside the room, but when she stared at Caroline, everything else faded to the background. If she didn't succeed in this war of wills—

"Fine."

Daughtry's heart pounded, but she kept her voice calm. "Get him to a safe place. I'll call the LexTals to pick them up." She paused. "I won't pull another vision until I hear from Cody that they're safe." Caroline appeared to be on the edge of losing her temper, but Daughtry had one more thing she needed. "I want my phone back. I'll only call from that." She was taking a gamble, praying that her bargaining power was large enough for Caroline to grant her request.

Because she really needed to activate the GPS on her phone.

"Fine. He'll be teleported out." Caroline gestured to one of the guards.

He left and reappeared a few minutes later with her phone.

She powered it on. Thank God, it still worked.

"Make the call."

Fingers shaking, she selected Cody's number from her list of contacts. It rang once. Again.

"Put it on speaker," Caroline ordered.

Not glancing up, Daughtry pressed the button. The phone continued to ring.

Come on, Cody. Pick up the damn phone.

"Daughtry?"

A breath rushed out of her lips. "Cody. Listen, it's me—"

"Are you okay?"

"Yes," she said. "Look, the Dalshie have me and Tyler."

Cody cursed.

"They're letting him go, but I have to stay—"

"No, you can't. We'll find you. You just have to hang in there a little longer." His voice was so fierce and if he'd been standing in front of her, his anger would have battered her across the bond.

"I'll be fine."

"No, you won't."

"Shut up and listen to me," she snapped. "Cody . . . she'll keep hurting him." Silence met that statement and Daughtry pressed on. "The Dalshie will teleport Tyler out. You have to meet them. Call me back when everyone is safe."

"But—"

"I *have* to do this, Cody. Don't argue with me. I'll be fine." *Maybe. Okay, probably not.*

"Bullshit. You can't—"

"Okay, time's up," Caroline said, interrupting them and striding over to grab the phone. She put it up to her ear. "You'll receive the coordinates in five minutes." She hung up and slipped the phone into her pocket. "Satisfied?"

No, but what could Daughtry say? She was making up this shitty plan on the fly. She hadn't been able to double-check the settings on the phone to make sure the locating feature was activated. All she could hope was that with it powered on the LexTals could track her.

"You. Take care of it."

The indicated guard nodded and left the room. Would they actually let Tyler go free? It seemed too much to hope.

She forced the thoughts away. *This* was the only chance they'd get.

Caroline pulled out the phone and punched in a text message. "There. I've sent the coordinates. Now do it."

"No."

"No?" Caroline raised a perfectly groomed eyebrow.

"Not until I talk to Cody again."

Caroline rolled her eyes. "You don't trust me?"

She huffed out a bitter laugh. "You've hurt the people I love. Hunted me like an animal. I agreed to cooperate, Caroline, but I won't bow down to you." A shake of her head. "I'll be damned if I'll act like a sniveling servant who abides your every wish. Now. Let. Me. Talk. To. Cody."

The phone slapped into her palm, and she selected Cody's name again with steady fingers, adrenaline making her dead calm as she put it up to her ear.

She hoped it didn't end up making her just dead.

Cody picked up on the first ring. "We've got him."

"Is he okay?"

He paused a second too long.

"Cody?"

"He's alive. Barely."

She looked up at Caroline who shrugged as if to say, *What did you expect?*

Fuck. Daughtry's heart pounded in her chest and it made it difficult to hear her own words over it. "What if he—"

"He won't," Cody said. "But you can't worry about him. You have to stay safe. We're coming for you. Delay her, but don't do anything stupid." His words were fast, trying to say as much as possible. "I'm sorry, so sorry. And I love you, cowgirl. With everything I've got."

"I love you, too," she whispered.

Caroline cleared her throat.

"I have to go."

"I know."

"I know. *God.* I know, cowgirl—"

Caroline plucked the phone out of her fingers and ended the call.

Daughtry didn't protest, just blinked back the tears in her eyes, shoring up her spine. Part of her wondered why Caroline had allowed the call at all. Then again, talking to Cody, hearing his voice, his worry, was as torturous as the visions.

The smirk on Caroline's face showed that she knew it.

What else could be a better reminder of everything she'd be giving up?

Dread hit her full in the stomach. How she was going to survive this? And at what cost?

THIRTY-FIVE

"PULL IT."

Daughtry took a deep breath, forcing herself to stare at Caroline full-on.

She would survive this the same way she'd survived the past year: by looking at the next hour, the next minute, the next second as just another speed bump. She'd endure, just as always.

Her magic flowed forth effortlessly.

The blackness in her mind jumped, battering at the door holding it in place. She had to blink back tears. It hurt, her mind threatening to splinter into pieces, and she bit her lip, yanking the vision to the forefront of her mind, vowing to study every puddle and blade of grass. There *had* to be some way to find the key, to alter the vision for good.

To not turn into a monster.

This time the process was different. Easier. Without fear holding her back, she was almost detached from the violence. Instead of the images flying into her brain, she controlled them.

With a simple thought, the action froze. Another flick of her mind, and it sped up. She could even zoom in or out—

She walked across the field. The mud sucked at her feet, its wet cold seeping through her shoes, chilling her skin. The hot rancid breath of the Dalshie puffed onto her cheeks and raised the hair on her arms.

It felt real.
Yet she saw nothing that looked like a key.

Her Dalshie stepped forward, slipped in the mud, fell to his knees.
The sword came down—

Wait.
She rewound the vision—

As she walked closer, she noticed the stick again, the one that had looked so unnatural before. There was something strange about that sharp piece of wood. An odd mass of air surrounded it, making it appear just the slightest bit blurry. Magic. A sick power that made her skin crawl.

She shrugged off the reaction and reached for the stick. Could it be simple enough to remove it?

Her hand was an inch away when she saw something glitter in her periphery. The action on the field faded, the noise of clanging metal and shouting spectators muting. The colors drained away until she stood in the middle of a silent black-and-white movie. Only two things stood out.

Daughtry turned her attention to the glittering objects.

And finally understood.

There were *two* keys.

But which was the right one? How did she choose?

As a Dalshie, didn't the guard deserve the worst possible death?

Her power ached to focus on the sharp stick imbedded in the ground, to pull it just a little higher.

She could see it easily.

The man would step on the stick, impaling his foot straight to the bone and, injured early, he would struggle to mount a defense. Instead of a quick beheading, his ashing wouldn't happen until his opponent had reduced him to his respective parts.

Or she could encourage the bird down from the sky. The distraction would be enough for her Dalshie to inflict his own death blow on his opponent. The guard would live. For now.

Daughtry knew what she wanted. What her magic wanted.

It screamed for her to have her vengeance.

This guard would participate in her torture. He'd kidnapped those children, done God-knows-what to Tyler. She should make it worse for him, make him feel one iota of the fear and pain he'd inflicted on others.

She reached for the stick . . .

Then came the memory of Tyler's warning, of Daniel's gasped out words to stay strong. But no, even they wouldn't fault her. He was only a Dalshie. After everything the guard had done, he deserved—

No one should have this power.

The thought ripped through her, knocking loose the threads of darkness that had crept out of the locked box and tangled themselves into her mind.

The risk—the temptation to play jury and executioner, to play God—was too great.

The truth slammed into her.

There was only one way to prevent the blackness from infecting her with its lust for power. Only one way to stop the death. To save Cody.

To save *herself*.

Her magic expanded, violet strands stained with black.

It burned through the hold on the bond, bursting through the barrier so that her mind was finally free to connect to Cody's. The darkness arrowed for him immediately. She had to be quick. She wouldn't risk hurting him.

But *finally* she could feel him. Talk to him. Revel in the warmness of their connection.

For just a few seconds more.

"I should have told you before. I'm sorry, I shouldn't have run from you." She pulled the knife out from the back of her pants. *"I love you."*

Cody's mind lurched into hers. *"No! Don't!"*

Daughtry barely heard Caroline shout. "No!" Hardly registered the footsteps pounding across the stone floor toward her.

"Tell me you love me."

"I love you. Please, don't do this. We're—"

"I'm so sorry."

She positioned the blade between her ribs and plunged it straight into her heart.

It hurt.

Then it didn't.

Her vision went dim and hazy. Hot blood poured down her

front, warming her cooling limbs. She didn't even feel the hard stones as she fell limp to the ground.

A smile curled her lips at Caroline's blood-renting shriek of disappointment.

THIRTY-SIX

"YOU HAVE TO DO SOMETHING!" The voice was familiar, the smell of pine and sea salt comforting. Firm hands pressed on her chest, and Daughtry gasped, unconsciousness receding enough that she could feel pain.

"Stop!" she shrieked, agony pulsing through her every nerve fiber.

The voices and hands ignored her.

"I can't help her."

"Tyler, I swear to fucking God I will kill you right now," Cody snapped. "I'm holding onto her blood by a hairsbreadth. I can't heal her too."

"I *can't* do it."

"I've never asked you for anything. I need your help." Cody paused. "Do you want me to fucking beg?"

"No! For God's sake. *No.*" Regret dripped off every word.

"Then why?" The hands shifted on her chest, and she moaned in pain. "You know we have to save her. I can't—"

Another voice, sounding very far away, chimed in, "Do it, Tyler. We have to move."

Dante, her slowing mind realized.

"I can't. I won't," Tyler said, and this time rustling accompanied his words. Daughtry struggled to open her eyes, to understand, but her strength failed her.

Dead silence descended.

Daughtry felt Cody's despair abruptly shoot through her. The bond was back.

Just in time for her to die.

"You won't die," he growled. "Tyler, please. We'll worry about the consequences later."

"He's right," Dante said, closer now. "You have to try."

Nobody moved for a long moment, then the pain ramped up, and her body fought viciously for a peaceful end against the self-inflicted injury. She cried out.

"Okay," Tyler said. "*Okay.*"

Power—burning, itching—pushed into the wound. It thrust past her skin into her heart and shoved at the point of the blade that was still in her chest. The sharp metal was forced out agonizingly, millimeter by millimeter.

It hit the stones with a *clang*, but the sound was fuzzy to her ears. The pain of the healing was stealing her consciousness.

"Cody." The word was quiet, almost lost in the sounds of the room.

"I'm here."

A pause followed, filled with too many emotions for her addled mind to comprehend.

"I'll always be here."

DAUGHTRY'S EYES felt crusted shut. She reached a hand up to rub them.

"Ow!" she gasped, her eyes flying open. A large IV was

attached to the side of her wrist, the needle biting into her flesh as she moved. Startled, she looked around, scanning the room for familiar sights.

"I'm here." Suz came into the light. "How are you feeling?"

Daughtry grimaced, delicately moving her wrist to prevent the needle from jabbing her. "Thirsty," she said, her voice rasping.

A straw appeared at her lips, and she greedily drank down the proffered glass of water. Dry throat abated, she laid her head back. Just that tiny bit of movement had exhausted her.

Suz fussed with the blanket, shifted the pillow behind her neck, and whispered a soft goodnight before retiring to a cot on the far side of the room. Daughtry lay prone but awake, her mind racing, reaching out to something she didn't understand.

Something important.

Exhaustion won out over puzzling, and she'd just settled in, eyes sliding closed, when the door to the infirmary flew open.

A muscular hand prevented it from slamming into the opposite wall.

Her breath caught.

Shadowed in the dim light, the muscular man strode forward. A long scar marked the side of his jaw and neck.

"Cowgirl?" he asked. A scent drifted forward, tickling her nostrils. It was a distinct smell. Familiar.

"Daughtry?"

It took a moment for the fog around her mind to lift. "Cody?" Every muscle in his body relaxed when she spoke his name. "You're really okay?"

She hadn't dared to hope.

The fear of the relentlessness of her visions had seemed too great. But Cody was there, alive, his fingers strong and warm as they interlaced within her own.

He smiled, and the simple quirk of his lips made her heart swell.

"If I've told you once, I've told you a thousand times, cowgirl"—he pressed a soft kiss to her lips—"You need me, and I'll always be there." Then he slid into the bed and pulled her into the unwavering strength of his arms.

THIRTY-SEVEN

THE DALSHIE WALKED INTO A DANK, dark cell, letting her red-haired, green-eyed glamour fall. It was as effortless as breathing to assume the form, but she much preferred her gleaming ebony skin.

She was angry, eager to let her rage loose. The future she'd been working toward had been close. *So close.* Teetering-on-the-ends-of-her-fucking-fingertips close.

They'd stolen that from her.

When the LexTals had stormed her compound, she'd had no choice but to run. She hated running, hated that she needed a two-bit Oracle who didn't know her way around a vision. And she hated that she'd been forced to abandon her favorite house.

Turning tail and fleeing wasn't her style.

She clenched her fingers into tight fists, not flinching when her nails cut into her palms. The wounds were inconsequential, would heal before her next breath.

Her rage didn't fade as quickly.

Willing the torches to life, she regarded the woman lying on the stone floor in front of her.

Her brother was the source of her fury.

Cody was responsible for the deaths of her strongest soldiers. For losing Daughtry's powers. She couldn't wait to cut him to shreds. Why had she ever resisted the urge to do so? She should have said the hell with her cover and eliminated him the first moment he'd given her attitude. But she hadn't.

Unfortunately for her, he wasn't here to pay for that insolence.

A smile stretched her lips. But his sister was.

"So Caroline, what should we play with today?" Her fingers trailed across the small table. Untraditional torture objects were mixed with the classics. Letting her fingers wander, she bypassed the Taser and a pair of rusty scissors before settling on the wooden spoon. She was feeling creative.

"Fuck you," Caroline said, a raw, guttural sound.

"You never learn, my dear." She picked up the wooden spoon and lit it with black flames summoned in her palm. "But, don't fear. I'm more than willing to remind you."

She traced the flaming wood down her prisoner's cheek, chuckling as cries of pain echoed off the brick walls. Her free hand followed in the spoon's wake, trailing along the burns riddling Caroline's breasts and stomach.

She soaked up the screams—the scent of burning flesh—like they were sunshine.

"Ah yes, talk to me just like that." She lifted her hand, watching the ragged rise and fall of Caroline's chest. "Tsk. Tsk. I'll make it better." She thrust the splintering wood in-between Caroline's naked thighs. Cody had killed her most-skilled Dalshie, her lover she'd spent a decade training.

Now his sister would pay the price.

Caroline's shrieks rose and rose until—

They cut off.

She sighed. Torture was no fun when the victim was unconscious.

Her hand wavered over the bucket of ice-cold water but, in the end, she tossed the spoon aside and strode out of the room.

Enough pleasure. It was time for her next move.

—Dark Phoenix, now available on Kindle Unlimited.

PHOENIX SERIES

Phoenix Rising

Dark Phoenix

Phoenix Freed

ALSO BY ELISE FABER

(see a full listing and descriptions at www.elisefaber.com)

Roosevelt Ranch Series (all stand alone)

Disaster at Roosevelt Ranch

Heartbreak at Roosevelt Ranch

Collision at Roosevelt Ranch

Regret at Roosevelt Ranch

Desire at Roosevelt Ranch (November 3rd, 2019)

Billionaire's Club (all stand alone)

Bad Night Stand

Bad Breakup

Bad Husband

Bad Hookup

Bad Divorce

Bad Fiancé (Oct 6th 2019)

Bad Boyfriend (Jan 19th, 2020)

Gold Hockey (all stand alone)

Blocked

Backhand

Boarding

Benched

Breakaway

Breakout (December 15th, 2019)

Life Sucks Series (all stand alone)

Train Wreck

Phoenix Series (rereleasing October 21st, 2019)

Phoenix Rising

Dark Phoenix

Phoenix Freed

Phoenix: LexTal Chronicles (rereleasing soon, stand alone, Phoenix world)

From Ashes

KTS Series

Fire and Ice (Hurt Anthology, stand alone)

ABOUT THE AUTHOR

USA Today bestselling author, Elise Faber, loves chocolate, Star Wars, Harry Potter, and hockey (the order depending on the day and how well her team -- the Sharks! -- are playing). She and her husband also play as much hockey as they can squeeze into their schedules, so much so that their typical date night is spent on the ice. Elise is the mom to two exuberant boys and lives in Northern California. Connect with her in her Facebook group, the Fabinators or find more information about her books at www.elisefaber.com.

 facebook.com/elisefaberauthor

 amazon.com/author/elisefaber

 bookbub.com/profile/elise-faber

 instagram.com/elisefaber

 goodreads.com/elisefaber

 pinterest.com/elisefaberwrite